Critics and authors can't get enough of
Jennifer Hillier's suspense-packed novels

Praise for *FREAK*

"This book freaked me out—in a good way. In a word, 'frightening.' Jennifer Hillier creates a **truly scary killer** in Abby Maddox, **the female version of Hannibal Lecter**—smart, cunning, and wickedly evil. I was engrossed on page one, couldn't put the book down, and breathless at the ending. Be prepared for a late night's reading. Then sleep with the lights on—if you can. This one **blew me away**."

—Robert Dugoni, award-winning and *New York Times* bestselling author of *Murder One* and *The Conviction*

"Hillier introduces **a new kind of serial killer**. . . . *Freak* will keep you turning pages long after bedtime."

—*BookLoons*

"[A] **creepy** psychological thriller."

—*Fresh Fiction*

"*Freak* is **difficult to put down**."

—*National Post*

"If you like **rockin' thrillers** that just won't quit, with plenty of twists and turns, you'll really enjoy *Freak*!"

—*My Bookish Ways*

"Hillier's thriller is addictive. . . . Leaves readers hungry for the next."

—*Kirkus Reviews*

"Readers beware: what flows through these pages is not always easy to stomach, but I dare you to take your eyes off the page. . . . *Freak* features the return of a fabulous cast of characters from *Creep*. . . . Chilling, action-packed, heart rate–escalating, and terrifying. . . . If you want a read that will have you on the edge of your seat for hours, give these two novels a go!"

—*Indigo*

"Exhilarating. . . . Fast-paced. . . . A shocking final twist."

—*Gumshoe Review*

"If your tastes run to the style of the great fifties *noir* authors . . . Hillier is what you've been waiting for."

—*The Globe and Mail*

"Another really good book from Ms. Hillier, an author I will be keeping an eye out for in the future."

—*Mama Knows Books*

"Thrills and danger just keep coming. . . . Hillier really nails the little details like the description of Highway 99 in Seattle. Those seemingly insignificant things are what push a novel from great to excellent."

—*My Book Views*

"Hillier's so good at hitting all the right suspense beats. . . . An innate writing talent also exists, doubling the page-turning pleasure."

—*Horror.com*

But I'm a creep, I'm a weirdo
What the hell am I doin' here?

—"Creep" by Radiohead

Be sure to read Jennifer Hillier's acclaimed debut thriller

CREEP

"Top-of-the-line thriller writing. . . . You better call in sick—you're not going anywhere until you finish reading."

—Jeffery Deaver, #1 *New York Times*
bestselling author of *Edge* and *XO*

"Agreeably frightening . . . packs a considerable wallop."

—*Publishers Weekly*

"Fast-paced entertainment."

—*National Post*

"A chilling and graphic portrayal of a sociopathic obsession."

—*Chatelaine* magazine

"Suspenseful plotting and solid character development. . . . This fast-paced page-turner will keep fans of Lisa Gardner and Chelsea Cain guessing."

—*Library Journal*

"Engaging. . . . Hillier pulls off [a] sleight of narrative hand with remarkable skill."

—*Booklist*

"Quick-paced, smartly written psychological suspense that will surprise readers. . . . [A] shocking ending."

—*Fresh Fiction*

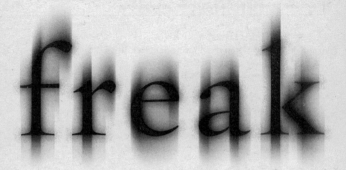

freak

JENNIFER HILLIER

POCKET BOOKS

New York   London   Toronto   Sydney   New Delhi

Pocket Books
A Division of Simon & Schuster, Inc.
1230 Avenue of the Americas
New York, NY 10020

This book is a work of fiction. Any references to historical events, real people, or real places are used fictitiously. Other names, characters, places, and events are products of the author's imagination, and any resemblance to actual events or places or persons, living or dead, is entirely coincidental.

First Pocket Books paperback edition May 2013

POCKET and colophon are registered trademarks of Simon & Schuster, Inc.

For information about special discounts for bulk purchases, please contact Simon & Schuster Special Sales at 1-866-506-1949 or business@simonandschuster.com.

The Simon & Schuster Speakers Bureau can bring authors to your live event. For more information or to book an event, contact the Simon & Schuster Speakers Bureau at 1-866-248-3049 or visit our website at www.simonspeakers.com.

Manufactured in the United States of America

10   9   8   7   6   5   4   3   2   1

ISBN 978-1-4516-6455-3
ISBN 978-1-4516-6456-0 (ebook)

For my parents,
Nida Perez Allan and Roberto Pestaño

ACKNOWLEDGMENTS

It takes a dedicated and supportive team to get a book published, and I'm very blessed to work with such amazing people.

Huge thanks to my feisty and fabulous agent, Victoria Skurnick of Levine Greenberg, for always fighting for me, and for always knowing exactly what I need to hear. We're a good fit, and I hope we work together for a long time.

My team at Gallery Books is incredible. My editor, Kathy Sagan, was instrumental in getting this book as shiny and polished as it is, and I've enjoyed every moment of our creative brainstorming. I also need to thank assistant editor Emilia Pisani for her wonderful ideas and line notes, which made the book so much better. I am grateful to have my publicist, Stephanie DeLuca, working so hard on my behalf. Editorial assistant Natasha Simons is always a pleasure to work with. Big thanks to my copy editor, Thomas Pitoniak, for all his hard work. And of course, I'm so very grateful for the continuing support of Louise Burke and Jennifer Bergstrom.

April Gibson, my publicist at Simon & Schuster Canada, is an all-around awesome person, and I'm lucky to have her in my corner.

My friends and family think it's so cool I'm a writer, and you know what? It is. But it would be very challenging to write full-time if they didn't believe I could do it, and the love and support I receive every day from these wonderful people means everything to me.

My mom, Nida Perez Allan, thinks everything I do is great, and while I suspect deep down that maybe not *everything* I do is amazing, I love her for being my biggest fan.

My dad, Roberto Pestaño, continues to teach me so many important lessons about love, life, and finding the right balance between the things I want to do and the things I need to do.

My brother, John Perez, isn't much of a fiction reader, but he's proud of his little sister and he doesn't make fun of me, and that's all I need.

Special thanks to Tim Allan, Liz Perez, and Evelyn Tiu, for being great partners to the people I love the most.

Both my Pestaño and Perez families, in North America and in the Philippines, have been generous with their support, and I love you guys more than you know. I'm also blessed to be part of the Hillier and Philpott families; your kind words have lifted me up many times.

I'm fortunate to have kind, funny friends who've been by my side through all the crazy ups and downs of trying to get published (and, hello, *life*), and if they weren't keeping me sane and making me laugh, I don't know that I could have written this book. Big hugs and inappropriate squeezes go out to Annabella Wong, Dawn Robertson, Brian Hanish, Micheleen Beaudreau, Teri Orrell, Lori Cossetto, Jennifer Bailey, Jennifer Baum, Nancy Thompson, Marsha Sigman, and Benoît Lelièvre.

Big thanks to my Twitter pal Jeremiah for lending his name to a character. Feel free to RT this.

I'm also grateful to my lovely friend Mónica Busta-mante Wagner, who helped me with the Spanish phrases in this book. *Gracias*.

To all the amazing writers I've met through the blogosphere, Twitter, and Facebook: You're all rock stars! I am so lucky to be part of an incredible community of artists who support each other the way we do.

And lastly, to Steve Hillier: none of this would mean anything without you. You know that.

CHAPTER : 1

There was something fucked up about a job where cocaine was overlooked, but cigarettes would get you fired.

In a stall in the bathroom of the Sweet Chariot Inn in downtown Seattle, Brenda Stich (professional name: Brianna) shook out another line of the wondrous white powder onto the back of her hand and snorted. It took about three and a half seconds for the shit to kick in, and thank God for it. It had been a long three days with the guy from New York, and she was delirious with exhaustion. The bitterness dripped down the back of her throat and she swallowed. The coke coursed through her veins, and just like that, the world was back in high definition.

Okay. All right. Much better.

She exited the stall, grateful the bathroom was empty so she could fix her makeup in peace. Brenda had been hoping for a night off to recharge, but Estelle's text didn't leave room for argument. You never argued with Estelle. You worked when she wanted you to, and there was really no such thing as a night off. The Bitch even had all the girls on that new birth control pill where you only bled three times a year, so forget using your period as an excuse.

You were always on call, twenty-four hours a day, seven days a week. If you were what the client wanted, and you weren't available, they'd go elsewhere. And Estelle hated to lose money.

Hated, of course, was an understatement. They didn't call her the Bitch for no reason.

Brenda checked her makeup in the bathroom mirror one last time. She'd done a decent job covering her dark circles, but her eyes were still red. No problem. An escort always had five things in her purse at all times—condoms, lube, a cell phone, breath mints, and Visine. And sometimes drugs, though of course Estelle never tested for that. If drugs helped her girls work, so be it. Brenda dug out her bottle of Visine and squeezed a few drops into each eye, blinking to move the fluid around.

Better.

Estelle might not test for drugs, but she did have the girls screened regularly for venereal diseases, and no one was able to work during the seventy-two-hour period it took for the tests to come back. Unfortunately Brenda wasn't due for testing for another week. Dammit, she should have gotten tested today—at least then she'd have had the next three days off. Her last appointment, which had ended only a few hours earlier, had been a fast-talking businessman from Manhattan, in town for four days and determined to make the most of it. He'd had a voracious sexual appetite, made even worse by Viagra. Brenda had once had a conversation with a veteran escort named Charlotte (real name: Carla), who'd spoken of the pre-Viagra days with longing. "Back then, they'd pop after five, six minutes. Ten if they were trying to impress me. Nowadays? The fuckers'll go all night, thanks to all the fucking drugs. Pun intended."

Brenda's New York client had indeed gone all night, every night, for the past three nights. She'd showed him a good time and he'd tipped her nicely (a fat wad of twenties was stashed in the bottom of her purse beneath the lining, and no, she didn't have to share this with the agency), but now she was sore and there was a bruise on her knee from where she'd slammed it into the bed-post during one particularly acrobatic session.

Man, what she wouldn't give for a cigarette. But smoking on the job was a big fat no-no. The clients could always smell it. And taste it. Estelle didn't care if you did blow, but if you smoked a cigarette and the client com-plained, you were done. Unlike cocaine, cigarettes weren't considered a performance-enhancing drug.

She backed away from the mirror to see her full self. She looked good. Tight dark blue jeans were tucked into sleek black boots, and a thin white sweater showed off everything it was supposed to without revealing any skin. A short fitted jacket completed the ensemble. Her makeup was deliberately subtle, and her long, dark hair was left loose and straight, as per the client's request. He had specifically asked for a Girlfriend Experience, which meant she was to provide a very relaxed, "date night" type of encounter, with lots of easy conversation, foreplay, and non-kinky sex, topped off with cuddling and sweet talk afterward. Tonight, the sexy tight dresses and five-inch stilettos had been left at home, and that was fine by Brenda. GFEs, as they were known in the business, were her specialty.

She left the bathroom and headed toward the elevators, nodding to the uniformed concierge in the main lobby. He nodded back, looking bored. She'd seen him before, having had business in this hotel several times, but she didn't have to pay him off—Estelle would have taken care of that. Estelle's girls never handled money, because the Bitch didn't trust anybody. In fact, the client would have paid for Brenda's services yesterday, by cash or PayPal. Once Brenda got the text that payment had been received, it was on like Donkey Kong.

No background checks were ever done. The clients always preferred anonymity, and that was the risk you took in this business. A little scary, yes, but the job paid better than anything else she could do, like waitressing or retail sales. And it was putting her through school. Besides, it wasn't like she was working the streets, something Brenda would never do. Even sex workers had standards.

She was, however, required to check in with the agency five minutes before her scheduled appointment time. The check-ins were primarily to ensure that Brenda had arrived on schedule. She was not required to check in after the appointment was over, because frankly, Estelle didn't care how long she stayed with a client once she had received her money. It was *always* about the money. Brenda could probably work for a different agency, some place with more stringent safety measures, but none paid as well as Estelle did, and that was a fact.

The client was made fully aware in advance of the

required phone calls, but Brenda often wondered what Estelle or her assistant, Lynne, would actually say to the police if it turned out they had to call the cops. *"Hello, nine-one-one? My escort's not answering her cell phone and I'm worried she's being beaten and murdered by her client. Could you send someone over to the hotel?"*

And, oh yes, at this price point, they were always *clients*, never *johns*. And Brenda was never a hooker, prostitute, working girl, or whore. Always an *escort*. At five hundred dollars an hour (50 percent of which went to Estelle), it would have been damned insulting if someone called her a hooker.

She knocked on the door to room 1521 and waited. A moment later, the door opened. Brenda pasted a smile on her face, feeling a bit more alert now that the coke had fully kicked in. But her smile faded as she took in the client, who was definitely not what she was expecting.

His face, already flushed with excitement, lit up at the sight of her. "You look great," he said, breathless. "Just perfect. Exactly what I asked for." The door opened wider. "Please, come in."

Brenda hesitated, wondering if she should call Lynne to make sure they knew just how old this particular client was.

"I know." His smile was impish. "A little younger than you were expecting. But I'm eighteen, I swear. It's actually . . ." He poked his head out the door and checked down the empty hallway. His face reddened even more and he lowered his voice slightly. "It's actually my first time. Hope that's okay. I paid and everything."

Of course he'd paid. Brenda had already received confirmation of that. Okay, so he was young, probably still in high school. What was it to her? Actually, his inexperience would make for an easy night. At least he wouldn't have any weird requests.

She stepped inside. The door shut behind her.

"Not a problem," Brenda said. "Let me just check in with my agency, and then I'm all yours."

Turning away, she pressed two on her speed dial, murmured a few words to Lynne, and disconnected. She turned back to her young client with a smile. "There, all done. I'm Brianna. So happy to meet you." She reached forward to give him a hug, as she always did at the start of a Girlfriend Experience.

She didn't see the knife on the bed—long, sleek, and shiny—until a minute later when he had a hand over her mouth so tight she couldn't breathe.

She struggled against him, legs kicking out in front of her, hands clawing at the arm that was wrapped around her waist like a steel trap, but her efforts were futile. For a kid, he was surprisingly strong. Then a fist slammed into the side of her head, and her knees went out.

Fuck me, Brenda thought as the room turned hazy. She felt the sharp tip of the knife graze her throat, and if she could have screamed, she would have.

CHAPTER: 2

From the bits of conversation swirling in the hallway, the woman hadn't been dead long, six hours, maybe eight at the most. Female, mid-to-late twenties, long, dark hair, jeans, naked from the waist up. Her brassiere, sweater, boots, and jacket had been found crumpled in the corner of the room and had already been bagged for trace. The DO NOT DISTURB sign had not been placed on the exterior door handle, so housekeeping had entered the room at 9:02 that morning after a short knock. The Filipina maid, upon seeing the dead body, had screamed herself silly. It was the calm businesswoman across the hall who'd called 911.

Jerry Isaac stood just inside the doorway of room 1521 at the Sweet Chariot Inn, not entirely sure why he was here. He wasn't a cop anymore, had been retired from Seattle PD for two years, and had no business being at a crime scene. But the phone call he'd gotten from Detective Mike Torrance, his old partner, had left no room for argument. So Jerry had come, though he couldn't begin to understand what a murder victim had to do with him.

His cell phone rang. Reaching into his jacket

pocket, he checked the call display. It was his office. Danny. He answered it.

"Only have a minute to talk," he said to her, instead of saying hello.

"No problem. I just need your okay to order more toner for the copy machine. It's a hundred bucks." Danny was a no-nonsense girl, and Jerry liked that about her. She was a graduate student in criminal justice at Puget Sound State, and she'd started her internship at his private investigations company back in September. Hiring her had been a great move, and Jerry would be sorry to see her go when her internship ended next month.

"Go for it," he said.

"Thanks." She hung up.

He put the phone back in his pocket and remained a few feet back from the scene, not wanting to intrude on the multiple conversations taking place among the officers in the room. The scar across his throat itched like mad underneath his knit turtleneck, and he refrained from scratching it, knowing it would only make it worse. The wound had been inflicted a year before by a woman who was in prison awaiting trial for a crime much worse than her assault on him, and it still hadn't fully healed. Probably because he kept pawing at it.

But he couldn't help it. Every time Jerry thought of Abby Maddox, his scar itched. Every time his scar itched, he thought of Abby Maddox. There was no getting away from the memories, especially since her face was constantly on the news these days. Nothing was sexier to the public than a beautiful villain.

Mike Torrance, looking like his usual scruffy self in

a rumpled shirt and old sport coat, was standing near the top end of the king-sized bed, only inches away from the dead body. He caught Jerry's gaze and nodded. Clearing his throat noisily, he said, "Everybody out of the room for a few minutes, please."

The room emptied, curious faces looking at Jerry as they passed him at the doorway. He didn't have a badge, but they could tell he wasn't quite civilian. After thirty years in PD, you could never lose your "cop look," even if you were retired and wanted to.

Torrance beckoned him forward. Reluctantly, Jerry stepped closer. He had no desire to look at a dead body, but apparently he had no choice now.

"Thanks for coming," Torrance said.

Jerry stared at the half-naked body sprawled on the bed. She was faceup, hair fanned out over the pillow, eyes blank and staring at the ceiling, naked breasts spilled to each side, jean-clad legs askew. Her arms were positioned awkwardly, as if she'd been flailing when she died. Multiple bruises and contusions dotted her torso.

It was a lot to take in, and Jerry realized he'd stopped breathing. He took a long gulp of air. The scene might not have been so bad, if not for her face.

From the neck up, the dead woman's skin was a hideously swollen blend of purples, blues, and yellows. It immediately reminded Jerry of something, and it took him a few seconds to think of what it was—a kid's toy marble, of all things, minus the hair. *Christ*. A wave of nausea rolled in his gut.

Something was off about the woman's neck. At first glance, it looked split in half. And yet, there was no blood. A closer look might help explain things, but Jerry couldn't bring himself to do it. He stepped away from the bed.

"Why am I here, Mike?" His soft, raspy voice filled the quiet room, and it still surprised him to hear it. Gone was the deep, smooth baritone he'd once taken for granted. He had Abby Maddox to thank for that. "You pulled me off a stakeout for this?"

Torrance studied him. "Your eyes are bloodshot. You been up all night?"

"Yeah, I was on a job," Jerry said. He didn't bother to elaborate. What he did as a private investigator was none of Torrance's business. "And I have to get back to it. So why don't you tell me why you called me here."

"This will only take a second."

"What will?" He kept his voice low. There were only three bodies in the room—his, Torrance's, and the dead girl's—but Jerry didn't want anyone outside the room to hear him. The door was still propped open, cordoned off with yellow crime scene tape. "Come on, man. You know I could never stomach this shit."

He had never been good with dead bodies, and Torrance damn well knew that. During his time at PD, Jerry had worked vice, narcotics, domestic violence, robbery. Never homicide.

"See that?" Torrance's gloved finger hovered a few inches away from the woman's neck. "Take a good look at how she was killed."

Jerry sighed. Clearly Torrance wasn't going to explain anything to him until he saw what the detective wanted him to see. Moving closer to the foot of the bed, Jerry leaned forward, his eyes fixing on the spot where Torrance was pointing.

He saw it then. *Holy hell.*

"Zip tie?" Jerry might not have believed it if he wasn't actually looking at it. The plastic tie was transparent, which is why it wasn't visible from farther back. Somebody had strangled this poor girl with a piece of plastic you could buy at any hardware store for a few pennies. The tie was pulled so tight that the skin of her neck was bulging out like a squished balloon on either side. It was the goriest thing Jerry had ever seen that didn't involve blood.

It would not have been a fast death.

"Have you ever seen anything like this before, Mike?" Jerry said, trying to wrap his mind around it.

"Death by zip tie? Not personally, but considering it's about the cheapest murder weapon I can think of, it makes me wonder what kind of message it's supposed to send." Torrance pulled out another pair of latex gloves and offered them to Jerry. "Put these on and help me roll her over. Just a little. There's something else you need to see."

"No way." Jerry ignored the gloves and backed away from the bed again. Maybe he wouldn't have been so horrified at touching the body if the dead woman had been fully clothed. But she wasn't. Jerry couldn't fathom his hands on her cold, bare skin. "I can't do that."

"She's dead, pal. She isn't gonna mind. You really need to see this."

Adamant, Jerry shook his head. Giving up, Torrance placed his gloved hands under the dead woman's shoulders and lifted. It took some effort, but he got the body up about a foot.

In the bright morning light of the hotel room, it only took Jerry a second to process what Torrance wanted him to see. The woman had been lying in her own blood. The sheets underneath her were soaked with it. The deep red shade was shockingly stark against the hotel's crisp white linens, and it was more blood than Jerry ever wanted to see in one place at one time.

Stomach churning, he forced himself to take a good look at the dead woman's bare back.

"Somebody carved her." Jerry was speaking more to himself than to Torrance. He stared at the gashes, which ran from her shoulder blades to her waist. "Man, this is so many kinds of wrong."

"Can you make out what the words say?"

It was difficult to see past the blood smeared all over her, but after a few seconds, he saw that the letters (*Carved into human skin!* his mind shrieked unhelpfully) spelled out the words FREE ABBY MADDOX.

Jesus Christ. He had not been expecting to see *that*. Hell, no.

And beneath that, more gashes, but Jerry couldn't bear to look any longer. The dead girl had a serial killer's name carved into her body. It was horrific enough, thank you very much.

He sprang a few steps back from the bed, feeling Torrance's eyes on him, waiting for him to say something. Jerry felt numb. The best he could muster was, "What the fuck, Mike?"

"This is actually the second one." Torrance lay the

body back down gently. "The first one was found a week ago, the day after the prosecuting attorney announced that Maddox was being formally charged with murder. We didn't want to alert the media then because we didn't want to give the killer the publicity he was so obviously seeking. But now, with this second one, it's clear what we're dealing with. The murders are pretty much identical. The first victim also had long, dark hair and was slender, mid-twenties. She was also strangled with a zip tie in a hotel room."

Jerry was listening but not processing. A moment ago, he couldn't bear to look at the dead body, and now it felt like his eyes were stuck. He took it all in, her breasts, her shiny hair, the bruises, the cuts, her bloated face. She'd been alive once, and someone had killed her. Someone had carved her, writing words on her like fucking graffiti on a brick wall.

It was all too much.

He bolted from the room and made it out to the hallway, breathing hard and ignoring the questioning faces of the other cops who were probably still wondering what the hell he was doing here in the first place.

Torrance was behind him a moment later. He took Jerry's elbow and guided him down the hallway, out of earshot from the others. "You all right, pal?"

Jerry glared at him, still breathing hard. The hotel hallway air was slightly scented and this did nothing to help his nausea. "Pictures would have sufficed, my man."

"I really needed you to see it for yourself. I need your help with this."

"I'm retired."

"From PD, yeah. But your brain isn't retired, is it?"

"Who is she?"

"We're still working on the ID."

"'Free Abby Maddox.'" Jerry began to pace the hallway. The white-hot itch at his throat screamed for relief and he tugged at his turtleneck, not daring to scratch. It would be too hard to stop once he started. "Somebody has a sick sense of humor. Who the hell would want that psychotic bitch out of prison? She's exactly where she belongs."

"There's no end to the utter fuckery of the human race, pal." Torrance peeled off his latex gloves and ran a talc-powdered hand through his hair, leaving little bits of white in his short, bushy strands. "Maddox is a beautiful woman. She was big news last year when it was discovered she was Ethan Wolfe's girlfriend, and then she went on the run, and then she got convicted of assault. All that media attention was crazy enough, but now with her murder trial coming up? It's about to get ten times worse. And I'm sure there would be no shortage of wack jobs who would love to see her go free."

"She got nine years for what she did to me, and she's served a year so far. Now she's facing a possible life sentence with this murder charge. In what world would she ever go free?" Jerry cracked his knuckles, a habit he'd long given up trying to break. "You want to send a message, you write letters. You picket outside the prison. You don't go and kill two innocent women just to tell us you think Maddox is innocent of murder."

"Not just women. Women who look a lot like Maddox. What better way to get our attention?"

Jerry's left temple began to throb. "This is crazy. She's a serial killer. And now *another* serial killer is wanting her to go free?"

Torrance was quiet for a moment. Then finally he said, "She assaulted you, yeah. But is she really a serial killer?"

Jerry stopped pacing and glared at his former partner. "Fuck you, Mike."

"I'm just saying—"

"I don't want to hear it." Jerry's jaw was clenched so tight his molars were aching. "I'm sick of people suggesting she couldn't have killed anyone. That she was a victim of Ethan Wolfe herself. You weren't there, Mike. It wasn't your throat she cut."

"Easy." Torrance put a hand on Jerry's shoulder. "I'm not trying to be a dick—"

"Then stop being a dick." Jerry shrugged his hand off. "It's really not that hard."

Torrance lifted both hands in a sign of surrender. A few tense seconds passed. It was as good an apology as Jerry was going to get, and finally he gave his old partner a grudging nod.

The detective pulled out a pack of Marlboros and shook one all the way out before realizing he was in a hotel hallway and wasn't allowed to smoke. He stuck the cigarette in his mouth anyway, but didn't light it.

"I'd bet my left nut Maddox knows something about these current murders," Torrance said. "Think about it, pal. Because of you, the prosecuting attorney had an airtight case for first-degree assault, but everyone knows that what the PA really wants is to nail Maddox for murder. Finally, in a highly publicized press conference, the PA announces they've got enough to charge her, and a trial date is set. Then within a week we have two dead bodies with Abby Maddox's name carved on them? At the very least, that's a pretty good delay tactic, don't you think?"

Jerry sighed. "Why don't you just ask her?"

"We tried. Maddox doesn't want to talk to us." The cigarette bobbed up and down between Torrance's lips. "So I was thinking, maybe you could give it shot. Go see her at the prison."

Jerry couldn't help but laugh. It came out a bark, short and bitter. "And in what alternate, fucked up universe would I want to do that?"

"It's either you or Sheila Tao."

"Excuse me?" Jerry's head snapped up. "What are you talking about?"

"Maddox has been asking to talk to Dr. Tao ever since she was arrested a year ago." Torrance wouldn't meet Jerry's gaze. He knew better. "I never told you because I knew you'd flip out. I know how protective you are of your friend."

"Which is exactly why you should have told me." Now both temples were throbbing. Jerry started pacing again. "You're insane if you think I'm letting Sheila anywhere near that bitch."

"I knew that's what you'd say. And I agree, which is why we never contacted Dr. Tao. What she went through with Ethan Wolfe was enough. Plus I don't need her huge fiancé breathing down my neck like he did for the seven weeks Maddox was on the run." Torrance plucked the cigarette out of his mouth and rolled it between his thumb and forefinger. "So that's why I'm asking you to go see her. She'll talk to you. And we need answers, pal." He looked down the hallway toward room 1521.

Jerry said nothing. He didn't know what to say, and frankly, he was feeling pretty resentful at being ambushed.

His scar continued to scream for relief. Unable to take it anymore, he pulled down the collar of his turtleneck and gave his throat a good scratch. It felt wonderful until it started to burn, as was always the case. Forcing himself to pull his hand away, he examined his fingernails. There were specks of blood under two of them.

"It's just one visit to the prison." Torrance was watching him carefully. "Just to find out what Maddox knows. And what she wants. Did you see the other thing on the body that was carved beneath her name? Come on, let's go back into the room."

"Fuck that."

"Come and look at this first, and then you can tell me to fuck off." Torrance was moving down the hallway before Jerry could say anything else.

He didn't want to follow. The image of the dead girl was already etched into his brain permanently. While he felt awful about her death, there was nothing he could do to change it. Getting involved wouldn't help anything, other than to make his life worse than it already was. He'd already been scarred by Maddox, and in more ways than just the four-inch-long welt across his neck.

On cue, his scar screamed, and he scratched it again, drawing more blood. His personal life was already in the toilet. Work was busy and stressful. The last thing he needed right now was face-to-face contact with the psychotic bitch who'd tried to kill him.

Down the hallway, he saw Torrance reenter room 1521. Whatever it was that his former partner wanted him to see, it couldn't possibly change his mind about talking to Maddox. Right?

Shit.

Two seconds later, Jerry was striding toward the room.

What was that thing about curiosity killing the cat?

Yeah. That.

CHAPTER: 3

Morris didn't want to marry her. It was becoming painfully obvious. Dr. Sheila Tao was a professor of psychology, an expert on human behavior, and yet somehow she had missed all the signs. Because she hadn't wanted to see them.

She picked at her small bowl of honeydew and orange slices, which may as well have been cardboard, for all she could taste. Across the table in the brightly lit restaurant, her fiancé ate his own fruit contentedly, blue eyes focused on the giant flat-screen television mounted above her head. She sighed. She should have known better than to agree to eat brunch at a place that had TVs in it, especially when they needed to have a serious talk about the wedding. Unfortunately, Morris didn't seem to be in a talkative mood.

Their server refilled Morris's coffee, her pierced eyebrow raised at the sight of Sheila's barely touched fruit. "Is the melon okay?" she asked.

"It's fine." Sheila forced a smile. "Just not as hungry as I thought."

The server topped off Sheila's coffee. "I'll have your eggs out in a minute."

If Morris was listening to this exchange, he didn't show it. Clearly ESPN was much more interesting. Sheila had no idea what game he was watching, or even what sport, and she didn't care enough to turn her head to find out. Being a former NFL offensive lineman for the Green Bay Packers, Morris Gardener still loved football, but the man would watch anything with a score.

She caught a glimpse of herself in the mirrored wall behind him and saw that she looked pissed off, her full red lips pursed into a thin line, the space between her dark, almond-shaped eyes crinkled. Smoothing her hair, she arranged her features into a less hostile expression and turned her gaze back to her fiancé.

A few more moments passed before he finally broke away from the TV, and he smiled in surprise to find her watching him. "What's up, darlin'?"

"What's up?" Sheila knew she sounded pissy, but there was no way to pretend she wasn't pissed off. "What's up is I've been watching you watch TV for the past twenty minutes. If I wanted to watch you watch TV, we could have stayed home."

"Whoa, Nelly." Morris put his fork down and wiped his mouth with a napkin. "It's just sports highlights. Steelheads game doesn't start till noon. What did I miss?"

Reaching into her oversize purse, Sheila pulled out her wedding planner. She placed it on the table between them, moving the little tray of condiments out of the way so he would have a clear view of the thick leather binder. Morris's gaze dropped to it and his whole body stiffened. He leaned back in his chair, and Sheila might have laughed had she even a trace of good humor this morning. Ex-pro football player turned investment banker, six-four and two hundred sixty pounds, and yet here he was, scared of a goddamned wedding planner.

"Yes," Sheila said, reading his thoughts. "We are going to talk about the wedding."

"I didn't say anything."

"You didn't have to." She continued to make eye contact with him. "Morris, I'm going to ask you point-blank. Do you or don't you—"

"Okay, who had the ham and cheese omelet?" The cheerful voice of a server—not theirs, a different one—cut in. Exasperated, Sheila looked up into the face of the forcedly chipper young man who was balancing a large tray of food on a forearm full of tattoos.

"That's me," Sheila said.

"You must be the eggs Benedict, then." The server placed an oversized plate in front of Morris. "You look like an eggs Benny kind of guy. My favorite, too. Would either of you care for fresh ground pepper on your eggs?"

"We're fine," Sheila said at the same time Morris replied, "I would love some."

Morris grinned at her. Normally Sheila loved his smile—it made him look devilish and handsome—but at the moment she was too irritated to do anything but glare back.

She seethed in silence while the server dashed off to get the pepper mill. Then she seethed some more as Morris allowed the younger man to grind a generous amount of peppercorn onto his eggs.

"Need anything else at the moment?" the server asked.

"We're fine." Sheila's biting tone left no room for argument, and the server disappeared. Making a point not to pick up her utensils, Sheila looked across the table at her fiancé, whose mouth was already full of egg. "Morris. Please. We really need to—"

"I see Colin brought your breakfasts." Another ridiculously upbeat voice steamrolled over Sheila's words. "How does everything look? You're okay for ketchup and jelly? More cream for your coffee?"

Feeling as if she was about to lose it, Sheila glanced quickly at the server's name tag—their server now—then fixed her eyes on the young woman's pretty face. "Yes, Teri, we have our food, and the eggs are cooked perfectly. And no, we don't need ketchup or jelly or anything else. And before you can ask, we will not be needing more refills on our coffee. As a matter of fact, you can bring us the bill anytime. Just please, for the love of God, leave us alone. *Please*."

Teri's eyes widened and she backed away from the table with a what-the-hell-did-I-miss expression, one that eerily mirrored Morris's own from a moment earlier. Around them, heads turned, the other patrons looking over at their table with curious faces. Sheila didn't care if she was being loud. Let them all think she was a bitch. Maybe she was. It didn't matter.

Morris seemed overly absorbed in his breakfast.

"Look," Sheila said to him again, still not touching her food. "I'm just going to come straight out with it, and yes, we are going to discuss this right here, right now. We're not leaving here until you tell me why you don't want to marry me."

"Who says I don't want to marry you?" Morris's words were jumbled as he chewed. "When have I ever said that?"

"You won't even set a date." Sheila was making every effort to keep her voice down, but it wasn't working. The other patrons continued to stare. "The first time we planned a wedding, you were all over it. But this time? Every time the word *wedding* comes up, you find something else to do."

Morris swallowed, then took a long sip of his coffee. He wiped his mouth again, then took another long sip. It was a pathetic attempt at stalling. No problem. Sheila crossed her arms over her chest. She could wait all day if she had to.

Finally he said, "A lot has happened since we first tried to get married, darlin'. *Tried* being the operative word."

"So you're having second thoughts?"

"Of course not." He fiddled with a jelly packet. "I love you. I want to be with you."

"But you just don't want to marry me."

And then, just like that, Sheila felt it coming. Tears, hot and salty on her lower lids, threatened to spill over. She was horrified. This was not okay. Yelling in a restaurant was one thing; crying was another. Mortified, she touched her napkin to her eyes, hoping to cut the tears off at the pass.

"That's not it." Morris reached over and touched her hand, alarmed. He knew his fiancée wasn't a crier. "I asked you to be mine again, didn't I? You know I never say anything I don't mean."

"And yet we haven't set a wedding date."

He hesitated. "I don't think the timing is right."

"Oh God." Sheila pulled her arm away. The tears flowed freely down her cheeks and she blotted furiously, aware that everyone was staring. Through the haze she could see their server standing in a corner with a bunch of other restaurant employees, looking over and whispering furiously. She was putting on a show, apparently. Well, too bad. They could stare all they wanted. "I've been suspecting you felt this way for a while now, but I never thought you'd say you didn't want to marry me."

"But I didn't say that!" Morris's own frustration caused his naturally loud voice to become even louder. All chatter around them came to a complete stop. Great. Forget watching, now everybody in the restaurant was listening, too. "Don't put words in my mouth, Sheila. I'm not saying never. I'm saying *not now*."

"Same thing." Sheila's voice was dull. She wiped under her eyes. Dark blotches of mascara were transferring to her cotton napkin, and she knew she probably looked smudgy and clownish. She didn't care. All she could hear was that Morris didn't want to marry her, and the realization that her deepest fear was coming true was more painful than anything she'd felt in a long time. She'd almost lost him once. She couldn't believe it was happening again.

"Why don't we get our brunch to go?" Morris stared down an older couple at the next table who'd been watching them with great interest, and they finally looked away. "I feel like we're in a fishbowl."

"We're finishing our discussion here."

"Hon, people are staring—"

"I don't give a shit!" Sheila's voice was high and shrieky. "Let them look."

An awkward silence passed between them. Morris picked at his food, but it was clear he'd lost his appetite. Sheila's food stayed on her plate, untouched. Seconds ticked by like minutes. Slowly, the conversations around them resumed to normal levels. Finally Sheila leaned forward.

"I thought we were working through everything that happened," she said. "Or am I misreading things? I thought the counseling was helping us both. You know I'm in a good place."

"You're in an amazing place. I'm so proud of you."

"Then what's the problem? Talk to me. Tell me what you're feeling."

Morris sighed and put his fork down. He reached for her hand once again. "I just . . . I think it's too soon."

"It's been a year since everything happened."

"Yes, and maybe we need another year."

Another year? He couldn't be serious.

"Are you still thinking about . . ." Sheila stopped, not actually able to speak the name that was on the tip of her tongue aloud.

"Ethan." Morris said it for her, his voice flat. "Yes, I'd be lying if I said I wasn't thinking about him. Maybe more than I should be."

"Because of Abby Maddox being all over the news right now? Because I thought we had worked through that. I know it takes time, but—"

"Maybe the press has something to do with it, yeah."

Morris's jaw clenched and he was looking away—both surefire signs of his agitation—but he didn't let go of her hand. "It's definitely not helping. With all the media attention on Maddox right now, and the press talking about all the murders from last year, it's hard not to think of that . . . other stuff."

Sheila didn't ask him to clarify what he meant by that, because she already knew. She was a tenured psychology professor at Puget Sound State University, and around this time last year, she'd been having an affair with one of her teaching assistants, a graduate student named Ethan Wolfe. Yes, she'd been in a serious relationship with Morris at the time, and no, the affair had not ended well. In fact, it had ended so terribly that Ethan had nearly killed her. If it hadn't been for Morris . . .

Sheila closed her eyes. It hurt like hell to think of Ethan now, but her ex-lover was impossible to forget. Ethan Wolfe had fooled everyone. On the surface, he'd seemed like your average brilliant and charming graduate student. But underneath, he was a raging psychopath, and after Sheila's rescue, the dismembered remains of fourteen homeless women were found in the walls of Ethan's basement.

Fourteen dismembered bodies. And he'd only been twenty-three years old. The press had nicknamed him the Tell-Tale Heart Killer.

And even though he was dead, the nightmare still wasn't over. Abby Maddox, Ethan's longtime girlfriend, was front-page news once again, making it very difficult for Sheila and Morris to move forward. Though Abby was tucked away safely at Rosedale Penitentiary, serving out a nine-year sentence for first-degree assault on their friend and retired cop Jerry Isaac, it wasn't nearly good enough for the prosecuting attorney.

The King County PA, up for reelection next year and in need of good publicity, wanted somebody to pay for the murders of those homeless women found in Ethan's basement. Who better than his girlfriend Abby Maddox, who'd slashed the throat of a retired cop and had gone on the run for seven weeks?

Unfortunately, though, the evidence-gathering had been difficult. There was simply nothing linking Abby to the bodies found in Ethan's house. They couldn't prove Abby even knew about her boyfriend's proclivities. For months, it was looking like nothing was going to stick, and gradually, public interest in Abby Maddox waned. Things had blissfully quieted down for a few glorious months.

Until last week.

In a spectacular turn of events, the PA announced she finally had enough to charge Abby Maddox with the murder of Diana St. Clair. Diana had not been one of the victims found in Ethan's basement. She had not been homeless. On the contrary, Diana had been a fellow student at Puget Sound State, thought to have been romantically involved with Ethan Wolfe, her TA. She'd gone missing for a week until her body had turned up floating in the Sound. She hadn't drowned—of course not, Diana had been a contender for the U.S. Olympic swim team. She'd been stabbed to death. A year later, her poor parents were still demanding justice. It was believed that

Ethan had killed her, but with him dead, nobody had ever been charged with her murder.

Until now.

During the announcement, the prosecuting attorney had expressed confidence they could prove Abby Maddox knew about her boyfriend's affair, and that *she* had killed Diana in a jealous rage. The trial was set to begin a month from now. Meanwhile, the PA's investigation into Abby's involvement in the deaths of the homeless women would continue. There was no statute of limitations on murder.

And just like that, Abby Maddox and, by extension, Ethan Wolfe were back in the spotlight. Of course it had to be hard on Morris. But still, his words hurt like crazy.

"I need more time," Morris was saying. "That's all it is. A wedding right now just seems so . . ."

"What?"

"Out of place." Morris shrugged, helpless. "Everything still feels fresh. I can still remember the night I found you, the night I shot him . . ." He closed his eyes briefly. "I don't want those images floating around in my big head, even if they're pale and fuzzy and in pieces. Because I still see them, when what I should be seeing is you and our future. Not our past."

His words were like sharp needles, poking her over and over again. But deep down, Sheila knew he was right. She was pushing for this wedding because she was terrified of losing him, but if she continued to push, she *would* lose him.

"Okay," she said, relenting. "I hear you. I'm sorry I caused a scene."

"Don't apologize, darlin'. We should have had this talk months ago. It was cowardly of me to not tell you how I was feeling."

She held up her left hand, where a diamond the size of a small marble sat on her ring finger. "Should I still be wearing this?"

"Of course!" Morris kissed her hand. "Don't you dare take it off. You're my fiancée, and someday, you'll be my wife. When the time is right. When we're both . . . healthier."

Healthier. Nice way to put it. Morris was a recovering alcoholic, and she was a recovering sex addict, and a year ago, they had both fallen off the wagon. The road to recovery was a long one, and not a straight path by any means. Sheila knew that better than most.

"Can you live with giving it a bit more time?" Morris's voice was gentle.

She looked at him, looked at his handsome face in the glowy light of the restaurant, his kind eyes, his hopeful expression. The doubts were still screaming like banshees inside her chest, but she forced them down and nodded. "Yes." She wiped her eyes, feeling self-conscious. "God, I must look like hell."

"You're the most beautiful woman in the room right now." Morris kissed her hand again. "You hang on to that wedding planner. We'll need it someday soon."

"Sure." Sheila looked down at the leather binder. The tears were threatening her again. She willed them not to drop. "No problem."

CHAPTER: 4

Rosedale Penitentiary was a cold, lifeless place. Which was to be expected, considering it was a prison.

Abby Maddox sat facing her high-powered attorney, a man with a thick mop of silver hair and a ruddy alcoholic's complexion. They were in one of the prison "conference rooms," a laughable name for the space, considering it was only ten by fifteen feet, with painted concrete walls, a metal table, and four folding chairs. The steel was hard underneath Abby's ass, and she shifted periodically in her seat as her lawyer droned on. He had been speaking non-stop for five minutes. The man loved the sound of his own voice.

Which wasn't to say that Bob Borden wasn't a hell of a defense attorney. He was, and that's why she'd picked him. When word of Abby's arrest last year in Florida leaked to the media, a dozen criminal attorneys from prestigious law firms had contacted her, all offering to represent her pro bono. She knew right away she wanted Borden. His success rate at trial was impressive, he was male, and he'd been married for over twenty-five years.

And that last part was key. The more married a guy was, the more pliable he tended to be.

Abby nodded every few seconds to show she was listening, which she was, for the most part. Borden's animated gestures were difficult to ignore. Though he was in his mid-fifties, he was far from unattractive, dressed in a gray custom-tailored pinstripe suit and a teal necktie that brought out the bright blue of his eyes. The man was skillful, manipulative, and aggressive, and his intensity was exactly what she needed.

Borden's only weakness? His ego. *Men.*

"So where do things stand?" she asked when he finally paused. She was careful to keep the impatience out of her voice.

"They don't have much." Borden's gaze flickered to her lips, as they always did when she spoke. On cue, she licked them, watching as his breath quickened slightly. Really, it was too easy. It almost wasn't even fun.

"What do they have, then?"

"It's turning into a clusterfuck over there." His gaze lingered on her mouth for a few seconds more. "No doubt they're trying to find DNA and trace that will tie you to the murders of those homeless women. But if they haven't found anything yet, they're not going to. From what my sources are telling me, they're not even finding any of Ethan's DNA. He took great care to be clean, I'll grant him that. So our focus is on Diana St. Clair."

"And the professor's testimony?"

Borden waved a manicured hand. "Sheila Tao won't testify, I'll see to that. Anything she has to say about you is hearsay. She was locked in Ethan's basement for three weeks and nothing he said to her can be corroborated, so don't concern yourself with her."

Sheila Tao. The mere mention of the bitch made Abby want to scratch Borden's eyes out, just because he was there.

She kept her face composed. "So I continue to sit here and rot while we wait for the trial to start, and in the meantime the prosecuting attorney is still trying to pin the homeless women's murders on me. It's really not looking good for me now, is it, Bob? I'm already in for nine years because you said that was the best you could do."

"It was, Abby. And it won't be nine years, trust me. You'll be out in four for good behavior, and since you've already served a year, that's only three years left." Borden's smile was an attempt at reassurance. "It'll pass in no time."

The arrogant sonofabitch. Anybody in here could tell you that jail time was not quick time. The year Abby had spent in here already felt like ten.

"Actually, that's why I'm here this morning." The attorney folded his hands together. "There's been an interesting development."

"Tell me already." Abby worked at keeping her voice soft. "Or do you want me to beg?"

Borden's ruddy face turned a deeper shade of red. He adjusted his tie even though it didn't need adjusting. "A dead body turned up this morning at the Sweet Chariot Inn in downtown Seattle. It's an upscale boutique hotel, pricey but small. Adult female, twenties, Caucasian. The cops are coming to talk to you about it. My contacts at Seattle PD gave me the heads-up."

He'd thrown in that last line just so she'd know how

well connected he was. As if she didn't already know all about him. Abby knew more about her attorney than he'd ever realize. She knew that his kids were Jessica, Christian, and Hunter, ages seventeen, fifteen, and twelve respectively. She knew his wife was named Natasha, and that she was forty-six, and that she was fucking their Mercedes mechanic. Abby might be in prison, but she knew everything she needed to know about Bob Borden.

"The police are coming to talk to me about a dead body? Which has what to do with me?" Abby raised an eyebrow and gestured to her prison attire. "Look where I am. They can't possibly think *I* killed her."

"Of course not." Borden glanced up at the ceiling, as if to reassure himself that there were no cameras in here. There weren't, but his voice dropped, anyway. "But is there any chance you know who did?"

Abby leaned back in her chair, appraising her attorney. "Interesting question. What was the victim's name?"

"Brenda Stich. College student. She had more than a passing physical resemblance to you."

Abby cocked her head. "And it grows curiouser and curiouser."

"The name ring any bells?"

"Not remotely." Abby drummed her fingers on the table impatiently. "Is this really what you came here to ask me, Bob? I live in a six-by-nine cell surrounded by guards all day. What could I possibly know about a murder?"

"I do have a reason for asking." Borden continued to

watch her intently. "It seems your name was found at the scene, carved into the dead girl's body. I'm told the exact words were 'Free Abby Maddox.'" He paused for dramatic effect. "I'll confirm once I receive photos."

She stared at him, tempted to ask him to repeat what he'd just said, even though she'd heard him perfectly. Keeping her face straight and her tone appropriately somber, she said, "You know I have some disturbed fans, Bob."

"Yes, you do."

Abby wasn't being arrogant with her use of the word *fans*. She was well aware of her social media celebrity status. There was a fan website called FreeAbbyMaddox .com. Someone had set up a Facebook page and it currently had over a hundred thousand "Likes." There were at least six fake Twitter accounts in her name. A bit twisted perhaps, but so what? After a year in here, she needed all the support she could get. Fans sent her all kinds of donations, which helped enormously in prison.

"Any fan in particular stand out?" he asked.

Abby allowed a small smile to play at the corners of her lips, never allowing it to fully materialize. "Nobody special comes to mind."

"They're going to check your mail. See who's been writing to you."

"That's a ton of mail. They won't find anything."

"That's their problem." Borden put his hand over hers.

A shudder of repulsion passed through Abby. Not that she let it show, of course. She didn't like to be touched unless she initiated it herself. But it was important to let him think she liked him. She needed him to work hard for her, especially since he was doing it for free. She allowed his hand to remain.

"What's happened here, Abby—as much as it's a tragedy that a woman was found dead, of course—is not necessarily a terrible thing," Borden said. "For you, I mean. There are indications that this murder wasn't the first. Another woman, also resembling you, was killed a week ago, but I haven't received definitive word from my sources yet as to whether the two murders are related. They likely are, though."

Abby sat up straighter. "They think it's a serial killer?"

"A serial killer who's obsessed with you. Somebody desperately wants you out of prison. And whoever he is, he went to great lengths to send the police a message."

Abby wanted to smile, but she held back. A smile would not be an appropriate reaction to news like this. "So the killer carved 'Free Abby Maddox' into the woman's back. That's a serious way of sending the prosecuting attorney a message, Bob."

Her lawyer paused, a slight frown passing over his face. Immediately, Abby bit her lip. *Shit*. The man missed nothing, which was exactly the reason she'd picked him. Had Borden specifically said that the carving was on the woman's *back*? Maybe he hadn't.

She squeezed his hand, and it immediately had the desired effect because his face reddened. "Those poor women." Her voice was husky. "How did she die, Bob? Blood loss?"

"Actually," Borden said, his tone matching hers, "she was strangled with a zip tie before she was carved. You know those long plastic doohickeys you can buy at a hardware store?" He grimaced. "It's actually a very efficient way to kill somebody. The ties are cheap, they're quick to tighten, and once they're on—"

"You can't get them off unless you cut them off," she finished. "With scissors."

"Exactly. No blood. No mess. No fuss."

Abby said nothing as she processed this. It was a rather horrific way to die, wasn't it? She closed her eyes for a moment, picturing what the death would have been like. She imagined the sound the zip tie would make as it was pulled tighter, ridged plastic against ridged plastic, and how it would feel cutting into her throat, cutting off air, cutting off the ability to even take a breath, small hands clawing at the plastic to try and tear it off, but to no avail. The world eventually going dark, until there was just . . . nothing.

A zip tie. Who knew something so cheap, so readily available, and so easy to hide in a pocket would be so effective?

Fucking brilliant.

"There's more," Borden said. "Beneath your name was another message." He paused again. He knew damn well he had her full attention and he was determined to soak up every second. Jesus, how did his wife stand him? "Two numbers. A two, a slash, and then a ten."

He let go of her hands and Abby resisted the urge to wipe her palms on her prison-issue slacks. She watched as he removed his pen from his breast pocket to scribble something on the yellow legal pad in front of him. He turned it around so she could read it.

2/10.

"Two-ten?" Abby frowned at his handwriting, her finger brushing over the page where he'd scrawled. "Is that a date? February tenth? What happened on February tenth?"

"Nothing, which is why they don't think it is a date." Borden tapped the notepad with his pen. "February ten doesn't correspond to anything. It's not your birthday, it's not your incarceration date, it's not linked to anything relevant they can find. Not even anything to do with Ethan, as far as they can determine."

"So then what does it mean?"

"The police think it's the kind of number you would see at the bottom of a limited-edition print."

Abby waited. Her attorney interpreted her silence as confusion.

"You know when artists make prints of their work?" Borden said. "And at the bottom, they sign it, beside the number of prints that will be in circulation? The dead woman who was found a week ago—who's probably linked to this murder—was also strangled with a zip tie. Your name wasn't on that one, or we'd have obviously heard about it then, but there was a number carved on that body as well. One-ten." He scrawled it again for clarity.

1/10.

"I see." Abby picked up the piece of paper and stared at it, tilting her head. "So it's a *counter*. As in, one out of ten. Two out of ten."

"Yes. They think so."

She spoke softly, almost a whisper. "So there'll be

eight more victims? Victims who look like me, with my name carved into them?"

"Possibly."

Abby leaned forward and took both his hands in both of hers, enjoying the flush that spread across his cheeks once again. "So you're thinking I might have some leverage here. The police are going to assume I know something."

"Do you know something?"

She shrugged and said nothing. A moment passed. Borden didn't push. She knew he didn't care whether she was innocent or guilty—he was her lawyer, for fuck's sake. All he cared about was winning.

Borden smiled at her, the rush from their skin-to-skin contact going straight to his head. "It's okay. Even if you don't know anything, there's no reason to let them think otherwise. For now, anyway. This could definitely be to our advantage, if we play it right."

"So tell me how to play it."

He squeezed her hands tighter. "Just keep doing everything we talked about. I've been getting some calls from television shows wanting to interview you, and we can work with that, too. You might be in prison, but you *are* in control here, Abby. Don't you ever forget that."

Abby laughed. God, men could be so stupid. "Come on, Bob. As if I ever could."

CHAPTER: 5

The lovebirds were still inside the restaurant. How long did it take to eat lamb souvlaki, anyway?

Jerry didn't have the time to be sitting outside a Greek tavern. He was scheduled to meet Maddox in an hour, and the drive to Rosedale Penitentiary was a little over that, maybe fifty minutes if he really stepped on it. But none of that seemed to matter at this moment. Abby Maddox could wait. He'd been on an overnight stakeout when Torrance had called that morning, and he wanted—no, needed—to see how it all played out.

He sat cocooned inside the tinted windows of his brand-new navy blue Jeep Grand Cherokee, bought last month after his old Honda Accord finally died. The afternoon was dark and wet, typical for a Seattle winter. With the rain pelting against the windshield, he was in the perfect spot to observe the entrance to the restaurant without being seen. An older Sony DSLR camera was in his lap, mounted with a 180 lens. Not the best one he owned, but good enough for the few shots he would take when the couple finally finished eating and came out.

Jerry didn't love being a private investigator, but he

didn't hate it, either. It was simply something to keep him busy since his retirement from Seattle PD two years ago. Jerry was still a young man, only fifty-three, and retirement in the cliché sense—golfing, vacations to Florida, early bird specials at the local diner—had never appealed to him. Relying on referrals from his cop friends, he'd started the business one month after his last day at PD and had been lucky to have a steady stream of clients from the first day he'd hung his shingle. The income wasn't making him rich, but it supplemented his pension decently. He specialized in cheating partners and missing persons. There always seemed to be an abundance of both.

This job was the former. Not Jerry's favorite type of work by any stretch, because in infidelity cases like this, emotions always ran high. And he hated delivering bad news, which he almost always had to do, because if a husband or wife *suspected* their spouse was cheating, the spouse almost always was. There was something to be said for marital instincts.

Jerry knew all about marital instincts. He'd been married for over fifteen years. He had damned good marital instincts.

The glass door of the restaurant finally opened and the woman exited first. Her date held the door for her as she went through, laughing at something she'd said. Arm in arm, the pair strolled down the sidewalk to where the man's Range Rover was parked in the pay lot. The woman narrowly avoided stepping in a puddle, and she grabbed her date's arm for support. Jerry allowed himself a tight smile in the privacy of his Jeep. *Not cool making her walk in the rain, buddy,* he thought. *You should have had her wait in the restaurant while you went to get your fancy car. That's what I would have done.*

Rolling his window down a few inches, Jerry poked the lens of his Sony through the opening and took several photos in rapid succession. Pictures weren't his strong suit, and nobody had requested these today, but he felt compelled to bang out a few shots anyway. You never knew if you'd need them later. Plus it was easy taking pictures of this woman. Her smile was infectious, and Jerry thought she looked extra beautiful this afternoon, her long coat unbuttoned over a knee-length green dress, one he hadn't seen before.

As far as her lover went, Jerry had done a thorough background check, and not that much had come up. The man's name was George Jackson and he was the head basketball coach at Puget Sound State University. His income was roughly $160,000 a year, obnoxiously high considering the Steelheads had been the losingest basketball team in the Pacific Northwest for the past three years straight. Jackson was forty years old, making him six years younger than the woman on his arm. An upstanding, taxpaying citizen with no criminal record.

The wind picked up suddenly, catching the woman's dark hair and pulling it back off her face. Even from this distance, Jerry could see the gorgeous diamond hoop earrings she wore, the stones glinting like little stars at her lobes.

Diamond hoop earrings that the woman only wore on special occasions.

Diamond hoop earrings that had been an anniversary present five years ago.

Diamond hoop earrings that Jerry had spent hours picking out at the jewelry store, because that was the kind of thing a husband did for his ten-year wedding anniversary.

Through the long lens of his camera, Jerry watched as another man held his wife's arm, leading her toward a shiny white Range Rover. He watched as Annie climbed into the passenger side, still laughing as her date climbed in beside her and started the engine.

A minute later, Jerry pulled out onto the street behind them, careful to keep one car back. Not that he had to worry about being spotted. Neither was expecting he'd be behind them, and of course Annie wouldn't recognize the brand-new Jeep.

Like the last six times, he was planning to follow his wife and her boyfriend back to Annie's apartment, because that's where George Jackson, the college basketball coach who was thirteen years younger than himself, richer, and in much better physical condition, had picked her up.

Like the last six times, Jerry needed to see the good-bye kiss. He needed to see the man's arms around his wife in that passionate embrace that always seemed to top off their dates together.

Even though it stung like hell. Even though it aggravated him. Even though it caused the scar at his throat to itch like crazy from the stress. It was all as fresh and real as it had been six months ago when Annie had left him. She may have done the leaving, but it was Jerry who'd done the hurting.

He knew he had to stop following her. None of this was healthy.

The Range Rover turned left toward Annie's place, and at the last second, Jerry turned right, which would take him to the freeway. There was someone he needed to see before he headed to the prison.

He'd had enough self-punishment for one day.

CHAPTER:6

Sheila cared about Jerry a lot, but he was her close friend's soon-to-be ex-husband, and the whole situation was awkward as hell.

Jerry was one of Morris's closest friends. Marianne (or Annie, as only Jerry was allowed to call her) was Sheila's best friend, and the four of them had been through a lot together. But in a marital separation, it was always more than just the couple who split. Social circles fractured right along with the marriage. Sheila hadn't seen Jerry in a couple of months at least, and she had no idea why he was here now, sitting in her office with a big manila folder in front of him. The morning had been difficult already, and she thought she'd escape to the university to catch up on some work. She sensed now that that wasn't going to happen, and she pushed the papers she'd been grading aside.

Jerry didn't look good. Tired and skinny, he was dressed in a black turtleneck to hide the scar on his neck. He seemed to only wear turtleneck sweaters these days, and it was not a good fashion choice for him. They only made him look skinnier.

"Sure you don't want coffee?" she asked him again.

"I can grab you a cup. If I'd known you were coming, I'd have stopped and picked up some muffins."

Jerry shook his head and glanced at his watch. It made her nervous that he wasn't smiling. Usually he was always smiling.

"I only have a few minutes," he said, his voice raspy and raw. Even after a year, it still surprised Sheila to hear it. "I'm glad I tracked you down here. I stopped by your house and nobody was home. Where's the big guy today?"

Sheila smiled. Jerry always referred to Morris as the "big guy," even though the two men were about the same height. Morris, however, outweighed Jerry by about seventy pounds. "Out, schmoozing clients from Hong Kong."

"Investment bankers work on Saturdays?"

"If you consider golf, dinner, and poker to be work," Sheila said drily. "I was lucky to see him this morning. He probably won't be home till midnight." She winced, trying not to think about the scene she'd made at brunch earlier.

Jerry glanced at his watch again. "I'm actually glad he's not around. It was you I came to see. I need to talk to you about something important."

"Something about you and Marianne?" The words were out before Sheila could stop herself. Shit. She hadn't wanted to bring up Jerry's wife, and now she had done just that.

Jerry looked surprised. "No. Why would you think that?"

"I—" Sheila stopped. She'd already stuck her foot in

it and wasn't sure what to say next. "Shit," she said instead.

Jerry was quiet for a moment. He drummed his fingers on her desk. "I know she's seeing someone," he said finally.

"Jerry . . ."

He lifted a hand, his expression pained. "That's not why I'm here. But since you brought it up . . . I saw her with him the other day. It's pretty obvious they're . . . close."

"You saw Marianne the other day?" Sheila looked at him closely. "You saw her, or you followed her?"

Jerry wouldn't meet her gaze.

"Oh, Jerry." She sighed. "That's not the way to get her back."

"I didn't say I wanted her back."

"Of course you do. She's your wife. You love her. Fifteen years of marriage is a long time."

"She left *me*."

Sheila was growing more uncomfortable by the second. "You know why she did."

"Because I pulled away," Jerry said, frustrated. "I know I was terrible to live with, for months. Maybe I still am, I don't know."

"It was a difficult time for us all, Jerry." Sheila hadn't wanted to have this conversation with him, but she supposed now it was inevitable. They were friends, after all, and it wasn't realistic to think they could sit alone in her office and not talk about something major that was affecting them both. "People cope with it differently."

"Your hair is longer." Jerry looked at her, his eyes soft. "Like Annie's. You look more like her."

Sheila and Marianne were both of Chinese descent, and yes, Sheila had let her dark hair grow out over the past year. It now fell well past her shoulders. "We've been mistaken for sisters more than once," she said with a smile.

Jerry sighed deeply and tugged at the collar of his turtleneck. "Anyway, that's not why I'm here. I was at a crime scene this morning. There was a body found at a hotel downtown."

Sheila was instantly intrigued. Despite the craziness of last year, she still had a thing for true crime. "Yes, it was all over the news this morning. I heard it on the radio as I was driving in to the office. What happened?"

"A young woman was murdered." Jerry cracked his knuckles. "She was strangled, then carved."

"The news didn't say anything about her being carved." Sheila found herself both fascinated and repulsed. "Do they know who did it?"

"They're working on it. You remember my old partner, Mike Torrance?"

She nodded. Detective Torrance had interviewed her at length after her rescue from Ethan's basement. Mid-forties, scruffy, gruff voice, generally unsympathetic and a borderline jerk. Morris couldn't stand the guy, and Sheila couldn't say she blamed him.

"He called me over to the hotel. Wanted me to see the body." A dark look flitted across Jerry's face. "Not my idea of a fun Saturday."

"I don't understand. You're retired. What does a murder victim have to do with you? Did you know her?" Sheila sat up with a start. "Oh God, Jerry, I'm so sorry—"

"No, no, it's nothing like that," Jerry said. "I didn't know her, but she . . ."

Sheila waited for him to continue. After a few seconds, impatience and curiosity got the better of her. "Okay, out with it already. What does a dead body in a hotel room have to do with you? Or me? Because you wouldn't be here if this didn't have something to do with both of us."

Jerry sighed, and it was then she noticed how deeply the lines were etched into his forehead. He'd really aged in the last few months, and Sheila didn't have to wonder how bad his scar looked under the turtleneck. There was a reason he was still wearing them. Marianne had tried for months to get him to go to a plastic surgeon who might be able to improve its appearance, but apparently Jerry had never been willing to discuss it.

"The victim had the message 'Free Abby Maddox' carved into her back." Jerry spoke clearly but softly, his rasp worse than ever.

Sheila froze. She opened her mouth to speak, but nothing came out.

"The cops think Seattle has a new serial killer on its hands," Jerry said.

Her gaze fell to the manila folder sitting on the desk between them, and she finally found her voice. "Is that what's in there? Pictures?"

"Crime scene photos. Do you want to see them? You don't have to look if you don't want to, but I brought them in case you did."

She hesitated, then reached forward and slid the folder toward her. Taking a deep breath, she flipped it open, bracing herself. The first sheet was a typewritten page of notes, and she skipped past it to the color photographs underneath.

The images were difficult to process. At first glance, they weren't nearly as gory as she was expecting—she'd seen much worse on TV and in the movies. The only difference was, in these photos, the women were real people, and now they were dead.

And not just dead. *Murdered.*

"That first picture is of Stephanie Hooper," Jerry said, his voice taking on a mechanical quality Sheila had never heard before. "Age twenty-four. You can see she has an uncanny resemblance to Abby Maddox, though of course nobody would have picked up on it at the time. She was found in a hotel room downtown a week ago."

Sheila peered closer at the photo. The woman was lying atop a rumpled bed, dressed in tight jeans, naked from the waist up. "What's that around her throat?"

"Zip tie."

"You're kidding."

"If you look at the next picture, it's a shot of her at the morgue, and you can see the carvings on her back."

The next one was worse. Under the harsh lights of the morgue, the bruises were clearly visible, and FREE ABBY MADDOX was carved deeply, and rather neatly, into the woman's back. The victim's skin color was unnatural, and with her lying on the cold steel table, it was easy to forget that she had once been alive. Breathing. Vibrant. The thought pinched something deep inside Sheila, filling her with a profound sense of sadness. She looked up at Jerry. "I can't make out the second carving beneath the name, it's too small. What is it?"

"It's a one, then a slash, then a ten," Jerry said.

Sheila frowned. She didn't get it.

"Look at the next photo. If you want to. Though you definitely seem to have a better stomach for this stuff than I do."

Obligingly, she turned to the next picture. And felt another pang.

"Victim two was Brenda Stich." Jerry cracked his knuckles again, something he always did when he was stressed. "This is the one they found this morning. Different hotel. Age twenty-six. As you can see, she was also a Maddox clone. She also died of asphyxiation by zip tie."

Sheila inhaled sharply. Even though Jerry had told her what to expect only moments before, it was something else entirely to see it in full color. The words FREE ABBY MADDOX were indeed carved deeply into the woman's back, and the blood from the wounds was smeared all over her skin.

It took her a second before she could speak. "What's that underneath Maddox's name? Same as the last girl?"

"Sort of. Only this one says two-slash-ten."

It was too much to process. Taking one last look at the picture, Sheila closed the file, relieved there were no more photos. Hands trembling, she clasped them together again, trying to regain her bearings. She knew Jerry was about to explain everything. Problem was, she was no longer certain she wanted to hear it.

"Rape kits on both vics came back negative." That distant tone again. Jerry sounded as if he were reciting.

"Both women had engaged in intercourse recently, but there's nothing specific to indicate sexual assault. The first one, Stephanie Hooper, was a student at the University of Washington. The second one was enrolled at Seattle Pacific, though she only went part-time."

"Both college girls," Sheila said. "And the zip ties? Any significance with those?"

"None the cops can think of. They're cheap and impossible to trace."

"And the knife?" Sheila said. "Was the same one used to carve both women?"

"Someone's been watching *CSI*." Jerry gave her a wan smile. "It's not definitive, but it appears that the same knife was used in both murders, something longish, sharp, and smooth. The carving was likely done postmortem." He paused. "The number on the first vic was never released to the media. At first they thought the one-slash-ten corresponded to a date of some sort. But with this next vic—"

It hit Sheila then.

"He's counting them." Horrified, she tried to wrap her mind around it. "One out of ten. Two out of ten."

"Yes."

"And they think there might be eight more victims?"

"They do, yes. And so I have to talk to Maddox today. At the prison. Find out what she knows." Jerry glanced at his watch again. "I'm late."

Sheila blinked. "That's funny, I think I misheard you. I could have sworn you just said you were going to talk to Abby Maddox today."

Jerry gave her a look.

"Give me a break!" Sheila felt her face grow hot. "Tell them to go to hell! Why would you—"

"It was either me or you. Maddox has been asking to speak with you for the past few months."

Sheila sat up. "And why wasn't I informed of that?"

"They didn't want to upset you. You've been through enough."

"That's not for anyone to decide but me." Aggravated, Sheila pushed her chair out from the table and stood up. "You should have told me, Jerry."

"I only just found out myself."

Sheila started pacing the floor. "Why does she want to talk to me?"

"I don't know," Jerry said. "I feel like it's a ploy. But whatever she knows, she won't reveal it to the cops. She'll only speak to you. I'm hoping she'll settle for me instead. If she knows anything about what happened to that poor girl this morning . . ." His voice trailed off.

Sheila turned around to face him, and saw him tugging at the collar of his turtleneck again. He saw her watching and stuck his hand back in his lap.

"And you agreed to go?"

"Yeah. And I didn't want you to hear about it from anyone else but me." He sighed deeply. "Those bodies, they change everything. She's made it clear through her lawyer that she might know something about the murders. At least, that's the way she and her attorney are playing it."

"I'm going with you. If she's asking for me, then I need to see her."

Jerry looked horrified. "Oh, *hell* no. And I'll give you

three good reasons." He leaned forward. "First, I don't trust the bitch. She's playing games, and you don't need to be subjected to her bullshit, not after everything you've been through. And second—and this is an even better reason—Morris will kill me if I let you anywhere near her."

"Don't be silly," Sheila said, although she couldn't necessarily be certain that Morris wouldn't at least knock Jerry on his ass. "I'll tell him tonight when he gets home that I went to see her. I don't even have to bring you into it, really. What's the third reason?"

"The postcards."

Sheila fell silent, remembering. A year ago, while Abby Maddox was on the run from the police, she had sent Sheila postcards, taunting her. It was how they'd tracked her. It was how she'd gotten caught.

"I'm not worried," Sheila said. "I can handle her."

"She's got a bone to pick with you," Jerry said. "And I'm sorry, but I'm not comfortable with that."

"It's not up to you. Or Morris, for that matter." Sheila stood over him and crossed her arms over her chest. "I'm not scared of her, Jerry. Toward the end, I wasn't even scared of Ethan, really."

"Let me repeat. Morris will kill me." Jerry enunciated every word. "He won't like this, Sheila. Not one bit."

"Let *me* repeat. It's not up to him. If Abby's been asking to see me, then of course I need to go." She gestured to the manila folder on the desk. "What happened to those young women isn't right. They're pawns in a sick game, and if there's anything I can do to stop this from happening to someone else, I need to do it."

The look on Jerry's face told her he was choosing his words carefully. Finally he pushed his chair back and stood up. "Okay, we'll go. But be honest with me. What do you really think, looking back on it now? You still think Ethan was telling the truth? That Abby masterminded all those killings, and that his only role was the disposal of the bodies?"

"It wasn't his only role, remember. Let's not forget that he hunted them and raped them, too." Sheila's voice was hard. "During my time with Ethan in the basement, yes, I really did believe he was telling me the truth. It all seemed entirely plausible that Abby was running the show, especially after she—" She glanced at Jerry's throat and decided not to finish the sentence. "And then she took off, and was on the run for weeks. Of course it all made her seem incredibly guilty."

"And now?"

"You know what they say about hindsight." Sheila shut down her computer and reached for her purse. "When I look back on it now, it's clear Ethan would have said anything to get me to feel sorry for him. He was so manipulative and he lied about almost everything else—why not Abby? He wanted my sympathy, my understanding. He had every reason to lie about her. But that doesn't mean she wasn't involved somehow."

Jerry nodded and followed her out of the office.

"So what does she want?" Sheila said as she locked the door behind her. "Obviously she couldn't have killed these two women herself because she's been in prison for the last year. But if it turns out she does know something about it, what does she expect in return?" They made their way toward the elevators.

Jerry looked away before answering. "I would assume she wants to cut a deal before her murder trial starts next month. And she'll probably want immunity so she can't be charged with the murders of the women found in Ethan's basement."

Sheila felt her mouth fall open. "And you're okay with this?"

Pulling down the collar of his turtleneck, Jerry showed her his scar. In the fluorescent light of the hallway, it was raw and fat and purple, and much worse than Sheila imagined. She'd only seen it once before, shortly after he'd left the hospital a year earlier, and it pained her to see it didn't look much better now. *He must pick at it twice a day,* she thought.

"I know how it looks." Jerry's voice was strangled. "I know how it looks because I live with it every day. I sound like Marlon Brando when I talk because she permanently damaged my vocal cords." He let go of his collar. The knit material bounced back, but not all the way. "So in answer to your question, no, I am not okay with any of this. But it's not about me now, is it? It's about the women who are turning up dead with her name carved into them."

He was angry, but Sheila understood it wasn't directed toward her. She pushed the down button for the elevator.

"Listen," Jerry said. "Are you really sure about this? Because if Morris—"

"It's not up for discussion, Jerry."

He opened his mouth to respond, then a second later snapped it shut.

They stepped into the elevator, Jerry not saying another word, as Sheila knew he wouldn't. After fifteen years of marriage, he had to know damn well you couldn't argue with a woman once she'd made up her mind.

CHAPTER: 7

Rosedale Penitentiary was just outside Gig Harbor, about an hour south of Seattle. Sheila and Jerry made the drive in record time, but the stress of facing Abby Maddox had caused Jerry to scratch his throat the entire way. When they finally arrived at the prison, his scar was bleeding and his collar was sagging.

They sat in the parking lot as Jerry changed into a fresh turtleneck he'd been keeping in the backseat. It was hard not to notice how skinny he'd become, all bones and ribs jutting out from his dark skin.

She looked out through the rain-spattered windshield of the Jeep at the building sprawled out before them. She'd never been to a prison before, and Jerry had mentioned it had been a while since he'd had cause to step inside one himself. It wasn't anything close to what she'd been expecting. Unlike the prisons in *The Shawshank Redemption* and *Escape from Alcatraz*—which were the only prison movies she'd seen—there was nothing theatrical about Rosedale. It might have passed for a high school, if not for the twenty-foot-high fence topped with coiled razor wire surrounding the premises and the guard tower that overlooked the recreation yard.

Was she up for this? Sheila had only been face-to-face with Abby Maddox once, and that was a long time ago. Abby had come by the psychology building at the university to visit her boyfriend, and Ethan had introduced them briefly. She remembered being struck by the younger woman's beauty.

Sheila flipped down the visor mirror and dug through her purse for her signature red lipstick. Maybe it was silly, but the lipstick brightened her face, instantly making her feel more empowered. She didn't want to see Abby Maddox feeling anything less than her best.

They left the Jeep and made their way toward a set of thick double doors painted a gaudy bright blue. The prison lobby, if that's what it was called, was large and empty. Dark tile on the floors, beige walls, benches, lockers, and vending machines were on one side, and a long counter sat right in the middle with a metal detector beside it. A stern-looking corrections officer, dressed in a starched white uniform shirt with epaulets at the shoulders, nodded as they approached. Her name tag read SGT. E. BRISCOE. She didn't look surprised—or particularly happy—to see them, but Sheila suspected it might just be her face, which seemed stamped with a permanent scowl.

"Good afternoon. What can I do for you?"

"We're here to see Abby Maddox," Jerry said, sounding like a cop. Sheila had to smile.

The CO didn't blink. "Identification, please."

Jerry slid his driver's license across the counter, along with another card Sheila didn't recognize. Fishing in her oversize purse, Sheila pulled out her driver's license as well. The corrections officer looked everything over, typed something into the computer, then checked something off on a clipboard sitting next to the monitor.

"Detective Isaac, welcome. I'm Sergeant Briscoe." The CO stuck her hand out and Jerry shook it. Sheila noticed he didn't bother to let the woman know he was technically retired from PD, and therefore no longer a police detective. "Got a weapon on you, sir?"

"Nope."

"Just to let you know, no cigarettes, no chewing gum, and no cell phones allowed."

"Didn't bring any of those, either."

"Please sign here." The CO pushed the clipboard toward him and Jerry scrawled his name in the designated spot. Sheila did the same. Passing them a small plastic bin, she said, "Keys, coins, anything with metal. Belt, too." She glanced at Sheila's purse and frowned. "Bags go in the lockers, right behind you."

Sheila headed for the row of metal lockers that resembled the kind you'd find in a train station. Most were already taken, but she found one at the bottom that was free. Extracting the key, she returned to the desk. Jerry was already waiting for her on the other side of the metal detector.

"Go ahead and step through," the guard said, and Sheila did as she was told. Nothing beeped.

The CO led them down a long, brightly lit hallway. Toward the end were several doors marked CONFERENCE 1, CONFERENCE 2, and CONFERENCE 3. The guard unlocked Conference 2 and gestured them inside.

"We're doing it here?" Jerry looked around dubiously.

The room was small, no bigger than ten feet by fifteen feet, with a table and chairs in the middle.

"It's what Seattle PD requested when they called." The CO pointed to the walls, which were bare. "It's a conference room, no mikes and no cameras." She made as if to leave, then paused and turned back. "When they bring Maddox in, do you want her kept in handcuffs?"

Jerry and Sheila exchanged a look. Sheila hadn't thought about that at all. She personally didn't feel any fear where Abby Maddox was concerned—anxiety, yes, but not fear—but who knew what Jerry was thinking? The woman had attacked him, after all.

"No, I suppose that won't be necessary," Jerry said, but the rasp in his voice was more pronounced.

The guard nodded. "It'll be a few minutes. She's in the Close Custody Unit, which is on the other side of the property."

The CO closed the door and they were alone. There were no windows in this room and it didn't take long for Sheila to feel claustrophobic.

"Not quite what I expected," she said.

"Nothing like Alcatraz," Jerry agreed, and they exchanged a smile.

"What was that other card you handed the guard?" Sheila asked. "Along with your driver's license?"

"Temporary police consultant ID." Jerry pulled it out of his pocket so she could look at it. It was a plain, laminated white card with his name and photo, with the Seattle PD logo prominently displayed. She noticed it was set to expire in exactly thirty days. "It's my all-access pass." He rubbed his collar again.

"There's nothing they can give you for the itch?" she said softly.

"Nothing that works," Jerry said, aggravated. He softened his tone. "It's usually not that bad. It's worse when I'm stressed. Like now." His hand went to his collar and he rubbed against the material gently.

"I'm nervous, too." Sheila wrung her hands together, feeling warm though the room was cool. "This is definitely not something I planned on doing today. Or ever, for that matter."

"Sure you're ready for this?" Jerry was watching her. "It's not too late to wait outside if you want to change your mind."

But it was too late. Because as soon as the words were out of his mouth, the door unlocked and opened.

And just like that, there she was. Abby Maddox, in the flesh.

The young woman stood just inside the doorway to the conference room, expression serene, eyes a deeper blue than they looked on TV, hair longer. She seemed thinner in her loose-fitting prison-issue uniform, and also older than her twenty-four years, but not for any physical reason. It was the way she carried herself, the way she stood there.

The corrections officer who escorted Abby from her cell—a very handsome man in his early thirties, Sheila couldn't help but notice—removed her handcuffs.

"I'll be right outside, sir." The corrections officer was addressing Jerry. The name on his gold tag read OFFICER M. CAVANAUGH. "Just bang on the door when you're finished."

"No problem," Jerry said.

"You're all right here?" the CO said to Abby.

"I'm good, Mark. Thanks."

First-name basis with the corrections officer? Was that allowed? Sheila watched the two of them closely. It was subtle, but anybody really looking could see there was a familiarity between them that extended beyond the inmate/guard relationship. Obviously Abby wasn't shy about making friends, and Sheila wondered just how deep that friendship went. The CO nodded once more and left the room, shutting the door behind him. It locked automatically.

Abby arranged herself in her chair, taking her time, and Sheila took a moment to study the inmate. Even after a year in prison, the younger woman's skin was luminous. Shiny black hair, longer now, spilled over one shoulder. Her eyes, an unusually intense shade of blue-violet, resembled Elizabeth Taylor's, as did her full, naturally rosy lips. You almost forgot she was dressed in drab gray prison scrubs. It was hard not to stare.

Abby stared back at Sheila openly, her eyes taking in every inch of Sheila's face. After a moment, Abby finally turned toward Jerry, her gaze lingering at his throat a second longer than necessary.

"I didn't think you'd actually come." Her voice was low, husky.

It was unclear whom she was speaking to, so Sheila responded. "I didn't know you'd been asking to see me. I only just found out."

Abby nodded, then turned her attention back to the

private investigator. He was rubbing his throat through his turtleneck once again. Abby caught the gesture and a small smile turned the corners of her lips. "How've you been, Jerry? You look well."

It was a lie and all three of them knew it. Jerry looked older, skinnier, and more tired than he'd ever looked before Abby Maddox entered his life.

"You look exactly the same," he said stiffly.

"I appreciate you both making the trip all the way down here." Abby's tone was polite. "I'm sure you're both very busy. I don't get that many visitors."

"I'm surprised," Jerry said. "You're practically a celebrity. I'm amazed they're not lining up."

"My visitor's list has to be approved by the superintendent. Needless to say, most of the people who request visits don't get approved. But they obviously made an exception for you two." Abby smiled. "I heard you were reinstated, Jerry. Or, should I say, *resurrected*."

"Where'd you hear that?"

"The proverbial grapevine. So you're a police officer again?"

"Nope. I'm just helping out with one investigation."

"And that's why you're here. My lawyer told me this morning you might come. Your cop friend was here earlier." Abby's eyes narrowed slightly, a sign of displeasure. "Torrance? What an asshole."

Sheila looked down to hide a smile.

"You told Detective Torrance you wanted to talk to Dr. Tao." Jerry's jaw was clenched. "She's here now, so talk. Start with the dead bodies with your name on them. I think you know damn well this is just the beginning."

"I don't know anything for a fact."

Jerry sighed and looked at Sheila. Abby had been in the room less than three minutes, and already the private investigator was frustrated.

"Why were you asking for me, Abby?" Sheila forced herself to keep her tone light and open. "Was there something you wanted to discuss with me?"

"There's quite a bit I'd like to discuss with you, Sheila. But not here, not now. It would be a private conversation." Abby's expression was difficult to read. "You were with Ethan when he died. I have so many questions. Best saved for another time."

Sheila nodded, not exactly sure how to respond. The use of her first name jarred her a little. Certainly Abby wanted some kind of closure; Ethan had been her lover, after all. But Abby was a convicted felon and possible serial killer. Sheila felt her heart harden. She owed this woman nothing.

"Can we cut to the chase?" Jerry's hoarse voice was strained. "We're here. I'll ask you again. What do you want?"

"What does anybody in prison want?" Abby's smile was sad. "I want to get out of this hellhole. I don't want this to be my life. They've charged me with the murder of Diana St. Clair, and there could be more murder charges coming for the bodies they found in Ethan's basement if the prosecuting attorney gets her way. There's a very good chance I'll die in here."

"My heart bleeds for you."

Abby's smile faded.

Jerry cracked his knuckles. "So let's focus. What do you know about the body that was found this morning?"

"It's not that simple."

"Bullshit," he said, exasperated. Sheila noticed his hands were under the table and his arms were rigid. His scar was probably burning.

As if sensing his internal struggle, Abby's gaze fixed on his throat again, and this time it stayed there. "Is it bad?" she said softly. "The scar?"

"Bitch, go to hell."

Abby didn't flinch. "I wasn't trying to be rude. I know what I did to you."

"You've got five more minutes." Jerry's words were slow and deliberate. "Either you tell us what you know, or we're out of here. And once we leave, we're not coming back."

Abby's gaze flickered to Sheila, and then she was focused on Jerry again. "I know you hate me for what I did, but I want you to know that I panicked. Ethan, he . . ." She paused and took a deep breath. "It wasn't a good relationship. He wasn't a good person. I spent eight years of my life with someone who turned out to be a monster."

Sheila said nothing. Neither did Jerry. An uncomfortable silence descended over the room.

Abby leaned forward. "I sit in a tiny cell all day. All I've had is time to think. And I think if you got to know me—"

"I don't want to know you," Jerry said, his jaw working.

"I understand. You're still angry."

"Who says I'm angry?"

"You'd have to be." Abby looked at Sheila, then back to Jerry. "What I did . . . it's scarred you in a lot of ways, and not just physically. Anyone paying attention can see that."

Jerry blew out a breath. "Okay, you've apologized. Now for the last fucking time, tell us what you know. You've got three minutes left."

"I don't know who the killer is," Abby said.

"Fine." Jerry stood up, pushing his chair back on the linoleum floor so hard it screeched. "Thanks for wasting our time. Let's go, Sheila."

"Wait."

He ignored Abby and headed for the door. Sheila stood up.

"Jerry, *wait*." The urgency in Abby's voice caused him to turn around. "Please don't go yet. I don't know who the killer is, okay? But I know I can help you."

"How?"

"I know where the next victim is."

Holy shit. Sheila sat back down, glancing at Jerry, but his dark face was impossible to read.

"Okay then." Still standing, he pulled a small black notepad out of his back pocket. "Give me a name and I'll call it in right now, have somebody pick her up before she gets hurt."

"I didn't say I knew who, I said I knew *where*." Abby looked up at Jerry, her eyes never wavering from his face. "And she's already dead. Before I tell you anything more, there are certain things you need to agree to."

Jerry sat back down. "What things?"

Abby reached into her pants pocket and pulled out a folded piece of paper. "Read this first. From my lawyer to you."

Jerry unfolded the paper. Sheila craned her neck, but from where she was seated, she couldn't make out the words. As Jerry read, the lines in his face grew more pronounced.

When he finished, he looked up, incredulous. "Tell me you're joking."

The younger woman didn't smile, but her eyes were shining in a way that made Sheila very uneasy. "I never joke when it comes to my freedom."

It was the first honest thing Abby Maddox had said.

CHAPTER: 8

They'd finally left. A good first meeting all around, Abby Maddox thought. Dr. Sheila Tao had been exactly what she'd been hoping for—open-minded, inquisitive, fearless. And not totally unsympathetic, as Abby had thought she might be. A long shot, but maybe there was something to work with there. Slowly, things were clicking into place.

The handcuffs weren't necessary, but she was a high-level offender and protocol was protocol. Anticipating the hateful cold metal bracelets, Abby held her wrists out, but instead of snapping them on, Officer Mark Cavanaugh just smiled at her.

"God, I've missed you." He leaned in.

Before his lips could make contact, Abby said, "Where have you been the last three days?"

His lips were less than an inch away from hers. Pulling back, he looked down, not answering. Which told her everything she needed to know.

"Again?" Abby said, her voice cold. "I thought you said it was under control."

"I called in sick. I haven't been feeling well—"

"Bullshit." She touched his chin, tilting his face up

with her hand. "I don't care if you're an alcoholic, Mark. I'm not your wife. I'm not going to get in your face for drinking too much, because I actually don't care if you drink yourself into oblivion. Your body, your life, your choices. But not right now, do you understand? Right now I need you strong and I need you focused."

She let go of his chin. His head dropped again. A moment later, he looked up at her, his dark eyes searching her face. He leaned in.

"Not here," she said.

"Come on, nobody's watching." Mark's hand was still holding her wrists. His touch was gentle, his fingers grazing the delicate skin of her palm. A tingle went through her. "It's the conference room," he said. "No cameras, remember? I've missed you so much."

He was right, this was probably the one place in prison they could be this close without the risk of anybody seeing anything. Turning her face up to his, she parted her lips and allowed him to taste her. She moved in close and rubbed against him, feeling him harden beneath his scratchy uniform pants. He groaned softly, as she knew he would, and his lips moved down to her neck. One hand pulled her closer.

Mark was a good-looking guy, with a hard body to match underneath the CO uniform, but that wasn't why Abby was into him. It was really very simple. Abby was into Mark because he was into *her*. The desire in his dark eyes, his eagerness to please her, his willingness to risk himself to do whatever it took to make her happy—she knew she could use him.

He steered her back toward the table, then hoisted

her up onto it, his hands moving fast underneath her cotton top. She felt his fingers graze her breasts over her ugly prison-issue brassiere, fumbling to find her nipples. His other hand reached for her pants, tugging at the elastic waistband. He snaked a hand inside, moving aside her underwear, and she sighed. For three minutes, she closed her eyes and allowed him to pleasure her, his fingers touching all the right spots. She came quickly and quietly, moaning softly in his ear as she reached orgasm.

She opened her eyes to find Mark watching her, a satisfied grin on his face. *Men.* All he'd done was something she could do to herself anytime she wanted, but you'd think the guy had just won the Super Bowl.

"My turn," he said, reaching for his belt buckle.

She stopped him. "No."

"Come on, I'll be quick." He leaned in again, his breath hot on her neck. "I promise. I just want you so fucking bad—"

"I said no." Abby's voice was soft but unyielding.

He saw that she meant it. Grudgingly, he stepped back, adjusting the material around his crotch with a grimace. "What's the matter with you? This is the perfect opportunity."

She slid off the table, tucking her shirt back in and smoothing her hair with her hands. "This is a delicate time for me, you know that. I have to be extra careful. I can't take any chances right now, and I can't have any violations. If all goes well, I'll be leaving here soon. You want that for me, don't you?"

Mark's chiseled face was sullen. "I don't know, actually. I like having you here, close to me. I get to see you every day."

Abby sighed. He might be pretty, but he was oh so stupid. She gave him a reproachful look. "That's a bit selfish, don't you think? A minimum-security prison means more freedom for me. The possibility of getting outside more. Walking around unrestricted. More visitation. Maybe even a private cell. It's not like you couldn't put in for a transfer."

"Really?" His face lit up. "You'd want me to?"

"You're my boyfriend. Sure I would." She held her wrists out. He dutifully pulled out the handcuffs and snapped them on. He kept them so loose, it almost didn't matter that she was wearing them, but she hated the feel of the metal against her skin. "Celia was telling me about that place. She says there are a lot of little nooks and crannies where two people can sneak off and be alone for a few minutes without anybody noticing." Celia was Abby's cellmate, and she'd said no such thing.

"I'm your boyfriend?" Mark smiled. "I like that."

Of course that would be the one thing he'd jump on. So fucking predictable. All married men were. "Unless I'm just a fling."

"Of course not." He moved in close and kissed her again. "You're so much more than that. I think about you every minute of every day. I dream about you. When I wake up in the morning, I'm hard because—"

"We should go," she said. "They're going to wonder what we're still doing in here."

Sighing, he unlocked the door and led her out, his arm on her elbow. Both of them nodded to Sergeant

Briscoe, who was standing a few feet away from the door as if she'd been about to come in. She frowned at them, her middle-aged eyes narrowed into slits. Her gaze lingered on Abby's face a little longer than necessary. Abby smirked. Briscoe looked away.

"Hey, Sergeant," Mark said easily enough, guiding Abby past the older woman and down the hallway.

"Officer Cavanaugh." Briscoe's voice was flat.

The COs were always careful not to refer to each other by their first names. It was prison policy, a way to keep their identities safe, not that it made any difference. It wasn't hard to find out what you needed to know. It had taken Abby five seconds to learn Mark's first name.

"How much longer before you get me what I asked for?" she murmured as she and Mark headed down the hallway. They paused in front of the double doors at the back of the building, and a second later were buzzed through. They had to cross the quad in order to reach the Close Custody Unit where Abby was housed. "I need a replacement. I can't go any longer with one that isn't working properly."

"Oh yeah, I meant to tell you." Mark stared straight ahead, not smiling. Out here, there were cameras everywhere, and someone would be watching. His tone, though, gave away his excitement. "The new one's under your bunk. Make sure Celia doesn't see it."

"That might be a little difficult."

"The less who know, the better." They paused at another set of doors, and waited a moment. Finally Mark yelled, "Open!" and a second later, the doors buzzed open.

Mark steered Abby past the guard's booth to a glaringly bright blue metal door a few feet away. Pausing for a moment, both of them looked through the huge glass windows at the three tiers of cells inside. The common area in the center was busy. The other inmates were socializing, everyone dressed in identical gray scrubs with the letters DOC stamped on the back. Branded like cattle.

Mark sensed the shift in her mood. "Chin up, baby," he said in a soft voice. "It won't be for much longer."

No, it wouldn't. Because Abby had a plan.

Abby watched the activity inside the CCU. She didn't have friends here. The place was a fucking zoo. Every day she woke up to noise—inmates yelling, fighting, singing, cackling with laughter. Abby missed her freedom, yes, but what she missed most of all was the *quiet* of the outside world. This place might have been somewhat bearable had it just been quiet.

Freedom could not come soon enough. If she was in here for much longer, she was going to lose her mind.

Mark removed her handcuffs. The door to the CCU buzzed open and Abby stepped through, adjusting her posture so she was standing perfectly straight. Nobody had ever messed with her in here, but that didn't mean they wouldn't. She always had her eyes open.

"Check your bunk," she heard Mark say in a low voice before the blue door shut behind her.

A few moments later, alone in her top-tier cell, Abby did check. And it was exactly where he said it would be. She smiled.

Game on.

CHAPTER:9

There was one simple reason Jerry didn't like cemeteries. They were full of dead people.

Standing a safe distance away (lest any dead bodies spring up from the earth and attack him), he watched Mike Torrance pace a little too close to the perimeter of the eight-by-four hole being dug by a couple of workers. Off to the right sat a small forklift, not yet in use.

"Maddox better not be lying." The detective stopped and glared at Jerry, as if it would somehow be his fault if she were. "I swear to God I'll show up to every fucking parole hearing for the rest of her sentence if she's lying about this."

"You and me both."

"I can't believe she wouldn't give you anything else other than the location." Torrance started pacing again. "You *did* try, right?"

"What did you expect, Mike?" Jerry snapped. It had been a long day already, it wasn't nearly over, and the question was insulting. "This whole thing is a chess game to her, and she's the reigning grand master. We're lucky she's even letting us play. I told you, this is what she does."

Jerry had questioned Maddox at the prison for over

an hour. Sheila had sat quietly, listening but not interrupting. Of course he'd tried to get as much information as he could, but Maddox wasn't stupid. Quite the opposite. She held all the cards and damn well knew it. She would tell the police what she wanted them to know when she was good and ready, and not a moment earlier. He could still picture the look on her face as she spoke—serious, but slightly amused, enjoying every second of their undivided attention.

"She'll be mid to late twenties, dark hair, slender. She'll resemble me. But you knew that already," Maddox had said to him, her eyes shining in a way that had made Jerry uneasy. "She's buried somewhere in Heavenly Rest Cemetery. Her body will be underneath someone else's casket. Check for graves that are fresh; she was probably killed in the last couple of weeks or so."

"Name?"

"No idea."

"And you know all this how?"

"I'll tell you tomorrow, when you come back to tell me I was right."

"And why the hell would I believe you?" Jerry's jaw was clenched and the words were almost painful to spit out.

"Because you know I can't bullshit about something like this." Maddox had been unfazed by his frustration. "It's a simple matter of checking, Jerry. If you don't find a body, then you know I'm lying. If you do find a body, then you know I have something to offer your investigation. Right now, all we have is trust."

She was fucking deluded if she thought he'd ever trust her, but okay, she had a point.

"Tell me this at least," Jerry had said. "How'd he manage to get the body in the ground before the casket was buried?" He paused for a moment, trying to re-create the scenario in his head. "That doesn't even seem plausible."

"It's all in the timing." That glint appeared in her eyes again, and it was unnerving. "And when you see that I know what I'm talking about, I'd like you to come back tomorrow with my deal in place. You. Not the cops or the PA."

"Tomorrow's Sunday."

"Not my problem. You'll figure it out."

Jerry and Sheila had stood up to leave, but before he could knock on the door, Maddox said quietly, "By the way. Say hi to Ethan for me."

"Excuse me?" He turned back to face her.

"Heavenly Rest Cemetery, where you're going to dig up the body?" Maddox looked up at them with moist eyes. "It's where Ethan is buried."

And now here they were, digging by the light of the moon and a few spotlights, the nasty chill in the air only adding to the misery of it all.

They'd been at it for an hour, but since "six feet under" really was six feet under, progress was slow. Luckily, Heavenly Rest had only had one burial in the last two weeks, for one Mrs. Doris Wheaton, age ninety-two, according to the background check they'd run on the way over. Her burial had taken place only ten days earlier, so the ground remained soft and unsettled. Still, it was slow going, because the dirt had to be moved carefully. They didn't know what they might find.

On the other side of the cemetery, a small, plain

tombstone marked Ethan Wolfe's grave. Jerry had passed it on the way over, pausing only briefly to look down at the Tell-Tale Heart Killer's name etched into the stone, just above the dates of his birth and death. It made him wonder again why it was in *this* cemetery, of all places, that the newest victim was hidden. Everything about this felt contrived. He couldn't shake the feeling they were being set up.

The full moon was a formless blob behind the clouds and the light cast strange shadows over the trees and tombstones. Heavenly Rest Cemetery was downright spooky at night. It was set high on a hill overlooking Seattle, and while the twinkling lights of the city below were pretty, the heavy mist made the cemetery feel eerie. He tried not to think about the decomposing bodies only a few feet beneath him, about the maggots and other little insects making their way through the rotting flesh, about the bones of the skeletons that would eventually remain. He shuddered, and it wasn't from the cold.

Jerry's grandmother had died of cancer when he was ten years old. She'd lived with them in his family's house, in a small room at the top of the stairs, and he was often entrusted to watch over her whenever his mother worked or was too tired. His responsibilities consisted of bringing his grandma her biscuits and juice, and sitting with her while she watched *Jeopardy*.

He had loved his grandmother, and so at first, helping with her care had been fine. But as the months passed and she grew weaker, it became not so fine. Jerry had watched his grandmother deteriorate from a laughing, vibrant woman who could spank him just as easily as hug him, into a withered mess of skin and bone.

And then there were the *smells*. The room she'd died in had smelled like her for weeks after her death—a sickly blend of stale breath, antibiotic ointments, and urine. Jerry hadn't been able to set foot in her room for a long time because the smells always brought back powerful memories of her death.

He had been present at her burial, laying the final white rose on the casket before it was lowered into the ground. And then later that night—and for weeks to come—he'd had nightmares about her being deep in the earth, her frail body slowly rotting into nothing. Even though his mother had spent years trying to tell him that cemeteries were among the safest places you could be, and that God was always watching, Jerry had never felt comfortable being in places where people were laid to rest.

To his left, a few feet away, stood a man who actually looked pleased to be here. Roger Aubrey, age fifty-five according to his DMV info, was the cemetery's head caretaker. They'd knocked on his door on the way over, disrupting Aubrey's date with his satellite dish and a bag of Cheetos. While they weren't exhuming Doris Wheaton's body and therefore did not require the permission of Wheaton's family to dig up her grave, they did require the cooperation of the caretaker to determine which grave sites were fresh.

Jerry ambled over to the man and smiled apologetically. "Sorry to have disrupted your evening, Mr. Aubrey. We appreciate your cooperation in locating the grave site, but you really don't have to stick around. We'll put everything back the way it was."

The man's attention stayed focused on the diggers for a moment longer before turning to Jerry. "Oh no, I wouldn't dream of not being here." His voice was high-pitched and excited. "I've been caring for this cemetery for the past two years. It's my job to make sure everything gets restored properly."

"Well, then, let me ask you a question." Jerry tucked his hands deeper into his pockets. "Have you seen anyone hanging out near this particular grave since the burial two weeks ago? Or the weeks leading up to it?"

Aubrey shook his head. He was balding, and the wind blew the few hairs of his comb-over the wrong way, revealing a shiny pink scalp that glowed in the uneven light. "Not that I've noticed. We don't keep records on who visits. When the gates are open, people can come and go as they choose."

"And what about the day of the burial? Were you here?"

"I was, yes." Aubrey squinted, deep in thought as he continued to watch the diggers. "It was a small service. Only a dozen or so people, and most were dressed in scrubs."

"Scrubs?"

"I assumed they were nurses or caregivers from the retirement home the deceased lived in before she passed away." Aubrey chewed his bottom lip. "They seemed sadder than her grandson did. He kept checking his watch, as if the funeral service was keeping him from something more important. Very sad."

"Sir, let me ask you something else." Jerry's low tone got the caretaker's full attention, and the rotund man finally pried his eyes away from the grave site. "In your expert opinion, how would somebody go about getting a dead body—one that isn't in the casket that matches the name on the gravestone—into the grave before a burial? How is that even possible? Don't you check to make sure the hole is . . . empty . . . before you lower the casket in?"

Aubrey's eye twitched. "It's all in the timing," he said, echoing what Maddox had said earlier at the prison. A tingle went up Jerry's spine. "It's certainly not unheard-of to bury other things in a grave along with the casket, though it happens a lot less than it used to. It used to be that graves were dug a few days early and covered with tarp until the burial. But animals used to get stuck in the graves, you see, and it was always a pain—not to mention a danger—to remove them in time for the service."

The caretaker suddenly made a wheezing sound, alarming Jerry, until he realized the man was laughing.

"I remember this one time, a deer fell into a grave and broke her leg," Aubrey said. "Must have been there all night, and boy, was she spitting mad the next morning when we tried to get her out. Animal Control finally had to shoot her." He laugh-wheezed again.

"Funny," Jerry said.

"I've been in the caretaking business for a while now, and you hear stories like this, but you never think it'll happen in *your* cemetery. Urban myths, you know?" Aubrey blinked rapidly several times, an annoying facial tic. "It's kind of an old-school thing to do, hiding a body under a casket."

"How do you mean?"

Aubrey seemed delighted at the question. He held up a chubby finger. "One, it's risky. Graves are dug late at night before a burial, and you'd have to know in advance one was being dug because there isn't a large window of time between the digging and the service." He held up another chubby finger. "Two, look around. We're right in the middle of the cemetery. You'd have to be lucky that nobody sees you dragging a dead body across all this open space." A third chubby finger joined the other two. "And three, if you're going to kill someone and dump the body, why not just dice it and dump it in the Sound? Like on *Dexter*. Neat, clean, minimal risk of getting caught, water washes away all trace evidence."

Jerry studied the caretaker. "You've given this some serious thought."

The man shrugged. "Everything you need to know about killing is on television these days."

Jerry couldn't dispute that, but before he could respond, Torrance's voice cut in. "We've got the casket!"

His former partner was gesturing him over, and Jerry reluctantly stepped closer to get a better look.

A moment later, a rectangular concrete box was lifted out of the ground with a forklift. Roger Aubrey had explained to them earlier that the casket would be inside a grave liner, which was made of solid concrete and probably weighed a ton. Inside the casket, of course, would be Mrs. Doris Wheaton, who'd been dead for over two weeks. Thank God they wouldn't be opening it. The victim, according to Abby Maddox, was supposedly buried somewhere *underneath* Mrs. Wheaton.

The grave liner was carefully placed about ten feet away on the ground. Jerry watched as the workers who'd dug the hole moved away from it, almost instinctively. He didn't blame them. At this time of night, with the wind and the mist and the grave liner and the twitchy caretaker, the whole thing seemed like a scene out of a bad vampire movie. All that was missing were the wooden stakes. It was creepy.

Torrance thanked the workers for their help and told them to get a coffee. They couldn't leave for the night—they'd have to eventually put the casket back in the grave—but for now, they weren't needed. The workers didn't argue and left quickly.

Torrance shone his Maglite into the hole.

"See anything?" Gingerly, Jerry stepped closer. He shone his own flashlight down into the grave, afraid to find out what, exactly, was in there. But it turned out to be anticlimactic—all he could see was a hole full of dirt.

"Somebody get down there and start digging," Torrance barked.

The two crime scene technicians from Seattle PD—a young female and an older male—had arrived twenty minutes earlier. They'd been sitting at the back of their truck watching the whole thing from about ten feet away, sipping coffees from Tully's. At the sound of Torrance's voice, they looked at each other, uncertain. Neither looked happy to be here.

"Well, there's a first time for everything," the male tech said, hopping down and grabbing his kit. "Let's saddle up."

They brought their gear over to the hole, nodding to

Jerry as they passed. The female tech, whose name was Jessica Grieg, tugged at the harness around her waist to make sure it was secure. Jerry thought she looked about twenty-one, though surely she was older than that. Fixed to Grieg's harness was a length of bungee cord, the other end of which was strapped to her partner, whose name was Vic Chernovsky. Grieg then slipped on a hard hat with a small light attached.

Face grim, she snapped the bulb light on and began a careful descent into the grave as her partner bore her weight. When she reached the bottom, she pulled something out from her kit that looked like a small spade, and started digging.

"Aren't you going in, too?" Torrance asked Chernovsky.

The male tech shook his head. "Not enough room. You don't want us bumping into each other, stepping on the remains we're trying to find." He studiously kept the spotlight pointed down at his partner.

Twenty long minutes passed.

Finally, Grieg called out, "I've got a body!"

Jerry and Torrance both shone their lights down. Sure enough, a hand and leg were exposed. Obviously female, obviously slender. Jerry's gut rolled.

Torrance frowned. "Where's the head?"

Grieg was squatting, brushing away the dirt to uncover the victim's head. A moment later, Jerry caught sight of long, dark hair and a bare shoulder. His heart lurched; Maddox hadn't been bluffing.

"She's facedown." Grieg looked up at them and squinted as their lights hit her face. "You want me to turn her over?"

"Not yet," Torrance said. "See if you can clear away what's on her back."

Grieg nodded. Using a small brush, she delicately dusted the torso, revealing stark cuts on the victim's back. The wounds were pressed with dirt, and against the dead woman's pale skin, the words were easy to read.

FREE ABBY MADDOX.

And beneath those three words, another carving: 3/10.

"Sonofabitch." Torrance stared at the body for a few seconds longer before turning to face Jerry. "Three-ten. You know what this means, right?"

"It's the third body."

"Right." Torrance frowned. "The third body found, but it's been here for ten days. We know that, because it had to be left here right before Doris Wheaton's casket was lowered in."

"Right." Jerry had no idea what Torrance was getting at.

"Think about it, pal." Torrance stepped closer to him. "It's been here for ten days, which means she was killed *before* Maddox was formally charged with murder. Which means she was killed first. And yet, the killer marked her three-ten."

"The third one found, but the first one killed." Jerry sucked in a breath as the realization hit. "Shit. That means the killer knew exactly when we'd find her. This was planned out well in advance. You think the other seven are dead already?"

Torrance didn't answer. He pulled out his phone. "I'm calling right now so we can get Maddox's deal in place. You ready for another trip to prison first thing tomorrow?"

It was a stupid question. Of course he wasn't ready. It was the last thing he wanted to do.

But Jerry was all in. No going back now.

CHAPTER : 10

A pparently no place was sacred.

Jerry saw the reporter and cameraman as soon as he turned in to his office building's parking lot, and swore under his breath. Would this day never end? He was dead tired, and his first instinct at the sight of the camera was to turn around and head home. But the only things waiting for him at his house were a few cans of sardines and some leftover Thai food from the night before.

The reporter was hovering at the building's back entrance, a petite woman with pale blond hair shellacked to her head. She looked vaguely familiar. As Jerry approached, the cameraman switched his light on. It beamed right into Jerry's face, temporarily blinding him.

"Mr. Isaac, good evening. I'm Bernadette Barkley from *The Pulse*. We're profiling Abby Maddox. Can I ask you a few questions?"

Bernadette who? From the what? Jerry shook his head. "Sorry, no time." He lifted a hand, attempting to shield the bright light of the camera from his eyes.

Of course the reporter acted like she didn't hear him. "Mr. Isaac, in light of Abby Maddox's recent charge for the murder of Diana St. Clair, our viewers are wondering how you feel. Do you think she's capable of murder?"

Was there no end to the amount of stupid questions a person could be asked? "How do I feel?" Jerry stared down at the reporter, who was a good foot shorter than himself. "How do I *feel*?"

Looking directly into the camera lens, he pulled down the collar of his turtleneck, giving them a clear shot of his scar. He could only imagine how ugly it would look on TV, especially in high definition, and the thought brought him immense satisfaction. "*This* is how I feel, ma'am."

And then, deliberately slowing his cadence so there'd be no misunderstanding, Jerry spoke directly into the camera, squinting against the bright light. "Now get that camera out of my face, motherfucker."

He was inside the building before the woman could respond. Thankfully, they weren't allowed to follow him inside, but he latched the door behind him anyway.

The building in Fremont where Jerry leased office space was old, and he could hear the music blaring through the thin door before he was even halfway up the back stairs. He frowned. It was nearly midnight, and there should be nobody in the building at this time of night. Instinctively, he reached for a gun he no longer carried. He sighed. Old habits never died.

It had to be Danny playing the music, though he couldn't figure out why she'd still be in the office this late. He took the stairs two at a time, the noise growing louder with each step. He inserted his key into the doorknob only to find the door unlocked, and he frowned again. *Dammit, Danny*. His twenty-three-year-old assistant was a smart girl, but she obviously had no sense of self-preservation. Seattle was a safe city for the most part, but they worked in the PI business, which meant they saw their share of angry spouses. An unlocked door at midnight was never a good idea.

Jerry sighed. Time for another lecture on the importance of safety.

He pushed open the door and sure enough, Danny Mercy's back was turned and all he could see was her caramel-hued ponytail bobbing to the music. Heading straight for her desk, he reached for the speakers and pulled the plug. The sudden silence blared, and she jumped.

Danny whipped around. "What the hell, dude? You scared the crap out of me!"

He shrugged out of his coat, not caring that drops of rain were splattering across his assistant and her computer. "That was the point. The music was too loud, Danny."

She made a show of wiping a speck of moisture from her cheek. "So? It's midnight, nobody's here—"

"And you didn't lock the door."

"Oh." The annoyed look on her face was instantly replaced by an expression of contriteness. "*Lo siento, jefe.* I could have sworn I locked it."

He sighed. Good enough. He was too tired to lecture her anyway. "Still taking those Spanish classes, huh?"

"*Sí, señor.* My friend Pedro was helping me practice, but he just moved away, got a job in El Paso."

"What are you doing here?" He shot her a look. "English, please."

She shrugged. "I left one of my textbooks here, then decided I might as well check my email. Didn't feel like going home yet." Her eyes narrowed. "What are *you* doing here?"

"I run the place," he said. Seeing the look on her face, he softened his tone. "Didn't feel like going home, either."

He plopped down on the two-seater sofa in the reception area and stretched his long legs out. At the sight of his skinny ankles, covered in his usual white athletic socks which starkly contrasted with his black faux leather sneakers, Danny smiled. He grinned back. All right, so he wouldn't be modeling for *GQ* anytime soon. Life would go on.

"You look tired." His assistant's face was kind. "Long day?"

"Day from hell. You don't want to know."

But of course she did—she always did—and so he filled her in quickly on the events of the day, from the body at the Sweet Chariot Inn, to his face-to-face with Abby Maddox, capped off with all the horror movie fun at the cemetery.

Danny listened raptly, nodding every few seconds, never once interrupting. Other than her superb organizational skills, her ability to listen and not ask questions until he finished speaking was his favorite thing about her.

"'Free Abby Maddox,'" Danny repeated when he finally wrapped it up. "You know there's a site called FreeAbbyMaddox.com?"

"Are you serious?"

She typed it into her computer and he tilted the monitor toward him. Soon the screen was filled with images of Maddox's face. Some were from her days at Puget Sound State, two were taken the day she was arrested and hauled back to Seattle, and there were a few photos of her during the trial.

"It's not your typical fan site," Danny said. "At first I thought it was a place that just had articles about her, but people post all kinds of stuff, and a lot of it's sexual. A lot of sickos out there, you know? As soon as you mentioned 'Free Abby Maddox' being carved on the body, it made me think of it."

Jerry's face was grim. "Good work. I'll text Torrance."

She rolled her eyes. "That'll take you thirty minutes; you're terrible with text. Let me send him an email."

He was too tired to argue. Her fingers flew across the keyboard and a minute later it was sent.

"So tell me," his assistant said, looking up at him. "You and Dr. Tao actually talked to Abby Maddox today?" Danny had been a student in one of Sheila's classes a couple of years before, and like all Puget Sound State University students, she was well versed in the Ethan Wolfe/Sheila Tao/Abby Maddox trifecta. She'd even had Ethan as her TA for a term. "What was that like for Dr. Tao?"

"Sheila's a pro. Wasn't intimidated at all."

"Doesn't surprise me. She's about the coolest professor I ever had. I very nearly applied to the graduate psych program because of her."

"Nah, you're right where you should be," Jerry said. "The world has enough psychologists. What it needs is more criminologists, like you're going to be. Just wish you weren't leaving me next month. You'll be hard to replace. You're the best intern I've ever had."

"I'm the only intern you've ever had." Danny smiled. "So what does Maddox know?"

"We're still trying to figure that out. I don't know if she can give us the killer's name, but she seems to know more about what's going on than anybody else. I have to go back to the prison tomorrow. Great way to spend a Sunday." Jerry's face sagged as soon as the words were out of his mouth. "I'm going to take a wild guess and say that Maddox has been corresponding with the killer. Everything is just too coincidental."

"Heavenly Rest is where Ethan Wolfe is buried."

"Yeah. That's right." Jerry blinked in surprise. "How'd you know that?"

"You know I followed the case. Everybody did." Danny fiddled with the papers on her desk, not meeting his gaze.

"It's okay," Jerry said, but he felt a twinge at the back of his neck. He hated to admit it, but her interest in Ethan Wolfe bothered him, not that he blamed her. "Wolfe went to your school, and so did Maddox. I get it."

"It's just . . . she's a psychopath." Danny's voice held an undertone of wonder. "I majored in psych, and I know a psychopath when I see one. And now I'm a criminal justice student, *hello*. I wouldn't let my guard down around her, you know?"

"Smart girl."

"By the way . . ." She hesitated. "There was a reporter hanging around outside today."

"I spoke to her. You'd think they'd get tired of me saying 'no comment.' Right when I thought all that crap was dying down . . ." Jerry looked at his assistant sternly. "Remember, don't ever talk to them."

"Give me some credit, dude."

Stifling a yawn, Jerry watched as she typed something into her computer. A moment later, another invoice was printed and added to the stack. He could feel his eyes wanting to close, and knew he should be signing off on those invoices before he passed out completely, but he couldn't seem to get up off the sofa. The loveseat here was more comfortable than the one he had at home— Marianne had taken most of the "good" furniture with her when she'd moved out.

"Listen, it's late. I'm heading home." He forced himself to sit up, eyes bleary. "I don't want you here alone. Want me to drop you somewhere?"

"I've got my bike."

"We'll put it in the trunk. Come on, I'll drive you home."

She shut down the computer and followed him out. He carefully locked the door behind them and they headed down the stairs to the parking lot behind the building.

"So, what's next?" Danny was in front of him and her ponytail bounced along with her as she skipped down the steps. "You said you found a third body. What happens now?"

"It's back to the prison first thing in the morning." Even just saying the words, Jerry felt the weight of it all on his shoulders. He honestly couldn't think of a place he less wanted to go. "So Maddox can sign off on her deal. Then, she talks. And tells us what she knows."

Danny pushed the back door open and headed for her bike, which was chained to the rack beside the door. "Sounds easy enough. Can I come?"

"Where? To the prison?"

"No, to the Taj Mahal." Danny rolled her eyes. "Yes, the prison."

"I guess it's not a terrible idea." Jerry popped the rear hatch on his Jeep and lifted her bike up. "I could use the help."

What he didn't say was that he could use the *buffer,* someone else in the room with himself and Maddox to keep things civilized. It had helped having Sheila there today, and he dreaded going back alone. He didn't trust himself around Abby Maddox.

Danny climbed into the Jeep's passenger side. When Jerry got in beside her, she said, "So you think she's been corresponding somehow with the killer. That's really sick when you think about it."

"Damn skippy." He started the engine and pulled out of the lot.

"You think he writes to her?"

"Don't know, didn't ask."

"What would the letters say?"

"Don't know, haven't seen them yet."

"Does she—"

Jerry finally laughed. "I don't know. You can ask her yourself tomorrow."

Danny snuggled back into the seat, her young face glowing in the light. He could tell she was excited to meet the notorious criminal, and while it was irritating, Jerry really couldn't take it personally. She was just a kid. She wasn't trying to offend him.

Ten minutes later he pulled up in front of the converted warehouse she called a loft. He'd seen where she lived once before, in the daylight, but right now it looked positively unsafe. It was surrounded by abandoned buildings and Jerry was pretty sure one of them had been a crack house at some point.

"You should move," he said, rolling down the window. He kept his eye on the small group of men smoking near the building's entrance. "I don't like the unsavory looks of your neighbors."

Danny chuckled and reached for her bag. "Two of those unsavory guys are my bandmates. We practice in the abandoned building next door. Some kind of machinery used to be manufactured there, and the whole place is soundproofed. We can play as loud as we want."

Okay, so maybe that was pretty cool. Danny was the lead singer in an alternative rock band—Jerry couldn't remember the band's name, or maybe he'd never asked her—and he could see that a warehouse would be the perfect place to rehearse.

But playing music here was one thing. Living here was another. He didn't care if the real estate analysts had declared this neighborhood an "up-and-coming" area of Seattle. In his opinion, it was much too industrial to feel like home.

"Seven sharp, okay?" he said as they got out of the Jeep. He popped the back and hefted her bike out. "Be outside on time. Don't make me buzz you. We have to be at the prison by eight."

"Why so early?" Danny stifled a yawn and pointed to her friends. "I still have a couple of hours of rehearsal tonight."

"You're kidding. It's midnight."

She gave him a look that made him feel old. "It's the only time we could all meet. We have a gig tomorrow night at the Pink Elephant. You should come. Show starts at eleven."

"Hell no. Way past my bedtime." Jerry pointed at her and raised an eyebrow. "And girl, I come back for you tomorrow and you're not waiting for me outside, I keep on driving."

"Chill, dude. I'll be ready."

CHAPTER 11

Morris was red, Morris was heaving, and Morris was pacing. None of these things was a good sign, but all three combined? Sheila clutched a pillow to her chest and braced herself for the onslaught. Maybe she should have waited till morning to talk about this. They'd both had a long day, and midnight wasn't the best time for a serious discussion.

He pointed a large finger at her and she cringed. "You'd better explain this to me before my head explodes."

"Morris—"

"What in the *world* would possess you to go to a prison and talk to that psycho bitch?" Morris shouted. The sound actually hurt Sheila's ears and she wondered if the neighbors could hear them. Morris was not a soft-spoken guy to begin with, but at full volume, she could feel the walls shaking. He continued to stomp around their bedroom, not waiting for an answer. "I'm gonna kill Jerry for bringing you there. Goddammit, he knows better. Abby Maddox is dangerous, Sheila. She's a murderer—"

"We don't know that yet," Sheila said.

He stopped and turned, his face growing redder. "Excuse me? We don't know that? Since when don't we know that?"

She clutched the pillow tighter. "You need to hear me out. I know what I'm doing."

"All evidence to the contrary."

"Morris, please." Sheila reached over and put a hand on his arm, her go-to technique for calming him down. Thankfully, it worked. His breathing slowed slightly. "Just listen for a minute."

"Talk."

Sheila chose her words carefully. "If there's a chance I can help solve these new murders, then I need to try, okay? I know more about Ethan and Abby's relationship than anybody else. I can get her to talk to me, I know I can." She took a deep breath. "You know what I went through with Ethan. You know he blamed all the murders back then on her."

"And you said you believed him."

"Because I did at the time. I'd been in his basement for three weeks, thinking I was going to die. Believing what he said about Abby gave me hope, because it meant that if she was the murderer, then *Ethan wasn't*. Which meant that maybe, just maybe, I'd survive."

She didn't want to think about it now, but it was impossible to keep the images out of her head. A lot had happened in Ethan's basement. Awful things, terrible things, things she hadn't told anybody about, not the cops, not her therapist, not even Morris. *Especially* not Morris. And she never would.

"But let's be honest here." Sheila's voice quivered.

"Ethan was a sociopath. Looking back now, he lied about absolutely everything. Why wouldn't he lie about Abby, too?"

Morris didn't speak. Sheila could tell by his face—brows furrowed in concentration, jaw set, eyes fixed straight ahead—that he was processing what she was saying.

"The bodies were all found in Ethan's basement," she said quietly. "He had a kill room. He had all the tools to . . . dispose of them. And considering what he did to me . . ." She swallowed and took a second to gather her thoughts. "I don't know what Abby's involvement was in those murders last year, but I no longer believe anything Ethan said to me. I'm not saying she didn't do them, but I can no longer say for certain that she did. It's up to the prosecuting attorney to figure that out. What I do know is that women are being murdered *now*. And if there's any way I can help . . ." She allowed her voice to trail off.

She had explained her reasons as best she could. Morris was either on board, or he wasn't. There was nothing left she could say.

An uncomfortable silence filled the room. Then finally, he said, "And there's no one else?"

A wave of relief passed over her. "No," Sheila said, letting out a breath. "Nobody who could get to her like I could."

Morris continued to pace, something he did when he was working out a complicated problem. His executive assistant liked to complain that he had wear patterns on the carpet in his office. "I'm sorry, darlin', but this whole thing is a big fat steaming pile of cow dung. And you're stepping right in it. She's using Jerry. She's going to use you, too."

"Maybe so, but I can handle it. So can Jerry. You have to trust us. You have to trust me."

Morris's jaw worked.

"What's really bothering you about this?" Sheila asked softly. "Talk to me."

He stopped pacing and sat down beside her on the bed. "Okay, here's the thing. Whenever I'm doing a deal, the one thing I've learned is to always be one hundred percent aware of what's in it for the other guy. It's easy to focus on what *we* want—hell, you're a psychologist, you know this is what people do. We see the world through our own filters. We focus on our own needs."

"Yes, that's human nature."

"But it's dangerous to see the world this way. It's dangerous to focus on what we want, and not give any thought to what other people want. If I'm doing a deal and I'm not completely aware of what the other guy wants, I'm gonna get screwed. Happens every time." Morris's brow furrowed. "The important question here is not what Abby knows. The important question is, what does Abby *want*?"

And just like that, Morris had nailed it. That was the exact right question to ask, and Sheila had to smile. "Her freedom," she said. "Most of all, she wants her freedom."

"Exactly. And she has nothing to lose. And that's what's scaring me." Morris leaned toward her, his blue eyes fixed on her face. "In my experience, darlin', people with absolutely nothing to lose and everything to gain are the most dangerous people around."

Sheila nodded. She couldn't disagree. Abby Maddox's freedom was hanging in the balance, and of course the woman would do anything possible to save herself. Abby would grasp at anything she had to, would use anyone she had to. She was a survivor.

Sheila knew all about survival. Maybe more than most people.

"Okay," she said, meeting Morris's gaze firmly. "I hear you. I will keep my eyes wide open, and I promise you I'll be careful."

"But you're still going."

"As many times as it takes." Sheila squeezed his arm again. "I have to do this, Morris. Please try and understand that. I can't *not* help. Please don't ask me to step away when there might be something I can do. You didn't see those pictures. You didn't see how young they were." A lump caught in her throat.

Morris sighed and ran a hand through his thick brown hair. The sigh told Sheila the argument was over, and she finally let go of the pillow she'd been squeezing.

"I'd like it on the record that I am adamantly opposed to this." His voice was gruff.

"Consider it recorded. Adamantly."

"When are you going?"

"Tomorrow afternoon. Jerry's visiting her in the morning with her new deal."

"Can I go with you?"

"Absolutely not." Sheila smiled, but her tone left no room for further argument.

He finally lay down on the bed. Crisis averted. Sheila snuggled up beside him, resting her head on his burly chest, and breathed in his scent. She loved the way he smelled. Clean and citrusy and warm. Always warm.

"Speaking of Jerry, how is our friend?" Morris nuzzled the top of her head.

"He's not great." She snuggled closer. "I'm worried. He's so skinny."

"He's always been skinny."

"Not like this. I have to wonder if he's even eating. With Marianne out of the house . . ." She looked up at her fiancé. "Do me a favor and call him? Take him out, stuff him with food, get him talking. I don't think he has anybody to confide in. He tried talking to me, but I can't do it. It wouldn't be fair to Marianne."

"Hon, I've tried. He doesn't return my calls."

"Try again. Please. He needs support through all this. He's just afraid to ask for it."

Morris frowned. "I'll call him, but I don't think he'll talk to me about his love life. We're guys, darlin'. We talk about sports. The stock market. The size of Kim Kardashian's ass. We don't talk about personal stuff."

"He's our friend." Sheila's voice was soft but firm. "He was there for you when you needed him. So you be there for him, too. Even if you have to force him to let you help."

"All right." Morris kissed her forehead. "I'll call him tomorrow, see if he wants to go to that Chinese monkey place."

Despite her concern, Sheila laughed. "The Golden Monkey, right! That's his favorite restaurant. I thought you hated dim sum. You said that place was gross."

"It's growing on me. But don't you dare tell him I said that. I need something to bust his balls over."

"I won't breathe a word. It'll be our ancient Chinese secret."

Morris groaned. "Honey, that's terrible."

"So is the Golden Monkey."

Jerry was exhausted. Arriving at a women's prison at eight o'clock on a Sunday morning was not his idea of a good time, especially since he was just here the day before.

He and Danny were met by a long lineup inside the lobby of Rosedale Penitentiary. The prison had seemed quiet yesterday afternoon, but Jerry and Sheila had come after visiting hours. Mornings were obviously when most families arrived.

Yes, families. The lobby was filled with husbands, grandmothers, and young children who all seemed to know the drill. They were probably here every week. How many of the inmates were mothers? The thought was disturbing.

Jerry was surprised to see Mike Torrance waiting inside the lobby. Torrance seemed equally surprised to see Danny.

"What are you doing here?" Jerry asked as he shook hands with the detective.

Torrance nodded to Jerry's assistant and held up a thin manila envelope. "I have Maddox's deal here. Signed by the prosecuting attorney first thing this morning. Bob

Borden's been notified and he's probably already here." He smiled, a sharklike grin. "He's not expecting me, though."

"Thanks for running it down. So you'll leave it with me?"

"Nope," Torrance said. "I'm giving it to her personally."

"I don't know if that's a good idea, Mike—"

But his former partner had already turned away, heading straight for the corrections officer manning the reception desk and bypassing the long lineup. Jerry and Danny followed, ignoring the hostile stares of the other visitors who were annoyed they'd cut in line.

"Lineup starts at the back, sir," the corrections officer said to Torrance. Jerry recognized her from the day before, the one with the permanent scowl. Her tone matched her face. "We'll get you processed as fast as we can."

Torrance flashed his badge and stared her down. "I'm here on official police business, Sergeant . . . Briscoe," he said, peering at the name on her uniform. "And it's very time-sensitive. Abigail Maddox is expecting us."

The CO glanced at his badge and punched something into her computer. "Detective Torrance, yes, of course. Right this way please." She noticed Danny and Jerry standing behind him. "Detective Isaac. Oh, and hey, Danny. Didn't see you on the visitor's list. You three are together?"

At the CO's use of the word *detective*, Torrance raised an eyebrow and looked at Jerry, who raised an eyebrow and looked at Danny. His assistant knew the CO?

"They're with me, yes," Torrance said.

"Any of you bring weapons?"

"I'm carrying." Torrance's face changed once he understood what she was getting at. "Oh, come on, Sergeant. Seriously?"

The corrections officer was unfazed. "Sorry, Detective. Prison regulations. I'll need to keep your weapon and holster. We'll lock it up tight for you, don't worry." She looked over at Jerry's assistant with disapproval. "Maddox is high custody level, Danny. You know you're supposed to get preapproval from the superintendent first."

Danny managed to look chastised and hopeful at the same time. "I know, but there was no time, Sergeant. One-time exception? Please?"

The CO sighed. "Fine, but get your name on the list if you want to come back after today."

"Thank you." Danny headed toward the lockers, where she stowed her purse.

"You and the CO know each other?" Jerry said when his assistant returned.

"I used to volunteer here, remember?" Danny looked at him and waited. When he didn't reply, she said, "Last summer, for a few weeks, before I started grad school? I told you about it at the interview."

Jerry frowned.

"It was on my résumé?" Danny looked irritated.

He honestly didn't remember.

A few moments later they were being escorted down the same long hallway. The corrections officer unlocked the door to Conference 2.

Jerry stifled a sigh. "Back here again."

The CO unlocked the door and pushed it open. An older gentleman was already seated at the metal table, briefcase in front of him. Jerry recognized him immediately from Abby Maddox's assault trial. Slick suit, silver hair, flashy paisley tie. Bob Borden.

Maddox's attorney almost spit out his coffee when they stepped in. The door closed and locked behind them, and just like that, the room got even smaller.

"Mr. Isaac." Borden stood, his chair scraping the linoleum floor, making a screechy nails-on-a-chalkboard sound. "This meeting was only supposed to be with you."

Jerry took a seat, not bothering to introduce anybody. "What can I say, I'm a popular guy. I don't travel without my entourage. Looks like we're going to need an extra chair."

Torrance stepped forward and stuck his hand out toward the lawyer. "Detective Torrance, Seattle PD."

Borden's arms stayed firmly fixed at his sides. "I know who you are, Detective, but you have to leave."

"Excuse me, I don't—"

Borden cut him off. "My client made it very clear she'll only speak with Mr. Isaac." He gave Danny the once-over, seemed to decide she was insignificant, then turned his attention back to the detective.

Torrance's face turned a deep shade of red. "I don't give a shit what your client said, Mr. Borden. Women are being murdered and she knows who's doing it. I'm lead detective on the fucking case. So you tell your goddamned client—"

He was cut off by a discreet cough, and everybody turned around. Abby Maddox, hands cuffed in front of her and dressed head to toe in the same gray prison issues she was wearing the day before, stood in the doorway watching them. Her face was a mixture of amusement and wariness. In the sudden silence, the sound of Danny's sharp intake of breath was heard by all.

Maddox scanned the scene, her blue-violet eyes glancing over the red-faced detective, the apprehensive lawyer, the smirking private investigator, and the wide-eyed student. Finally her gaze settled on Mike Torrance. "Tell his goddamned client *what,* Detective?"

Torrance stiffened. "I was just going to say that I don't see why you'd object to speaking with me."

Borden pulled out a chair for his client, and Maddox took a seat. She raised her wrists as the corrections officer who escorted her—Officer Cavanaugh, same guy as yesterday—unlocked her handcuffs and then stepped back toward the doorway. The CO didn't leave.

Maddox rubbed her wrists. "Because I think you're an asshole, Detective. Do you need me to be any clearer than that?" Her smile was sweet, a complete contradiction to her icy tone. "Bob, kindly tell the detective that if he doesn't leave, the deal is off and I'm going back to my cell."

Borden looked at Torrance reproachfully. "Do you really need me to repeat that?"

The detective's already mottled face turned a shade deeper, which Jerry wouldn't have believed possible if he weren't seeing it for himself. Danny was watching the whole awkward scene with huge eyes.

Heaving a big sigh, Torrance headed for the door, which the CO opened for him.

Danny spoke up. "Maybe I should go, too, so you guys can talk privately." She made a move toward the door, but Maddox reached out and touched her arm.

"No," Maddox said, and Danny stopped. "That's okay. You can stay."

Danny glanced uncertainly at Jerry. He shrugged and gestured for her to sit. She took the last remaining chair, which put her directly across from the inmate.

"You gonna be okay here?" the CO asked, addressing Maddox.

"I'm good, Mark, thank you." The inmate flashed him a brief smile, and he left the room, the door locking behind him.

Maddox appraised Danny thoughtfully but said nothing. Danny met her gaze with a nervous smile.

"Did you bring the paperwork?" Bob Borden said, his steely eyes focused on Jerry.

Jerry pushed the manila folder toward the attorney.

Pulling a pair of reading glasses out of his breast pocket, Borden scanned through the documents quickly. He looked up, brows furrowed. "This isn't as we discussed."

"That's what they're offering."

"The deal we discussed was immunity for all the murders, including the bodies found in Wolfe's basement."

"The PA agreed to dismiss the murder charge for Diana St. Clair, and your client will be moved to a minimum security facility for the assault on me. No way the PA is going to agree to immunity on the other murders." Jerry's jaw was clenched. He hated everything about this deal, but there was nothing he could do about it. "I'd say that's pretty sweet."

"I don't understand," Maddox said, addressing her attorney. "You said I'd get probation and time served for the assault, and you also said you'd make sure they couldn't charge me with anything else. Now you're telling me it's just a prison transfer? It's still prison. And they can still get me for the bodies in Ethan's basement?" Her voice, normally soft and husky, was growing loud.

"Yes, what's the glitch?" Borden shot Jerry a glare. "What are we missing? You want her help with these new murders or not?"

Jerry glared back at the man. "This is the deal they gave me to present to you. I'm not authorized to make changes. You want to whine to someone, call the prosecuting attorney. Sign it or don't sign it, I don't give a shit."

"I don't want to spend any more time in jail, Bob," Maddox said to her lawyer.

"Shoulda thought of that before you cut my throat," Jerry said before Borden could respond.

Maddox turned back to him, silent for a moment. "I see," she finally said. "So it's you who wouldn't agree to probation. You want me to stay in jail."

"Oh, come on." Jerry finally met her gaze, ignoring the wild itch inside his collar. "We both know you're an intelligent woman. So don't sit there and pretend like you don't know how much I despise you. Your future is of no interest to me."

"I think we're remembering what happened that

night differently." Maddox's voice was steady. "The night everything . . . happened."

"Nope. I remember it perfectly." Jerry leaned forward. "I know you did those murders last year, okay? All of them. I don't have proof, and neither does the prosecuting attorney yet, but I know you did them. Or at the very least, you helped Ethan cover them up. It's the reason you tried to kill me. It's the reason you ran."

She glanced up, as if checking to make sure none of this was being recorded. She didn't have to worry. There were no cameras in here.

"What can I do to change your mind?" she asked.

"Not a goddamn thing."

Maddox leaned back in her chair and appraised him thoughtfully. "Wow. You really hate me."

"Yes. I really do."

She stared at him a moment longer, then said, "I'll need a moment alone with my attorney."

Jerry nodded and he and Danny left the conference room. The CO, stationed outside the door, looked over at them curiously, and Jerry took Danny's arm and maneuvered her a few feet away down the hallway. He didn't trust Officer Cavanaugh, or Mark, as Maddox called him.

He lowered his voice. "Listen, Danny, I have to ask. When you were a volunteer here, did you have any contact with Maddox?"

His assistant blinked. "No, none."

"Why didn't you mention last night or this morning that you used to volunteer here?"

"Dude, I assumed you knew. Check my résumé if you still have it. It's right on there."

Jerry rubbed his throat through his turtleneck. "She's bad news, Danny."

"I know that—"

"I mean it." Jerry put his hands on Danny's shoulders and turned her to face him. His assistant was petite, only five-four. He had a good foot on her and she had to crane her neck to look up into his face. "I know you find her fascinating, but Abby Maddox is a master manipulator, Danny. She was Ethan Wolfe's girlfriend for eight years. She's extremely good at getting what she wants. She'll say whatever she has to say to get you on her side. Don't get chummy, you hear me? And whatever you do, don't turn your back to her. And for God's sake, don't trust her."

"I got it." Danny seemed spooked by his intensity and she backed away slightly. "Honestly, Jerry, I got it."

The door to the conference room opened and they were called back inside.

Once they were seated, Borden spoke. "Everything looks to be in order."

"Good." Jerry kept the surprise out of his voice. He didn't think in a million years Maddox would agree to the deal, but somehow, her lawyer had talked her into it. Wonders never ceased. "Then all your client has to do is put her signature at the bottom."

"Do you want to read it over?" Borden said to Maddox. "It's fairly straightforward, but I can summarize each paragraph if you need me to." Jerry couldn't help but notice that the attorney's tone was different when he spoke to his client. Gentler. Less authoritative.

Maddox shook her head. "If you tell me it's fine, Bob, then I'll sign it right now."

Looking pleased, Borden took a silver-plated ball point pen out of his briefcase and placed it in front of her. "So you understand that you're receiving immunity for any charges involving Diana St. Clair's death in exchange for helping the police catch a murderer. If the information you provide leads to an arrest, you'll be transferred to a minimum security prison for your current conviction, where you'll serve out the remainder of your nine-year sentence for first-degree assault. However, with good behavior and a successful parole hearing, there's no reason to think that you won't be out in the next three years, since you've already served a year. You'll still be a very young woman when you get out, Abby."

Maddox took the pen, scrawling her name at the bottom of the last page. Then she fixed her gaze on Jerry. "It's not exactly how I hoped it would be, but I'm still grateful you helped make this happen, Jerry."

"Wasn't up to me."

Maddox handed the silver pen back to Borden. "Thanks, Bob. You can go now."

The attorney was taken aback. "You sure? I can stay if you—"

"We'll be fine." Her tone was dismissive. "It's Sunday, Bob. Go play with your kids."

Borden's face flushed, but he nodded and put the documents in his briefcase. "I'll be in touch. Call me if you need anything." He knocked on the door for the CO to let him out.

When he was gone, Maddox leaned back in her chair. For somebody who'd just found out that she wasn't getting out of prison anytime soon, she didn't look too upset. If anything, she looked quite satisfied. An uneasy feeling settled over Jerry. It was as if she knew all along this would happen. As if her plans had come to fruition exactly as she'd expected.

He couldn't shake the feeling he'd just been played.

Maddox's eyes danced over Jerry's face. "So how was your trip to the cemetery? Did you find what you were looking for?"

"We did. She was right where you said she would be." Jerry cracked his knuckles. "You signed the deal. Now start talking."

Maddox folded her hands in front of her. "I've been getting letters from the killer. Not that I really believed he was the killer, until just now. People will say anything to get my attention."

Jerry waited for her to continue. Exasperated, he said, "Well? Are we going to see these letters?"

"Bob told the CO to get them from my cell. They should be here in a few minutes."

"How many letters has he written you?"

"Not sure. Maybe a few."

"Why didn't you say something sooner?"

"What would I say?" Maddox looked irritated. "I get a lot of letters, Jerry. And all of my mail is checked before it gets to me, anyway. I have zero privacy here. You should be grateful I remembered anything at all."

"How do you know he's the killer? Did he actually tell you where the body is buried?" Danny's voice was surprisingly firm.

Maddox turned to the younger woman. "There was a letter that mentioned Heavenly Rest. That stuck with me. And he said something about 'three-ten' being hidden there, which didn't make sense until my lawyer told me that the bodies were numbered."

"Did you put that specific letter aside, at least?" Jerry said, cranky.

"Well, that would be too easy now, wouldn't it?" Maddox said with a wry smile. "Sorry. It's in the pile with all the others."

The headache started in Jerry's left temple. "Do you at least remember the guy's name?"

"Of course not." Maddox frowned. "Come to think of it, I don't know if he always signed the letters. But after a while I was able to recognize his writing style. I guess we'll have to read through them all."

"How many letters we talking?"

As if on cue, there was a knock at the door. The male CO was back again. In one hand he carried an enormous garbage bag full of mail, and his bicep, exposed by the short sleeve of his uniform shirt, flexed obnoxiously as he hoisted the bag up. Jerry rolled his eyes.

"Where would you like these?"

Maddox patted the table. "Just dump them right here, Mark."

The CO did as he was instructed. Jerry stared as heaps of letters fell out of the bag and onto the table. It took almost a full minute to shake them all out, and when the CO was finished, the pile was a foot high and four feet in diameter.

"Holy crap." His assistant's voice echoed exactly what Jerry was thinking.

"What can I say?" Maddox said. "I'm a celebrity. At

least reading them gives me something to do to pass the time."

"Let's get to work," Jerry said, grimacing. "Faster we get through this, faster we're outta here."

Danny turned to the CO, who was still standing by the door. "Um, Officer Cavanaugh? Please tell me there's coffee."

"Sure, I can grab some for you." He glanced around the room. "Should I bring three cups?"

"Bring the whole damned pot." Jerry looked over at the mountain of mail, the throbbing in his temple growing worse. "We're gonna need it."

CHAPTER: 13

Jerry ran out of steam by noon. The conference room was too damned small for the three of them. They were making some progress on the letters, which were largely tame and uninteresting. It didn't help that Maddox was slow getting through them, as if she were reading them all for the first time. Hungry and headachey, Jerry was in a foul mood, and if he didn't get out of here soon, his head might well explode.

Okay, so maybe his aggravation had a lot to do with Maddox and Danny getting along so well. The chitchat between them was mindless enough—prison gossip, PSSU news, etc.—but hadn't he just told Danny not to get friendly? She was a smart kid, and was obviously making conversation to keep things running smoothly, but it was irritating to hear them talk and laugh as if Maddox were . . . normal.

He snapped off his latex gloves and the sound made the chatter stop. To Danny he said, "Can I talk to you in the hallway for a moment?"

Exchanging an "uh-oh" look with Maddox, Danny followed Jerry out of the room.

"Everything okay?" she said when the door shut behind them.

Once again, Officer Cavanaugh was standing nearby, and Jerry took Danny's arm and pulled her a little farther down the hallway.

"What's the matter?"

"You're getting a little chatty with the criminal." Jerry didn't bother to hide his aggravation. "What did I tell you about watching yourself around her?"

"What did I do?" His assistant looked confused. "We're just reading letters and making small talk. That's all."

"I don't want you letting your guard down around her." Jerry leaned in. "I mean it, Danny. You can't trust her."

Danny backed up a step. "I'm not deaf, Jerry. I heard you the first time. I'm just trying to keep things pleasant. One of us has to, don't you think? You want her to open up, to keep cooperating, don't you?"

He sighed and leaned against the wall. His head hurt. She was right. He was overreacting.

"Why don't you go get something to eat?" Danny was watching him closely. "You can grab a sandwich from the vending machine and sit outside. It's a nice day. Take five, cool off."

Jerry rubbed his temples. "I don't know." He was starving, which only added to his irritation, but he didn't feel comfortable leaving Danny alone with Maddox. Who knew what the psychopath would say without him around to supervise?

Danny sighed. "Fine, it's up to you. But your eyes are bloodshot, you've got that look on your face that tells me you have a killer headache, and you need to eat some-thing." She looked up at him and saw he wasn't convinced. "I'll tell the CO to come in with me, okay? Have a little faith. Despite what you think, I can take care of myself. You never give me enough credit, Jerry."

Not that Jerry trusted that CO, either, but again, he knew Danny was right. He hadn't hired her because she was a ninny. "Okay. Ten minutes. Maybe less."

He walked her back to the conference room, made sure the guard went in with her, then headed over to the front desk to ask where he could find some food. A few minutes later, he was sitting outside under a tree, eating a candy bar and drinking a soda. The cool, crisp air on his face helped, as did the rare pocket of sunshine, and he felt his headache begin to subside.

He checked his phone and saw that he had a missed call. Morris. After bringing Sheila with him to the prison yesterday, he wasn't sure he wanted to check the voice mail. His headache had just improved, after all. He closed his eyes. He really hadn't slept in the past two days, and it was beginning to catch up to him.

Someone tapped him on the shoulder and he jumped. Opening his eyes, he looked up at the shadow looming over him.

"Thought you were only going to be ten minutes," Danny said, a little breathless. "I've got some names for you to give to Torrance."

"You finished the letters?" Jerry said, surprised. He checked his watch. Thirty minutes had passed. Dammit, he hadn't meant to leave her alone so long. "There was still a big pile."

"That's the best part. I didn't have to finish the letters. Once you left, Abby totally opened up to me. She gave me a bunch of names." Danny handed him a scrap piece of paper. "These are the people who write to her the most frequently. I'm not sure if they're all real names—some of these might be nicknames, or fake—but it's a start."

Jerry took the paper from her. "Nice job," he said, unable to keep the admiration out of his voice. "Might make an investigator out of you yet."

"Ha. She liked me, that helped. And dude, if any of these pan out, I want a glowing—and I mean *glowing*— evaluation."

Considering her internship was unpaid, Jerry was hardly in a position to argue. Hell, he was of a mind to let her write her own damned glowing evaluation just for allowing him to get out of this prison and away from Maddox much sooner than he'd thought.

He called Torrance as they headed back to the parking lot, passing along the names Danny had just given him. Torrance said he'd look into them.

"Before you hang up, thought you'd want to know that I finally got an ID on the third vic," his former partner said. "Claire Holt, age twenty-six. Ran her prints through the database; she got picked up for a DUI a few months back. It looks like she was working as an exotic dancer in Portland for a few years before moving here a few months ago."

"And did she start stripping here?"

"Yup. Weird, right?"

Jerry knew exactly what Torrance was referring to. No woman would move to Seattle to strip for a living. There was far more money to be made in the exotic dance trade in Oregon, where the industry was thriving.

"She had to have moved here for another reason." Jerry was thinking hard. "School? Boyfriend?"

"I'm guessing school since she attended UW part-time," Torrance said. "I'm heading to the Perfect Peach now. I'll find out what they know."

"The Perfect Peach? Never heard of it."

"Wasn't around when you worked vice. It's on Highway 99, north of the bridge. Want to meet me there?"

Jerry hadn't planned on getting involved any more than he had to in the investigation, but it wasn't like he had anything else to do once he dropped Danny off.

"Give me an hour," he said.

CHAPTER: 14

Abby stared at the pile of letters. It was funny how you didn't realize you were in a good mood until the good mood suddenly disintegrated. She had no desire to go back to her cell.

The door opened and Mark was back. He'd taken a quick smoke break, not that she was ever supposed to be left alone, but it wasn't like she was going to tattle on him. Seeing him made Abby feel a little better, but not much. He was simply a tool, nothing to get excited over, nothing that made her feel anything in particular.

He closed the door behind him. "You all done? Need help getting this stuff back in the bag?"

"That would be nice."

They started stuffing letters back into the Hefty bag. Mark was watching her closely. "What's wrong? Thought you'd be feeling good about how things went today. Everything's happening exactly how you wanted it to."

She looked at him closely. "You been drinking today?"

He looked away immediately. "It was only a couple of gin and tonics, no big deal."

"We're so close to getting everything we want, and

you're pulling this shit?" Abby slammed her hand on the table, and he looked back at her, startled. "If you get fired, you will fuck everything up for me. Don't you know that? What do I need to say to you for you to hear me?"

"Relax," Mark snapped. "You already look too much like my wife, and now you're starting to sound like her, too? I had a few drinks on my break. I needed something to take the edge off. Being with you, helping you do all this . . . it's not easy, Abby."

"Don't compare me to your wife, you asshole." God, he was such an idiot. If she didn't need him, she'd have cut him loose a long time ago. "You're not going to push me around the way you push her."

He looked at her, his jaw clenched. "Everything's going just fine," he said. "Why are you trying to pick a fight?"

There was no point in arguing with stupidity.

"I'm just hungry," Abby said. To hell with it, she didn't feel like fighting. She didn't want him to know how low she was feeling, how desperate she was getting. It was important never to show weakness around anyone. But every day, it felt like the prison was getting smaller and smaller.

"Chow hall is serving tuna casserole, green beans, and some kind of cake," Mark said.

She grimaced. Disgusting.

"I can get you some pizza." Mark put the bag down. "Briscoe's birthday was today."

"Real pizza?" Perking up, Abby's mouth began to water. She couldn't remember the last time she'd had real food. "From an actual pizza parlor?"

"Giovanni's. Thick crust. There's some left; you want me to get you a couple slices?"

"God, yes."

He was back a moment later with two giant slices of pizza smothered in cheese, tomato sauce, mushrooms, pepperoni, and sausage. Nothing like the poor excuse for pizza they served occasionally in the chow hall. It smelled heavenly. Abby inhaled deeply before diving in. While she ate, Mark continued to funnel her letters back into the bag.

"How's the new smartphone working out for you?" The door was closed and locked behind him, but he still kept his voice low.

Abby savored the flavors in her mouth. It was like she'd been eating in black-and-white for the last year, and now she was eating in Technicolor. The only downside to this? Having to go back to bland prison cuisine the next day. "It's perfect," she said, her mouth full. "Much better than the last phone."

"Internet signal okay?"

"It's good enough." She reached for the bottle of water beside her. "I'm not complaining. The only problem is, Celia found it."

Mark froze. "Shit, Abby, I told you—"

"Don't worry, I took care of it."

"And what the fuck is that supposed to mean?"

He had balls, she'd give him that. But he was forgetting his place, and that was unacceptable. "Watch how you speak to me, Mark," she said softly.

The CO's jaw worked. Clearly he had things to say, but he didn't talk back. Wise decision. Controlling his tone, he said, "So how did you handle it?"

Abby finished off her first slice and licked her fingers. Even the grease was yummy. "Celia doesn't know it came from you, if that's what you're worried about. I let her make a couple of calls on it."

"Christ, Abby—"

"Just to her family. The kids don't know the difference and her husband will never say anything."

"You should have hidden it better."

"I thought I had." Abby picked up her second slice of pizza. She wanted to savor it, but knew she had to eat quickly. She couldn't hang out in the conference room forever. "But she found it, and letting her use it once in a while is the best way to ensure she'll keep it quiet."

"I'm not concerned about her telling a CO about it." Mark leaned against the wall, looking unhappy. "I know she'd never do that. I'm concerned about her telling another inmate, who'll tell another inmate, who'll tell another inmate, and next thing you know, the damn thing's being passed around all over the CCU. And that's when a guard finds it."

"Mark, seriously. Relax. I told her if anyone else found out about it, I'd destroy the phone completely." Abby reached out and put a hand on his arm. "Thanks again for getting it for me. I know it was a huge risk."

He relaxed slightly, as she knew he would.

"What time are you off?" she asked, changing the subject.

"I was off an hour ago."

That brought a smile to her face. Putting her pizza down, she pulled him close and gave him a kiss. "What did you tell the wife?"

"That I stayed late for Briscoe's birthday thing. It's partly true." Mark smiled ruefully. "By the way, did your lawyer hear back from that TV show? The one that was willing to pay?"

He was referring to the current events show *The Pulse,* currently in negotiations with Bob Borden for an interview with her. Abby needed the money. She and Ethan hadn't been married, and when he'd died, she'd had no idea where his money went. It definitely hadn't been willed to her.

"Yes, and he's trying to arrange the interview for to-morrow morning. They want to air it this week." Abby finished the last few bites and sidled closer to him. "So what's going to happen with us when I get out? You going to run away with me?" She was half-joking.

He caressed her, not seeing the humor. "I've never loved anybody like this, Abby. I'm leaving her to be with you. You know that."

It was the right answer, and now he deserved his reward. In a husky voice, she said, "Come here."

He didn't hesitate, moving his chair beside hers so that they were both facing the door of the conference room. Sliding her hand under the table, she massaged him through his uniform pants. He was already semi-erect.

Unzipping his fly, she snaked her hand inside his slacks and wrapped her fingers around him, feeling him grow harder, and then she leaned over and put her mouth on it, varying the pressure, letting his breathing dictate how fast or slow she should go.

A few minutes later, he groaned, and she knew he

was close. Applying more pressure, she lengthened her movement, using her tongue to flick all the spots she knew drove him crazy. His hands gripped the edge of the table and she moved her face away just in time.

She removed her hand from his pants and cleaned herself off with a napkin.

Mark opened his eyes a few seconds later, a lazy smile on his lips. He zipped himself up and tucked in his shirt. "You're unbelievable."

"I know," she said, kissing him.

There was a short knock on the door, and they pulled apart just before it swung open. Sergeant Briscoe was in the doorway, keys in her hand. The middle-aged CO stared at the two of them, frown lines further aging her face. Then her gaze fell to the paper plate, where a lone bit of pepperoni still sat, evidence of the pizza that had once been there.

"I was going to remind you it's chow time, but I see you've already eaten." Briscoe's voice was sharp. "Why isn't Maddox back in her cell?" she said, addressing Mark.

Suddenly she sniffed the air, and her eyes, naturally narrow and suspicious, grew even smaller.

Abby wanted to laugh. Could Briscoe actually smell what they had just done? Probably, not that it mattered. This was Mark's problem. Amused, she watched the two COs stare each other down, and thought—not for the first time—that Elaine Briscoe might be an attractive woman if she could just stop scowling. The woman clearly needed a good lay.

Mark stood up. "That was my pizza, Sergeant."

"Officer Cavanaugh, can I see you in the hallway for a moment?" Briscoe turned to Abby. "Get all this cleaned up and prepare to go back to your cell. I'll find someone to escort you."

Mark didn't look back at her as he exited the room behind Briscoe. Abby didn't care.

She grabbed her bag of mail, and a moment later, a different CO, someone Abby didn't know too well, was in the doorway to cuff her and lead her back to the Close Custody Unit.

As she passed Mark and Briscoe in the hallway, her gaze turned briefly in their direction. Their low, heated voices made it clear they were arguing about something. Briscoe was angry, as was Mark.

She passed them with a knowing smile.

A few minutes later, she was back in her cell. Celia was in the bunk above hers, headphones over her ears, watching a rerun of the *Real Housewives* of whatever city on her TV. Abby lay back in her bed for a minute, then rolled over and reached for her phone, stashed in the air vent just beside her bunk. Downloading her emails and text messages, she saw one that made her smile.

Borden had just texted to let her know that the television interview with *The Pulse* was a go, and that the show had agreed to pay her the money she'd requested. It wasn't much, but it was better than nothing. She was to meet with Rosedale's superintendent the next day to work out when Bernadette Barkley, the cheesy blonde who'd be interviewing her, would be arriving. She hid the phone back in the air vent and closed her eyes.

She wondered if Bob Borden realized how unethical

it was to text her in prison, knowing full well inmates weren't allowed to have cell phones. Then again, ethics weren't the man's strong suit.

The same corrections officer who'd escorted her to her cell appeared again at her door a moment later. "Maddox. You have a visitor." Her lips pursed. "Again."

Abby sat up with a grin. Right on schedule. Everything was falling into place.

ighway 99, also known as Aurora Avenue North, had always been seedy. It was lined with motels that rented rooms by the hour, twenty-four-hour massage parlors, and gentlemen's clubs, though the word *gentlemen* seemed laughable. Jerry hadn't been down this way in a few years, not since he worked for PD.

He pulled up in front of the Perfect Peach, finding a spot right beside Torrance's unmarked. The building was nondescript save for the large mural painted on the exterior stucco wall, which left no room for misunderstanding that this place was, indeed, a strip club. The mural portrayed a glossy young woman with Jessica Rabbit proportions who had a giant fuzzy peach painted where her ass should have been. One slender arm pointed toward a big black door. There were no windows.

Coming in from the daylight, Jerry needed a moment to get used to the darkness. He stood for a moment inside the doorway until his eyes adjusted. The pulsing music assaulted his ears, and he wondered how anybody could work in a place so dark and so loud.

A huge bouncer, dressed in all black and possessing

arms the size of cannons, informed him politely that the cover charge was twenty bucks. Jerry pulled out his police ID. The bouncer waved him in.

He spotted Torrance at the bar talking to the bartender, a woman in her fifties with dyed jet-black hair. Though the lights were dimmed and Jerry was about fifteen feet away, he could still tell she was wearing too much makeup. As he made his way toward them, he glanced around at the patrons. On a Sunday afternoon, the place was almost dead, and the few customers that were here were older and alone. They were all fixated on the small, round stage, elevated about four feet from the floor, where the current dancer had breasts resembling cantaloupes. The rest of her body needed a good meal and a few days out of the sun, as her overtanned skin was looking a bit crispy. She was working the pole energetically enough, but her face showed boredom. He wondered what she was thinking about. Her rent, probably.

Jerry said hello to Torrance, who nodded back. The bartender tossed a white towel over her shoulder and left.

"Something I said?" Jerry said, bemused.

"She's getting the manager." Torrance picked up the glass in front of him and took a long sip. It looked like water. "She's only been working here a few weeks. Doesn't remember Claire Holt."

A moment later a muscular man wearing a shiny gray button-down shirt and black dress slacks approached them. Short, about five foot six, he had a thick, dark goatee and a clean-shaven, shiny bald head. He stopped in front of the two men, his eyes narrowed into suspicious slits even though nobody had said anything yet.

"Ken Eisler." He didn't offer his hand. "I'm the owner."

"Detective Mike Torrance, and this is Jerry Isaac," Torrance said smoothly, flashing his badge. "Sorry to take you away from your busy day, Mr. Eisler, but we need to ask you a few questions about Claire Holt." Though he didn't always intend to, Torrance had a way of saying everything with a smirk.

The man bristled. "Who?"

Torrance pulled out his iPhone and scrolled through it. He held up a DMV picture of the deceased. "Claire Holt."

Eisler's face registered surprise. "Oh, right. That's Candy Castle. All the girls change their names when they work here. She was only here for three months, then left a few weeks ago. What did she do?"

"Is there someplace quiet we can talk?"

Eisler led them through the club to a back room marked PRIVATE, which turned out to be his office. It was nicer than Jerry expected, with dark chocolate walls featuring colorful prints, a well-preserved antique desk in the corner, and a couple of shelves stuffed with business books. Eisler pointed to a couple of chairs and closed the door. The sounds of thumping bass mercifully went away. Soundproofed. Jerry didn't know how the man could work otherwise.

"Drink?" Eisler took a seat behind his desk. He opened his top drawer and pulled out bottle of Patrón Silver and a couple of shot glasses.

Torrance shook his head. Jerry did the same.

Eisler poured himself a shot and downed it in one smooth gulp. "So what happened to Candy?"

"She was strangled to death." Torrance's voice was purposefully flat. It was the tone he used for shock value, when he wasn't speaking with the victim's family or close friends. Jerry knew he wouldn't be mentioning the zip tie, or the carving of Abby Maddox's name on Holt's back.

Eisler leaned back in his chair. He seemed genuinely surprised. "Shit. She was a nice girl. What happened?"

"That's what we're here to find out," Torrance said. "When did she start working for you?"

"Four months ago. I think she was from Portland."

Torrance nodded. "And she left last month?"

Jerry pulled out his notepad and began making notes. Eisler hadn't seemed to notice that he hadn't yet said a word.

"About that time, yeah. She was a good dancer, so it was a no-brainer to hire her when she came in to audition." Eisler sighed heavily. "I had a feeling she wouldn't stick around long, though. When dancers come up from Portland, it's usually because they don't want to be dancers anymore. They do it till they get settled and then they try to find other work. Portland's where it's at, really. I'm thinking of moving my club down there to—"

"Why did she quit working for you?" Torrance said.

Eisler blinked. "You mean you don't know?"

Torrance and Jerry exchanged a look. "We're asking you," Torrance said.

The club owner clasped his hands together and his

thick lips pursed slightly. "She said she wasn't making enough money here at the club. She had big dreams; you know the type."

"What type is that?"

"The wannabe actress-model type. The wannabe famous type."

"And that's why she left?"

"She wanted to be in a different industry," Eisler said, clearly choosing his words carefully. "Come on, I know you guys know this."

"Explain it to us anyway." Torrance's face was unreadable.

The owner paused, then said, "Maybe it's better if I show you." He typed something into his computer, then turned the monitor around so they could see. There was a pause as Jerry and Torrance processed what they were looking at.

Jerry needed a moment to soak in the photographs. Claire Holt—Cassandra, on her website—was wearing a tiny gold bikini, the fabric just sheer enough to show the outline of her nipples and pubic region, though she wasn't technically nude. The pictures were actually quite classy, close to *Playboy* quality. At the bottom was a link that said FOR BOOKINGS, CLICK HERE.

"So she's a call girl," Jerry said. "Is this website legal?"

"It's not illegal." Torrance's normally stoic face was thoughtful. "She's got the disclaimer saying you have to be over eighteen to enter her site, and she's not blatantly saying she's a prostitute."

"The pictures kind of suggest it, though," Jerry said dubiously.

Eisler's smile was grim. "She was a beautiful girl. Such a waste."

"How did you find her site?" Torrance asked. "She's using a different name."

"She told one of the girls here, who showed me." Eisler clicked on the bookings link, and the screen changed to a different website that said KANE MODELS. "Technically, she works for this agency."

"Kane Models? As in Estelle Kane?"

"The one and only."

"Estelle Kane runs a modeling agency," Torrance explained to Jerry. "It's legit, but rumor has it she has a healthy side business of the illegal variety." To Eisler he said, "We're homicide. We don't deal with vice matters. Do you know for a fact that she was working as an escort?"

"I don't know anything for a fact. But I do know that Ms. Kane is very successful at what she does. Her girls make a lot of money working for her and business is steady, legit or not legit."

"You know a lot about Estelle Kane."

Eisler smiled. "She used to work for me a few years ago. I was sorry to lose her, too. Gorgeous woman, had the most beautiful, creamy skin."

There was something distasteful about the way the man said the word *creamy*. Suppressing a shudder, Jerry asked, "Where can we find her?"

"I assume the best way to go would be through her website."

Jerry's cell phone rang. Pulling it out of his pocket, he glanced at the screen. It was Danny. "Be right back," he said to Torrance. Ducking out of the office and back to the thumping bass of the main area, he answered the call.

"Jerry?" His assistant sounded hyped up, excited. "It's me. I found something on—hey, where are you?"

"I'm, uh . . . I'm with Torrance." Jerry stepped closer to the wall as a stripper wearing nothing but a thong and pasties strolled by. She smiled at him and he averted his eyes.

"What? I can hardly hear you."

"What is it, Danny? I have to get back."

"Okay, here's the thing. One of the names Abby gave me—KillerFan—sounded familiar. It's been bugging me all afternoon. But then it hit me. He's one of the sickos who posts on FreeAbbyMaddox.com. He writes really weird shit." Danny sounded almost giddy. "Anyway, I tracked down his real name from the site. It's Jeremiah Blake. And get this: he's applied for visitation to see Abby Maddox six times. Out of the names I gave you, he's the only one who's tried to see her in person. The superintendent turned him down because he's not family and he doesn't know her personally."

"How would you know he tried to visit her in prison?"

Danny sounded annoyed. "Because I called Rosedale a few minutes ago. I still have friends there. Anyway, thought you'd want to know."

"Good work, kid." Jerry disconnected the call. A second later, the door to Ken Eisler's private office opened and Torrance stepped out. "You all done?" Jerry asked.

Torrance nodded. "Let's go back outside. I can't stand it in here. Can't hear myself think."

The two headed for the entrance. The cannon-armed bouncer opened the door for them and sunlight blazed into Jerry's face, temporarily blinding him. The club was so dark, Jerry had forgotten it was still daylight outside.

"So what now?"

Torrance was heading toward his unmarked. "Since we now know Claire Holt was a pro, it's got me thinking that all the other victims are, too. I'm going to have to talk to vice, see what they know about Estelle Kane. From what I've heard, they haven't been able to pin anything on her yet. Doubt they'll have anything useful for me, but you never know." He pulled a pack of Marlboros out of his pocket. "Was that Danny who called?"

"Yeah." Jerry filled him in on Jeremiah Blake as his former partner lit a cigarette. "Out of the ones who wrote to her, he seems to be the most obsessed. I think we should start with him."

"You do, do you?" Torrance raised an eyebrow and smirked. "Thought you didn't want to be involved."

"I'm already involved," Jerry said with a sigh. "But hey, I'm just the lowly consultant. Obviously it's your call."

Torrance stomped out his cigarette and reached for his phone. A moment later, he had an address. "All right. There's a Jeremiah Blake in Ballard. Might as well run this down, see where it goes. You coming with me, or you got somewhere else to be?"

"I'm coming."

"If this pans out, you'd better pay Danny a bonus. The kid's got a good brain on her."

"She doesn't get paid. But yeah. I know what you mean."

CHAPTER 16

It felt very different seeing Abby Maddox alone. With Jerry beside her, Sheila had felt safe. Without him, she felt . . . not unsafe, exactly, but exposed.

She sat in Rosedale Penitentiary's visitors' lounge and waited for Abby to arrive. The lounge was much more comfortable than the conference room she'd met Abby in the day before. No privacy, of course, but it was spacious and bright. Colorful murals decorated the walls. Natural light filtered in through the windows, which offered a pretty view of the manicured grounds behind the prison. Vending machines lined the back wall, and in one corner was an elevated guard's booth where a bored-looking corrections officer sat keeping an eye on things. There were lots of husbands and young children here today, and Sheila wondered what their mothers had done to be incarcerated.

The doors at the other side of the room opened, and Abby, escorted by a female corrections officer, was finally led inside. A small smile crossed her lips when she saw Sheila.

Heads turned. Whispers followed. It was obvious everybody knew who Abby Maddox was. Even the bored CO in the corner straightened up a little.

The guard uncuffed her and Abby took a seat at the table. "You look well, Sheila. I meant to tell you that yesterday."

"Thank you. You look well yourself."

Abby's eyes flickered over Sheila's face, missing nothing. "The longer hair suits you. And I've always admired your lipstick. Perfect shade of red." She cocked her head. "Chanel?"

"Dior," Sheila said.

"Expensive. Not that I'd expect anything less." Abby smiled again, her gaze dropping to Sheila's designer jacket and blouse. "You always look exquisitely tailored. Must be nice to have that kind of money to spend on clothes. And your engagement ring is blinding me from here. How big is that sucker? Three carats?"

"Four." Sheila kept her voice even. "And I've worked hard for everything I have."

Abby smoothed her prison issue shirt. "What do you think of my outfit?"

Sheila stood. "Can I get you a coffee?"

"Chocolate would be nice."

Sheila returned a few minutes later with two cups of coffee and two Kit Kat bars.

"Thanks." Abby ripped open the wrapper and took a bite, closing her eyes and chewing slowly. "It's amazing what you take for granted on the outside."

"How's the food in here?"

"Somewhere between edible and awful, but better than what I used to serve at St. Mary's." Abby broke off another piece of chocolate. "I'm amazed the homeless don't all commit crimes so they can come to prison."

St. Mary's Helping Hands was the soup kitchen where Abby and Ethan used to volunteer. It was now thought to have been Ethan's hunting ground, since several of the victims had passed through St. Mary's at one time or another. The memory was painful and Sheila shuddered.

Abby caught the movement. "Too soon to bring it up?"

"No, of course not." Sheila took a bite of her chocolate bar, but her mouth was dry and the sweet wafer tasted like cardboard. She took a long sip of her coffee and pushed the chocolate away.

At the next table, an inmate cradled an infant who couldn't have been more than six months old. Across from her sat an older woman—probably the inmate's mother—who looked haggard, as if she'd been up all night with the baby. Which she probably had been.

"That's Ruby." Abby's low voice cut into Sheila's thoughts. "Her mom brings the baby in every few days. Ruby assaulted a cop while she was being arrested for drugs. Automatic four years, so they tell me."

"I'm sure you've learned a lot about the penal system in the past year."

"More than I ever wanted to know, trust me. It's like getting a master's degree in criminal justice without the actual diploma."

"And I'm sure you're still learning. Especially now that you're helping with this new investigation."

"I guess you could say I have special insight," Abby said, her eyes gleaming.

"Because you've been in contact with the killer?"

The younger woman studied her. "That, and also because of Ethan. I *have* been up close and personal with a psychopath, Sheila. As have you."

They both fell silent for a moment. Clearly Abby wasn't ready to discuss the investigation yet. Sheila would have to ease her into it some other way, without risking the inmate clamming up.

"Do you want to talk about Ethan?" Sheila asked.

Abby seemed startled by Sheila's abruptness. "If that's all right with you."

"It's fine." Sheila made sure her hands stayed steady. "Where would you like to start?"

Abby sipped her coffee, pondering. Then a moment later, in the same tone one would use to ask if it was raining outside, she said, "Were you in love with him?"

Jesus. Sheila had assumed their conversation would focus more on what she had observed of Ethan's behavior in those last few weeks. She sure as hell wasn't expecting to discuss *feelings*. Her mouth opened but no words came out. She honestly didn't know how to answer the question.

"It's a simple yes or no, Sheila." Abby's husky voice was soft but firm. "I loved Ethan very much. I know he loved me, too. And yet he was involved with you for months, and now he's dead. I want to know exactly what kind of relationship you had with my boyfriend."

Well, *shit*. Abby wasn't pulling any punches, was she? Taking a deep breath, Sheila said, "I wasn't in love with Ethan. I cared about him, but not like that."

"Then like what?"

"It was . . ." Sheila struggled to find the words. She needed to be careful what she said, and how she said it.

She could never tell this woman she was a sex addict. It was something she worked very hard to keep secret, and outside of an extremely small circle of friends and the folks who saw her at Sex Addicts Anonymous every week who didn't know her real name, nobody knew. And Abby Maddox was the last person she would want knowing. "The relationship was strictly physical."

Abby's eyes closed.

A different person may have apologized, but Sheila wasn't sorry. She had paid for her mistakes with Ethan, a thousand times over. She was sorry she had ever gotten involved with him, yes, but not because of what the affair had done to *Abby*.

The younger woman opened her eyes again, her lashes moist. "I'm sure you knew Ethan had very specific demands. Demands that I couldn't meet all by myself. No woman could."

"Yes." This was so much harder than Sheila had been expecting. "What we had wasn't about love. It was about power. And dominance."

"On some level he must have loved you, though." Abby's voice caught in her throat. She almost seemed like she was about to break down, and Sheila was surprised by the amount of emotion she was seeing from the inmate. It certainly appeared real. "Otherwise, he would have killed you. Like he did those other women."

"He nearly did kill me."

"But yet, here you are." The ice in Abby's voice was unmistakable.

Sheila kept her expression neutral. "How much did you know? About what he was up to?"

The younger woman's expression was impossible to read. "I didn't know anything."

"You had no idea what was going on?"

"Didn't I just say that?" Abby's eyes narrowed and her voice went up a notch. "He lied to me. He lied to you. Why is that so surprising?"

"He said you—"

"I know what he said about me." Abby's face and neck flushed a deep red that started from her collarbone and worked its way up to her cheeks. Her posture, relaxed only seconds ago, was now rigid. "I know what he told you, and I know what you told the cops. It was all over the news, Sheila, or don't you remember? Because of him, and because of you repeating what he said—which, by the way, were all lies—I was practically convicted the moment I was arrested last year."

"But you—"

"Don't you dare interrupt me. I'm not done." Abby was heaving, and Sheila could feel the chocolate-scented hot breath on her face. "My boyfriend was a psychopath, okay? You should know that better than anyone. And yet somehow, you believed him when he told you I killed those women. You went and blabbed to the fucking cops about it. You were the reason I had to run."

"But you hurt Jerry—"

"Fuck Jerry! He cornered me, and I did what I had to do to get the hell out. I'm a survivor, Sheila, and so are you. You did what you had to do to survive in that basement, didn't you?" Abby's hands were clenched into fists. "Didn't you?"

Sheila blinked, almost paralyzed by the question.

Nobody but herself and Ethan knew the true story of what went on in that basement. She hadn't told a soul. But here was Abby, acting like she knew every detail about what had gone on, and maybe she did. Maybe Ethan had told her. The thought made her sick. "I did what I had to do to survive, yes."

"And so did I." Abby's voice shook with anger. "So don't you fucking sit there on your high horse and judge me. You might have a Ph.D. in psychology, but I've earned a degree in surviving a psychopath for eight years, so don't you dare presume to know anything about me. I'm half your age and twice as smart, and I don't deserve to be in this goddamned hellhole. I have a life waiting for me on the outside, a good life, with someone who loves me unconditionally and will do anything for me. Who, in fact, *has* done everything—"

Abby stopped abruptly and sat back in her chair, breathing hard. Sheila waited for her to finish her sentence, but it was clear she wasn't going to. She wondered who the "someone" was that Abby was referring to. The handsome corrections officer from the day before, perhaps?

The two women stared at each other across the table. Around them, faces were turned in their direction, and Sheila could sense several pairs of eyes watching their every move. It seemed as if the whole room had gone a few decibels quieter.

"I'm not judging you, Abby," Sheila said quietly, hoping to defuse her. "Ethan was a monster. He would have said anything to get his way. I know that now."

"Yes. But you need to admit that you used him, too."

"What?" Sheila said, startled.

"Admit that you used him until you didn't want him anymore, and that you threw him away." Abby's voice was like steel. "Admit that you're the reason he's dead."

Unbelievable.

"I won't do that," Sheila said quietly. "I will never do that. What happened wasn't my fault."

"Well, it's not mine, either. And I don't deserve to be here."

It took all of Sheila's willpower to stay calm and keep her face closed. She took a breath, needing strength for the lies she was about to spew. "You're not a bad person, Abby. But you got involved with a bad person and you made some bad choices. No, I don't believe you deserve to be here."

"Will you tell Jerry that?" Abby said.

"Of course I will." Of course she wouldn't.

Abby let out a long breath. Her fists unclenched and the blood in her face began to drain away. Around them, heads finally turned back around. Conversations resumed.

"I struck a deal with the prosecuting attorney this morning," Abby said, and just like that, her voice and posture were back to normal. Jesus, it was almost like talking to three different people. Her ability to switch gears reminded Sheila of Ethan. She tried to imagine the two of them together, and the thought was terrifying. "If they make an arrest, I'll be transferred to Creekside Corrections."

"Is that minimum security?"

"Yes. I heard it's not too bad. With good behavior, I could be out in three years."

Good God. That didn't seem right at all. "I hope your special someone is willing to wait for you."

Abby smiled. "I'm not even worried about it."

Sheila leaned forward slightly. "So, do you actually know who the killer is?"

Abby sat back in her chair, twirling a lock of shiny black hair in her fingers and looking quite content. "Maybe." Her smile made Sheila uneasy. "We went through my mail and we came up with some names. Jerry and Danny were here earlier today."

"Danny? Jerry's assistant?" Sheila was surprised Jerry would bring his intern to the prison. She remembered Danny Mercy quite well, having had her as a student a couple of years earlier. The girl was bright and quite personable. Then again, maybe that's why Jerry had her tag along. Someone like Danny, close to Abby's age, would probably be very helpful in getting Abby to open up.

"Yes. She's smart as hell."

Abby's expression was difficult to read, and it made Sheila uncomfortable, not knowing what the other woman might be thinking. She knew she needed to steer the conversation back to the murders. "I heard the women—the victims—looked a lot like you. And that the message 'Free Abby Maddox' was . . . left on them." She couldn't bring herself to say the word *carved*.

"I heard the same things."

"The killer must be someone who's quite taken with you."

"That's one way to put it."

"How would you put it?"

Abby shrugged and used her forefinger to draw imaginary circles in the air beside her ear, the universal sign for *cuckoo*. "People are screwed up, Sheila. You know that."

She nodded. "How do you feel about the victims?"

"You mean, do I feel empathy?"

"Yes."

"Well, of course I do," Abby said. "What kind of person would I be if I didn't?"

"But whoever's doing this, obviously they have some kind of plan to get you out of here and someplace nicer," Sheila said carefully. She knew she had to tread lightly here if she was going to keep Abby talking about this, which so far the younger woman seemed open to doing. "You've been given immunity from Diana St. Clair's murder. That's huge."

At the mention of Diana's name, Abby's face hardened. "As well I should be. I had nothing to do with her death. She was just another one of Ethan's victims."

The coldness in Abby's eyes chilled Sheila to the core. "But you would have gone to trial for a murder charge had these new murders not happened."

"Yes, and?" Abby cocked her head questioningly. "Why don't you just ask me whatever it is you're wanting to ask me?"

"Okay, then." Sheila sat up straighter and folded her hands in her lap. She looked straight into Abby's eyes. "Did you plan this? Did you have something to do with these new murders?"

The question brought a smile to Abby's face, and she leaned forward, her eyes glinting. "Does it matter if I did?"

Sheila opened her mouth to respond, but she

couldn't find the words. Had Abby just admitted she was orchestrating this whole thing from prison somehow? That she had allowed three young women to die in order to cut a deal with the prosecuting attorney? It was mind-boggling. Unconscionable. Depraved. And it wouldn't surprise Sheila one bit.

"I'm joking, Sheila." Abby leaned back again. She was practically purring. "Come on now. Of course I had nothing to do with it. And I feel terrible that women were killed just so someone could send the cops a message about me. But I'm a practical person, and I know I'm helping myself by helping the police." She shrugged. "What's so wrong with that?"

Before Sheila could think of how to respond, the corrections officer in the corner spoke into the mike.

"Visiting hours are over in five minutes," the CO said, his voice crackling slightly over the loudspeaker. "Please say your goodbyes now. Visitors, please begin making your way toward the exits. Thank you."

Around them, chairs squeaked as inmates and visitors stood up, murmuring words of endearment to each other and exchanging hugs. Abby stood up, too. "Well, thanks for coming, Sheila. It's been fun."

No, no, no. Sheila was right on the verge of getting Abby to admit something big here, she felt it in her bones. Abby knew more than she was telling Jerry about the murders, and now visiting hours were over? What timing. If only she had ten more minutes . . .

"Come visit me anytime." Abby's smile was cold. "If not here, at the new place. I think they'll be making an arrest very soon."

Sheila nodded, feeling helpless. The same corrections officer who'd brought Abby in had returned to escort the inmate back to her cell. Sheila watched as the younger woman was cuffed.

"By the way, Sheila," Abby said over her shoulder as the guard escorted her out. "You might want to watch *The Pulse* tomorrow night. I'll be taping an interview with them in the morning, and I'll be talking about my relationship with Ethan. I have no doubt you'll find it . . . enlightening."

Abby was out the door with the CO at her elbow before Sheila could respond.

Shit. So close.

CHAPTER: 17

I t took some serious driving skills to keep up with Mike Torrance's Steve McQueen lane changes. Jerry had forgotten about his former partner's death-wish driving, and he lost sight of the unmarked for a full minute on I-5 before spotting it again. The light rain was making the roads slick enough to be scary, and he was relieved when they finally exited the freeway.

He pulled up behind Torrance on Palmer Lane, parking on the street in front of the house where Abby's number-one fan and letter-writer, Jeremiah Blake, lived. The house was a brown-bricked rambler, older, set far back from the main street and flanked on either side by tall maple trees.

The driveway was empty but they could see lights on inside. Torrance rang the doorbell. A few seconds passed. Nobody answered. Torrance pressed his ear to the door briefly.

"Somebody's got to be home," he said. "I can hear music." He rang the doorbell again, then banged loudly several times.

It took another minute, but eventually the door opened. A kid who looked around fifteen stood there, staring at them with crust in his eyes. Hip-hop and the smell of old pizza wafted out into the cool afternoon air.

"Yeah?" he said. Tall, close to six feet and skinny, he had longish messy brown hair and a jawline full of pimples. He was dressed in stained sweatpants and a faded Puget Sound State Steelheads T-shirt that sagged around his ribs. His skin was pasty and his dark eyes had grayish circles, as if he hadn't been out of the house for a while.

"We're looking for Jeremiah Blake." Torrance eased closer to the door frame so that his foot was inside the house by about an inch.

"That's me," the kid said.

Torrance and Jerry exchanged a look. Surely this couldn't be the same Jeremiah Blake who was writing to Abby Maddox. The DMV records showed he was forty-five. This kid couldn't be out of high school. Torrance flashed his badge and Jerry did the same with his consultant's ID. "You're Jeremiah Blake? Are your parents home?"

The kid took a step back, his eyes widening at the sight of Torrance's badge. "My dad's not here. His name's Jeremiah, too. What do you—"

"Can we come in?" The detective's face was like stone. "Or would you rather talk outside where all your neighbors can see us?"

The kid poked his head out onto the stoop and looked around. Indeed, one of the neighbors next door, a middle-aged man who had just pulled into his driveway, was observing the three of them curiously. "All right, come in," he said reluctantly, opening the door wider and taking another step back.

Torrance and Jerry stepped into the house. The three of them stood in the front foyer in a triangle, eyeballing each other. The hip-hop changed to heavy metal, an assault on Jerry's ears.

"How about you turn that off for a little bit?" Torrance said, his eyes crinkling at the noise. "So we can talk."

The teenager shrugged and turned for the hallway. The two men exchanged a look and then followed him. The house wasn't big and they were in the kid's bedroom a few footsteps later.

Blake's room was small, cluttered, and generally a disaster. The floor was a mess of dirty clothes, old fast-food cups, and crumpled cheeseburger wrappers. A large tube television sat in one corner, the screen frozen on a scene of an eerily real cartoon man shooting a bunch of other men, blood spraying out of their chests where they'd been hit. The video game box sitting on top of the TV said "Gears of War 3." Wow. So much blood for one video game. The last game Jerry could remember playing was Galaga, over three decades ago.

Wrinkling his nose, he sidestepped a pizza box that was open but empty aside from a few bits of hardened cheese left behind. Empty Twizzlers wrappers—the family pack size—were everywhere. The tiny bedroom held a rank blend of body odor, old gym shoes, and stale food—a special scent also known as teenage boy. Jerry's sister's son had a room just like this one, but with one noticeable difference.

In this room, every inch of wall space was covered with posters. Some were of rock bands Jerry had never heard of—the Killers, Foo Fighters, Act of Mercy. And intermingled with those were posters of serial killers. The faces of Ted Bundy, Charles Manson, Ed Gein, and even Ethan Wolfe lined his walls. And those were just the ones Jerry recognized.

Blake didn't have any posters of Abby Maddox, probably because there weren't any available, because technically she wasn't yet a convicted serial killer. But there were several printouts of Maddox's face taped strategically around the room. They were in black-and-white but the kid had colored in Maddox's eyes with pencil crayon in the exact right shade of blue-violet.

Jerry suppressed a shudder.

Blake flipped the stereo off then turned around. At the sight of them, he jumped, not realizing they were right behind him. Jerry followed Torrance's gaze to the kid's laptop, which was sitting open on the bed and powered on. The browser was showing a website called *The Serial Killer Files*. Blake saw them looking and quickly tapped a button with his finger. A second later, a screen saver popped up, the band logo for Act of Mercy. A skull with a bullet hole in its forehead. Nice.

"I see you're a fan of criminals." Torrance's hawk eyes moved over the posters slowly, missing nothing. "Got some good ones here."

"Um, are you guys allowed to be in here?" Blake's gaze flickered back and forth between the two men. "My dad's not home. That's who you want, right?"

"Actually, I think it's you we're looking for," Jerry said amiably.

"How are old you, son?" Torrance's face was unreadable. His eyes scanned the posters a moment before coming back to Jeremiah Blake's face.

"Eighteen."

"Got any ID?"

"Why?"

Torrance sighed.

The kid reached for a pair of jeans crumpled beside the bed and fished around in the pockets. He pulled out a tattered wallet, and from that, a stained high school ID card. He handed it to Torrance, who scrutinized it before handing it to Jerry. Yup, this Jeremiah Blake was eighteen. Christ. Other than his height, he looked so much younger than that.

But the good news was, at eighteen, he could be questioned without parental supervision. Jerry handed the kid's ID back to him.

"Who else lives here?" Torrance asked. "Besides you and your father?"

Blake swallowed, his large Adam's apple bobbing painfully in his scrawny throat. "It's just the two of us. My dad has a girlfriend that sleeps over sometimes, but not . . . not lately."

"And what about you? Do you have a girlfriend who sleeps over sometimes?"

The kid's face reddened. "I . . . I don't have a girlfriend. Look, I think you guys should tell me why you're here. Or else I . . . I'm going to have to ask you to leave."

Torrance smiled and looked away. It was Jerry's cue to speak. "You're a fan of Abby Maddox?" he asked, his voice a little less raspy than usual.

"Um. Who?"

Instinctively, Jerry stepped forward a couple of inches. Torrance stepped back. It was amazing how easy it was for them to slip back into their old routine.

"Abby Maddox," Jerry said patiently. "You know, the infamous attempted murderess and girlfriend of the Tell-Tale Heart Killer. She's been all over the news lately—TV, newspapers, Internet, blogs. You have at least a half a dozen pictures of her on your wall. Good job nailing the eye color, by the way."

Jerry took another step toward him, prompting the kid to sit down on the bed since there was nowhere else to go. He looked up at the two men. "Yeah, I know who she is. Everybody does. So what?" Blake stared at Jerry sullenly, then suddenly his features lit up with recognition. "Hey, wait a minute. I know you! You're . . . that guy. You're the . . ."

Oh, to be eighteen and barely coherent, Jerry thought, stifling a sigh. "Yep, I'm that guy."

"You're not a cop anymore." Blake's tone was accusatory. He frowned, his eyes going right toward the ID clipped to Jerry's breast pocket. "You're just a—"

"He's a cop on *this* case," Torrance interjected smoothly. "That ID is real, son."

"So you don't think Abby Maddox deserves to be in prison." Jerry looked down at the kid, who looked confused and desperately unhappy, as if he wished the bed would swallow him up. "You don't think she's guilty of attempting to murder me."

"*Hells* no!" Blake said hotly, and once the words were out, his face turned a deeper shade of red. "It's just . . . I'm sorry what happened to you and all, but come on, dude. She's gotta be fucked up, you know? Being with Ethan Wolfe for so long. That's bound to mess with her head." He looked at Jerry earnestly. "I don't think she meant to hurt you, honestly."

Torrance wisely stepped forward. He placed a hand on Jerry's shoulder and Jerry took a step back. "Was that your blog I just saw on your computer? *The Serial Killer Files*? What do you write about on there?"

"Serial killers, duh." Blake scratched his head and little flakes of dandruff floated to his shoulders. "I do profiles. I guest post all the time on other sites, too. I'm pretty much the go-to guy for killers." He lifted his chin, obviously proud of himself.

"Is that like a hobby?" Torrance asked. "Whatever happened to stamp collecting? Or sports?"

"It's not a hobby, it's my job. And killing *is* a sport," the kid said with a grin. Jerry shuddered.

"Abby Maddox has heard about your blog, and she thinks you're a total freak." The lies rolled off the detective's tongue with ease. When Blake showed surprise, he added, "She gave us all your letters, too. She said you're a stalker and she wants you to stop writing her."

"No way, she didn't say that." Blake started picking at a pimple on his chin. "I never wrote anything bad, and I've only sent like a dozen. She'd never say that. Is that why you're here?"

"Has she ever written you back?"

"No, but—"

"Why would you keep writing her, then? Wouldn't you think that after the first, say, two letters, that if someone hasn't written you back, it means they're not interested?"

The kid's thin shoulders slumped. The pimple on his chin was oozing blood and pus. He grabbed a tissue and pressed it to his face. "If she wanted me to stop, why wouldn't she just tell me to stop." It came out a statement, not a question, and the kid suddenly seemed defeated. Jerry almost felt sorry for him. Almost.

Blake looked up at Jerry. "Maybe when you see her next time, you could tell her I'm not a freak. Tell her I'm her biggest fan and I've written like, twenty blog posts about her. I think she's amazing, and I'd love to interview her for my site. Will you tell her that?"

"That you're not a freak? Sure, I'll tell her." Jerry kept his face expressionless. "As for the blog interview, you do know she's not allowed to access the Internet, don't you? How can she even read your blog?"

Blake's face fell again and he was quiet for a moment. "Right," he said. "Look, what do you guys want? I got stuff to do."

Jerry pulled the chair from the desk and sat down across from him. "We want to know where you've been the last few days."

The kid looked at Torrance as if he was wondering whether this was a real question. He looked back at Jerry. "I was home."

"All week?"

"Yeah."

"You don't go to school? Work?"

"I work part-time at Fred Meyer." Blake was referring to the locally owned Northwest superstore. "I'm a stock boy. At the one in Ballard."

"But you weren't working there this week."

"Hells no. I was home."

"Can anyone verify that?"

"No." Blake began to fidget. "My dad works all the time. He works on a crab boat, and he's gone for a couple weeks at a time. Look, what's this about? Did something happen? Do you think I did something?"

Jerry stood up and put the chair back near the desk. "There was a murder downtown. A woman's body was found in a hotel yesterday morning."

"And you think *I* did it?" Blake finally stood up again, his ears red and his eyes wide with surprise, and maybe even a little excitement. His reaction disturbed Jerry. "Because I . . . I write a blog about serial killers and I have a boner for Abby Maddox? Like, who doesn't? That's kind of a . . . a . . ."

"Stretch?" Torrance said helpfully.

"Yeah," Blake said, his head bobbing back and forth between Torrance and Jerry. "I'm not a murderer just because I *blog* about murderers." His eyes widened. "Hey, is there some connection between Abby and the victim?"

It was a surprisingly intelligent question for a kid who didn't seem that bright.

Torrance didn't answer. Instead, he dug into his breast pocket. "How about a cheek swab?" He held up what looked like a long Q-tip wrapped in a skinny Ziploc bag. "Just so we can rule you out."

The kid's eyes showed real fear. "You want my DNA?"

"It just takes a second. One swipe and this all goes away. We'll never have to bother you again."

"I don't know." Jeremiah Blake's eyes were darting all

over the place, reminding Jerry of a rabbit stuck in a hole. "I . . . I guess."

"Great." Torrance leaned in. "Open up." The kid did as he was instructed and Torrance swabbed the inside of his cheek. Sticking the Q-tip back in the plastic bag, Torrance sealed it and put it back in his pocket. "Thanks for being so cooperative. We'll get out of your hair now. Listen, stay available, okay? Don't go anywhere or it'll look really suspicious. We might have to chat with you again."

The two men made their way out of the room and back down the hall, where the air seemed fresher. Blake followed behind.

"Hey, can I do an interview with you?" The kid touched Jerry's arm. "I think my readers would want to know your side of the story. I don't know if you've been keeping up, but, like, dude, you don't really come across as a nice guy in the press."

"*Hells* no," Jerry said, closing the door behind him.

CHAPTER: 18

Jeremiah Blake was one creepy kid.

Jerry had been scrolling through the eighteen-year-old's blog for the past hour, and he was starting to feel like he needed a hot shower with disinfectant soap and a good scrub with one of those scratchy long-handled sponges. While the kid's writing was good, the content was damned twisted. Detailed profiles of serial killers, dissections of killing methods and crime scenes . . . was this what kids were into these days? *The Serial Killer Files* was a very active blog—lively discussions ensued in the comments section after every post. Jerry didn't think he'd ever understand why people were so turned on by death.

There were voices out in the reception area and he wondered who was here. Torrance had asked him to work at an unoccupied desk at the East Precinct, but Jerry had declined, preferring the familiarity and comfort of his own office. The last time he'd been at the precinct had been the night Maddox had—

He scratched his throat and forced the thought out of his mind. A few seconds later, Torrance poked his head in.

"Busy?"

Jerry peeled his dry eyes away from the computer, grateful for the distraction. "How'd it go with the neighbor?"

Torrance lumbered into the office and plopped himself into the chair across from Jerry's desk. He'd stayed behind on Palmer Lane to talk to the man who lived next door to the Blakes. "Went well. He was only too happy to dish."

"Hold that thought. Hey, Danny!" Jerry called through the open door. "Come in here for a sec."

A moment later his assistant was in the doorway. "What's up?"

"Can you go through all the posts on Jeremiah Blake's blog? From a year ago, onwards. I feel nauseated. You have a stronger stomach for this stuff than I do."

"Everybody has a stronger stomach for this stuff than you do," Torrance said. Jerry gave him a look.

"I've been reading some of the posts already," Danny said. "It's not that bad. Just profiles of murderers and some of the victims, and photos of—"

Jerry lifted a hand. "Just read them all, please."

"And what am I looking for, exactly?"

"Anything that strikes you as weird," Torrance said. "Trust your instincts."

"He blogged about you guys, by the way," Danny said. "On the FreeAbbyMaddox site. I've been keeping tabs on it. He said the cops paid him a visit. Earned him some credibility, and now all her fans think he's cool."

Torrance looked at Jerry. "Didn't I tell him not to say anything?" He looked back at Danny. "What else has he written about there?"

"All kinds of stuff. Whoever runs the site must not care who posts, so there's a lot of stuff to sift through. The site attracts a lot of freaks, all obsessed with Abby Maddox."

"It's gonna take a while to find out who runs it," Torrance said to Jerry. "The IP address that registered the site tracked all the way to India."

"She has fans in India?" Jerry couldn't fathom anyone in India having heard of Abby Maddox, let alone caring enough about her to run a website in her name.

"That's doubtful," Torrance said, and Danny grinned as if she knew what his former partner was about to say next. "I'm guessing the site owner has likely rerouted the—" He stopped when he saw the look on Jerry's face. "You know what, why don't we just wait and see what they find out."

Danny laughed.

"All right, that's enough, you two," Jerry said. "I'm not that dumb when it comes to technology. Get to work on that blog, Danny. Great job so far."

When she had closed the door behind her, Torrance said, "So listen, I looked up the other names Danny gave me and none of them look like possibles. I questioned all of them, and every single person has an alibi for where they were when one of the victims was killed. Jeremiah Blake, on the other hand, doesn't have an alibi for any of them."

"And the madam? Estelle Kane?"

"Having a hard time tracking her. Heard she might be out of town; I'm working on it. So far we know Claire Holt was a pro. The first two, no way to tell right now.

If they were escorts, their friends and family don't seem to be aware of it, but that's no surprise."

Jerry frowned and glanced back at his computer screen, still showing Blake's blog. His picture was in the top right corner and it showed a smiling, rather mangy-looking kid. Jerry pointed to it. "I don't know, Mike. The kid's clearly weird, socially awkward, stays at home all day playing video games . . . he's like the poster child for 'angry misfit.' It's almost too perfect."

"If it fits, it fits." Torrance shrugged. "His high school is closed tonight, but I'm going to stop in first thing tomorrow and see what else I can find out about him. His school records should tell us something."

"All right, so what did the neighbor say?" Jerry asked.

"He had some good info, actually." Torrance reached for his pack of Marlboros, saw the look on Jerry's face, and stuck it back in his breast pocket. "The kid, believe it or not, was some kind of genius. Really high IQ, graduated from school two years early."

"You're kidding me. He could barely string a sentence together."

"That, my friend, is his brain on drugs." Torrance sighed and shook his head. "The neighbor said he's had some serious mental and emotional issues ever since his mom died when he was five. He became painfully shy, didn't feel comfortable around other kids, and always kept to himself. The neighbor said the kid could have gone to any college he wanted, full academic scholarship. But he refused to apply, started getting into weed and who knows what else a couple of years ago, and since his father's away all the time, nobody really did anything about it."

"How nice of Jeremiah Blake Senior to take an interest in his son's well-being."

"Point is, we shouldn't underestimate him. He's young, but his IQ's probably double what ours is. He's certainly capable of planning something like this."

Jerry shrugged. "So what? That doesn't mean the kid's *smart*. There's a difference between book smart and life smart." He cracked his knuckles. "I still think it's too easy. If he was so smart, why are we looking at him? Why didn't he cover his tracks better?"

There was a knock on the door. Danny poked her head in. "Uh, guys? I think I found something."

"On Blake's blog? That was quick."

"I emailed you the link. When you log into your email, just click on it and it'll take you right to the page. Want me to do it?"

Jerry snorted. He found it both amusing and irritating that Danny always assumed he didn't know how to use email, or the Internet. Okay, so he was no technology expert, and more than once he'd sent out emails saying "Attached please find . . ." without actually attaching anything, but hey, he wasn't *that* bad.

He logged into his email program and clicked on the link Danny sent him. It was a blog post written six months earlier, and it was clear from the first sentence that this post was different from the others. It was a story of some kind, written in the first person. He read it out loud so Torrance could hear.

"'*Her long dark hair trails down her back and without turning around, she raises a hand and beckons me closer. She faces the wall, her palms flat on the surface, and I move forward until I can feel her through my clothes. I slowly peel off her blouse, sliding it up and over, and her skirt, sliding it down and under, until she is naked and panting and breathless with her desire. She wants me. She spreads her legs and I reach between them and—'*.

"Skip to the end," Torrance said.

"*'I enter her,'*" Jerry said, ignoring him, "*'and listen as she gasps my name over and over again. I stroke her hair, murmuring her name, and I tell her how much I love her, how good it feels to be inside her, and as she climaxes, I pull it tighter, and tighter, until I can no longer hear her, until she is quiet and still and no longer breathing. I am satisfied.'*"

"Oh hell." Torrance reached forward to turn Jerry's computer screen around so it faced him. "Did he really write that?"

"It sounds like a lot of the sex fantasy stuff that gets posted on the FreeAbbyMaddox site. He said in the comments section underneath that it was just a short story." Danny was still lingering at the doorway. "Fiction. He made it up."

"I know what a short story is, Danny," Jerry snapped, giving his assistant a dirty look. "What was the reaction?" he said to Torrance.

"Mixed." The detective had taken hold of his mouse and was scrolling down the page.

Danny looked thoughtful. "I know writers say fiction is just made-up crap, but personally, I think even made-up crap's gotta come from *somewhere*."

Torrance looked up. "I think I agree with you," he said to her, and they exchanged a smile.

Jerry sighed and stood up. "I've had enough for

today. I'm going home to sleep and I might not come in tomorrow. Lock up the office, okay?" he said to Danny. "All lights off and don't forget the alarm."

His assistant gave him the same dirty look he'd given her a moment earlier. "I know what locking up is, Jerry."

CHAPTER: 19

She didn't mind the job. She really didn't.

She knew it was customary for a lot of the escorts to complain about what they did, to pretend they hated having sex for money, as if being all moral about it somehow made them better people. So ridiculous. It didn't matter what you thought about what you did, it mattered what you *actually did,* and if you fucked for money, you were a whore. Plain and simple. Alessandra (real name: Alice Bennett) didn't get what the big deal was. Whoring was better than waitressing, working retail, and cleaning houses. All shit she'd done to earn money before she started stripping, and before she'd hooked up with Estelle.

It was easy work. The clients paid the modeling agency directly and so she didn't have to worry about handling money. Condoms were a must. And she wasn't one of those stupid girls who'd fuck bareback for an extra five hundred under the table—so not worth it, too many diseases. The way to survive in this business was to treat prostitution like the job it was. Be smart, be polite, give the client what he wanted (or she—Alice's specialty was couples), keep your nose clean (because drugs fucked up your judgment), and everything would be just fine.

Alice was more tired than usual tonight, having worked the last three days straight. But the money had been too good for her to pass up this last-minute Monday night request, and she knew the 5-hour Energy drink she'd downed a few minutes earlier would kick in soon. After tonight, she was taking a couple of days off. She needed to study. Midterms were coming up.

She strode down the hallway of the Phoenix, a boutique hotel just outside the shopping district. She passed a mirror but didn't bother to glance over—she knew she looked good. Long, dark hair, loose and flowy (she'd been raking in some good money since she'd gone from blonde to brunette—who knew?), jeans, boots, T-shirt, leather jacket. She'd been booked for a GFE tonight, and while they weren't her favorite—too much talking, not enough doing—she was up for it. Estelle had agreed to discuss upping her percentage to a fifty-fifty split instead of the standard forty-sixty all the girls got, once she hit the one-year mark. Which would be in two weeks.

She knocked on the door. It opened immediately.

"Right on time," the client said.

She stared at him, then checked the number on the door.

"Alessandra, right?" he said.

"That's me," she said, looking him over dubiously. Tall but impossibly skinny, he had acne and a mop of hair that hadn't seen a barber in way too long. Hell, he was just a kid. "How old are you?"

"Come in, we'll talk inside." He opened the door

wider, and she stepped into the room. A second later, her phone rang.

She held up a finger and took the call. "Hi, Lynne."

The door closed behind her.

"Hi. Everything okay?" The voice of Estelle's assistant floated through the phone.

Not wanting to be rude in front of a client, Alice said, "Yes, I got here just fine. How's everything on your end?" This was code for confirming that payment had been received.

"Everything's clear over here. Payment was received via PayPal an hour ago. You're booked for two hours. Have fun and be safe."

"Okay then." Alice disconnected the call. It still seemed a bit weird—this was not her typical client. He was way too young and she was way too expensive.

But then again, what the hell did she care? He'd paid, he looked totally harmless, and he was smiling at her hopefully. And she had to admit, grudgingly, that his smile was rather sweet.

"Everything check out?" he asked. "I paid earlier, if that's what the call was about."

"Everything's good." She smiled. "What's your name?"

"Jeremiah," he said.

She put her purse down on the dresser. "Let's get started then, Jeremiah." She stepped closer to him. Suddenly she heard a mewling sound, and noticed there was a pet carrier in the corner of the room. Alice frowned. "You brought your cat?" She was allergic to cats.

He smiled impishly and sat down on the bed. "Um,

I know I requested a Girlfriend Experience, but . . . I've always wanted to try something a little different. I'm not sure I'm into all the cuddling, you know?"

Thank God. Neither was she. "Not a problem," Alice said. She sat beside him on the bed. "What did you have in mind, then?"

He reached into a plastic bag sitting beside the bed and pulled out a pair of silk scarves. Blushing slightly, he said, "I thought maybe . . . I thought maybe we could do something with these scarves. I've got some . . . bondage fantasies."

She laughed and took one of the scarves from him. "Sweetie, this isn't kinky. You want kinky, I can give you kinky. Too bad you didn't request it. I have a whole suitcase full of gear I could have brought." She patted the empty space on the bed between them. "Come closer and tell me exactly what you want. Don't be shy."

"It's kind of embarrassing, and I don't know if you'll want to . . ."

She put a hand on his arm and dropped her voice to a throaty purr. "Baby, I've heard everything you can imagine. You paid good money for me to be here, right? Might as well make the most of it." She leaned forward. "Here's a not-so-secret secret, Jeremiah. I'm a sure thing. All you have to do is tell me what you want."

He smiled. "Okay."

Moments later, she was naked from the waist up, and her arms were over her head and secured to the bedposts, one on each side.

He hovered over her, straddling her, his eyes feasting on her naked breasts. One hand cupped her tentatively, a finger caressing her nipple, which hardened in response. It didn't feel good and it didn't feel bad. It just was what it was: work.

He leaned forward and she braced herself for his kiss. She didn't particularly like kissing—another reason she wasn't crazy about GFEs, too much kissing and not enough fucking—but she readied herself anyway, smiling up at him and parting her lips.

He stopped an inch short of her face. His breath smelled like Twizzlers and old pizza. "Hang on," he said. "I've gotta turn the TV on. There's something I want to watch while I do this."

"Whatever gets you going, honey," Alice said.

He reached for the remote control and flipped through the channels, turning up the volume. Then he pulled off his shoes and socks. Turning back to her, he said, "The show starts in a few minutes. So, you said to tell you what it is I want."

"What *do* you want?" she said, looking up at him with her best wide-eyed expression. The faster she got him hard, the sooner she'd be home in her pajamas watching *The Real Housewives of Orange County*. "Tell me all about it, baby."

"Open your mouth."

She smiled and did as she was instructed. Before she knew what was coming, he'd stuffed his sock in it. Then he punched her in the face.

Alice felt her nose break. The pain was sudden and intense. She screamed, but the sounds were muffled at best.

"I'm gonna do things a little differently tonight, Alessandra," he said, and punched her again. "Because I gotta speed things up. I gotta get things moving. You understand, don't you?"

Of course she didn't. Her face was on fire, and she could feel tears leaking down her temples. She looked up at him, right into his eyes, which were shining with glee, and realized at that moment that he was totally, positively, absolutely crazy.

She tried twisting to get away from him, but there was nothing she could do. Her arms were tied to the bed. She tried screaming, but the scratchy cotton of his sock in her mouth only gagged her. The mewling coming from the corner of the room grew louder, and Alice thought now that it didn't sound like a cat at all.

He hit her again and everything went dark.

CHAPTER: 20

The *Pulse*'s feature with Abby Maddox was scheduled to start in two minutes. The nightly cable news show, which had been struggling with ratings for the past year, had won the interview battle over the notorious inmate. It was a huge score. The show had wasted no time in sending that cheesy blond journalist Bernadette Barkley down to Rosedale, and while the interview wouldn't be airing live—it had been taped much earlier in the day—it was about as current as it would get.

"Like she's not all over the news enough already since her murder charge," Morris said, frowning at the television. "Do we have to watch this garbage?"

"Can you make tea?" Sheila kept her voice light and offered her fiancé a smile. "I'd love some tea."

Morris huffed out of the room and Sheila remained still on the sofa, one ear cocked toward the kitchen. A moment later she heard the water steaming in the kettle. Okay, good. Giving him something to do ensured his head wouldn't be exploding in the next five minutes. Maybe he'd even go downstairs to the den to watch something else, but she knew better.

Sheila turned the volume up on the television, not

realizing she was chewing on her lower lip until it began
to throb. The show's introduction and teaser told viewers
what was to come. They were calling this episode "Up
Close and Personal with Abby Maddox." Unbelievable.
The woman practically had her own reality show.

Morris was back with two steaming mugs. Sheila
took hers gratefully and gave it a tentative sip. Earl Grey,
one teaspoon of honey, just the way she liked it. She
murmured a thank-you to Morris and smiled. He didn't
smile back.

Bernadette Barkley's steady cadence voiced over a
biography of Abby that lasted about five minutes. She
started by summarizing the inmate's relationship with
Seattle's notorious Tell-Tale Heart Killer. Ethan Wolfe's
face appeared on the screen then, and Sheila found herself holding her breath. It wasn't one of the photos that
had been playing on endless rotation all over the news
lately. In this picture, Ethan was outside the psychology
building at PSSU, sitting on his vintage Triumph motor-
cycle. He was wearing jeans and a worn leather jacket,
his short light brown hair looking almost blond under a
rare patch of Seattle sunshine. He looked incredibly
handsome, which is probably why the show had chosen
to use this photo.

Even after a year, it was difficult for Sheila to see the
face of her ex-lover and kidnapper. She could feel Morris's eyes burning a hole into the side of her cheek,
checking for her reaction, and she was careful to keep
her face neutral. Slowly, so he wouldn't hear it, she let
out a long breath of air.

The screen then flashed to a photo of Jerry. Sheila

had unfortunately seen this picture several times. Last year, only a day after the assault, a reporter who'd disguised himself as an orderly had snapped a picture of the private investigator asleep in his hospital bed with his throat bandaged.

That got a grunt out of Morris. "He hates that picture. Figures they'd use it."

"Makes for good TV," Sheila said ruefully.

"On the run for seven weeks after her lover, Ethan Wolfe, was discovered to be the Tell-Tale Heart Killer," Barkley was narrating in a sweet and almost salacious voice, "Abby Maddox was captured and charged with the assault of retired police detective Jerry Isaac. She's been incarcerated at Rosedale Penitentiary just outside Gig Harbor, Washington, for the past year, having received a maximum sentence of nine years for the first-degree assault of a retired police officer. But in a huge turn of events, the King County prosecuting attorney formally charged Maddox last week with the murder of Puget Sound State University student and swimming star Diana St. Clair, who allegedly had an affair with Maddox's lover, Ethan Wolfe, while all three were students at the university. The highly anticipated trial was set to begin a month from now."

A picture of the swimmer flashed on the screen. They had chosen to use the one of Diana in her swimsuit, looking tanned and lean, holding up a gold medal from her last college championship win.

Barkley's bright green eyes were sparkling. "But in yet *another* astounding turn of events, *The Pulse* has learned that another series of murders is happening in

Seattle *right now*. So far there are three victims, and it's possible that Abby Maddox may have information on the killer. She is currently cooperating with Seattle police and the King County prosecuting attorney's office to help find Seattle's newest serial killer from inside her prison cell. Sources tell *The Pulse* that should an arrest be made, Abby Maddox will be immune from prosecution for her alleged involvement in the Diana St. Clair murder."

Hearing it like this—the whole story summarized in a matter of breaths—made Sheila feel dizzy. "Jerry told me the police weren't going to tell the media they had a serial killer on their hands," she said, frowning. "He said they were planning to wait until they had concrete proof all the murders were related."

"The show obviously has sources inside." Morris's voice was flat, and Sheila risked a glance at him. He was staring at the TV with a granite jaw. "Doesn't matter how they know; the cat's out of the bag now. It's going to be chaos."

The screen changed to show Abby Maddox in an interview room at Rosedale. She was dressed in her usual prison attire, but the show had obviously provided her with a makeup artist, and the inmate looked more stunning than ever. Abby made Bernadette Barkley, seated across from her at the cold metal table, seem old and garish, even though the blond TV personality couldn't have been much older than thirty-five.

Barkley began the interview. "Thank you for agreeing to speak with me, Abby. How have you been?"

Abby smiled. "I'm in prison. I've been better."

"Ever since your arrest last year, the public has been

fascinated by you. Are you aware of the media attention surrounding you?"

Another smile. "I've seen myself on the news a few times, yes. I have a TV in my cell."

"Tell us a little bit about life in here."

Abby shrugged. "There's not much to tell. Monday through Friday, I tutor inmates in English and math to help them get their GEDs, and on weekends I read books and write in my journal."

"You have a degree in mathematics from Puget Sound State University, is that right?"

"I do, yes. Before my arrest, I was only a few courses shy of receiving my master's."

"Can we discuss how you met Ethan Wolfe?"

Abby tucked a lock of hair behind her ear, and on cue, the camera zoomed in closer to her face. Her blue-violet eyes were soft and sad. "I was sixteen, living in a group home at the time. We met in high school, in history class. He was by far the smartest kid, almost genius smart. It was . . ." She smiled at the memory and shook her head. "I didn't stand a chance."

"You never knew your parents?"

"I don't remember my mother at all. She left when I was two. My father drank himself to death when I was seven. I grew up in foster homes and group homes. Ethan . . . Ethan was the only real family I ever had."

"Eight years together, that's a long time," Barkley said, her voice softening. "You must have been deeply in love with him."

"He was the love of my life," Abby said simply, and Sheila knew she was telling the truth. "My soul mate."

That got another grunt out of Morris.

"You never knew that he was a murderer?" Barkley said.

The inmate's eyes hardened. "Everybody asks me that, and I'll tell you what I told them: Of course I didn't know. How could I know? He hid it from everyone, especially me. Even now, I can't . . ." Abby closed her eyes, and the camera zoomed in closer still. A single tear fell from her lashes and made its way down her cheek. The effect was quite dramatic. "I can't reconcile the Ethan I knew with the Ethan I've seen in the news. I never knew him that way."

"Bullshit," Morris spat, and Sheila put a hand over his arm.

"You met with Dr. Sheila Tao yesterday, his victim, who was also his professor at PSSU. Can you talk about that?"

Sheila held her breath.

"I'd rather not. What she and I discussed is between us."

Sheila exhaled.

"But I will say this," Abby said, and Sheila stiffened again. "Despite the fact that she slept with my boyfriend for three months, she didn't deserve what he did to her. Dr. Sheila Tao is a recovering sex addict, and she couldn't help it. I feel no animosity toward Dr. Tao. In fact, I appreciate very much that she came to see me and that she cares how I feel."

There was a pause as the camera flashed to Bernadette Barkley's expertly made-up face, which was showing equal amounts of ill-disguised shock and glee.

Sheila's mouth fell open. "Oh God," she said, her voice faint. The room began to spin and her whole body started shaking. "Oh God, oh God, please tell me she didn't just say that."

Morris looked equally stunned, but he recovered quickly. "Honey, it's okay—"

"It's not okay!" Sheila shrieked, jumping up from the couch. Her cup of Earl Grey tea landed on the carpet, spilling dark brown liquid onto the cream-colored threads. "She just told the entire country that I'm a sex addict! Oh my God . . ." She burst into tears.

Morris was up in a flash, his big arms around her torso. "Darlin', just breathe," he said, stroking her hair. "Just breathe for me, okay? In and out, there you go . . ."

Trembling violently, Sheila buried her face in his chest. "I'm ruined," she said, a sob escaping her. "Oh God, Morris, I'm ruined."

"Of course you're not," he said, his voice deep and soothing. "It's going to be all right. We'll get through this."

"Don't you understand?" Sheila looked up into his face, desperation seeping into every bone in her body. "I'm going to lose my job. The dean only allowed me to return last year on the explicit understanding that nobody would find out about my addiction or the affair I had with Ethan. The university board isn't going to allow a sex addict who sleeps with her students to teach there. I'm done, don't you get it? I'm done."

"We'll sue her." Morris's tone was firm. "We'll sue Maddox, and we'll sue the show. We'll say it's all lies."

"But it's not lies." The horror continued to spread

through Sheila like a flesh-eating disease. Her sobs were so deep they hurt her chest. "It's not lies, Morris. It's all true. And even if it wasn't, she *said* it. She said it on national fucking television, and it's out there, and it doesn't matter if I deny it. Everybody will think it, and that's all it takes."

Her knees buckled, but Morris held her up. He led her back to the sofa and she slumped into it, wishing she were dead. A moment later, she began to feel numb, and knew vaguely that it was her brain's response to the terrible, awful, mortifying thing that had just happened.

Because other than Morris, nothing mattered more to Sheila than her career. Without it, who was she? What good was she?

On the television, Barkley's sweet voice was still babbling.

"Abby, take us back to that night at the police station in Seattle, when you were alone with retired police detective Jerry Isaac. What really happened?"

Abby's gaze flickered to the table and then back up again. "At first, Jerry seemed like a friend. He didn't need to be at the police station, but he stayed with me because he knew I was scared. The police, they were so hostile, questioning me about Ethan's whereabouts. Jerry was very helpful at first, very protective. But then he began to make me . . . uncomfortable. The way he looked at me . . ."

"How did he look at you, Abby?"

"It's hard to explain." The inmate was practically whispering. "I just suddenly became aware that we were alone in the break room, and he was talking about Ethan a lot, and I got nervous. He told me I wasn't allowed to leave, and kept hinting that I was going to be arrested, that I'd be put in jail forever because the police thought I was involved in Ethan's crimes. I felt cornered. I felt a desperate need to get out of there. It was like I couldn't breathe."

"And then you assaulted him," Barkley said, her voice oozing sympathy.

"I really don't remember anything that happened except that I panicked."

"You sliced his throat, you crazy, lying bitch!" Unable to take it anymore, Morris let go of Sheila and was up off the sofa again. Pacing like a caged bear, he pointed at the screen, the blush on his neck a dark red and climbing fast. "Why are they letting this psychopath have an audience? We all know she's lying."

Sheila was still too numb to speak. Yes, Abby was completely lying about Jerry, but what did it matter? It was he said/she said, and the public would believe what they wanted to. Abby was a young, beautiful woman, and Jerry had been coming across as cold and surly in the media. Sheila had no doubt that the public would believe Abby, because hell, it was more fun that way.

"It was a combination of things," Abby was saying. "I'd only ever been with Ethan. I wasn't used to other men being so close to me. I knew they were going to arrest Ethan, I knew that the life we had was over. There didn't seem to be a way out of the mess Ethan had created, and I felt smothered. Jerry kept saying I couldn't leave. I remember panicking. I don't remember anything after that."

"You cut his throat," Bernadette Barkley said solemnly. "Even if you felt smothered, as you put it, that's not typically what most people would think to do as a defensive maneuver."

The words hung in the air for a moment. Abby dropped her gaze. When she finally spoke, her voice was clear and she looked at Barkley steadily. "I have no explanation. All I could think about was getting as far away from him, from the police station, from everything, as I possibly could."

"So you're in the break room kitchen, you had the knife in your hand . . ."

"I don't remember that."

"Was your intention to kill him?"

"I don't remember, but I'm certain it wasn't."

Barkley's face was the picture of skepticism. "It's a tough scenario to believe."

"Well, that's why I'm in here, isn't it?" Abby said, meeting the blond woman's gaze directly. "I've never once said I didn't do it. I'm saying that in my mind, it was self-defense. But none of that matters now. They gave me nine years, and I'm serving out my sentence."

"I caught up with Jerry Isaac as he was arriving at his office the other night," Barkley said. "I asked him to comment on your murder charge. Here's what he had to say." She nodded, and an image of Jerry in the parking lot of his office building in Fremont appeared on the screen.

Bernadette Barkley was shown sticking a microphone in Jerry's face, who already looked exhausted and pissed off. "Mr. Isaac," the journalist said in a crisp voice, "in light of Abby Maddox's recent charge for the murder of Diana St. Clair, our viewers are wondering how you feel. Do you think she's capable of murder?"

Morris finally stopped pacing and sat back down on the sofa.

On the television, Jerry glared down at the petite blonde, his dark features forming an even darker expression. "How do I feel?" he repeated, and Sheila immediately thought, *Uh-oh*. "How do I feel?"

Looking directly into the camera lens, Jerry yanked down the tight-knit collar of his black turtleneck, exposing the ugly scar, purple and puckered and angry. It glowed in the light of the camera. His tone was clipped and harsh, the words spoken slowly and enunciated clearly despite the rasp in his voice. "*This* is how I feel. Now get that camera out of my face, motherfucker."

Of course *The Pulse* censored the profanity. There was a bleep in place of the word *motherfucker,* but Jerry's exaggerated lip movements left no room to dispute what he'd said.

Despite his aggravation, Morris laughed. Hard. Sheila might have laughed, too, but there was nothing remotely funny about this interview. Nothing at all.

The screen changed back to Bernadette Barkley. "When we come back, we'll talk more about Abby Maddox's life growing up as an orphan in Nebraska, her relationship with the Tell-Tale Heart Killer, Ethan Wolfe, and the pet rat she used to have."

Commercial break. Thank God.

"Pet rat?" Morris muted the television, wrinkling his nose. "That's disgusting."

"Turn it off," Sheila said dully. Every muscle in her body ached. "I don't want to see the rest of it."

"You don't want to hear them discuss the new murders?"

Sheila shook her head, more tired than she'd felt in a long time. "They can't discuss that. Abby would be interfering with the investigation if she did, and it would kill her deal. And I have no desire to hear about her pet rat, or anything else she has to say." She closed her eyes, leaning back against the sofa. "I've had enough. Turn it off. Please."

Her fiancé did as she asked. "Honey, trust me, it's going to be okay."

Sheila opened her eyes and looked up at him. "I think that's the first time you've ever lied to me, Morris."

CHAPTER: 21

The hotel room at the Phoenix smelled like vomit. And there was nothing like the smell of vomit to make you want to vomit, too.

The body was a few feet away, naked torso exposed, the carvings on her back as plain as day. Her long, dark hair streamed over the side of the mattress and the one eye that Jerry could see was swollen and glassy. Cause of death was the same—zip tie around the throat—and Jerry felt an eerie sense of déjà vu. But he knew this one was different, because this victim had been beaten. Badly. Face and head. The three women before her had not. The killer's behavior was escalating.

The victim's fingerprints were on file from a petty theft when she was eighteen, for which she'd received a fine and probation. She'd been identified as Alice Bennett, age twenty-four, originally of Topeka, Kansas. She was found by the assistant manager of the hotel an hour after checkout time when calls to the room by the front desk had gone unanswered.

The assistant manager of the Phoenix had entered the room around 1 p.m. and had gotten a very close, if unwelcome, look at the dead woman. She'd been covered with a sheet, he said, and he'd assumed she was sleeping. When she didn't respond to his greeting, he'd shaken her. And then saw more than he wanted to.

"I barfed," Dave Puckett said, ashamed. The guy was barely out of hotel management school. He'd nearly vomited on the body itself, but managed to move away at the last second to empty the contents of his stomach on the carpet at the foot of the bed instead. The pile had since been cleaned, but the stench remained. "I know I should've done it farther away because I might have destroyed trace evidence and everything, but it was all I could do not to hurl *on* the body, you know? I'm really sorry. Hope I didn't screw things up for you guys."

Everybody was a fan of *CSI*. Sometimes it was helpful. Sometimes it was a pain in the ass.

What had caused Puckett to vomit was not the blood. The assistant manager insisted he was okay with seeing her bloody face; apparently he was also an amateur mixed martial arts fighter, and bloody faces were part of the job. No, what had grossed Puckett out was that when he had shaken the woman in an attempt to rouse her, the sheets covering her torso had fallen away, revealing the deep carvings on her back.

That, and she was being eaten by a rat. An extremely large, disgusting, pink-tailed rat.

"A rat?" Torrance had said dubiously when he heard this. "You have rats in your hotel?"

"Of course not," Dave Puckett had said indignantly. "We charge three hundred a night for a standard room. This was not our rat."

Crime scene had since caged the rat, found hiding in the bathroom. Jerry's own stomach rolled at the thought of those rodent teeth tearing chunks of flesh from the woman's skin. Whoever had put it there had *wanted* the woman to be eaten.

The carvings on her back still said FREE ABBY MAD-DOX, and below that, 4/10. But this time, surrounded by rat bites, the message seemed much more urgent.

There had also been a newspaper lying beside the body. Abby Maddox had made the front page of the *Seattle Times* this morning, and above her face—a screen grab from her feature on *The Pulse* the night before—screamed the headline ABBY MADDOX LOVES RATS.

The killer had a sick sense of humor.

Crime scene had just finished up. Everything had been photographed and bagged and was in the van, ready to be taken to the lab for analysis. Jerry watched as two guys in crime scene bodysuits carefully rolled the body onto a gurney, then rolled it out into the hallway.

"You can get out of here," Torrance said. "I don't need you for a while. I'm still running down Estelle Kane's whereabouts and I haven't heard back yet from the techies about where the FreeAbbyMaddox site is origi-nating from. Whoever owns the site has taken great pains to hide his location. I'll touch base with you later."

Jerry didn't argue. The dead woman's partially eaten face was still seared in his brain, and he needed to take his mind off it.

In his Jeep a few minutes later, he checked his phone and saw that Morris had called again. Damn, the big man was persistent.

Sighing, he highlighted the number and pressed SEND.

::::

There were only two reasons Morris would want to see him, Jerry thought. He either wanted to discuss Jerry's failing marriage (which Jerry had no desire to do, despite Sheila and her fiancé's concern) or he wanted to pound Jerry to a pulp. Neither thought was appealing, but if Jerry had to choose, he had a better chance of surviving the former. Jerry and Morris were the same height, but the former NFL offensive lineman turned investment banker outweighed him by at least seventy pounds. Jerry had been on the receiving end of a Morris punch once before, and it hadn't felt good.

The Golden Monkey, Jerry's favorite dim sum restaurant (well, okay, his favorite restaurant, period), was busy and loud as always. He took a lot of heat for telling people how much he liked this place. The decor was dated and tacky, all peeling wallpaper and stained carpet and bathrooms that had seen one too many customers. The cuisine, however, was delicious. A person could easily stuff himself for ten bucks, fifteen if he was really hungry.

Servers in bright pink vests maneuvered dim sum carts around the tightly spaced tables, while harried waiters darted around refilling water glasses and teapots. Morris hadn't said much to Jerry yet other than the usual pleasantries, and that was fine by Jerry. He watched now as his friend stabbed another *siu mai* with his chopstick, Morris's ham-sized hands looking ridiculous as he tried to navigate it out of its bamboo container. The *siu mai*—a steamed pork and shrimp dumpling wrapped in egg noodle—was delightful, though Jerry knew the big guy would never give him the satisfaction of admitting it.

"Try this." Jerry pushed something toward Morris he knew his friend hadn't tried before. "You'll like it."

Morris eyeballed it suspiciously, then seemed to decide it looked safe enough. A generous ball of shrimp rested on a slice of green pepper, doused in black bean sauce. He watched as Morris carefully maneuvered one out of the serving plate and directly into his mouth.

"It's good." Morris chewed slowly. "Tasty."

"Have another."

Morris swallowed. "You're trying to keep my mouth full so I can't cuss you out for what you did."

Jerry put down his chopsticks and braced himself. "All right. Let me have it."

"You took my fiancée to see Abby Maddox." Morris's frustration was clear, even over the clanking and chattering of the busy restaurant. A few heads turned in their direction briefly at the sound of his booming voice. The server pushing the dim sum cart nearest them shot them a disapproving look. "Are you on drugs? I'm telling you, Jerry, if we weren't such good friends, I'd—"

"I'm sorry." The apology was lame and Jerry knew it. "I tried to talk Sheila out of coming, man, I really did. I only stopped by her office to tell her about the murders myself so she didn't have to read about them in the papers. I thought I was protecting her—I never thought she'd want to come along. And in my defense, once she'd made up her mind to talk to Maddox, there was nothing I could say to change it."

"Yeah, she is stubborn, that one," Morris said grudgingly. Then he frowned. "I just don't understand why *you're* helping them. You're not even with PD anymore. Why get involved?"

"What was I supposed to say?" Jerry was getting so tired of everybody's shock over this, when to him it was a no-brainer. "There's a serial killer at work, and Maddox might be able to lead us right to him. What was I supposed to tell them? 'I'm still mad the bitch cut me last year and so I don't care if ten women get murdered, I'm not helping you?' Come on, man. This is the right thing to do."

"The deal concerns me, okay?" Morris lowered his voice and Jerry had to strain to hear him. "Abby Maddox is a menace to society. She was Ethan Wolfe's partner in crime. The thought of her getting out . . ." He stopped, shuddered, looked away.

"You didn't see the dead bodies yesterday, Morris," Jerry said quietly. "These women, they've barely lived their lives, and some animal is snuffing them out one by one and carving Maddox's name into them, just to get her attention. Much as I want to see that psycho bitch locked up for the rest of her life for what she did to me—and what I know she did to those homeless women last year—she's the lesser of two evils right now. I don't have the luxury of saying no."

Morris said nothing, which to Jerry meant he understood. They sat in silence for a few moments, neither man feeling the specific need to talk. The dim sum carts kept rolling by, and both of them continued to pick out dishes.

"So how's Sheila doing?" Jerry finally asked. "I, uh, saw the interview on *The Pulse* last night."

"You mean Maddox telling the whole world that my fiancée's a sex addict?" Morris grimaced and took a long sip of his water. "She's not doing well, amigo. She's got a meeting with the board of directors at the university later this afternoon."

"Damn." Jerry put his chopsticks down. "Is she going to get fired?"

"I don't know. I'm hoping that at worst, they put her on probation." Morris rubbed his face, the worry showing in every wrinkle around his eyes and mouth. "She decided she's going to come clean about her addiction, and she got letters this morning from her therapist and her meeting leader at SAA to show the board how hard she's been working on her recovery."

"But the affair . . ."

"Wolfe was twenty-three when Sheila got involved with him, and while it's frowned upon, there's nothing specific in her employment contract that says she can't be romantically involved with a student of legal age. Because she's tenured, they can only fire her on the grounds of moral turpitude, but they'd have to prove that her actions adversely affected her ability to teach. Which they haven't. She's received nothing but positive ratings from her students this past year." Morris sighed. "And the reason I know all this is because we met with a lawyer first thing this morning."

"Shit, man." Jerry shook his head. "I'm so sorry."

"Me, too." Morris stabbed at another *siu mai* and chewed without enthusiasm. "Her career's everything to her. If she loses her job, I don't know what she'll do."

"She'll land on her feet. She's strong."

"Tell *her* that. I've never seen her so down." Morris leaned back in his chair. "You know, what I don't get is why Maddox would blab it to the world. Sheila said she didn't even think Maddox knew about her sex addiction."

"Because she's a game-player, Morris." Jerry met his friend's distraught gaze with a steady one of his own. "She likes to play games. You remember the postcards she sent Sheila."

Morris nodded. The year before, when Maddox was on the run, Sheila had received four postcards in a two-week span, all of them from Maddox, all of them taunting her and threatening her safety.

"She likes to mess with Sheila, but I don't think she'll ever hurt her," Jerry said. "Maddox is a lot of things, but the one thing she isn't is stupid. She knows if anything ever happens to Sheila, she'd be the prime suspect. Besides, she has eight years more on her sentence."

"She could be out in three with good behavior."

"Yeah, but still, three years can change a person." Jerry didn't really believe this last part, but he knew it was what his friend needed to hear. In his experience, once a psycho, always a psycho. But telling Morris what he really thought—especially since there was nothing he could do to change it—would not be helpful at all.

The big guy finally nodded. Jerry nodded back. Both men reached for the last *char siu bao,* a white, doughy dumpling filled with steamed pork.

"You take it." Jerry pushed the bamboo container toward his friend.

"Damned right, I will," Morris said, but he split it in half, making a point to place the slightly smaller bit on Jerry's plate. The dough had cooled a little, but the sweet-and-sour barbecued meat inside was still warm and gooey.

A moment later, Morris cleared his throat. "So have you talked to Marianne lately?" His deep voice was carefully nonchalant.

"You know I haven't."

"You should call her."

"Annie's the one who left." Jerry stiffened. "She's made her decision."

"Yeah, but you're still married," Morris said.

"A technicality I'm sure she'll remedy soon." Jerry knew he sounded bitter and hated himself for it. "I'm expecting the divorce papers any day now."

"That's what you want?"

"No," Jerry said tightly. "Of course not. If I thought I could fix it somehow, if I thought I could apologize enough, I would. But we've been separated for six months. And now she's moved on."

Morris stopped eating. "What do you mean?"

"Annie's seeing someone. It looks serious."

"Who?"

"George Jackson," Jerry said.

Morris's face was blank.

"You know the basketball coach of the PSSU Steelheads?"

"*That* guy?" Morris almost choked. His eyes were as round as dinner plates. "You're kidding me. That guy's the losingest coach in the Pacific Northwest! He's an embarrassment! That's . . . oh wow, man. That's awful."

Despite his misery, Jerry chuckled. He should have known that Morris, of all people, would understand. It was bad enough his ex-wife was dating someone. But *that* guy? It was nice that someone else got just how humiliating it really was. "Unfortunately I don't think the Steelheads' win-loss record matters to Annie."

"I'm sure it's not serious. He's way too young for her."

Jerry winced.

"Sorry." Morris grimaced, looking like he wanted to kick himself. "I didn't mean that the way it sounded."

Jerry didn't respond. He'd said all he wanted to say about the matter.

His cell phone rang as he was chomping down the last bit of *char siu bao*. Pulling the phone out of his breast pocket, Jerry checked the screen and saw that it was Torrance. "Sorry, man, I gotta take this." He turned away from the table and answered.

"Where are you?" The detective's voice was gruff in Jerry's ear. "I can barely hear you."

Jerry glanced at Morris, who was checking out the next dim sum cart and pointing at the things he recognized. "Having lunch. What's up?"

"We found a hair, and it's not the vic's. Want to meet me at the morgue?"

And just like that, Jerry's appetite was gone. "Sure. I'm on my way."

"You're bailing on me?" Morris said when Jerry disconnected the call. "But I just got a bunch more stuff. You have to tell me what's edible and what's not."

"It's all edible," Jerry said. "Everything you picked is good." He reached for his wallet.

"Nah, I got this." Morris waved him off. "Go on. Save the world."

Sticking his wallet back in his pocket, Jerry clapped Morris on the back. He was relieved that he and the big guy were okay. Their friendship was important to him, even more so since Annie had left.

"Man, I'd be satisfied with just saving a life," Jerry said. "Thanks for lunch."

CHAPTER: 22

I f the executive vice president's boardroom was de-
signed to be intimidating, it was working. Sheila had
never felt so small.

She'd had to cancel her late afternoon class to be at
this meeting, and the three faces seated across from her
now at the long mahogany table were infinitely scarier
than the three hundred faces that would have attended
her lecture.

There was the vice provost of undergraduate educa-
tion (who, though married, had drunkenly hit on Sheila
at a Christmas party three years earlier), the young di-
rector of human resources, whom Sheila had met with
twice after she'd returned to the university following
her stay in rehab the year before, and an older woman
Sheila knew was high up in the chain of command, but
whose specific title she couldn't remember.

Sheila's immediate supervisor, Dean Simmons, was
seated quietly beside her, and this made her even more
nervous. Normally a smiling, cheerful man, the dean
hadn't said anything to anyone once he'd entered the
boardroom. He'd brought with him a thick red folder,
which he'd placed on the table between them. Sheila had

no idea what could be inside, and she was afraid to find out.

The preliminary discussions were over, and all she could do now was sit and listen to what they had to say. Her back ached from the tension, which was so thick in the room it was hard to breathe.

"In light of everything that happened last year with you and Ethan Wolfe, we think it's best if you leave the university." Louise Jardin, the woman whose job title Sheila couldn't remember, was speaking, her thin red lips pursed in disapproval. "PSSU never really recovered from your incident last year, and now, with news of your . . . sex addiction . . ." She said the words with such distaste, Sheila wondered if the old lady would choke on them. Jardin didn't finish her sentence.

"My incident?" Sheila repeated. "Recovered?" She sat up straighter, trying hard to keep her tone professional and even. "I'm sorry, but what kind of recovery was needed for the *university*? I was the one who was kidnapped, if you recall. I was held captive for three weeks by a man who turned out to be a serial killer."

"Yes, but he was your student," James Schneider, the vice provost, said. His raspy voice reminded Sheila of Jerry, though that was the only similarity. His steely eyes were fixed on her face. "You had an affair with your student, Dr. Tao. That's not something the board can overlook."

"With all due respect, sir, you overlook it all the time." Sheila gripped the arms of her chair, needing the support, though she continued to speak politely and firmly. "I can think of four professors who've been involved with their students, and they've all received nothing more than slaps on the wrists. I think it's wholly unfair that you would single me out for making what I fully admit was an error in judgment, and there's no precedent for firing a professor because of a romantic involvement with a student."

The board members exchanged looks. "Dr. Tao—" Jardin began.

"Please allow me to finish," Sheila said. "Ethan Wolfe was my student at one point, yes. He took two classes with me as an undergrad. But at the time we got involved, he was no longer being taught by me. I was his thesis adviser, but he was not technically my student. He was a teaching assistant in my class, whom I supervised. He was twenty-three years old—of legal age—and a fellow employee of the university."

"Dr. Tao is right," Lara Duncan, the woman from human resources, said. "What they did, however inappropriate, isn't technically against university regulations."

"There's not a day that goes by that I don't regret the relationship I had with Ethan Wolfe." Sheila softened her tone, though it remained professional. "It was a mistake. But you must know I paid for it. I almost died because of it. I don't believe I deserve to lose my job over it."

Louise Jardin leaned over, whispering something in James Schneider's ear. Schneider nodded, then whispered something to Lara Duncan. The exchange went on for a few minutes as Sheila waited in agony. Finally, Jardin straightened up and faced forward.

"Dr. Tao, we don't disagree that there isn't a precedent for firing a tenured professor due to inappropriate conduct with a student," Jardin said. "You're right, it's never been done before. But the issue here today is that your face and name are all over the media. It was one thing last year when you were a victim of a serial killer, but now you're being perceived very negatively by the public. Your affair with Ethan Wolfe made headlines today, and your sex addiction makes it even worse. I'm told that the psychology department has received several calls from concerned parents this morning threatening to withdraw their kids because they don't feel comfortable with a sex addict teaching them. Isn't that right, Dean Simmons?"

Sheila looked over at her supervisor, who sat with a stoic face and nodded. The dean would not meet her gaze.

Sheila didn't have to look in a mirror to know her cheeks were bright red. Reaching into her briefcase, she pulled out two envelopes and placed them on the table. "I have a letter here from my meeting leader at Sex Addicts Anonymous that describes the efforts I've made over the past year toward my recovery. I also have a letter from my personal therapist that confirms I've been in therapy for sex addiction for the last twelve months, and that I finished an eight-week program at the New Trails Treatment Center in Oregon after I was released from the hospital last year."

"We weren't aware you were at a treatment facility last year," Schneider said.

"That was my call." Dean Simmons finally spoke up, his voice heavy. "Dr. Tao asked for a leave of absence for medical reasons, and I signed off on that. I saw no need last year to inform anybody as to the exact reason she needed time away."

"And you're not obligated to inform anyone," Lara Duncan said to the dean, her voice reassuring. "Dr. Tao had a note from her doctor, and that's all you'd need as far as HR is concerned."

Sheila's eyes were moist and she willed herself not to cry. "Ladies and gentlemen, please. I've built my career here. I want to stay here. I love my job."

"I believe that," Jardin said, frowning. "But Puget Sound State enrollment numbers have dropped ten percent this past year. Now while we can't say it has anything directly to do with last year's fiasco—"

"If they've dropped, they've dropped because we had a serial killer prowling the campus," Sheila said. "Not because I had an affair with said serial killer."

"The board disagrees," Schneider said, his face like stone. "In my opinion, you are an embarrassment, Dr. Tao."

"James, that's unfair," Dean Simmons said, and Sheila turned to him in surprise. The dean pushed the thick red folder forward. "I have here Dr. Tao's student reviews for the past three terms. There are more than three hundred here, and they're all positive. Every single one. And I spoke to the Student Union this morning. Dr. Tao has received fourteen nominations so far for Professor of the Year. Which, as you may recall, she has won not once, but twice before. I believe strongly that Dr. Tao is an asset to my department, and to this university, and I would hate to lose her." He fixed his gaze on Schneider. "We all have demons, James. We all have personal problems. We all make mistakes. Dr. Tao's have unfortunately been made public, and she will be dealing with that embarrassment for quite a while. Rather than punishing her, we should be throwing the prestige of the university behind her. She deserves our full support. She certainly has mine."

Sheila almost wilted in relief. Underneath the table, Dean Simmons placed his hand over hers and gave it a quick, hard squeeze.

"You should know that I won't leave willingly," Sheila said when she found her voice. "I won't apologize for loving my job, and this university. If you fire me, I will have no choice but to sue." The words were ugly, and she hated to say them, but at this point, there was nothing left to lose.

"But we would allow you to leave on your terms," Louise Jardin said, in an attempt to sound reasonable. "You would, of course, finish out the remainder of this term, at which point we would announce that you've left the university to pursue other endeavors. We are prepared to offer you a year's salary as compensation for a quiet departure."

A year's salary. Wow. They really wanted her gone. Sheila fought the tears that were threatening to spill over. "I'm sorry, Ms. Jardin, but if you want me gone, you will have to fire me. In which case, I hope you're prepared for a long and lengthy legal battle." She made a point to look at James Schneider. "Which, I can assure you, would probably embarrass everyone. My attorney is waiting for my call."

Schneider's face reddened. The room went silent. Lara Duncan from HR looked down to hide a smile.

"We'll need a moment to confer," Schneider finally said, his voice stiff. "If you could please wait outside, Dr. Tao."

Sheila stood up, feeling all eyes upon her as she walked around the table and out into the hallway. The door shut firmly behind her, and she leaned against the wall, breathing hard.

Jardin and Schneider were a couple of assholes, there was no doubt about that, but that didn't matter. Sheila loved Puget Sound State. She was in no way ready to leave. She was only forty, for Christ's sake, and she'd been planning to teach for at least another twenty years. What the hell would she do if she lost her job? She loved academia, loved being in a grand lecture hall, loved watching the faces of her students light up as a concept that was previously confusing to them finally made sense. She loved the debates, the questions, the exchange of ideas. Who was she if she wasn't a professor of psychology?

The door opened a moment later and Dean Simmons gestured for her to come back inside. Sheila squared her shoulders and followed him in, taking her place back at the table.

"Okay, Dr. Tao," Louise Jardin said. Her face was flushed, and it was clear that the discussion Sheila had been excused from had been heated. "You shall remain a professor here at Puget Sound State. But you're on probation for the next three terms, and should any other incidents occur with students, or should your sex addiction affect your teaching negatively in any way, we will have no choice but to let you go. Long, lengthy legal battle be damned."

James Schneider nodded. So did Lara Duncan, but the corners of her lips turned up slightly.

Beside her, Dean Simmons touched her arm and smiled.

Sheila let out a breath. "Thank you, everyone," she said. "I promise I won't let you down again."

She exited the boardroom for the last time, keeping her feelings in check until she got back to her office a few minutes later, where she closed the door and slumped into her chair, utterly exhausted.

Sheila had managed to save her job, but barely. Goddamn that Abby Maddox. The psychopath had not only ruined her reputation, she had nearly damaged Sheila's career, something Sheila had spent half her life working on and which meant everything to her.

She hoped the bitch burned in hell.

CHAPTER: 23

Jerry didn't want to look, but it was hard not to stare at the body. He'd already seen her at the hotel that morning, but here, under the bright white lights of the morgue, no detail was spared.

Alice Bennett's nose was broken in two places, eyes swollen shut, lips split, and she was missing two teeth. Both cheekbones were smashed. Her head was split open and there was gray matter and blood matted through her dark hair. The zip tie was pulled so tight she wouldn't have had a chance in hell of getting the damned thing off, even with scissors or a knife. The skin above and below the zip tie was bloated. Bite marks dotted her torso and neck, and one ear had been chewed off completely, thanks to the damned rat.

Whoever had done this to her had really gone to town. The question was, why? Why bash her in the head and the face, and *then* strangle her with a zip tie? Why the rat? Why such anger?

The medical examiner was eerily calm as she pointed out the things she wanted them to see. How anybody could do this job was beyond him. Jerry would rather pick up garbage at the side of the road all day than work with dead bodies.

Phoebe Castor, however, seemed to enjoy her job, and even managed to look rather cute dressed in scrubs and a pair of oversized goggles. Bending over the body on the table, she extracted a green pine needle with some sort of tool that resembled tweezers. "Don't get too excited, boys." The ME's dark eyes were bright behind her glasses, her expression serious. "It's from an evergreen."

"Perfect, since we live in the Evergreen State." Torrance jammed his hands in his pockets as if he were afraid to touch something. "There are only about a hundred million fucking evergreens here."

"But how many are in that area of downtown Seattle where she was found?" Phoebe said, unfazed by Torrance's gruff tone. Cleary she was used to the homicide detective's surly demeanor. "Not very many, I think."

Jerry said nothing. His stomach wasn't feeling too good. The dim sum was churning in his gut, and the four Tums he'd chewed when he got here didn't seem to be helping. It wasn't just the poor girl on the table, beat up and carved up, that was getting to him. It was the smell in the room, a nauseating mixture of formaldehyde, bleach, and decomposing human being. Dead bodies, he was discovering, had a very specific odor, one that was strong enough to seep into the fibers of your clothing and never come out. There was nothing quite like the sweet decay of rotting meat.

"It looks like these carvings were made by the same weapon as what we found on the previous victims," Phoebe was saying. The body was now turned face down, and the ME's gloved finger was tracing the pattern of the letters. "Long, sharp knife, maybe not quite at surgical quality, but not far off. But the letters are different."

"How so?" Torrance stood over the body, his eyes scanning every inch of the victim's back.

"With the other three victims, the letters were neat and evenly spaced, like the killer took the time to make the carvings legible." Phoebe peered closer at the body. Jerry turned his face away, content to listen to her voice rather than look. "But this time, they're messier. The spacing is uneven, and shallower, as if they were done fast."

"So he was in a hurry?"

"Maybe. Or he was acting on some kind of emotion." Phoebe straightened up and pulled her glasses off. They left red marks on her cheeks, but she was still adorable. "That part's up to you guys to figure out."

Jerry looked down at the folder in his hands, open to show a color printout of Alice Bennett's driver's license photo. Her looks had been far above average, and it was hard to reconcile the DMV picture with the body on the table. Whoever had killed her had wanted to destroy her beauty. Jerry wasn't a profiler and truthfully didn't think much of the profession, but any layperson could see that whoever had killed her had wanted to make her as ugly and horrific as possible.

"Four vics," Jerry said. "Four vics and the best lead we have is a socially awkward teenage freak with a genius IQ and a strange obsession with serial killers."

Torrance shrugged. "Like I said, if it fits, it fits."

"Should we go pick him up?"

"Still waiting for the DNA test to confirm that the

hair found on her really is Blake's. Judge won't sign the warrant otherwise. Soon as we get the call, we're gone." Torrance's face was dour. "I had a tough time getting him to consider this one. Because Blake's so young. No criminal record, no nothing other than his blog and the posters on his walls."

The phone rang in the small room, and all three jumped a little. Pulling her latex gloves off, Phoebe reached for the phone. She murmured into it for a few seconds and then hung up. "Guys, the hair analysis came back. DNA is a match for Jeremiah Blake. You've got your Jack the Zipper."

"You did not just say that. That's gotta be the cheesiest nickname ever." Torrance groaned. "Which is why it's gonna stick."

Jerry was disturbed. "But he's just a kid," he said, more to himself than to Phoebe or Torrance.

"Yeah, and the kid's a killer," Torrance said. "So let's go get him."

CHAPTER: 24

It wasn't too late to turn back. Even though she knew the client had paid and was waiting for her on the other side of the hotel room door, it wasn't too late to change her mind.

Or was it?

Tammy Kachkowski (professional name: Tara) stood in the hallway of the Watercrest Hotel and raised her hand to knock. But her fist stopped a few inches short of the painted steel door. Shit, she really didn't know if she could do this. Taking a deep breath, she took one step back, running her fingers through her long, dark hair, attempting to calm herself. Her heart was beating so hard and so fast, she could almost hear it.

Was she really ready for this? Yes, she needed the money, and no, she wasn't a virgin. God knew she'd had her share of crappy boyfriends and one-night stands. And really, that's all this was, right? A one-night stand? Only with two very important differences: There would be no expectation of a relationship on her part, and she would get paid. Quite well.

But if anyone found out what she was doing, she would never live it down. Her poor but stoutly religious parents would certainly disown her, and her friends? Forget it, they'd never speak to her again. She'd be a pariah if word of this ever got out.

And oh God, what if the guy was ugly? Or worse, had terrible hygiene? What if he liked it rough? The client had requested a two-hour Girlfriend Experience, and Estelle had been adamant that Tammy take it, because GFEs were a good way to get started in the business. They mimicked real dates, with conversation and flirting and everything. There wasn't supposed to be anything kinky, no toys, no bondage, and definitely nothing back-door.

Tammy closed her eyes and took another deep breath. She now understood why a lot of the girls drank and did drugs. Alcohol would have helped a lot right now. She stepped forward and raised her hand again, but before her knuckles could make contact with the door, it swung open. She stared at the client in surprise.

He was younger than she expected, maybe a few years younger than herself, and while not handsome, he was far from ugly. Thank God—she was worried he'd be really old. On the contrary, he looked like he was still in high school. Skinny, dressed in jeans and a black T-shirt, he was barefoot, his hair still damp from a shower. She could smell soap and water. Okay, cool. Maybe this wouldn't be so bad, after all.

"Hello," he said with a shy smile. "I was worried you were going to change your mind. I saw you through the peephole."

Tammy felt her face flush. "I'm sorry. I . . . I was just thinking that . . ."

He opened the door wider. "Come in," he said. "We'll talk inside."

She stepped into the room and the door closed behind her. "I just have to—"

"Check in with your agency," he said, still smiling. He turned the lock and fastened the latch. "I know the drill. Take your time."

She turned away from him slightly, placing her purse on the dresser and reaching for her phone. Lynne from the agency picked up right away.

"I'm here." Tammy lowered her voice, but the client didn't appear to be eavesdropping. He had gone to sit at the edge of the bed and was flipping through the TV channels. "God, I'm so nervous," she said. Her heart continued to thump in her chest. It was almost painful.

"Relax, honey," Lynne said. Tammy had never met Estelle's assistant—she'd only met Estelle herself, at the interview—but the woman had always been kind to her over the phone. "It's going to be okay. Just listen to what he wants, be yourself, and try and have fun. The first time's always tough, but I know you can do this. It's nothing you haven't done before. Pretend like you're on a date."

Easier said than done, but Tammy knew she was just trying to help. "Do I call when I'm finished?"

"No need, unless you want to," Lynne said. "I know you made it there on time, and that's all I need to know. Good luck, honey."

Tammy stuck her phone back in her purse and turned to the client. Sucking in a breath, she stepped forward. "I'm Tara," she said.

"I'm Jeremiah." His eyes flickered up and down her body, even though she was fully clothed in jeans and a sweater. "Wow, you're really beautiful."

"Thank you." She sat down beside him on the bed, wondering what to say next. *Think.* What would she say if she were on a date and really liked him? She leaned in a little, nudging his shoulder with her own. "You smell great. I like your T-shirt. Act of Mercy . . . that's a local band, right? I think they played at my college pub once." She traced the logo with her finger, a white skull with a bleeding bullet hole in its forehead. "They were pretty good. The lead singer is very talented."

"You've heard of them?" The client seemed surprised. "They're not that big yet. I'm a huge fan, try never to miss a show. Just saw them play the other night at the Pink Elephant."

She grinned at him. "You must have fake ID."

That won her a laugh. "I do, yeah," he said. "I'm only eighteen."

"I'm twenty-two," she said, then stopped. Shit. Was she supposed to tell him that?

"I like older women. So did my dad. He had a thing for . . ."

"What?" she said.

"Girls like you. Working girls." He leaned in and kissed her. Surprisingly, he was good at it. His tongue traced the outside of her lips. "Mmmm. You taste good."

"I'm not really a working girl," Tammy said, trying not to sound defensive. "This . . . this is my first time."

He shrugged. "You're getting paid, aren't you? Makes you a working girl in my book. My dad would have loved you. He'd always tell me, why buy a girl dinner when you can just buy the sex?"

It felt wrong for him to stereotype, but she wasn't in any position to argue. He continued to kiss her, and she found herself becoming aroused. His hand slid under her sweater, and in response, she ran a hand up his thigh. He was already hard.

"Lift your arms up," he said, nuzzling her ear. "I want to undress you myself."

She obliged. He pulled her sweater up over her head, and she heard the crackle of electricity as the fuzzy cotton rubbed against her hair. "Static," she said, and they both laughed.

He pushed her gently back onto the bed and started kissing her stomach. She stiffened at first, feeling a little exposed without her top on, but after a few seconds she had to admit he was damned good at what he was doing. Pulling down the front of her lace bra, he licked her nipple, and she sighed with contentment. Yes, okay, very nice. Would it always be like this? If so, this would be the easiest way in the world to make money.

She closed her eyes, enjoying his tongue on her breasts, losing herself in the experience. Seriously, this was awesome. She felt the client—dammit, what was his name again? Oh, right, Jeremiah—move on top of her, and she spread her jean-clad legs slightly so she'd be able to feel his erection better.

Then something cold pricked her neck, and her eyes flew open.

He was staring into her face. "Don't move," he said.

"You move and it will slice right through your neck, and that's not how I want to kill you."

He had a hand over her mouth before she could scream.

And then the door busted open.

The client looked up and smiled. "What took you guys so long?"

CHAPTER: 25

Jeremiah Blake confessed to four counts of first-degree murder.

Torrance had wanted an additional charge for the attempted murder of Tammy Kachkowski, the young woman they'd pulled the kid off of, but she had refused to talk to the police, insisting that nothing had happened. She hadn't had sex with him, he hadn't hurt her, and she said that if Jeremiah Blake was charged with anything having to do with her, there was no way in hell she would testify. Torrance wasn't sure he wanted to push it. A student at Puget Sound State (she refused to admit she was a call girl and had acted outraged at the insinuation, as her parents were Catholics, fuck you very much), Kachkowski just wanted to go home and forget the whole thing ever happened.

They didn't need her testimony, anyway. The kid was making their job ridiculously easy. Jeremiah Blake knew everything about the crime scenes. The knife they'd found on him was the same knife used on all the women. He knew how the bodies were positioned, which ones had tattoos, which ones dyed their hair so the "curtains matched the carpet," and he could even remember their perfume. He'd happily described what it felt like to sink his knife into their skin, and the delight he'd experienced in choking them to death with a skinny little zip tie.

"You have to admit, the zip ties are cool," Blake had said with a grin. "Cheapest things ever, easy to conceal, and once you get one on . . ." He'd pretended to claw at his throat, bugging his eyes and sticking out his tongue, a parody of someone choking to death. Dropping his hands, he'd laughed. "It's not coming off."

Jerry had wanted to strangle him.

They had their man. Jeremiah Blake was their Jack the Zipper . . . an idiotic nickname, yes, but no one could deny it fit.

And yet, something still nagged in the back of Jerry's mind. Call it intuition. Call it a hunch. Instinctively, something just seemed off. But he couldn't seem to pinpoint what it was.

Blake was alone now in Interview Room 2 at Seattle PD, and they watched him on the monitor in a different room. The kid hadn't lawyered up and he'd refused to call his father. Instead, he'd talked up a storm, answering all their questions with enthusiasm and smiles. Blake actually seemed to be *enjoying* police custody. He probably figured it would make a great blog post or two. Jerry wondered if the kid actually understood the gravity of his situation, and could only conclude that he didn't. Being a teenager was probably the only time in your life when you felt utterly invincible.

They continued to watch him, each man processing his own thoughts. The kid was leaning back in his chair, hands splayed on the desk in front of him, rocking back and forth on the chair's two back legs like Jerry used to do when he was in high school so many moons ago.

"Bet he falls backwards in his chair within an hour," Torrance said, munching on a slice of leftover pizza he'd found in the break room.

Jerry said nothing, not taking his eyes off the monitor. Though they had the volume muted, he could tell Blake was singing.

"Okay, what feels wrong to you?" Torrance asked.

"You can tell?"

"Pal, it hasn't been that long. I remember that look. What's bugging you?"

Jerry sighed and tugged at his collar. "I don't know. It was all just . . . way too easy."

Torrance finished the last of his pizza and wiped his palms on the thighs of his slacks, even though there were napkins right beside him. "Yeah, maybe. But guess what, that's the way it goes sometimes. Not all homicide investigations are hard, and thank God for that. That doesn't mean anything's wrong."

"Okay, I'll give you that." Jerry cracked his knuckles. "But play devil's advocate with me for a bit here. Why would the kid confess? Why make it *that* easy?"

"Why not?" Torrance said, but his tone wasn't challenging. Jerry smiled a little. This was how they used to work back in the day, tossing ideas back and forth. "He's exceptionally bright, like you said, but he's not street smart. Maybe he knew he'd be caught at some point, anyway. Hell, maybe he *wanted* to get caught. Maybe he planned it like this. You spent thirty years in PD, you know how many genuinely fucked up people there are out there."

"But what's in it for him?" Jerry said. He stood up and started pacing; the movement helped him think more clearly. "He's killed four women. He was fairly strategic about it. The third one found was actually the first one killed, so we know he's got decent planning skills. He carved up the bodies, so we know he likes the drama. Hell, he blogs, so he obviously enjoys having an audience. But if he's in prison, he can't blog. No Internet access. No way to make money off this."

"Who says he's in it for the money? You saw his walls. The kid idolizes serial killers. He's obviously in it for the fame." Torrance stared at Blake through the monitor. "I hear everything you're saying, pal, but you're forgetting one very important fact. *Jeremiah Blake is a fucking psycho.* Psychopaths don't operate with the same rules of logic the rest of us do. You're trying to make sense of something that will never make sense."

Jerry nodded grudgingly. He knew that everything his former partner had just said was true. And yet . . . "Have you tracked down his father?"

Torrance shook his head. "He works on a crab boat called the *Della Rosa*. And apparently it's somewhere in the middle of the Bering Sea right now. Still trying to get ahold of the boat."

"The dad's never around." Jerry frowned. "No wonder the son turned out to be a freak."

The speaker buzzed again. Torrance reached over and smacked the button. "Yeah?"

"Mike, there's a woman here to see you." It was the front desk calling. Jerry recognized the voice as belonging to the desk sergeant, a man nearing retirement who never sounded excited about anything. "Name's Estelle Kane. Says you've left her messages."

"Have her meet me in Interview Room three." Torrance stood up and grinned at Jerry. "Perfect timing. The madam is here."

"Do we need her?" Jerry asked. "After all, the kid confessed."

"Might as well cross the *i*'s and dot the *t*'s."

Jerry was still distracted by the rocking motion coming from the monitor. Blake's mouth was open wide, and Jerry turned up the volume, listening for a few seconds. "What the hell is he singing? Is that an actual song? It sounds terrible."

Torrance chuckled. "He's not much of a singer, but it's definitely a real song. Never heard it before? It's by Talking Heads." He looked at Jerry, whose expression must have been blank, because the detective repeated, "Talking Heads? They were big in the seventies and eighties? Dude. You're not that old."

"*Dude*. I was listening to Rick James in the eighties." Jerry pursed his lips. "Kool and the Gang. Earth, Wind and Fire. Real music."

"And all good stuff," Torrance said amiably enough. "But I don't think any of those guys could write a song as fitting as the one Jeremiah Blake's singing right now."

"Which is?"

"'Psycho Killer.'" The detective smiled grimly. "It's perfect, no?"

:::::

"I don't recognize him." Estelle Kane shook her head, staring at the monitor. "I don't actually meet our clients in person, Detective. All bookings are done over the phone or online."

"His name is Jeremiah Blake."

Her face twitched. If Jerry had blinked, he might have missed it. "Don't know that name," she said.

"And what exactly is it that your company does, Ms. Kane?" Torrance asked. He was leaning against the wall beside her, toothpick dangling out of his mouth.

"We're a modeling agency. If you've been to the site, which you obviously have, it's fairly self-explanatory."

"Cut the shit."

She glanced up at him, her expertly made-up eyes showing no reaction to Torrance's harsh tone. "You asked me. I'm telling you."

"I think we both know what you do. Everybody knows."

Kane smiled slightly, then checked her manicure. Her nails were long and glossy, the tips painted white. "Do they? I don't think so."

She was not at all what Jerry expected. He assumed she'd be at least twenty years older. In his mind, madams were old, cynical, retired prostitutes who couldn't pull tricks themselves anymore and so they got younger women to do it, taking a nice cut for themselves.

Kane, as it turned out, was closer to the Heidi Fleiss variety. She was thirty-two and beautiful. Honey blond hair hung in waves down to the middle of her back. Long, dark eyelashes framed wide green eyes, and her tan was either purchased from a premier salon or earned on the beaches of the French Riviera. Her skin was flawless, her full lips glossed to perfection. She sat with her long legs crossed, wearing a fitted gray dress and nude-colored stilettos with red soles. Jerry didn't know anything about women's attire, but her outfit certainly looked expensive.

She appraised the monitor for a minute longer with eyes that had probably seen too much for someone so young. "What is it he did?"

"He killed four girls who worked for you."

"I only have one employee, Detective. My assistant, Lynne." Kane looked bored. "All the models are independent contractors. If I approve them, they get a profile on my site, I help them with their photos, and all payments go through me. For my services, I take a percentage. It's really very simple."

"Claire Holt didn't work for you?" Torrance said. "What about Stephanie Hooper? Brenda Stich? Alice Bennett?"

Kane looked up at him, her face difficult to read. "Yes, they all did. *As independent contractors*."

"Well, now they're all dead. *As doornails*."

She stared at him as if she were waiting for the punch line. "I hope you're joking."

Torrance tapped on a folder on the desk. "I've got pictures. Say the word."

Kane looked away.

"You don't keep track of where your girls are?" Jerry asked.

"Why would I? Once I approve them, *as models*, their profile goes up on my site. The client simply clicks on the one he wants, and books."

"I don't understand," Jerry said. "What's the incentive for the girls—sorry, *models*—to partner with you? Why wouldn't they just run their own websites? Take their own payments?"

Kane rolled her eyes. Clearly his question was moronic. "Because I have a reputation. I'm sure you've seen the amount of trash that's advertised on the Internet. All of my girls are . . . professional. Classy. Educated. Because of this, I can charge premium rates and ensure repeat business."

"You forgot to mention they're clean, too," Torrance said, the toothpick bobbing up and down between his lips. "Am I right? All your girls are free of venereal diseases?"

Kane didn't answer.

"And how do your clients pay?" Jerry asked.

"The only way to do it is online, via credit card or PayPal. Our website is very interactive."

"And how do you run background checks?"

"I don't."

Jerry stared at her, incredulous. His temple began to throb. "You send these girls out without background-checking the johns?"

Kane didn't answer.

"Lady, you're a piece of work."

Kane's face turned to stone. "Perhaps I should call my attorney."

Torrance sighed. "We're homicide, not vice, Ms. Kane. We know what you do for a living, okay? And personally, I don't give a shit. Your so-called modeling agency is another department's problem. What I do give a shit about is that I have a murder suspect in the next room who's killed four women who all worked for you. I need to know what you know."

"I want immunity."

"We can work something out, I'm sure. Right now, it's a good idea to foster goodwill, don't you think? You give, I give. I got no problem with that."

"It depends on what you want to know."

"Tell us what you know about Jeremiah Blake," Jerry said. "Start there."

Kane chewed her lower lip for a moment, then her face regained its composure. "Fine. I recognize the name. I've seen it in the past on credit card payments. He was a regular client for a few years, but I don't know that I've seen him book anyone recently."

Jerry looked at Torrance questioningly. "The father was a client, too?"

Torrance leaned in toward Kane. "I'm not interested in your clients from the past few years. What I want are the credit card numbers and/or PayPal email addresses of the clients who *last* booked Stephanie Hooper, Brenda Stich, Claire Holt, and Alice Bennett."

Kane was quiet for a moment. Finally she said, "If it gets out that I gave you this information, I'm ruined, Detective. My business is all about discretion."

"You give, I give, remember?"

Kane turned away, pulled out her phone, and made a quick call, jotting something on a small pad she kept in her purse. Then she tore out the page, handing it to Torrance.

The detective frowned. "Just one email address?"

Kane nodded. "The same client booked all four women through PayPal."

Torrance handed the slip of paper to Jerry. The email address she'd scrawled was JB@serialkillerfiles.com. He looked up at his former partner. "Seriously, Mike? It's too easy."

Torrance shrugged. "Who cares? It's done. We got him."

Jerry frowned at the monitor. The kid was still rocking back and forth in his chair in the interview room. Dammit, maybe his instincts *were* off. The evidence was all there. Everything fit. Yet still . . .

The kid's chair tipped all the way backward, and a second later Jeremiah Blake was sprawled on the floor.

"Told you he'd fall," Torrance said.

CHAPTER : 26

Marianne Chang used to be Sheila's therapist, but they'd both decided last year that Sheila would be better off working with someone else. Someone who could be objective. Someone who wasn't a friend. Because Marianne *was* Sheila's friend—her closest girlfriend, by far—and right now, her friend was giving her a look that was equal parts worry, sympathy, and anger.

"I agree with Morris. You shouldn't have gone to the prison. Whatever you said to her the other day obviously set her off." Marianne sipped the vanilla latte Sheila had brought, and leaned back in her plush white chair. It was early for both of them, but with their schedules, sometimes the hour before classes and patients was all they could manage. "Thank God you saved your job."

"For now." Sheila wrapped her fingers around her own coffee to keep her hands warm. Staring out the window of Marianne's office, she sighed. "But they made it very clear that one more slipup and I'll be out the door on my ass."

"You won't slip up, I'm not worried. How's your therapy going?"

"Really well. We're working through a lot of my

childhood stuff." Sheila grimaced and took a sip of her latte. "Not fun, but, you know . . ."

"Necessary."

Sheila nodded.

"Are you planning to visit Abby again?"

"I've tried, but she's taken me off her visitors list." Sheila didn't bother to conceal her frustration. "She's got some balls on her, I'll give her that. She knew exactly what she was doing when she told the world that I had an affair with Ethan, and that I'm a recovering sex addict. She knew damn well what it would do to my career. And if that crazy bitch thinks she can—"

"Careful," Marianne said.

"What?"

"You sound like you're about to stoop to her level." Marianne put her coffee cup down on the table between them. "Don't do it. Don't play her game."

"Yes, but she—"

"Listen to me." Marianne leaned forward and fixed her gaze on Sheila. "You remember how Jerry was last year? After he was finally released from the hospital?"

Sheila did. It had been a terrible time for Marianne. Jerry had been bitter, disillusioned, angry. His kind and humorous nature had all but disappeared, and even now, a year later, he hadn't quite gotten it back. He had changed.

"His bitterness seeped into every part of him, and then by extension, it seeped into every part of us." Marianne closed her eyes, remembering. "He was so filled with hostility, always talking about wanting 'that bitch to go down.' It consumed him. It drove us apart."

"I remember."

"What Abby Maddox did to you, announcing your secrets on television, is the metaphorical equivalent of her cutting your throat. But guess what? Just like Jerry, you didn't die. You saved your job." Marianne's tone was firm. "I'm not saying it's not going to be challenging from this point on, trying to improve your reputation while ignoring what people are saying about you. But you can't buckle. You can't let her win. Whatever you're feeling about her, you have to let it go. As cliché as it sounds, you have to rise above it."

Sheila was silent. Of course her friend was right. The anger and bitterness would eat her up if she let it. Finally, she nodded.

"I read this morning that the police made an arrest. They found Jack the Zipper?"

Sheila sipped her coffee. "Turned out to be a teenager. He confessed. It's over."

"And this means Abby gets transferred."

"To minimum security." Sheila sighed heavily. "She gets immunity for the Diana St. Clair murder."

"But not the murders of those homeless women."

Sheila shook her head. "They could still charge her with those, but it doesn't look like they can pin anything on her. Abby Maddox could very well go free in three years. God help us."

"But only if she has a successful parole hearing," Marianne said. "Which, between you and Jerry, I doubt it would be."

"Good point. I guess that does make me feel better."

"Speaking of Jerry . . ." Marianne's voice was soft,

tentative. "I know you've spent a little time with him lately. How's he doing?"

"He's okay." Sheila wondered how much she should say. "He's . . . he knows you're seeing someone."

Her friend's mouth dropped open. "You told him?"

"Of course not."

"So he's been following me," Marianne said. Sheila looked away. Suddenly her friend laughed. "I knew it. I thought I saw him one morning, driving by, scoping out my house. New Jeep?"

Sheila nodded reluctantly.

Marianne laughed harder. "I know him too well. God, I love that man."

"He loves you, too." Sheila smiled. "He misses you."

A comfortable silence descended upon them, and Sheila resumed looking out the window. The view of downtown Seattle from Marianne's office was lovely, and she wondered—not for the first time—what it might have been like to go into private practice. She never thought she'd want to be anything other than an educator, but after yesterday's meeting, it might well be something she'd be forced to consider one day.

"I miss him, too." Marianne's choked voice broke through Sheila's thoughts, and she turned her head back, shocked to see that her friend was crying. "I miss him so much, Sheila."

"Oh, honey." Setting her coffee down on the table, Sheila went to Marianne, putting her arms around her. "I know it's been hard. I'm sorry. What can I do?"

Marianne shook her head, sniffling. "Nothing. It's just . . . I think about him every day. It's still hard, imagining a life without him in it. But I'm still so hurt. The way he shut down, and shut me out . . ."

"Of course you're still hurt." Sheila gave her a sad smile. "But as I told him, there's no right way to cope with what he's been through. Or what you've been through. It takes time to heal, and sometimes, that healing needs to happen separately."

"You think I'm being too hard on Jerry?"

"I think marriage is hard, period." Sheila gave her a squeeze. "You guys went through a terrible time last year, and Jerry didn't handle it well. But I do think it's fixable . . . assuming you want to fix it. Nobody's saying you have to."

"I don't know what I want," Marianne said, the tears beginning to flow again. "I just know I miss him."

"Maybe you should tell him that. Start there. See what happens." And then, delicately, Sheila asked, "How are things going with the new guy? George, right?"

"It's not serious. We have fun together, that's all. He's . . . easy. Which is what I need right now."

Another silence, again not uncomfortable, followed. Both women stared out the window, lost in their own thoughts.

Then quietly, Sheila said, "Morris wants to postpone the wedding."

It was Marianne's turn to be sympathetic. She leaned her head on Sheila's shoulder. "Well, shit. I guess nobody's healing as well as we'd like."

Sheila gave her friend another hug. "At least we have each other."

CHAPTER: 27

Jerry was beginning to feel claustrophobic in Jeremiah Blake's garage, but it was still better than being in the kid's bedroom, which really did smell terrible. Earlier that afternoon, they had found a box under Blake's bed that likely contained personal items from the victims—an earring, a bracelet, a necklace, a ring. Jerry had found himself relieved that it had not been a box full of unwashed underwear—or worse, body parts. The way this case had unfolded, nothing would have surprised him.

Elsewhere in the house, traces of blood had been detected in both the kitchen and the adjoining dining room, and it appeared that the walls and floors of both areas had been scrubbed down with bleach recently. There was no way to know yet if the blood specks belonged to any of the victims, or if it was someone else's altogether. Unfortunately testing would take a few days.

Jerry wasn't sure what they were supposed to find now in the garage, and he was growing impatient. Searching through people's stuff was tedious. He tripped over a box of old books and cursed.

"We're supposed to be looking for evidence of other crimes," Torrance explained, poking through yet another shelf full of tools. Four more cops were still inside the house, searching. "Do you not want to be here for this? You're so testy today."

"I'm just having a hard time picturing the kid doing it. We're missing something. I'd bet my badge on that." Jerry slumped on top of a plastic crate, his long, skinny legs splayed out on the dirty concrete.

"If you had one," Torrance said with a grunt.

Jerry fingered the temporary ID clipped to his belt. "You know what I mean. I feel it in my bones. You know those instincts never go away."

Torrance's gloved hands were picking through a black Hefty garbage bag. He'd found it in the backseat of the red 1969 Corvette that was propped up on wooden blocks and probably didn't run anymore. The 'Vette might have been a sweet ride at one point, but whoever had taken it apart didn't seem to know how to put it back together again. The wire shelves at the sides and back of the garage were all filled with car parts.

"Old clothes." Torrance's face wrinkled as he got a whiff of the garbage bag's contents. "There's vomit on some of them. And urine. Fucking worst smell ever."

Jerry wasn't sure about that. Dead bodies smelled pretty bad, too. "All men's clothing?"

"From what I can tell, yeah." Torrance tied the bag up and shut the door of the Corvette. "No idea if they're Blake's or his dad's. Man, I need air, I'm gagging."

The detective pressed a button on the wall and the garage door opened slowly. They'd left it closed so as not to attract the attention of Blake's neighbors, but the stench of vomit and urine was too much.

Jerry turned toward the incoming fresh air, his headache subsiding a little once the cool breeze hit his face. "So what now?"

Torrance sighed. "This is just routine, pal. To see if there's anything more we need to know about our young serial killer. But Blake did confess, we have his DNA on the last one, and he kept souvenirs that I bet we can trace to the vics. What more proof do you need?"

Jerry mulled it over. "Why zip ties?"

"Why not?"

"What's he trying to accomplish by carving Maddox's name on the bodies?"

"You'd have to ask him that."

"Why did he threaten us with ten possible victims? He was caught after number four."

"Again, you'd have to ask him that, but you have to admit that getting us to believe there could be ten murders created a sense of urgency," Torrance said. "Maybe he thought he could actually kill ten women and get away with it, or maybe the final tally never mattered. Who the hell knows."

A shadow appeared behind them, and both men whirled around.

"Hi there." It was the man from next door Jerry had noticed a couple of days before, whom Torrance had already questioned. He was dressed in a business suit and holding a briefcase as if he'd just come from work, which he probably had. "So you've arrested him, then?"

Torrance frowned at the intrusion. "Hello again, sir."

The man nodded to Torrance, then stuck his hand

out toward Jerry, who shook it. "Hi there. Cameron Frye. So, did you guys arrest Jeremiah?"

Torrance didn't blink. "Yes, we did."

"For drugs?"

"No," Torrance said. "For murder."

The neighbor took a step back. The look of shock on his face was almost comical. "Christ. I thought he might have done it, but wow, I didn't really let myself believe . . . poor JJ."

Jerry and Torrance exchanged a look. "Who's JJ?" Jerry asked.

"Jeremiah's father," the neighbor said, confusion crossing his features. "His full name is Jeremiah Jonas Blake, but he goes by JJ, and the kid goes by Jeremiah." He raised an eyebrow. "You guys should know that, since JJ is the one who's dead."

"Jeremiah's father is dead?" Jerry said, his eyes widening.

"You guys just told me he was." Frye took another step back. "Wait, what's going on?"

Torrance stepped forward. "Maybe you should tell us, sir. What makes you think Jeremiah Blake Senior is dead?"

"That's not the murder the kid's arrested for?" Cameron Frye looked like he wanted to run. "Oh, shit, I—"

"Start talking, Mr. Frye," Torrance said.

"I haven't seen JJ in almost five weeks." Frye's gaze flickered from Torrance to Jerry, and he continued to back out of the garage. "He's never been away this long."

"We were told he works on a crab boat."

Frye clutched his briefcase close to his body, as if

wanting to seek comfort from it. "Well, yes, JJ is a crabber. Difficult work, but it pays well, and they need the money. His wife died of cancer twelve, thirteen years ago. He's been raising Jeremiah alone, which isn't easy. As I told you before, the kid's had a lot of emotional problems. I don't know the details, but I know he doesn't socialize with other kids. He's in his head a lot."

Torrance and Jerry both nodded.

"But JJ's jobs don't usually last this long. Two, three weeks, tops. JJ always lets me know when he's going to be away so I can keep an eye on the house. Jeremiah's eighteen now but he's not very responsible. I was expecting JJ back about two weeks ago, but I haven't seen him. I asked Jeremiah about it, and he got all weird on me."

"Weird how?" Torrance asked.

"Like he knew the answer but didn't want to tell me." Frye saw the looks on their faces. "Hey, I'm a father to two teenage girls. I can tell when kids are lying."

"Why didn't you mention this to me before, Mr. Frye?" Torrance's eyes narrowed. "I asked you all kinds of questions about the kid then. Why didn't you tell me what you suspected at that time?"

"Because I know it sounds crazy. I don't know that I even really believed it, or even that I do now. It's just, I saw you guys come back, you said murder, and I just assumed . . ." The neighbor's voice trailed off, and he shrugged, helpless.

Torrance stepped closer, invading the invisible boundary of Cameron Frye's personal space. Reflexively, the man took yet another step back. "Tell us why you suspect Jeremiah Blake killed his father. I don't care how crazy it sounds, just talk."

Frye looked around but the street was quiet. He stepped a little farther out of the garage. "Okay, indulge me for a second." He pointed to the grass. "Gentlemen, take a good look at the lawn."

The two men followed Frye's gesture to the front yard, where the grass was very green, but long and unkempt. Weeds were cropping up in several spots near the edges of the driveway. It didn't look horrible, but it did look as if it had been neglected for a few weeks.

"Jeremiah hasn't mowed the lawn since his dad left," Frye said. "That was five weeks ago. And trust me, if he thought his dad was coming back anytime soon, he'd have kept it looking good. To me, that means he knows his dad isn't coming back."

Torrance looked dubious, but the man's reasoning actually resonated with Jerry. Whenever Annie went away for a conference, the house would be messy right up until the hour before she was due back. If Jerry didn't know exactly what time she'd be coming home, he'd clean up the night before, just to be on the safe side. It saved them both an argument.

Jerry's heart panged. The random reminders of his wife were always the worst.

"JJ is pretty strict about Jeremiah's chores," Frye was saying. "Sometimes, maybe a little too strict. Plus . . ." The neighbor's voice dropped even lower. "Jeremiah's been home every day for the past two weeks. JJ told me the kid either has to be in school or working—that's the rule if he wants to live at home. But he hasn't been going to work."

"You spying on your neighbors, sir?" Torrance's face was unreadable.

"No, of course not." Frye looked frustrated. "I keep an eye on things, is all. That's what I've noticed. Oh, and another thing . . ."

Torrance and Jerry waited.

"Jeremiah moved JJ's car out into the driveway late one night. The Corvette." Frye cleared his throat. "So two, maybe three weeks ago, I was up late getting a glass of milk—helps me sleep—and I heard someone tinkering around in the garage. I look out the window and see the 'Vette in the driveway. It doesn't run, you gotta push it, and Jeremiah would never touch that car without his dad around, he knows better. I thought, okay good, JJ's finally home and messing around in the garage, I don't have to worry about the kid anymore."

Frye scratched his head. "The next morning, the car was still in the driveway, and it was still there the day after, too. I finally saw the kid outside and asked him what his dad was planning on doing with the car. Jeremiah tells me he was the one who moved it out, because he was cleaning up the garage. I joked and said, 'You'd better not mess that car up,' and he just sort of smiled and said, 'Or what?' and walked away. I thought it was a strange answer, 'Or what?' What's that supposed to mean?"

Jerry turned and looked at the Corvette, back in the garage where it was supposed to be. Then he looked at the floor underneath. Something, a shadow, caught his eye, and he leaned forward to get a closer look.

And froze.

He turned back to Torrance, but his former partner wasn't looking at the floor. He was staring at the neighbor.

"So you think because he moved the car and because he didn't mow the lawn that the father is somehow dead?" Torrance didn't bother to mask the skepticism in his voice. "That doesn't make any sense, Mr. Frye. If he was missing, why hasn't Jeremiah reported him?"

"JJ, he's a good guy, okay? And he's my friend." The neighbor hesitated again. "But if I'm being totally honest here, he's not the greatest dad. If Jeremiah was my kid, I'd be home more. Jeremiah shouldn't be on his own so much. He needs a lot of guidance."

Torrance finally nodded. "So how would you describe the relationship between father and son?"

"Strained. Tense." Frye's brow furrowed. "I know JJ smacks him around sometimes. Don't get me wrong, the kid can be frustrating as hell, but I don't think that's right."

And yet he'd never once called Child Protective Services to voice his concerns, Jerry thought. Typical.

"Listen, Mr. Frye, we're still looking into things here. Do you have a phone number where we can reach you in case we have more questions?"

Frye recited his phone number, which Torrance typed into his phone. When the neighbor finally left, Jerry pressed the button to close the garage door.

"There's that look on your face again," Torrance said. "What's up?"

"Mike, look." Jerry pointed to the floor once the garage door was all the way down. "Look at the concrete underneath the Corvette. What do you see?"

Torrance stepped a little closer and peered down. Then, realizing he was casting a shadow over the spot he was trying to analyze, he moved a few inches to the side. Kneeling, he touched the concrete with his finger, then turned and looked around at the rest of the floor.

"Shit," the detective said softly. "The concrete under the 'Vette is fresh. It's not the same color as the rest of the garage."

Jerry nodded. "And it's not dirty."

"The kid poured new concrete here?"

Jerry squatted beside Torrance and touched the floor. "It's cured, but it's super sandy still. This is a new job."

"So that's why he moved the car out? To . . . redo the garage floor? Why?"

"Maybe he buried something. Or someone."

Torrance frowned. "You really think Jeremiah Blake killed his father? Why the hell would he do that?"

"Psycho killer, remember?" Jerry said. "You're the one who keeps telling me it doesn't have to make sense. I'm just telling you what I see."

CHAPTER: 28

I t turned out that even with a warrant, you couldn't just
go and tear up somebody's house. Not without special
permission. Never mind that the homeowner was possibly deceased and that looking for his body was the
reason you needed to dig up the garage in the first place.
You needed probable cause, not just a patch of fresh
concrete.

Like a confession, for example.

Jerry and Torrance were back at the King County Jail,
sitting across from a very bruised Jeremiah Blake. The
kid's left cheek was the color of eggplant and there was
a long scratch on his right arm. He looked miserable and
very, very vulnerable. He wouldn't say who'd jacked him,
of course, and Jerry couldn't help but feel a tiny stab of
sympathy. County jail was much worse than prison.
Blake might be eighteen, but he looked fifteen. He was
still just a kid.

"I thought they were putting him in a cell by himself," Torrance said to Blake's public defender, a young
woman named Shannon Koscheck, who looked fresh
out of law school and almost as pathetic as her client
did. Her mousy brown hair flopped over one eye and

she was constantly flicking her bangs out of her face. Her navy suit looked cheap and brand-new. Public defenders didn't make much.

Koscheck looked confused. "I just got here."

Jerry appraised the boy in front of them, who seemed extra skinny now that he was dressed in orange scrubs. "You all right, kid?"

Blake shrugged. "I'm fine. Just hungry. I'm missing chow right now."

Chow. The kid was learning the lingo.

"The kid's only been here for a day and already he's beat up," Torrance said to the corrections officer standing in the corner of the room. The CO shrugged, but whether it was because he couldn't care less, or didn't know about the situation, Jerry couldn't tell. Torrance sighed loudly and dug into his wallet, pulling out a twenty-dollar bill. He waved it at the CO, who looked at him questioningly. "Go find someone to get this kid a burger."

"That's not my job."

"That's why I said to *go find someone*." Torrance glared at the man, who looked genuinely confused. "Come on, someone in this place has to be going on break soon. Whoever goes can keep the change. Help me out here, man. I gotta question this kid and he's gotta eat."

The guard stepped over and took the money. "I guess I can ask somebody."

Torrance looked back at Blake. "What do you want? McDonald's? Burger King?"

"Carl's Jr.," the kid answered promptly. "The six-dollar burger. And curly fries and a chocolate milk shake."

The guard looked unhappy. "I'll be right back."

"Thanks," Blake said when the CO left. "That was nice of you."

"That's because he's a nice guy," Jerry said. "And I'm a nice guy."

"Look, kid, we're not gonna bullshit you, okay?" Torrance said. "We're not gonna play games. No good cop/bad cop routine, no tricks. You're too smart for that, anyway. We're here because we need to ask you some questions. You've been straight with us before, and I'm going to trust you're going to be straight with us now." He leaned in a little. "You've been very helpful in telling us everything we needed to know about the murders, and because of that, you've saved us a lot of time and energy. I spoke to the assistant prosecuting attorney assigned to your case. You plead to first-degree murder on all counts, you go to jail for life. But no death penalty. That's good news, right?"

"Don't say anything," Koscheck said to her client. "Let me talk."

Blake shot her a dirty look. "I'll say what I want, thanks. You work for *me*, remember." The attorney's face reddened. Blake focused on Torrance. "I can handle life. But no loony bin, okay? I don't want to go to a loony bin. I want to go to the Washington State Pen."

"That's up to the judge, but I doubt anybody will be recommending a mental health facility. The APA didn't say anything about that."

"Good. Will I be in gen pop?" Again with the lingo.

"Don't know," Torrance said. "Not up to me."

"Do you *want* to be in general population?" Jerry said.

"Look at me," the kid deadpanned. "Of course not. I'd be somebody's bitch inside of a week. I already had that at home, thanks." He stopped. "Shit. I didn't mean to say that."

"Oh, I don't know about that," Jerry said easily. "You're Jack the Zipper. You've murdered four women. You're a scary motherfucker. Serial killers get serious respect in prison. Everyone's going to want to be your friend. Plus you've got that whole twitchy don't-fuck-with-me thing going on. I predict you'll be very popular."

"Jack the Zipper?" Blake repeated, his eyes blank.

"That's what they're calling you." Torrance's voice was patient but Jerry could see the tension in his former partner's jaw. "Kind of catchy, no?"

"Yeah," Blake said, processing it. His face brightened despite the bruises. "Yeah, it is. They're seriously calling me that?"

"It's in all the papers."

"Which ones?"

"The *Seattle Times* did a piece just this morning about you." Torrance was a smooth liar. "Just a small article, not front page, but that's because you're not officially convicted yet and the police aren't releasing too much information to the media at this point. But I've heard a few people call you that. I think I heard it on KIRO Seven this afternoon as I was driving over."

"Yep," Jerry said. "Me, too."

"I haven't heard anything," Shannon Koscheck mumbled, but she may as well have not been in the room.

Blake's gaze shifted between Torrance and Jerry. After a moment he seemed satisfied they were telling him the truth.

The door to the room opened and the CO brought in a greasy fast-food bag and a sweating container of milk shake. Blake eagerly pulled out its contents, and a moment later the burger was a third gone, the kid's mouth was full, and the smell of ground beef and fries was everywhere.

"Hey, Jeremiah." Jerry watched the kid inhale his dinner. He spoke as if a thought had suddenly occurred to him. "What's your dad up to these days?"

Blake stopped chewing and swallowed. It seemed to go down a little slower than the previous bite. He took a sip of his milk shake. "I told you guys already. He's on a crab boat. Working."

"We've been looking for him," Torrance said.

"What for?" The kid wiped his mouth with a napkin. The burger, still warm, sat in its container. Blake glanced at it, but it was clear he'd just lost his appetite. "I'm eighteen. He doesn't need to be here for anything. I got my own lawyer and everything."

"Yeah, but he's your dad," Jerry said. "Don't you want him here?"

"He's busy," Blake said curtly. "I'm going to prison for the rest of my life. He can visit me anytime he wants. What's the difference if I see him now or later?"

"You don't think he'd want to be here to support you?" Torrance pulled his phone out of his jacket pocket. "What's the number of the crab boat? I'll call him right now, fill him in on what's happening with you." His fingers hovered over the phone's screen and he looked at Blake expectantly.

"I really think he'd want to know what's going on,"

Jerry said. "Unless there's some reason he can't be reached?"

Blake licked his lips. Sipped his shake. Ate a fry but didn't seem to enjoy it.

"Is he in trouble, Jeremiah?" Torrance reached over and stole a curly fry. "Should we send some cops out to find him?"

A long silence. For a moment, the only sound in the room was Torrance's jaw cracking as he continued to munch on curly fries.

"You won't find him," Blake finally said. He was beginning to look upset, rocking back in his chair, food forgotten. He started humming a tune Jerry didn't recognize.

"Don't be so sure," Jerry said, finally unable to resist a fry himself. It had cooled but was still damned tasty. He ate another one. "We have lots of resources."

"Jeremiah, is he dead?" Torrance softened his voice a little. In between his chewing, he managed to sound almost casual. "If he is, you can tell us."

"Don't say anything," the public defender said, but she needn't have bothered. Blake had gone to his happy place.

"I think he's dead," Torrance said to Jerry, who nodded in return. He focused his attention back on the kid. "The only question now is, where's the body?"

"Probably buried somewhere." Jerry's mouth was full of curly fries. "Maybe somewhere near the house."

"Or *at* the house."

"Or in the garage."

"Under the Corvette."

"Under fresh concrete."

"Just like Ethan Wolfe used to do it."

Shannon Koscheck put her hand on her client's arm. "Say nothing."

Blake shook her off. "What's the difference? I'm already going down for four murders. He was an asshole," he said to Jerry and Torrance, his voice cracking. He was starting to cry, and it made him seem even younger. "It was self-defense."

"Jeremiah!" his lawyer said, horrified. "Don't say another word until we discuss this in private."

"I don't want to discuss this in private." Blake focused his bleary eyes on Torrance. "I didn't mean to do it, okay? But I had no choice."

"You've got to be kidding me," Koscheck said under her breath.

And just like that, they had their confession. Torrance smiled and punched a few numbers into his cell phone. Turning away, he spoke in a low voice. Jerry knew that he was arranging for a team to go dig Jeremiah Jonas Blake Sr. out of the concrete garage floor.

"Tell us what happened with JJ," Jerry said.

Blake didn't hesitate. "He came home early, found weed in my room." His eyes widened. "Oh shit, I shouldn't have said that."

Torrance disconnected his call. "I don't think it matters, son. You've already confessed to murdering four women and your father. We're not going to get too excited about a little marijuana."

"Oh. Right."

"So he laid into you because of the dope?"

"Yeah. He was also drunk, so he was extra pissed. Usually, when it comes to weed, he just yells how that stuff will fuck with my head, smacks me around some, and that's about it. But this time, he threw a beer bottle at me. I ducked, and it hit the wall and broke and a piece of the glass cut my face." Blake moved his shaggy hair away from his jawline and showed them. Indeed, there was a small scar on his cheekbone. "I was scared and mad. I wasn't thinking. I went at him with the beer bottle and slashed at him. I cut his face. He shoved me against the wall and shook me, banged my head a buncha times. My dad's a big guy, you know?"

"Not a fair fight," Torrance said, the sympathy in his voice sounding sincere.

"I shoved the beer bottle into his neck." Blake's face had a faraway look as he remembered, his voice growing distant. "So much blood came out, it was so crazy. I thought it would spurt, you know? Like in the movies? But it didn't. It sort of gushed out, warm. His face—you shoulda seen his face. He was like, all surprised, and his eyes were all big and round. He clapped a hand to his neck but the blood just kept gushing between his fingers. Then he collapsed to the floor. Then he died." The kid blinked. "The end."

"And you buried him in the garage."

Blake nodded, looking distressed. "I didn't know what else to do."

"How long has he been in the garage, Jeremiah?" Torrance asked.

"Two weeks and two days."

Jerry shuddered.

"Will I get to go to the funeral?" Blake looked at them, his face crumpling. "He's my dad. I loved him . . ."

The kid broke down then, and the tears were painful. His attorney, not seeming to know what else to do, awkwardly patted her client's back.

"We'll plead out." The defeat was written all over Shannon Koscheck's face.

Torrance finished off the curly fries and nodded. "Damn right you will."

Jerry allowed himself a small sigh of relief. Finally, it was over.

He left the room, reaching for his phone. There was only one person he wanted to talk to.

CHAPTER: 29

Jeremiah Blake had confessed to the murders, and with Jack the Zipper off the streets and behind bars, Abby's transfer was executed the next day, thanks to Bob Borden's savvy legal maneuvering.

Abby was a little bit sorry Mark Cavanaugh wasn't here to see this momentous occasion, but the corrections officer had been fired a couple of days ago. Sergeant Briscoe, the old hag, had turned him in for drinking on the job. Briscoe was a petty, bitter woman, yes, but how many times had Abby warned Mark to be careful? She hadn't heard from him since the firing, and as of today, had no way of contacting him. She'd had to leave her phone with her cellmate, and while getting a phone at the new prison would be her first priority, it would probably take a few days.

The prison doors opened. The afternoon air was cool and refreshing, and even though she'd been outside at some point every day since she'd been incarcerated, the air somehow felt different now that she was no longer behind the fence. She'd only been at Rosedale for thirteen months, not long comparatively speaking, but it had felt like thirteen years. She stopped walking to take a deep breath, inhaling the scent of evergreens and sunshine. The corrections officer escorting her tugged on her arm.

Smiling, Abby said, "One sec."

The CO, an older man by the name of Bush, gripped her arm tighter. "Come on, Maddox, it's not like you're being released. You're just going from one prison to another. Let's go."

The gate in front of her buzzed open and Bush led her toward the bus waiting for her. It looked like a school bus, only gray instead of yellow, and it had the words WASHINGTON DEPARTMENT OF CORRECTIONS stenciled in large letters across the side beneath the tinted windows. Abby stepped up into the bus and gave the driver a warm smile. From inside his cage he nodded back.

She sat in the first row right behind him, as the only passenger, and caught her reflection in the rearview mirror. They'd put her in bright orange scrubs this time, protocol when moving from one prison to another. Bush removed her cuffs and took a seat behind her.

Creekside Corrections was technically a minimum security prison, but from what Abby had heard, it wasn't even really a prison in the traditional sense. She'd overheard a couple of inmates talking about it at chow the other day. She suspected they'd wanted her to.

"Visiting hours are every day from ten to eight p.m., and visitors can hang out with you in the rec room," the inmate named Delilah had said to her friend. With a name like Delilah, you would have thought she'd be pretty. She was not. "And you can do that new Be Smart program if you're good, get out of the prison, talk to kids about staying straight. It's like going to fucking summer camp."

"Well, shit," her friend Trix had said. They had both turned and eyeballed Abby, who had continued to eat her lunch at the next table as if she weren't listening. "What do I gotta do to get moved in there?"

"Get famous." Delilah's voice was louder than it needed to be. "Or fuck a guard. Take your pick." The two women had cackled with laughter.

Yes, Abby supposed now, looking out the window at the long stretch of wild grass racing along beside her, everybody had known about her relationship with Mark. Not that it mattered anymore. He'd provided a valuable service to her by getting her that smartphone, which she'd wiped clean of all messages and emails before leaving it with Celia.

Abby sighed. There'd be no time to relax once she got to Creekside. She needed to get friendly with a CO at the new prison immediately if she was to procure a new phone. It wouldn't be hard, but it would definitely take some work.

Stay focused, she reminded herself as she looked down at the cars passing by below. She saw faces looking up at the bus curiously, but they couldn't see her through the dark glass. *Stay focused and keep your eyes on the finish line.*

So far, the plan was working.

She leaned her head against the window, watching the world go by, looking at the sky and the trees, allowing herself to daydream a little. The hum of the bus was soothing.

"We're here," Bush said from behind her as they pulled up to Creekside's gate. Abby sat up in surprise. It felt like five minutes had passed. "Don't move until the bus stops. And don't move while I cuff you. I'd hate to bruise you on your first day in your new home."

Abby held her wrists out, looking thoughtfully at the building through the bus windows. Home sweet home. If it weren't for the modest-sized sign across the brick wall that said CREEKSIDE CORRECTIONS CENTER FOR WOMEN, she might have mistaken this building for a library, or something equally benign. There was even a landscaped courtyard at the front with wooden benches, flowers, and trees. A high fence surrounded the back of the property, but that was really the only evidence that this place was a prison.

She was off the bus a moment later and walking toward the gate, which buzzed open immediately. A few steps down a concrete path was another heavy metal door, where they buzzed her into the building.

Intake—also known as the "dirty room" because the inmates hadn't been searched yet—would take maybe ten minutes. Two guards were waiting for Abby in the dirty room, a petite older woman with a neat graying bob and a clipboard, and a younger female with a crew cut who wore latex gloves.

"I'm Sergeant Roland," the older one said. "This is Officer Pasco."

"Abigail Maddox," Abby said, and they all smiled.

Polite, calm, and respectful all around. They always were at Intake, because they didn't want you to freak out, as so many did on their first day. It took about a minute to get inked for fingerprints and cheek swabbed for DNA, and then Pasco said, "Open your mouth, please."

The CO's gloved fingers felt around inside Abby's cheek pockets and underneath her tongue, searching for any contraband. "Step into the bathroom, please, and undress."

Abby stepped into a tiny tiled room with no door, just a toilet against one wall and a shower stall with a thin curtain against the other, and quickly stripped. Lifting her arms up over her head, she turned toward the corrections officer, completely naked.

Pasco's glance lingered a split second longer than necessary on Abby's naked breasts, enough for Abby to catch it. She allowed Pasco to see her small smile, letting the woman know she wasn't offended. Hiding a smile of her own, the young CO gently probed Abby's armpits, then folded back Abby's ears. She ran her hands lightly through Abby's hair.

"Lift your breasts, please."

Abby placed a hand under each breast and complied.

"Wiggle your toes and lift your heels. Good. Now turn around and bend over, please. Cough twice, then spread your cheeks."

Again, Abby did as she was instructed.

"Ready for scars, birthmarks, and tattoos?" Officer Pasco directed the question to Sergeant Roland once the physical search was completed.

The older CO nodded and clicked her pen. "Ready when you are."

All of Abby's scars were noted on the clipboard.

There weren't many. A small one on her shoulder from where she'd once burned herself with a curling iron. A puckered scar on her arm from where her foster brother had burned her with a lit cigarette when she was sixteen. She'd met Ethan shortly after that incident, and he'd taken a bat to the foster brother's head when she told him what had happened.

Ethan. She felt a dull ache in her chest whenever she was reminded of him. Would she ever be able to think of him and not feel pain?

Abby only had one tattoo, and it was a purple butterfly at the base of her neck. In the body of the butterfly were the initials E.W. Lifting her hair, she waited patiently as Pasco snapped a photo.

"All right," Officer Pasco said. "Take a shower. Please wear the shower shoes and shampoo your hair."

Ten minutes later Abby was dressed in her prison issues—blue this time, much better than Rosedale's gray—and was led down the hall. Creekside seemed brighter than Rosedale, and a fellow inmate actually smiled at her as she passed.

A moment later Abby was seated in front of a round, soft-spoken black woman named Alicia Elkes, who was the superintendent of the prison. This was technically Abby's orientation. She listened politely as the superintendent gave a speech she had obviously given a hundred times before.

"We have just over two hundred offenders here, and we're nearly at capacity. That should give you some idea of how small this place is compared to the facility you just came from." Elkes's voice was soothing, almost musical. Abby thought of it as the "It's the first day of your sentence here and I don't want you to lose it" voice.

"Seems quite intimate," Abby said.

The superintendent smiled, her cocoa eyes searching Abby's face closely. "Not much gets by me. I have personally met and spoken to every single offender in my facility, several times, and I expect that over the next eight years of your stay here, you and I will get to know each other quite well."

"It won't be eight years." Abby returned the smile. "I plan to be on my best behavior. I want to be out in the real world in three."

"Good to hear." Elkes consulted the paperwork in front of her. "You have been assigned a cellmate, whom you'll meet shortly. We don't have many single cells here, but you might be able to earn one, in time, with good behavior. Another change you'll find is that the cells are dry. Your showers, toilets, and sinks will be down the hall from your cell."

Abby nodded.

"Everybody who comes here starts working in the kitchen," Elkes continued, "so that's where you'll be until we decide whether you might benefit from a different kind of job." The superintendent glanced down at Abby's file again. "I see you have a bachelor's degree. In what, may I ask?"

"Applied mathematics."

"And you were pursuing graduate studies?"

"Yes. In combinatorics and optimization. I'm almost finished, just three courses shy."

Elkes smiled and leaned back in her chair. "I can't

say I even know what that is, but it certainly sounds impressive. What did you plan to do with your degree?"

"Teach." It was the standard answer Abby gave everybody who asked. But the truth was, she had never really thought about it. She'd stayed in school to stay close to Ethan.

"Perhaps you could finish your master's in here. And we have a serious need for tutors, especially in the math area. I see you worked as a tutor at Rosedale. Your experience would be most welcome."

Inwardly, Abby shuddered. Tutoring inmates for their high school equivalencies had been torture, and she had no intention of doing that again here. "I definitely enjoy teaching."

"I have to admit, Miss Maddox, that I initially was not very happy when they told me you were transferring here."

"I understand."

"Do you?" Elkes's gaze stayed on Abby's face. "Allow me to share my concerns. You're not here because of your stellar behavior at a higher-security facility, as most transferred offenders are, nor are you here because you were convicted of a nonviolent crime. On the contrary, you're here because you were convicted of a *very* violent crime, but you managed to cut a deal with the prosecuting attorney in exchange for helping in the arrest of a serial killer. I have to tell you, it all leaves a very bad taste in my mouth."

Abby's instincts told her it was time to shut up.

"I should warn you that I am extremely intolerant of anyone or anything who might disrupt the harmony I've personally worked very hard to achieve here over the past ten years I've been superintendent. Creekside is a nice place, but don't let its looks fool you, Miss Maddox. It's nice for a reason, and that reason is *me*. I'm the head of this facility, and I run a very tight ship. Make no mistake, we are still a prison."

"I understand," Abby said again.

"I hope so," Elkes said. "Because I'm quite concerned that your notoriety will cause problems. I saw your interview on *The Pulse,* and I know you're quite the celebrity on the outside. In here, though, you are Offender 42891. I will not approve requests for reporters to visit you frequently. This is a safe, quiet environment, and I plan to keep it that way. Can I expect your full cooperation?"

"Yes, ma'am."

"Glad to hear it. If you treat me, your COs, and your fellow offenders with respect, we will certainly treat you the same, and your time here will be very easy. Respect is the only real currency here, Miss Maddox."

Abby wondered if the woman had that last line knitted on a pillow somewhere at home.

Elkes skimmed over the rest of Abby's file, then closed the manila folder and placed her hands on top of it. Her long, perfectly polished coral nails gleamed against her dark fingers. "So tell me, Miss Maddox. What do you hope to get out of your time here?"

Abby knew this question was coming, and she was ready with her answer.

"To grow, mature, and better myself. And to help others learn from my mistakes." Abby cleared her throat.

"Actually, ma'am, I'm quite interested in participating in the Be Smart program. I think I'd be a great asset."

"You want to talk to high school students?" The superintendent was surprised. The Be Smart program was relatively new, and it had inmates traveling in supervised groups to different high schools across the state, talking to kids about the importance of making the right choices and the consequences of making bad ones.

Abby nodded. "Yes. I know the program is in its pilot year, and that you've had difficulty getting funding. I think having me on board with my . . . notoriety, as you put it, could actually help you spotlight the program."

The superintendent appraised her. "I suppose it could. I do have an opening that needs to be filled quickly, so I'll consider it."

"That's all I ask."

"Okay." Elkes clapped her manicured hands together and then pressed a button beside her. "Now that that's all out of the way, I'll have a guard show you to your cell. You'll start working in the kitchen tomorrow. But for the rest of today, you're welcome to wander around the facility and figure out where things are. Don't hesitate to ask the staff anything you need to know."

"Am I allowed any visitors this afternoon?"

Elkes looked surprised. She checked her watch. It was only three-thirty. "I suppose so. Visiting hours go till eight. If their requests are in the system, that shouldn't be a problem."

Abby smiled sweetly. "Super."

A female guard who introduced herself as Officer Perez showed Abby out. No handcuffs—she simply escorted Maddox outside and across an inner courtyard, also landscaped with trees and flowers. It wasn't long before Abby was in her new cell, alone. Her cellmate, Officer Perez informed her, would be at work until four-thirty.

Abby sat on the bed and looked around. The cell was a little larger than the one she'd had before, and it was clear her new celly liked to read fiction. Paperbacks of John Grisham, Jeffery Deaver, and Stephen King were stacked on the shelves. Maybe the celly would let her read some of them. Not that she planned to be here long.

The intercom buzzed, startling her, and a second later a voice floated into her cell. "Maddox, you have a visitor. You may head to the visitors' center."

Abby stood near the intercom. "Can you tell me where that is?"

A pause and then, "I'll escort you. Meet me at the doors."

Officer Perez was waiting for her at the entrance to the tier. "Popular girl," she said with a raised eyebrow. "Been here ten minutes and already someone's here to see you."

Abby smiled. Right on schedule. Her heart raced in anticipation.

She followed the guard down a long length of hall-way, unable to help the bounce in her step. In a strange way this place reminded her of the math building at Puget Sound State—not very big, and very easy to nav-igate.

A shiver went through Abby's body as they passed through the double doors and into the secure visitors' center. The room was large and it resembled a college dormitory recreation room, with a few TVs, a couple of pool tables, several large sofas, and toward the back, several tables for sitting, eating, and conversation.

The CO turned to face her. "Since this is your first day, here's a quick rundown of the rules. You can hold hands. Any other form of touching—including kissing—can't last longer than five seconds. At no time are you allowed to exchange any objects other than photographs. There are cameras here and here," she said, indicating several cameras mounted to the ceiling, "plus there are guards in here at all times. We clear?"

"Clear," Abby said firmly.

"Have a nice time. You have until eight o'clock."

Abby stepped around the guard and walked purposefully through the room, ignoring the stares and whispers from her new fellow inmates and their guests. Her reputation had obviously preceded her, but she was used to it. Her visitor was waiting for her by the far window, and Abby smiled, her heart beating faster than it had in a long time.

Their embrace lasted the entire five seconds.

"God, it's good to see you," Abby whispered. "I've missed you so much."

"Everything is in place." Warm breath caressed her ear. "Soon, baby. Soon."

CHAPTER: 30

Jerry's relief at the investigation being over had lasted exactly one week. One measly week of reprieve, and here he was again. He cursed himself silently for not turning in his police consultant's ID immediately. It was now clipped to his pocket, but it had definitely lost all its appeal.

The body had been found at the Seabreeze Motel off Highway 99 that morning, only a few blocks down from the Perfect Peach. Not quite the same price point as the boutique hotels the previous victims had been found in. Except for the zip tie and the carvings, everything about this crime scene was weird, including the not-so-tiny fact that Jack the Zipper was locked up and couldn't possibly have committed this murder. As Danny would have put it, what the hell, dude?

Jerry looked down at the woman splayed out on the bed and was dismayed to realize that he was getting used to being around dead bodies. When Torrance had called him to the first crime scene—jeez, had that only been a couple of weeks ago?—he'd almost been sick to his stomach, but now, they were all beginning to blur into one another.

Torrance paced the room, thinking out loud. "This doesn't make sense. Jeremiah Blake is in prison."

"I told you we might have the wrong guy," Jerry said.

"Fuck that. No." Torrance shot him a look. "We have the right guy. I know we do. All the evidence points to that freak Blake. This is somebody else. The question is, why?"

Jerry had no answer.

His former partner stepped closer to the bed and frowned at the body. "Dark hair, naked from the waist up, zip tie around her throat, 'Free Abby Maddox' carved into her back. Okay, all of that is consistent with the rest of them. But this one's older, in her thirties. Plus the carpet"—he gestured to the floor, where bloodstains trailed from the door to the bed—"tells us that she was killed somewhere else and brought here."

"So then it's a copycat." Jerry shrugged. "Somebody wanted this woman dead for completely separate reasons and used Blake's MO to cover it up."

Torrance shook his head. "No, something doesn't fit. Blake's name and face have been all over the news. Why would the killer stage a copycat when he knows damn well we already arrested Jack the Zipper?"

"Maybe he panicked," Jerry said. "Or maybe, somehow, he didn't know the killer was arrested. We'll know more once we ID her. How much longer for the prints?"

"Any minute now." As if on cue, Torrance's phone rang. He answered the call, muttered a few words, then disconnected. Deep sigh. "Fuck. Her prints aren't in the system."

"Guess that would have been too easy."

They both fell silent, thinking.

"I stand by my original thought," Jerry finally said a moment later. "My guess is she got killed for totally unrelated reasons, and the killer panicked."

"I don't buy it," Torrance said, pacing. "That doesn't feel right to me."

"Well, you'll have to find out who she is and who she knows. Once you do that, you'll get some answers."

Torrance raised an eyebrow. "What happened to 'we'?"

"What?"

"You said *I'll* get some answers," Torrance said, looking at him closely. "As in me. What happened to 'we'? You don't want to help me with this?"

"Nah." Jerry shook his head. "I think you can handle it."

"You serious?" Torrance was surprised. "You're not going to see this through?"

"I already have seen it through. Jack the Zipper's in prison, and that's all I agreed to help with. Whatever this is, it's not my problem." Jerry gave his former partner a rueful smile. "I'm not interested in any more of this, Mike. I'm meeting a beautiful woman for lunch, and once I get back from it, I'm turning in my consultant's ID."

"Damn. I thought we were having fun, pal."

"Not my idea of a good time." Jerry held his hand out to Torrance, who shook it slowly. "I'm out, Mike."

::::

Jerry hadn't seen that smile in so long, and he soaked up every bit of it. It was like sunshine on his face. That one smile could cure world hunger, replenish the ozone layer, solve America's debt crisis. Okay, maybe he was exaggerating, but it really was the best smile he'd ever seen, and it filled him up just to be on the receiving end of it.

It felt natural being with Annie. He desperately wanted to reach over and touch his wife's hand, but he didn't want to push things. He didn't know if the smile held the promise of anything beyond this afternoon, and he had gone into this date refusing to have expectations.

He also didn't know where things stood between her and the PSSU basketball coach. He hadn't seen them together lately, but then again, he wasn't following her anymore.

Annie beamed at him, her face soft and glowy in the brightly lit tapas-style restaurant. They'd just finished lunch, and she was nibbling daintily at her crème brûlée, eyes closing with every bite. She loved crème brûlée. Jerry wondered if the basketball coach knew that.

"So tell me how the appointment went," she said. "Will the surgery be invasive?"

Jerry took the last sip of his wine. "He said it wouldn't be. I can expect to be under for a couple hours, maybe more. I'll never sound like Barry White, but he can do things to help with the scratchiness. And I'm still going to have a scar. Recovery should take a couple of weeks."

"But it will look better?"

"A lot better. Smaller, flatter, much less noticeable."

"Good." Annie smiled. "Then you can get rid of those turtlenecks. I miss seeing your scrawny neck."

"Hey now, honey." He laughed. "It's not that scrawny."

For the first time in months, she didn't bristle at his term of endearment. Instead, she laughed with him, diving back into her dessert.

He had screwed up his courage and called her the day before to invite her out to lunch. Dinner had seemed a bit too intimate. He'd been scared to make the call, worried she'd hang up or, even worse, be cold toward him. He'd pressed her speed dial number five times before finally allowing the call to go through. Morris had been telling him for a long time that his worst sin was pride, and he thought now that the big guy was right. Annie had agreed to the lunch right away, and had even suggested the time and the place. It made Jerry wonder why he didn't just call his wife ages ago.

"So." He fiddled with his empty wineglass as he formulated his next question. "How are things going with the basketball coach?"

Annie put her spoon down and wiped her lips carefully with her cloth napkin. Reaching into her pocket, she pulled out a small pot of lip balm. Jerry recognized it instantly. She'd discovered it in Paris when they'd gone on a tour of Europe a few years back, and had loved the stuff so much that she continued to order it online. Jerry remembered the taste—like honey and brown sugar.

She rubbed some balm on her lips. Her eyes were soft. "Is that really what you want to talk about?"

"You think it's weird?" Jerry met her gaze with a steady one of his own. "No matter what, we're still friends, aren't we?"

"It's not about that. It's just that I figured you already

know how it's going, and therefore don't need to ask. You follow us, don't you?"

Jerry felt his face grow hot. She knew about that? And here he thought he was being so stealthy, switching the old Honda for a Jeep she'd never seen . . .

Annie gave him a dry smile. "What? You don't think I know you? I married a cop turned PI. You might be unpredictable to everybody else, but not me. And I like the Jeep. It suits you."

Well, shit. There was nothing to say to that.

He couldn't help but notice she hadn't answered the question about her boyfriend, but before he could figure out another way to ask without sounding like a nosy prick, his phone vibrated. His hand reflexively went to his shirt pocket, but it stopped two inches short.

"Go ahead," she said. "Check it. I'm enjoying my dessert anyway."

"It's okay." Jerry put his hand back in his lap. "I can't imagine who it would be. I told Torrance earlier today that I was done. Things are picking up at the office but nothing that can't wait."

"I'm sure Danny can handle it."

"Actually, she has the week off. She's studying for midterms."

"She left you on your own to run the office?" Annie's voice held a trace of amusement. "And here I thought that girl was smart."

"She is smart." Jerry grinned. "The kid works damned hard. Hate to lose her now that her internship's all but done."

His phone vibrated again. Sighing, he pulled it out

of his shirt pocket. It was Torrance. The detective had left a voice mail and now he was sending a text message. Had his former partner not been listening when Jerry said he was finished? He clicked on the text.

CALL ME RIGHT NOW. URGENT.

"It's Mike," he said, frowning. "I guess I'd better call him back."

Annie sat up straighter. The frown lines crinkling her face told him she wasn't happy. "But you said all that was done. Abby Maddox is—" She stopped, realizing that she had just said the name they both hated out loud.

"I'm sure it's about something else." Jerry gave her a reassuring smile. "Be two minutes, hon. Order me another glass of wine?" It was only one-thirty. He didn't want the afternoon to end.

She settled back into her chair. "Sure, why not. I'll have one, too." She lifted a hand to signal their waiter.

Since it was raining outside, Jerry crossed the restaurant and ducked into the hallway where the restrooms were. He pressed a button on his phone, and it took only one ring before Torrance picked up. Jerry didn't bother with pleasantries.

"This better be good, Mike. I thought I made it clear—"

"Jeremiah Blake is dead."

Fifty points. That's how much Jerry guessed his blood pressure had just shot up. He knew Torrance wouldn't be telling him this if it didn't have everything to do with Abby Maddox.

Jerry counted to three, then said calmly, "What happened?"

"He was found in his bunk, strangled with a zip tie. Face looked like a fucking grape. And there was a message carved on his chest. It said 'I freed Abby Maddox.'"

"Christ." The images in Jerry's mind were horrifying. "Suicide?"

"That's what they initially thought, but now they're not sure. Someone snitched. It might be murder."

Jerry said nothing. He already knew what Torrance was about to ask.

"Pal, is there any chance you could go down to Creekside, throw your police ID around, see if you can get in to see Maddox? Just until I can get there. I'm stuck working on the vic we found this morning, which I'm still convinced ties to Blake somehow. Unfortunately a fresh dead body takes priority over a dead serial killer in prison."

Jerry squeezed his eyes shut, trying to process it all. I FREED ABBY MADDOX. What did that mean?

"And I've been thinking," Torrance said. "We know Blake was obsessed with Maddox, but remember how you kept saying it felt like we were missing something?"

"Yeah." Jerry held his breath.

"We were so focused on what Blake thought of Maddox that we never thought to ask what *Maddox* thought of *Blake*. When they cleaned out his cell, they found a cell phone. Can you believe that? A cell phone in prison? Apparently it's becoming a fucking epidemic, and I'm hearing it's the guards who sneak them in. There are a ton of texts in there from a couple of different numbers. We can't seem to trace them, but from the messages, I'd bet my left titty the texts were from Maddox. She's been communicating with Blake all along, praising him for his efforts, promising him the world. She played the kid, Jerry." Torrance was breathing hard. "She played him from the beginning, encouraging him to do the killings so she'd have leverage with the prosecuting attorney to cut a deal. I'd bet my badge she got him killed just to tie up the loose end."

Again, Jerry said nothing.

"Based on the texts between her and Blake, we might be able to get her on conspiracy charges for all four murders. I want the bitch to burn, pal. I need you."

Jerry glanced over to Annie, who was waiting for him at their table on the other side of the restaurant, a glass of red wine in her hand. An identical glass of wine was waiting for him at his seat. His wife was looking out the window at the rain, her face content, almost dreamy. They were having the nicest time they'd had together in over a year.

Was he really going to bail on the woman he loved most in the world to go talk to the woman he hated most in the world?

"I'm on my way."

Jerry disconnected the call. The violent itch at his throat, which had stayed blissfully dormant for the past week, was back with a vengeance. He scratched it long and hard before heading back to the table.

CHAPTER: 31

He was certain he had heard wrong. Mind you, his ears were usually pretty good. The one thing Annie always said he had going for him was that he was a great listener . . . when he was listening. Which he was now. Very intently. He had driven like mad to get from the restaurant to Creekside Corrections and had made it in just over an hour, and his ears were still ringing from speeding the entire way. Maybe he had misheard her.

"I am going to ask you to repeat that." Jerry stared at the superintendent, an attractive, curvy black woman who reminded him of an old girlfriend he'd had long before he married Annie. "What do you mean, she's not here? Where else would she be?"

"Abby Maddox was accepted into the Be Smart program." Alicia Elkes returned his heated gaze with a cool one of her own. "Ergo, she's not here. Because she's out. Doing her job."

"That's what I thought you said." Jerry felt like someone was playing a trick on him and that any minute, he was going to find out he'd been *Punk'd*. He gripped the sides of his chair in an effort to stay calm. The superintendent's office was decorated in a soothing mix of yellows and lavenders, but it wasn't helping. He forced a smile, but it probably came out a grimace, judging from the suddenly wary expression on the superintendent's face.

"Why am I just hearing about this now?" Jerry tried to soften his tone. "She's only been at your facility for one week. And she's in here for a violent offense." Despite his best efforts, his voice got loud again. "You let violent offenders out so they can *work*?" Glimmers of shiny spittle flew into the air.

Elkes pointedly wiped her cheek with a long, manicured fingernail. Her nail polish matched her lipstick. Bright coral. "We're a minimum-security prison, Mr. Isaac." She spoke slowly, obviously choosing her words carefully. "Do you understand that *one hundred percent* of our inmates will be released at some point? Therefore our focus is on rehabilitation, not punishment."

"But everybody here is a criminal."

She frowned at his choice of words. "They've committed crimes. They've broken the law. But the majority of our *offenders* are not bad people. They've just made bad choices. It's in the best interest of society that we prepare them for a life outside of prison in the hopes that they won't reoffend. The Be Smart program, if successful, will boost morale for the inmates and keep kids from going down the wrong path. Abigail Maddox is a perfect fit for Be Smart. I had no qualms about expediting her acceptance into the program."

"Because it's underfunded, and you were desperate for the publicity."

Elkes's face hardened, but she didn't respond. Which meant he was right.

Jerry sat staring at her in disbelief. What the hell kind of sick place would allow Abby Maddox to be part of a program that allowed her to go *outside*? He had heard of the Be Smart program, and while it sounded like it had potential, it involved inmates leaving the prison, something Jerry couldn't wrap his mind around.

"Do you people have any idea what Abby Maddox is capable of?" Jerry tugged on his turtleneck and willed himself not to scratch. "Do you know who you're dealing with here?"

"Mr. Isaac." Alicia Elkes sighed, folding her hands on top of Maddox's manila file folder. "I don't mean to overstep, but you are the retired police detective she assaulted, right? I realize this is personal to you. I'm sorry."

Yet the superintendent didn't seem sorry at all. A year ago, Jerry would have yelled. Nowadays, he no longer possessed the vocal strength to yell, and it was frustrating beyond all measure.

"Why didn't anybody notify me?" His voice was painfully hoarse. "Someone should have let me know that the woman who did *this* to me would be running around free during the day." He yanked down the top of his turtleneck and allowed the woman to get a good look at his scar. Her dark eyes widened as she took in all four inches of the purplish brown puckered flesh. It never failed to shock. "So as you can imagine, your news is not good news, ma'am."

Elkes rolled her chair back a few inches. "Mr. Isaac—"

"Call me Jerry. My father was Mr. Isaac."

"Mr. Isaac. Did you not just consult on a police

investigation where Miss Maddox helped solve a series of murders? Which is the reason she was transferred here?"

"I did what I had to do to save young women from being murdered. And I'd do it again. Because I survived. Others didn't." Jerry took a deep breath and tried to calm down. "But that doesn't mean I would have agreed to her participating in an outside work program, had I been consulted."

"It wasn't the Department of Corrections' job to consult you."

Fuck you. "Then there are flaws in your system."

"I never said it was perfect." Elkes sighed. "But you did catch the killer, didn't you? With her help?"

Jerry didn't know how to answer this. The issue wasn't that Jeremiah Blake was the killer. It was that *he hadn't acted alone.* "Jack the Zipper was an immediate threat."

"Yes, but Abby Maddox isn't." Elkes leaned back in her chair.

There was so much Jerry wanted to say, but he bit his tongue. Literally. He relaxed his jaw, tasting blood. "Where is her group right now? What school?"

"I am not going to give you that information." Elkes moved Maddox's file to the corner of her desk. "She'll be back in the facility in two hours. You're welcome to speak with her then."

Jerry rubbed his temple. The woman really didn't get it. "This can't wait two hours," he said, standing up. "The teenage killer she helped find? Jeremiah Blake? She may have arranged his murder."

He pulled out his phone. Torrance had emailed him photos of Blake dead in his cell, which Jerry hadn't wanted to see, but now he was glad he had them. He showed them to Elkes, whose dark eyes widened in horror. Her hand went to her mouth and she seemed unable to speak for a few seconds.

"Ms. Elkes, I need to speak with Maddox *now*. Wherever she is, you get her back here before somebody else shows up dead. Because I guarantee you somebody will."

"I—"

"Do it!" Jerry roared, his damaged vocal cords finally finding just the right groove. For the first time in a year, his voice thundered. He knew it wouldn't last. He leaned in and pointed a finger right in her face. "You listen to me, and you listen to me good, Ms. Elkes. I am heading to my car. In three minutes I'm going to call you and you are going to give me the location of Abby Maddox's Be Smart group. If you don't give it to me, I am going to personally contact the Department of Corrections and let them know what a pathetic facility you're running here. And then I'm going to give interview after interview about your lack of competency on every news outlet that's been hounding me for the past year, about what a ridiculous failure the Be Smart program is, and I'm not going to hold back. If somebody else dies and Abby Maddox is responsible, then I'm holding *you* responsible. Do I make myself clear?"

"I will get that information for you." Alicia Elkes's condescending, professional demeanor was finally beginning to crack. Obviously the things she cared most about were her job and the reputation of her facility, and Jerry had just threatened both. She was visibly upset, her lips quivering. "What else can I do?"

"Cross your fingers she's there," he said, and left.

CHAPTER: 32

Superintendent Elkes came through with an address. It took Jerry an hour to arrive at Grove High School, where Abby Maddox's Be Smart group was speaking. As soon as he saw the chaos in the parking lot, his heart sank.

A cluster of inmates, maybe a dozen or so, all dressed in bright blue button-down shirts and thick black slacks, were standing by the front entrance of the school. Abby Maddox wasn't among them.

Torrance hadn't arrived yet, and might not, depending on what the police officers here had to say to Jerry. Flashing his temporary police ID, which had expired a few days ago (not that anyone would notice), he headed toward a senior officer. Not senior in terms of authority, senior as in he had thinning steel-gray hair. Guy probably should have retired a few years back.

"Hey, Jerry!" Bill Wozniacki said, shaking his hand. "I heard you were consulting for the PD. Good to see you."

"Hi, Bill." Jerry forced a smile. He liked Bill, they'd worked together a long time back in the day, but he was in no mood for pleasantries. "Good to see you, too."

"How long you been retired now, bro? Three years?"

"Two."

"How's Marianne? I was just saying to the wife the other day—"

"Whatcha got for me, Bill?" Jerry said in his best no-nonsense voice. There was plenty of time for catch-up later.

Bill was a seasoned cop and he didn't blink. "The school called us about thirty minutes ago, telling us they lost one of the Be Smart inmates. We didn't even know it was Abby Maddox until we got here. Apparently someone set off a flare in the auditorium during the talk, which caused a ton of smoke and set the fire alarms and sprinklers off. Three hundred kids panicked, everybody rushed the doors, she slipped out."

"She slipped out?" Jerry repeated in disbelief.

"Heads are gonna roll, I know." Bill shook his head. "Anyway, she's gone, Jerry. We found Maddox's shirt, pants, and shoes stuffed into a trash bin behind the stage."

"So she had help," Jerry said. "If she'd ditched her prison garb, then someone brought her clothes. Shit."

"Not just clothes. A guard's uniform. Couple of the kids we questioned said they saw a CO slip out the back entrance, but they didn't realize it was Maddox."

Jerry strode over to where the rest of the Be Smart group was standing. There were seven inmates and two guards, one male, one female. "Which one of you is in charge?" he said, flashing his consultant's ID.

The male guard stepped forward. "I am." His name tag read DOS SANTOS.

"How could you lose her?" Jerry said, the rasp in his voice so pronounced he sounded strangled. "How the hell does that happen?"

Dos Santos looked helpless, his hand over his stomach. Jerry would be very surprised if the man still had a job tomorrow. "I had to step out to go to the bathroom. It was an emergency. That only left Officer Solomon to watch the group. The program's underfunded." He looked down and muttered, "I knew something tasted funny with the eggs this morning."

"Then you should have stopped after the first bite," Torrance's dry voice said from behind Jerry.

He turned to find his former partner looking slightly more disheveled than usual. "About time you got here." Jerry quickly relayed what they knew about Maddox, which wasn't very much.

"I already have an APB out on her. We'll find her." Torrance led Jerry away from the crowd a little. "And you'll never guess who else is missing."

"I don't know if I want to know."

"Mark Cavanaugh, the corrections officer from Maddox's first prison. I called Rosedale to talk to Maddox's cellmate about the phone, and she mentioned Cavanaugh got fired over a week ago and nobody's heard from him since. Apparently the CO and Maddox were intimately involved. Didn't you mention they were eye-fucking each other when you were there?"

"You have such a way with words," Jerry said drily, nodding.

"Anyway," Torrance continued, "Cavanaugh has two residences, an apartment near the prison and a larger home in Concrete that's been in his family for a long time. Guess what the family name is."

"No idea."

"Wheaton." Torrance paused to let it sink in, but Jerry was blanking on the significance of this. "As in, Doris Wheaton. As in, the name of the old lady whose grave we dug up at Heavenly Rest to find victim number three."

Jerry's mouth dropped open. "You're kidding."

"She was Cavanaugh's grandmother. The house in Concrete was hers. She had no other family, so Cavanaugh inherited it when she died."

Jerry closed his eyes, trying to process it all. "Where is Concrete, anyway? I've never heard of it."

"I had to Google-map it myself," Torrance said. "It's north. East of Mount Vernon. Population is like, less than a thousand. Anyway, I've got an APB out on Cavanaugh, too. For sure he's helping Maddox. She didn't escape by herself, and it's way too convenient that we can't track him down."

Jerry began to pace. First Jeremiah Blake, now Mark Cavanaugh. Was there anyone Maddox hadn't manipulated?

"I'd better call Sheila." Jerry's heart grew heavy as soon as he said the words. "Let her know that Maddox is out there. Christ. Morris is gonna flip."

He scrolled through his phone until he found Sheila's contact info and called. A moment later, he got her voice mail. He left a message, then tried her at the university. Finally he sent her a text message. The text would be the first thing she'd see when she finally checked her phone, which would save time.

"You should try Morris," Torrance said. "He'll know where she is."

Jerry hesitated. Things were good with him and Morris right now, and this one phone call was certain to shoot that all to hell. But of course Torrance was right—if anyone knew where Sheila would be, her fiancé would, and he was going to find out about all this, anyway. Jerry called Morris at the investment firm. Marcy, his executive assistant, answered and within a few seconds he was connected with the big man.

Jerry got right to the point. "Do you know where Sheila is?"

"Why?" Morris's deep voice was instantly wary.

Jerry took a deep breath and braced himself. "Abby Maddox is gone. Today was her first day with the Be Smart program, and, well . . . they lost her." He quickly explained what the program was about.

He heard Morris suck in a long breath and he steeled himself for the barrage he knew was about to come.

"They lost her?" Morris hollered in his ear. "*They lost her?* Are you kidding me?"

"I'm so sorry—"

"You're sorry? You're goddamned sorry?" Morris shouted, and Jerry winced. "I told you that this would happen. I told you she couldn't be trusted. Now what? She's coming after my fiancée? Did you try calling Sheila? Goddamn you, Jerry!"

"Well, that's just it, I can't seem to get ahold of her." Jerry spoke rapidly, hoping in some ridiculous way that talking fast would minimize the impact of his words.

A pause. Too long. Finally Morris spoke and Jerry

could hear the forced control in his friend's voice. Not a good sign. Morris yelling meant Morris was still in control. Morris calm at a time like this meant the man's huge head was about to burst. "Did you try her cell?"

"Yes. Twice. And I've texted."

"Her office?"

"Yes. Also twice. And I've left mess—"

"I'll call you back." Morris disconnected.

Shit.

"He's pissed?" Torrance said, stating the obvious. "I could hear him from here." He pulled out a pack of gum. It was Nicorette; his former partner was trying to quit smoking again. Jerry was betting it wouldn't last, not with everything going on right now.

"What do you think? Maddox has been missing for going on two hours now and we can't get ahold of Sheila. Forget pissed. He's about to blow a gasket." Jerry's phone rang. It was still in his hand and he looked down to see Morris's number. He took the call. "Hi, Morris."

"She didn't answer." Morris heaved in Jerry's ear. "I'm only gonna say this once, Jerry, so you listen up, my friend. *You had better find my fiancée.* Breathing, and in one piece. Because if something has happened to Sheila, if she's been snatched by that psychopathic bitch—who, by the way, I warned you both about—I will personally detach your head from your skinny, turtleneck-wearing, badly scarred neck. You got me, amigo?"

"I got you."

Click.

Jerry turned to Torrance. "Put out an APB for Sheila Tao."

Torrance's eyes widened. "On what grounds?"

"Will you please just do it? After what happened to her last time, I'm not waiting until she's nearly dead. That's not happening again." He felt like he was in shock. "It *can't* happen again."

"You know I need to have cause to put that kind of—"

"Come on, man," Jerry snapped. "You trust my instincts, don't you? Say whatever you have to say. Think of something." He softened his tone. "Please, Mike. She's my friend's fiancée, and my wife's friend. Please just do this for me."

Torrance nodded stiffly and turned away to make the call.

Jerry headed toward his car. If Sheila didn't turn up by tonight, he was fairly certain she was as good as dead.

And then so was he.

CHAPTER: 33

Sheila was feeling mellow. Bruno Mars's jazzy voice was singing about beautiful girls, the whole coffee shop smelled like cinnamon rolls, and the extra shot of vanilla in her latte was delicious. She smiled at Marianne. The impromptu yoga class they'd just finished next door had been exactly what the both of them needed. There was nothing like endorphins to make the world seem brighter.

"We should do yoga more often," Sheila said to her friend, taking another bite of the cinnamon roll they were sharing. "Thanks for talking me into it. I feel more relaxed than I have in months."

"That was the point," Marianne said with a smile. She seemed happy enough, but distracted.

"Feel like telling me what's going on?" Sheila said.

"I ended it with George."

"You're kidding." Sheila put her cup down. "I thought everything was going well. I thought you said he was . . ." She searched for the word her friend had once used to describe him. "Easy. I thought you said George was easy."

"He is. Was." Marianne sighed, looking frustrated. "He was laid-back, a good listener, easy to please, and

certainly not bad on the eyes. When we first started dating, those were the best things about him."

"And then?"

"And then . . . he got really boring." Marianne
clapped a hand over her mouth. "Oh God, I know that's
a terrible thing to say. But Sheila, I swear, all he ever
wanted to talk about was me or basketball, and both got
old really fast. It got to the point where I found myself
picking fights with him just so he'd show some personality, some emotion. How juvenile is that?"

Sheila couldn't help but laugh. "I understand, I do.
One of the things I love about Morris is his strong personality. He keeps me on my toes and never lets me get
away with anything. It's frustrating as hell at times, and
we butt heads a lot, but I can't say we're bored."

Marianne nodded, looking away, falling silent. Sheila
decided not to push. Over the loudspeakers, Bruno Mars
changed to Adele, who was longing for an old flame
who'd married someone else.

Sheila settled back into her chair, enjoying the low-
key vibe. She had turned her phone off before the yoga
class, and it occurred to her now that maybe she should
check her messages, see if Morris was wondering where
she was. She reached into her purse for her BlackBerry,
then stopped. No, this was her time with Marianne. Morris and the rest of the world could wait. She let the phone
fall back into her bag.

"I miss Jerry," Marianne blurted.

Sheila blinked. "I thought you just saw him a few
hours ago."

"Yes, and we had a great time. Despite everything,

I'd forgotten how much the man makes me laugh." Marianne looked glum. "Don't get me wrong, I'm still so mad at him, and I needed to get away from him and all his negativity. But . . . he's still the funniest guy I know. And a hard worker. And a romantic at heart. And I know he loves me. Be honest. You think I bailed on him?"

"Absolutely not," Sheila said firmly. "Things were rough for a while and you needed space. I really believe Jerry understood that, and that he still understands it. And you're right, he does love you, more than life itself."

"He said that to you? We didn't get a chance to get into it at lunch today."

"Almost every time we've talked," Sheila said, and it was the truth. "He'd take you back in a hot minute. You just have to decide if that's what you want, but I know he's hoping."

"How do I make that decision?"

It was a difficult question to answer. "I honestly don't know."

"We'd need couples counseling," Marianne said.

"Who doesn't? No shame in that."

"Things would have to change."

"Of course they would. It takes time and you both have to be one hundred percent committed." Sheila waved a hand. "What am I saying, you know all this already. No matter what, I want what's best for each of you, whether that means you're together or apart. But I do think you two belong together. I've always thought that."

Marianne took a deep breath. "Okay. I'll set up another date with him tomorrow. I think it's time to open up a real dialogue again."

"I think that's wonderful."

Marianne glanced at her watch. "Shoot, I have a patient in ten minutes. We should go, unless you want to stick around here? No, wait, your car's at my office. You'll have to come with me unless you want to walk back."

"No, that's fine, I need to get going, too," Sheila said. "I suddenly feel the urge to give Morris a massive hug when he gets home tonight. He's been really supportive with this whole Abby Maddox thing. Maybe I'll pick up dinner from that New York–style pizza parlor he likes and surprise him. If pizza doesn't show him how much I love him, I don't know what will."

It was just starting to rain when they got outside, and they sprinted across the parking lot toward Marianne's silver Mercedes before either of them could get too wet.

Marianne stuck her key in the ignition and turned it. The car made a loud screeching sound, and then nothing.

"That doesn't sound good," Sheila said.

"You've got to be kidding me." Marianne frowned. "The car's only a year old." Annoyed, she tried the ignition again. Same awful sound, and then nothing.

A knock on Sheila's passenger side window startled them both, and she looked up to see a familiar face through the glass. Surprised, she pressed the button to roll down the window. "Hello. What are you doing here?"

It was Mark Cavanaugh, the ridiculously handsome

corrections officer from Rosedale Penitentiary. He smiled at her. "I thought I recognized you. Dr. Tao, right?"

Sheila nodded, too caught off guard to do anything else.

"I had some matters over at the federal building to attend to, and whenever I'm up this way, I love stopping in at Java Jungle," Cavanaugh said. "Noticed you inside but thought it might be awkward if I said hello. However, I couldn't help but notice your car's not starting." He ducked his head a little to smile at Marianne through the open window. She seemed utterly dazzled. "Hi there. I'm Mark."

"This is my friend Marianne," Sheila said with a knowing smile. To Marianne, she said, "Mark and I met at Rosedale Penitentiary, where he works as a corrections officer."

"Nice to meet you," Marianne said when she finally found her voice. "I don't know what's wrong with my car. It was fine earlier."

"Try it again," Cavanaugh said, and Marianne complied.

"Hmmm. Sounds like it could be the alternator. Want me to take a look? I'm pretty good with cars."

"That would be great." Marianne pulled a lever and then hopped out.

The two of them disappeared behind the hood while Sheila waited in the passenger's seat, wondering what the problem might be.

A moment later, Marianne opened the driver's-side door and reached for her purse. "He says it's not the alternator. It might be the engine. Can you believe that? The car's still new."

"At least it's still under warranty," Mark Cavanaugh said from behind her. "They'll fix it, so it won't cost you anything except a whole lot of annoyance."

Frustrated, Marianne nodded at him, then turned back to Sheila. "Mark's offered to give us a ride back to my office so you can get your car. I'm going to make it back just in time for my six o'clock."

Sheila hesitated, feeling a tingle at the back of her neck. Something about this didn't seem right, but she couldn't put her finger on what it was.

"Sheila, seriously," Marianne said, exasperated. "I am so late."

Sheila grabbed her purse and got out of the car, shaking off the weird feeling. She was probably overthinking it. "Aren't you going to call AAA?"

"I will when I get back to the office. The car can sit here for a while. I'll run in and tell the yoga studio not to tow it. I can't be late for this appointment." In a low voice, she added, "My six o'clock has issues being left alone."

Cavanaugh and Sheila both laughed. Marianne jogged across the parking lot back to Yogalicious and disappeared through the tinted glass door.

An awkward silence descended. Feeling the need to fill it, Sheila said, "So how are things over at Rosedale?"

"They're good," Cavanaugh said with an easy grin. "Very busy, but I like it that way."

Sheila wondered if she should ask him about Abby. It had been clear to her that Abby and the CO had been close, but before she could think of how to phrase the question, Marianne was back.

"Okay, let's boot," her friend said, breathless. "Have I mentioned that I am so unbelievably late?"

"I'm parked over there," Cavanaugh said, pointing.

The two of them followed the younger man toward the back corner of the parking lot, where it seemed much darker since the floodlight on this side was out. Again, Sheila felt a tingle, but again, she was probably just being neurotic.

She noticed that Cavanaugh was dressed in civilian clothes, and the outline of his firm, perfect ass was evident beneath the soft material of his gray slacks. As they walked behind him, Marianne nudged and pointed. Sheila bit back a smile. It was, indeed, a great ass.

"Just give me a moment to move some papers out of the front seat," Cavanaugh said as they neared his shiny black SUV. It was a beast of a vehicle, a black Dodge Durango, with heavily tinted windows and shiny chrome rims. Flashy, but it suited him.

"No worries," Marianne said. "You're doing us a huge favor. I'll hop in the back."

Cavanaugh unlocked the doors. After shuffling a few things around, they all climbed in, Sheila in the passenger seat and Marianne behind her. The doors locked automatically when Cavanaugh started the engine.

Then an arm shot out from her left and Sheila felt a prick on her neck. It was the last thing she remembered.

CHAPTER: 34

Sheila awoke, her head pounding and fuzzy, her stomach churning, her throat dry.

Her first thought was as clear as it could have been under the circumstances: *I've been here before.*

Opening her eyes, she tried to look around, but her face was flattened against the cold concrete floor and her head wouldn't cooperate when she tried to lift it. Her arms were tied behind her back and she was lying awkwardly on her side in a fetal position. The only light in the room was coming from a bare bulb hanging from a wire above her head, and it was swinging, casting strange, moving shadows on the unfamiliar shapes around her. Trying not to panic, she took a deep breath, and the smell of must and mothballs filled her nostrils.

Her second thought was just as clear as her first: *Abby Maddox did this.* Sheila didn't know how, exactly, this was possible, but every instinct told her that Abby Maddox had brought her here. Where *here* was, Sheila didn't know, but it was the only explanation. Mark Cavanaugh would have no reason to do this unless someone had asked him to.

It was last year all over again.

You've got to be kidding. Seriously? You've got to be fucking kidding.

A low moan came from somewhere nearby. Alarmed, Sheila had enough of a surge of adrenaline to sit upright against the wall, but not without effort. Between her pounding head and her bound arms, it was a struggle to turn toward the source of the sound.

Eight feet away, she saw that Marianne was propped up against the wall as well, her head bleeding from one temple and her hair hanging in her face. Her arms were also fastened behind her, and she looked like a discarded doll with her yoga-pant-clad legs stretched out in front of her, askew.

"Marianne." Sheila meant to speak in a whisper, but her voice was louder than she intended. "Marianne, wake up."

Marianne blinked and focused her gaze on Sheila, her eyes clearing a bit in relief at the sight of Sheila's face. "Oh, thank God you're up. I was scared you had a head injury. You didn't respond when I said your name a few minutes ago."

"You're bleeding."

"So are you." Marianne grimaced. "I hit my head against the wall when he threw me down. It's throbbing like a sonofabitch."

"Dizziness? Nausea?" Sheila said, fearing her friend had a concussion.

"No, just a bad headache. But my ankles are sprained. Both of them. And I'm . . . I think I'm having chest pains."

"Oh God." Sheila sat up straighter, trying to focus. "You think you're having a heart attack?"

"No, no, it's a panic attack." Marianne took several deep breaths, but her calm voice wasn't fooling Sheila. "I've had them before. I just need to breathe and try and get my bearings."

Relieved, Sheila leaned her head against the cold concrete wall behind her and tried to get her own bearings. "Any idea how long we've been here?"

"No idea. My watch is gone."

"And Mark?"

"I woke up as he was leaving. I tried calling out to him, but he said he'd be back and left. I think we're in his cold cellar." Marianne pulled her legs closer to her body. She was shivering. "What the hell is going on? What does he want with us?"

"When I was at the prison, I got the impression he and Abby were close." Sheila shut her eyes, her head spinning. "I can only think that he's done this for her."

"But why? I thought you and Abby had come to some sort of understanding. That this was all over between the two of you."

"So did I. I thought after that TV interview, we were finally . . . even." The thought seemed ridiculous and naïve now.

"So what is this, some kind of twisted revenge plan?" Marianne's voice was bordering on hysteria, and that was not good.

"I don't know." Sheila was making every effort to stay calm. "I know as much as you do."

"This is not okay, Sheila!" Marianne said, her voice close to shriek level. "This is not—"

"Shhh, Marianne," Sheila whispered. "Please, try and

stay focused. We don't know where Mark is. We have to keep our heads together if we're going to get out of this."

A whimper. Marianne was crying.

Sheila looked around again, noting there were no windows. But there was an old wooden staircase on the other side of the cellar. "Hey, can you try and stand? I see stairs by the far wall. We need to get out of here before he comes back."

"I heard him lock the door," Marianne said, and her voice cracked. "And no, I can't put weight on my feet. I tried already. It hurts too much."

Sheila struggled to stand up, but she had no strength, and her bound arms were useless in helping her get traction. Anchoring her feet beneath her, she pushed her back against the wall, managing to raise herself up about a foot. Her quadriceps trembled with the effort. "Okay," she said. "I'm going to try and stand up, see if I can get up those stairs. This is an old cellar. Maybe the door's not that solid."

"You really think this is about Abby?"

"It's got to be Abby. It's the only thing that makes sense." Grunting with exertion, Sheila tried to straighten her legs, but just like that, her knees gave out. Her ass hit the floor painfully and she swore. A large wolf spider hovered nearby, and she flinched, hoping it wouldn't come any closer.

"But you said you no longer believed she was the true mastermind behind all those killings." Marianne sounded frustrated and confused. "You said Ethan was probably lying about that."

"I did believe it, and then I didn't, and now I don't

know what the hell to think." Sheila started to shiver. Her adrenaline had worn off and the cold was beginning to seep through her thin yoga clothes. "Listen, I'm going to inch my way closer to you. I'm freezing and you must be, too. Sitting against the wall is only making it worse."

Sheila wiggled across the concrete basement floor, groaning with the effort. It took a couple of minutes before they were finally touching. They pushed themselves against each other, and within a few seconds, Sheila already felt a few degrees warmer.

"My wrists are killing me," Marianne said with a groan. "What did he bind us with, zip ties?"

A wave of nausea went through Sheila as she realized that Marianne was right. *Zip ties. Jack the Zipper.* Jeremiah Blake—who was now in jail for five counts of murder, including the murder of his father—was the killer who had carved Abby's name on his victims.

After he'd strangled them with zip ties.

Oh God. Oh no.

Sheila could feel hysteria rising in her gut, and she did the only thing she could think of to stem it. She turned her head to the side, and vomited.

When her retching finally subsided, Marianne said drily, "I know you couldn't help that, sweetie, but the smell really doesn't help things."

Sheila managed a laugh at Marianne's attempt at humor. Her head felt a little bit clearer. She wouldn't tell Marianne about the significance of the zip ties, because her friend didn't need to know. Marianne was finally sounding calm and in control, and Sheila was determined to keep it that way.

"Are they going to kill us?" Her friend's voice was small.

Sheila was grateful the cellar was dim, because she didn't know if she could lie to Marianne's face. The answer was obvious to her. Yes, she was certain that Abby's intention was to see both of them dead. But she couldn't risk Marianne having another panic attack. She needed her friend alert and ready for whatever was going to happen next.

"I don't think so," Sheila finally said, hoping she sounded confident. "Abby's in prison, remember? She personally can't do us any harm from inside, and she's the one we'd really have to worry about. Cavanaugh's obviously been manipulated, and when he's back, we'll just have to work on making him see that he's throwing his whole life away by helping her."

"You think she's engineering all this from prison?"

"She's certainly capable of it. I'm starting to realize now that she's capable of anything. First Ethan, now her prison guard . . ."

"She sure knows how to pick 'em," Marianne said with a sigh. "I only met the guy for two minutes and I was already wondering if he was married or single."

"Okay, I'm going to try standing up again," Sheila said. "I need to get up those stairs."

She leaned against Marianne and tried to maneuver her body into a standing position. Her legs were frustratingly uncooperative, quivering like Jell-O. A few sweaty, grunting moments later, she was slumped next to her friend once again. "Shit! Why is this go goddamned hard?"

"Relax for a minute." Marianne's voice was soothing, and Sheila was grateful for it. "Rest and try again in a bit. It's that crap he injected us with. It makes you weak."

They sat in silence.

"So what's the plan once we get out?" Marianne said a moment later. "Please tell me you have one."

"I'm thinking."

"Think faster." Her friend's voice was edgy.

The two of them continued to sit, not talking. Sheila's mind ran through the possibilities.

What kind of contact had Cavanaugh and Abby had? They had spent time together at Rosedale, that much was clear. Sheila didn't know much about prisons, but certainly as a CO he'd have been able to orchestrate ways to be alone with her. Abby had been at Rosedale for a little over a year. Plenty of time for her to work her magic on him.

But now Abby was no longer at Rosedale. She'd been transferred to a minimum security facility Sheila couldn't remember the name of now. Was Cavanaugh visiting Abby at her new prison? Visits were monitored. It would have been too risky for them to plan this in a room staffed with guards. So how were they communicating?

And what motivation would Mark Cavanaugh have to help Abby? For him to commit kidnapping, assault, and eventual double murder? You would think as a corrections officer he would never want to be the one behind bars. Why risk it? What was in it for him? What had Abby promised him? She wasn't wealthy. The only thing she had to offer was herself, and while that was certainly enough, she had another eight years in prison, unless she somehow got out early for good behavior. Would Cavanaugh actually be willing to wait for her?

Unless . . .

No, she couldn't have.

"So?" Marianne's sharp voice cut through Sheila's thoughts. "Any ideas?"

Sheila closed her eyes, steeling herself for what she was about to say. "I have a feeling Abby's gotten out somehow. It's the only thing that makes sense."

Marianne's whole body stiffened. "Excuse me? Abby Maddox escaping from prison is *logical*? How the hell do you figure that?"

"I think Mark is in love with her. And would do anything for her. She handpicked him because he was a corrections officer—who better than a prison guard to help her bust out? What's the first thing she'd want more than anything in the world?"

"Her freedom," Marianne answered promptly, then sighed. "Shit."

"Exactly. And what's the second thing she'd want?"

Marianne paused. "To get away?" Her voice was uncertain.

"Well, yes, but she'd want to tie up loose ends first." Sheila wriggled closer, the zip ties cutting into her wrists. "And who's the one person she seems to hate most right now?"

"That's easy. You."

"Right. See, I'm the reason she's in jail. Ethan and I had an affair. I'm the reason he's dead. In her twisted mind, that makes me responsible for everything that's happened to her." Not that Sheila entirely disagreed. She really didn't. She just didn't feel she deserved to die because of it.

"And I get to come along for the ride." The bitterness in Marianne's voice was unmistakable.

"I'm sorry, Marianne." The apology was lame and Sheila knew it. "You so don't deserve this."

This time her friend said nothing.

A squeak caused them both to freeze. From the other side of the basement, they could hear a door opening. Footsteps tread carefully down the creaky stairs. Mark Cavanaugh had returned. Against her on the hard concrete floor, Sheila could feel Marianne's body stiffening again. Her friend felt like a statue. Even Sheila was having a hard time breathing properly.

But the key to surviving this whole thing, she knew from experience, was to find out what Mark Cavanaugh *wanted*. That was pivotal. Digging into Ethan's true desires had kept Sheila alive long enough for Morris and Jerry to track her down. It might keep her and Marianne alive long enough for them to do it a second time.

A figure approached. Under the dull light of the bare basement bulb, it was hard to see a face. Tall. Had to be Mark Cavanaugh.

Only it wasn't.

Dressed in tight jeans, knee-high boots, and a fitted leather jacket, Abby Maddox looked nothing like an inmate. Her hair had been cut short and bleached platinum blonde. She strode toward them and stopped a few inches away from their legs, looking down, seeming to relish the sight of the two women tied up and helpless. Her smile soon turned to disgust.

"Now that smells horrible," she said to Sheila, her gaze roaming over the pile of vomit to Sheila's right. "Not that I'm surprised. Ethan told me you had a weak stomach."

Sheila opened her mouth to say something, but nothing came out.

"What do you think, girls?" Abby said, tilting her head. She flicked the ends of her blond strands languidly. "About the hair. It's a wig. I didn't have time for a professional bleach job. But I like it. I think I can pull off being blond, don't you agree? They do say blondes have more fun."

Again, Sheila opened her mouth, but she couldn't find the words. She was too taken aback. Strategizing in her head was one thing—this had seemed like a totally solvable problem in theory. But now, face-to-face with Abby Maddox herself, in a damp cellar with her arms tied behind her back, it was a whole different playing field.

Abby seemed completely amused by Sheila's inability to speak. "Cat got your tongue, Sheila?"

"How'd you get out?" Sheila finally managed to say.

"Planning and patience. And a little help from my friends." Abby fixed her gaze on Marianne. "Well, hello, Annie," she said, and Sheila felt her friend jolt at the use of her nickname, something only Jerry called her. "I'm rather happy you're here, though I'm sure it sucks for you. But it's fitting, considering your husband is also someone on my shit list."

Marianne whimpered.

Abby's smile broadened. She moved closer and knelt

down, her face less than a foot away from Marianne's. "It's a nice feeling that I can do away with everyone who's fucked me over all at once. Not that you and I are really enemies, Annie, but since Jerry's not here, you'll do just fine. This would hurt him way more, anyway. And won't that be nice? How . . . serendipitous."

Abby Maddox stood up, brushing the cement dust off her jeans. She seemed impossibly tall, and impossibly dangerous. Her voice purred like a tiger's. "All right, girls. Ready to get started? This is going to be *so much fun*."

CHAPTER:35

As he and Mike made their way out to the tiny town of Concrete, Jerry wasn't completely surprised to see Morris's number on his phone. Because he hadn't been able to get ahold of Sheila himself, either, and it was now after 8 p.m. Wherever Sheila was, she should have responded by now.

Jerry prepared himself for another verbal ass-kicking. "Hey, man."

"She's not picking up her phone, Jerry," Morris said in his ear, his deep voice tight and controlled. "It's going straight to voice mail, amigo."

"We'll find her. We have an APB out on her and—"

"Fuck your APB!" his friend yelled. Jerry winced and moved the phone away from his ear. Torrance looked over, eyebrow raised. "My fiancée is missing, you blowhard. And I blame you!"

"I know you do." For once, Jerry was grateful for the rasp in his voice. It kept him from yelling back, which he really wanted to do, because Morris was right, it was his fault and he did blame himself. "And I promise you—*I promise you*—we will find her."

"Where are you right now?"

Torrance looked over again and shook his head. Jerry nodded. "We're heading for where we think she might be," he said.

"And what the hell's that supposed to mean?" Morris snapped, as Jerry knew he would. "Where are you, god-dammit?"

"We're heading north. We have a lead on—" Torrance's elbow drove into Jerry's ribs. The detective didn't want Morris knowing the details. "It's north. We'll be there shortly. We'll find her."

He could hear Morris heaving on the other end. "I don't understand this." From the uneven tone of his friend's voice, combined with all the huffing and puffing, Jerry knew that Morris was pacing. Probably wearing a path on his living room rug with his size-fourteen feet. "This cannot be happening. Not again. It's last year all over again."

"We don't know anything for a fact. She might not even be where we're going. For all we know, she's out shopping and her phone isn't charged. There's no reason to panic." Even as Jerry spoke, he knew the words were falling on deaf ears.

"What about Marianne?" Morris said, still huffing. "Maybe she knows where Sheila is."

"I left a voice mail. No answer." As Jerry said this, a small tingle went through him.

Morris apparently had the same tingle, because he said uncertainly, "Wait. I think they might have been to-gether today for a bit. Sheila said something about getting together with her . . ." His voice trailed off. Then, sound-ing even more uncertain, he said, "You don't think . . . ?"

"Nah," Jerry said aggressively, pushing away the sick feeling that was beginning to eat at his stomach. "Annie's fine, wherever she is."

"Call her boyfriend."

Ouch. "I don't have his number."

"Bullshit," Morris spat. "You're an ex-cop and a private investigator and your estranged wife is shacking up with some new guy. My ass you don't have the number. Call him."

Harsh, exceptionally harsh. Every word was a dagger through Jerry's heart, and he tried to remember that Morris's fiancée might be missing—for the second time in a year—and that her life might be at risk, also for the second time in a year. It wasn't that Morris didn't have a point, but man, it hurt like hell to hear him speak like this.

"I'll call him," Jerry said.

"Call me back."

Both men disconnected at the same time, not bothering to say goodbye. Jerry called information and asked for the number for George Jackson. Of course it was unlisted—the man was the losingest coach in the Northwest, and if his home phone number was made public, he'd probably get pranked all the time.

He then called an old friend from PD, who ran the name without asking questions. Jotting the number down in his notepad, Jerry swallowed his pride and called his wife's boyfriend. The man picked up on the second ring.

"Is this George Jackson?" Jerry asked.

"Yes, this is George." The man's voice was an enviable

baritone. Much like Jerry's voice used to be before his throat was slashed. "Who's calling?"

In the background Jerry could hear the sounds of an audience laughing. The television. Was Annie curled up beside him on the sofa, cuddling under a blanket? Or, God forbid, were they watching TV *in bed*?

He cleared his throat, wishing to God he could sound like his old self, if just for this one phone call. "This is Jerry Isaac."

"Jerry who—" A pause. "Jerry. Hey, man." Jackson's voice changed from pleasant to wary.

"You know who I am?"

"Of course."

"I'm sorry to call you out of the blue. May I speak with Marianne?"

"She's not here."

"Come on, man, tell her it's an emergency. I really need to speak with her."

"I believe you, but she's not here." Jackson paused again. "Is there something *I* can help you with?"

Jerry didn't know how to feel. Part of him was relieved as hell that Marianne wasn't lying naked next to this man, and the other part of him was suddenly terrified because now he officially didn't know where his wife was. "Any idea where she'd be?"

"You tried her at home? And on her cell?"

Jerry couldn't bring himself to answer such stupid questions.

His silence made the point he intended, and George Jackson sighed. "I don't know where she is, man. We're not seeing each other anymore."

Jerry sat up a little straighter. He could tell Torrance had overheard this last bit of conversation because his ex-partner's head seemed to be cocked a little closer than it had been a few seconds before. He really wished he wasn't talking about this with someone else in the car. "I'm sorry, I didn't realize that. When's the last time you saw her?"

"Listen, should I be concerned?"

"I could tell you that if you'd just answer my questions."

Another pause. "Couple days ago. As she was leaving my house."

An unnecessary jab. Through clenched teeth, Jerry said, "Did she happen to mention having any special plans this week?"

"No, nothing."

"Have you met her friend Sheila?"

"No, but I've heard a lot about her," Jackson said. "Why?"

"Any mention that she was going to see Sheila this week? This afternoon?"

"Uh . . . yes, as a matter of fact, I think she did mention that. She was going to suggest they start doing yoga again. I think she might have even mentioned that there was a class today. She was going to try and make Sheila go with her."

Jerry finally turned to Torrance, who met his gaze with an arched brow. "Do you know where?"

"There's a yoga studio not too far from her office. On Lenora and . . . Fifth, I think."

"Name?"

"I can't remember." Jackson sounded frustrated. "But we drove by it once. It's beside a little coffee shop and the sign for the studio is bright pink. You can't miss it."

"Thanks," Jerry said.

"Hey, man. Wait."

Jerry waited. He could almost hear the wheels turning in the man's head. The man who was no longer Annie's boyfriend, whom Jerry suddenly didn't dislike quite as much. "Yeah?"

"Listen, it feels funny asking you this, you being . . . *you,* and all—" Jackson cleared his throat, and Jerry took some comfort in the other man's obvious discomfort. At least he wasn't the only one feeling awkward. "But can you have her call me once you've gotten ahold of her? Or send me an email? You've got me worried."

"Sure, I can do that," Jerry said, and he meant it.

They disconnected. Immediately Jerry pulled up the Web browser on his phone and did a search for all the yoga studios in Seattle. There was one right at Lenora and Fifth, just like Jackson had said. He clicked on the website. The graphics were all done in bright pink. He called the number, and a moment later was speaking to a receptionist.

"My name is Jerry Isaac and I'm calling from the Seattle police. Can you tell me if a Marianne Chang or a Sheila Tao attended a class today? It's urgent."

"Hang on." The soft-voiced receptionist sounded all of sixteen. She was back a second later. "Sorry, my computer crashed a few minutes ago, and you know how older computers are, they just won't—"

"Miss, please, it's extremely urgent."

A short pause, and then her voice was a little crisper. "What did you say the names were again?"

Jerry spelled them both out.

"Yes, they were both here. They signed in for the four-fifteen class. Actually . . ." Jerry could hear her rifling through papers. "I remember Marianne. She came back after the class to let me know not to tow her car."

"I beg your pardon?"

"Her car," the receptionist said, sounding impatient. Noise in the background told Jerry the studio was busy. "She was having trouble with it, it wouldn't start. She asked me to make sure it wasn't towed. She was going to call triple-A but wasn't sure if they'd get to it before we closed. Hang on . . ." She put the phone down for a few seconds. "Yup, I just checked. Her car's still here. She said that she and a friend were being driven back to her office by some man and she'd call triple-A from there . . . Hey, if you talk to her, can you let her know that triple-A never showed up?"

"What man? Describe him."

"I didn't get too close a look but through the window I could see he was tall, dark-haired, good-looking. Really fit. Early thirties, maybe."

Jerry thanked her and hung up, feeling numb all over. After a moment he turned to Torrance. "She described someone who fits Mark Cavanaugh's description. Assuming that it's really him—and who else would it be?—it looks like they got into his car. Which means they have both Sheila and Annie." He choked as he said his wife's name. "God, Mike. They have my wife."

Torrance nodded, knowing that nothing he could

say at this moment would help. Keeping one hand on the steering wheel, he reached over and popped open the glove compartment, where his backup weapon was stored. Jerry took the Glock out and held it in his lap. Gripping it made him feel a little bit better, but not much. He didn't say thank you. He didn't need to.

The detective pressed his foot down harder on the gas and accelerated, and for once, Jerry was grateful that his former partner drove like a maniac.

CHAPTER: 36

The country house was in a small town called Concrete, population 842, according to the sign as they entered the town. It probably wasn't far off in terms of accuracy. There really was nothing to look at. Just a bunch of houses here and there.

Mark Cavanaugh's grandmother's home was at the south tip of Lake Shannon. A once-pretty house set on three acres, its days of glory were long past. Torrance pulled into the gravel driveway, and both men stepped out of the car, taking a moment to size up the house and their surroundings. The first thing that caught Jerry's eye was the shiny black Dodge Durango off to the side. Definitely Cavanaugh's ride, according to his DMV registration.

The property appeared to be abandoned. The grass was mixed with weeds as high as Jerry's shins and the house's exterior was peeling. A few of the shutters hung askew and a fading, warped wraparound porch framed dirty windows, some with cracks. Parked off to the side was an old blue Ford pickup, missing a bumper and a wheel. The house had apparently been in Cavanaugh's family for three generations, though it didn't look as if anyone had lived in it for years. Apparently Doris Wheaton, currently buried in the Heavenly Rest Cemetery, had been the last resident. She'd moved into a nursing home fifteen years earlier, and nobody had lived in it since. The town of Concrete was just too rural.

But behind the old house, Lake Shannon sparkled. The light from the full moon rippled off the waters, and there was a sense of calm and tranquillity. This could be a beautiful place if someone was willing to spend some money on repairs and maybe donate a little elbow grease.

Jerry took the steps up to the front entrance quickly and pounded on the door. No answer. Torrance followed suit, shouting, "Open up! Police!" but again, no answer.

With a grim look at Jerry, Torrance pulled out his gun and thrust his shoulder into the wood. The door opened with a cracking sound.

"I could live the whole rest of my life without ever having to break through a door again," Torrance said drily, rubbing his shoulder. "It's not like it is on TV. That shit hurts, pal."

Jerry heard him speaking but his brain didn't bother to interpret the words. He was too focused on looking for Annie. With Torrance's Glock in hand, he stepped inside the house and looked around, ears tuned for any possible sound.

There were no curtains on any of the windows and the electricity didn't work when Jerry flicked a few of the switches. The moonlight streaming in through the dirty windows was the only light inside, so he pulled out the pocket flashlight he always kept with him and switched it on. Torrance had his Maglite and the two of them proceeded to scope the house quietly.

They split up, Jerry taking the right side and Torrance the left, meeting back in the middle a moment later.

"Nothing?" Torrance asked quietly.

Jerry shook his head. Unless cobwebs counted.

They took the stairs, again splitting up, and again, neither man found anything. The house was sparsely furnished, the decor dated, and most of the closet doors were open, making it very quick to check.

"Maybe there's a shed out back or something," Torrance said.

Taking one last look around, Jerry nodded. The two exited the house and headed toward the backyard.

There was an old woodshed with windows and peeling paint, but it was stuffed so full of junk there was no way a person could be inside. Scoping the rest of the backyard with his frustratingly small flashlight, Jerry heard Torrance's voice.

"Found a root cellar!"

He sprinted over to where his ex-partner was, and in the ground there was, indeed, a root cellar. And the long grass surrounding it looked disturbed, as if someone had been there recently.

Oh God if she's inside please God let her be okay please God please. The thoughts, scattered and almost incoherent, traveled through Jerry's mind at the speed of lightning.

"It's padlocked," Torrance said. "We can break it, though. The warrant is for the entire premises."

"Do it."

"Watch yourself." Torrance aimed his gun and squeezed.

The heavy cellar door lifted an inch as the padlock blew off, then settled back down again. Jerry reached forward and pulled the door up and open, and stared at the long steps leading underground. It was pitch black.

"You want me to lead?" Torrance asked.

Jerry didn't bother to answer. He was through the doorway and down the stairs before Torrance could say anything else.

::::

The first thing that hit him was the damp smell.

The second thing that hit him was that with the door closed, there would be a total absence of light. He couldn't imagine Annie down here. The cellar would be cold and dark and terrifying.

Behind him, Torrance shone his flashlight over the walls and located a string hanging from the root cellar's ceiling. Torrance yanked on it and the room—surprisingly larger than Jerry expected—flooded with dim light from the bare bulb. There was obviously a generator somewhere, since the property didn't seem to have electricity.

The cellar was filled with crates, cobwebs, and boxes of something that smelled like it was rotting. Someone had also vomited recently, judging by the odor. Jerry flicked his small flashlight onto everything, but he wasn't being methodical enough about it—his light was haphazardly illuminating the space around him. He couldn't seem to slow himself down.

Torrance spotted the body first. "In the corner."

Those had to be the worst three words Jerry had ever heard, and his heart stopped. His legs suddenly felt like they weighed a thousand pounds and he couldn't seem to bring himself to move forward. He could see the body crumpled in the corner, away from the light. A pair of legs were visible from behind a stack of crates filled with canned vegetables.

"Is it—" He stopped, unable to finish the question.

Torrance moved forward quickly. He stepped around the crates, not wanting to disturb the scene. It was probably a good thing he was the one checking and not Jerry, who would have knocked the crates over in his quest to see who the body belonged to.

"It's not Annie," Torrance said, and Jerry felt his knees give out from the surge of relief that hit. They were the best three words he could have heard right now. "It's Mark Cavanaugh."

Jerry, legs now finally working, came up behind his ex-partner and shone his own little light down. Yes, it was indeed the former prison guard. Mark Cavanaugh, eyes wide open in surprise, was lying on his side. He looked ten times less handsome with his normally sharp features slack and pallid.

But then again, nobody looked good dead.

The CO was lying in a pool of something liquid, something that looked black until the light from the flashlight hit it, revealing it to be a deep, rich red. Blood, of course. Lots and lots of it, seeping from the deep gash at the man's throat, which might have mirrored Jerry's own a year earlier.

Normally Jerry would have been repulsed at the sight of that gaping wound, but his relief that the body wasn't Annie's outweighed any other feeling he might have had at this moment.

"She cut his throat." Torrance's voice was full of wonder. "Can you fucking believe that? Ballsy bitch. Guess she didn't love him after all."

"You should call it in."

Torrance nodded and stepped away. He pulled out his phone, but before dialing, he looked at Jerry and said, "I'm happy it's not Marianne. Or your friend, Sheila."

Jerry nodded, and Torrance called in the murder.

His former partner was back a moment later, his face even grimmer than before.

"What?" Jerry said.

"They got an ID on the body this morning, the one from the motel. The vic's sister filed a missing persons report. Guess who it is."

"I'm in no mood for guessing, Mike."

"Elizabeth Lee Cavanaugh."

Jerry froze. "Cavanaugh's married?"

"Well, obviously not anymore. When Elizabeth didn't show up to work today, the sister got worried, because apparently Cavanaugh's been on a bender and he's a mean drunk."

"So he killed his wife and covered it up, making it look like Jeremiah Blake did it?"

"That's my guess, yeah. Cavanaugh's got motive—he's in love with Maddox. And if he was drunk, it's likely he didn't even know Jack the Zipper had been arrested."

They spent the next few minutes looking around the cellar for clues. There was nothing to even indicate the women had been here, except . . .

A small object—very small, about the diameter of a quarter but much thicker—was caught in Jerry's flashlight beam. He stepped forward and squatted down, careful not to touch it. But as the realization of what the object was hit him, he felt his legs go out from under him again, and it was all he could do to keep his balance. He picked it up, staring at it with growing horror.

It was a tiny pot of Marianne's lip balm. The one she special-ordered from Paris, the one she was so fanatical about that she always had a pot in her purse, her car, and at home scattered throughout various rooms in the house. He'd know it anywhere. And he'd bet his left nut that Marianne had managed to leave it behind on purpose.

So that he'd know.

"They were here." He spoke quietly to Torrance, who sighed deeply from somewhere behind him. "Jesus Christ, Mike, they were *here*."

"I'm sorry, pal." Torrance's voice was heavy with regret.

Jerry heard him make another call, his former partner's gruff tone softening as he murmured information into the phone. He heard Marianne's name spoken, twice.

Jerry knew he needed to move, but again, his legs and arms wouldn't cooperate. He couldn't speak, couldn't think, couldn't breathe. He felt like a deer in the headlights, only there were no headlights, just this darkness around him, and the cold, dank smell of the cellar, and his absolute terror that his wife was in the hands of a serial killer.

Marianne's face was white as a sheet and she was having trouble breathing. Forget panic attack. Sheila was certain her friend was having a heart attack.

The two of them were tied up on the floor of an old van, Mark Cavanaugh's Durango having been left back at the house. Abby knew what she was doing—the van had obviously been prepared in advance.

Their legs were also bound with zip ties now, and it was impossible to move. They were covered with an old quilt that smelled like dirty gym socks, and while Sheila could breathe, the hot, stinky air made it difficult. Pressed up tight against Marianne, she could smell her friend's apple shampoo mixed with sweat, and the combined odors were stifling. Sheila tried to wiggle her body against Marianne so that she was flat on her back, which might make the air feel fresher. But with no usable limbs, changing positions even slightly was an impossible feat.

"Just pull over and let her out," she yelled again to Abby, but her muffled quilt-covered voice wasn't carrying well over the loud music.

Van Morrison's "Into the Mystic" was playing on the

radio, a song Sheila normally loved, though she knew she would never be able to listen to the song after this. Abby was singing along at the top of her lungs. Circumstances notwithstanding, her singing voice wasn't bad. Low and husky, a lot like her speaking voice.

"Abby!" Sheila shouted again through the thickness of the blanket. "Listen to me! Marianne is having a heart attack! She can't breathe! Pull over!"

Abby turned the music down and a short silence followed. Suddenly all Sheila could hear was her own breath peppered with Marianne's shallow breathing beside her.

"What's the problem back there?" Abby sounded annoyed.

"Pull over." Sheila spoke in her best authoritative voice, strong and crisp and even. "Marianne is having a heart attack, Abby. She is going to die."

"No, she's not." From the front seat, the younger woman's tone was dismissive. "She's in severe panic mode. It just feels like a heart attack. Don't worry, I've seen it happen a hundred times before." A snicker. "Okay, well maybe not a hundred times, but who's counting."

"You don't know that. She could be in real trouble." Sweat ran down Sheila's head in rivulets from the heat of the blanket and lack of air flow. Beside her, Marianne moaned.

"And so what if she is?" Abby's voice turned icy. "So fucking what, Sheila? What did you think was going to happen tonight? You think we're all going to the spa for mani-pedis? You think we dragged your asses up and out of that stinky root cellar and stuck you in the back of this shitmobile so we could all go joy-riding?"

Sheila sucked in a breath. So Abby really was going to kill them. It took her a moment to bring herself to speak. "What did you do to Mark Cavanaugh?"

A long silence.

Back in the root cellar, Abby had knocked them both out again by injecting them with yet another unknown substance. By the time she and Marianne had regained consciousness, they were in the back of this old van. Sheila had no idea how long they'd been driving. What she did know was that Cavanaugh had to have helped get them into the vehicle—no way was Abby strong enough to move them out of the cellar all by herself.

And yet, the prison guard was nowhere to be seen.

"Did you kill him?" Sheila asked.

Abby stayed silent. Sheila was going to assume her silence meant yes. And since she wasn't turning the radio back up, it was also safe to assume she was interested in hearing what Sheila had to say.

"I thought he was your friend," Sheila said.

Abby laughed. The sound was humorless, harsh, and brief. "Mark was an idiot, and a drunk. He almost fucked everything up for me. It was all going according to plan, but he got blitzed last night and killed his nagging bitch of a wife. And then he panicked and tried to make it look like it was Jack the Zipper who did it, not realizing they'd already caught the guy. It points the cops right to him, and by extension, *me*. I wasn't very happy about that. So yeah, I killed him, Sheila. Friends are so overrated."

"What about lovers?"

"Dime a dozen." Abby said this breezily, but Sheila could hear the edge beneath it.

"Especially now that you're free."

"Especially."

"But for how long?" They hit a bump in the road and something sharp on the floor of the van jabbed into Sheila's side. She tried to worm away from it. "How long until they find you? By now there's a massive manhunt. Why not just do your time? Your sentence wasn't that long. You might have been out in three years with good behavior."

"Or I would have had to do the entire eight," Abby said, and Sheila could tell her teeth were clenched. "And anyway, what are three years of your life worth to you, Sheila? Life is fleeting. I know that better than most. One day we're here, the next day we're snuffed out like birthday candles. I could fall down the stairs at Creekside, break my neck. Or one of those lowlife women could stab me in my sleep. Is that how I want to go? Every minute we live is a minute we're closer to death. Three more years in prison?" Another humorless laugh. "Might as well have been a life sentence."

"But, still, you—"

"Don't worry your pretty little head about it, okay? What happens to me is not your concern."

"Can you at least tell me where we're going?"

Abby turned up the radio. They were done talking for now.

::::

The drive was long and bumpy, and it wasn't long before Sheila's back was aching from whatever sharp object was digging into her. She was nauseated from breathing re-cycled hot air over and over again. Beside her in the dark, Marianne's raspy breathing had turned even more shallow. It didn't sound good. In fact, it was beginning to slow down. And her friend had stopped responding. She wasn't even moaning anymore.

Sheila screamed as loud as she could.

The van slowed down and Sheila felt them move from a smooth, paved road over to a gravel shoulder. They came to a full stop. The music shut off.

She heard Abby get out of the van, slamming the door behind her. The crunch of footsteps, again on gravel. A second later, the back door flew open and the blanket was ripped off Sheila's face. The cool night air felt glorious, and Sheila inhaled deeply while she could.

"Seriously, what the *fuck* is wrong with you?" Abby said, standing over them, her beautiful face the picture of exasperation.

Now that the van's back door was open, Sheila could see there were no other lights around them. No passing cars, no streetlamps, no lights from houses, nothing. In the silence, she heard the faint chirping of crickets. They were in the middle of nowhere.

"Marianne isn't doing well." Sheila did her best to sound stern.

"And I care about this why?"

"She's not part of this. She's sick. You need to let her go."

Abby took a seat on the back edge of the van's floor, sitting so that her legs were stretched out onto the road's shoulder. She used one hand to massage the side of her neck. "She's Jerry's wife," she said dismissively. "And I have a bone to pick with Jerry. He is, after all, the reason I got thrown in jail in the first place."

"You slit his throat."

"He left me no choice." Abby's voice was getting loud.

"Abby, please." Sheila softened her tone. "Please. Marianne hasn't done anything to you. She's not even with Jerry anymore. They split up. There's no reason to keep her here."

"Not like you, right?" Abby's eyes bored into Sheila's face. "Not like you, who got Ethan killed?"

Sheila closed her eyes briefly, thinking rapidly. "Let's just drop Marianne off at a hospital. Or at least somewhere where someone can find her and call nine-one-one. If you do that for her, I promise I will be quiet, I will stop yelling, and I will go wherever you want me to go. But just help her. Please."

"Aw." Abby cocked her head, her blue-violet eyes filled with icy amusement. "You guys are BFFs. I don't think I realized that till just now. How fucking adorable." She leaned into the van so that her face was directly in front of Sheila's. The blond hairs from her wig tickled Sheila's face. "First, let's be clear about something. You're coming with me whether you want to or not. This is not a negotiation."

"Yes, but—"

"I'm still talking." Abby's eyes searched Sheila's face. "You seem to like this chick, God knows why. She's been nothing but a whiny, crying little bitch since we met. Not like you, who's been through this before and has stayed pretty calm, I'll give you that. But clearly you're worried about your friend and she's distracting you, and we can't have that, can we? So here's an idea. How about I leave her *here*?" Abby gestured at the emptiness around them. "We're out in the middle of nowhere, in between two bum-fuck towns I can't even remember the names of. She can stay here, and maybe someone will find her. I'll do that for you, since you asked so nicely."

"She won't make it," Sheila said, desperate. "She's going to stop breathing soon, Abby. She won't be found in time. She needs a hospital."

"All right then. You've made your choice." Abby pulled something long and black out of the inside of her jacket. It looked like a skinny leather case, and Sheila stared at it in confusion, unable to make sense of exactly what it was. It wasn't until Abby pulled out something else from *inside* the case that Sheila finally recognized it.

It was fierce, like something out of a movie. Long, slim, supersharp. The blade was perfectly smooth and it gleamed in the dim light of the van. Abby held it up, caressing it with her finger.

Before Sheila could react, Abby reached forward and stabbed Marianne in the stomach. The motion was quicker and more violent than Sheila had ever imagined it could be. Blood spilled out, some of it landing on Sheila's hands and torso, and it was horrifically warm. The copper tang of it immediately filled the air.

"There." Abby wiped her knife on a patch of the van's carpet before sliding it smoothly back into its case. "Now it's no longer an issue. Now she'll die and you'll have nothing to worry about, and we can move forward. No more screaming or whining or begging, just like you promised."

Sheila cried silently, hot tears flowing down her temples. She opened her mouth to shriek, but nothing came out. Nothing at all, like in one of those nightmares. The van was a vacuum, sucking the air out of everything.

Abby leaned forward, directly into Sheila's line of sight. "Are you getting it now, Sheila? I'm not Ethan. I don't hesitate, and I don't fuck around. You feeling me now?"

Beside her, Sheila could feel her friend's body going slack. Abby moved away and reached to close the back door. With all her might, Sheila planted her feet on Marianne's thighs and kicked out. Marianne rolled out of the van and landed on the gravel shoulder with a sickening thud.

"Dumping the body already?" Abby smiled. "You don't like getting blood on you? I personally don't mind it, but of course I understand. Shall we just leave her on the road, then?"

Abby slammed the rear door shut and locked it. A few seconds later she had maneuvered the van off the shoulder and back onto the road. Sheila could hear her humming as she drove.

The air finally came back. Sheila screamed.

Unfazed, Abby turned the music up. A few seconds later, Sheila could hear the younger woman singing again. It was another song Sheila liked, and one she'd no longer be listening to. Assuming, of course, that she somehow survived this, which she no longer believed she would.

The song was an old eighties tune that Sheila had chair-danced to many times while listening to Internet radio in her office.

"Psycho Killer" by the Talking Heads.

As if Abby needed a soundtrack.

CHAPTER: 38

"There's no way to know where they'd be," Jerry said to Morris on the phone. "The house we thought they'd be in was a dead end."

"You sonofabitch," Morris spat in his ear. "This whole thing is your goddamned fault. I hold you personally responsible—"

"I know you do, and so do I," Jerry said quietly. "And I'm paying for it, okay? So is Annie."

Morris stopped huffing and puffing long enough to say, "What?"

"Annie's gone, too." Jerry couldn't keep the misery out of his voice. "Maddox has her, too."

Long silence. Then finally Morris said, "As angry as I might be with you right now—and trust me, I'd kick the shit out of you if I could—I wouldn't wish this on anybody. I'm sorry."

"Thank you."

"Find them." Morris ended the call.

In the dark car, Jerry turned to Torrance, who was once again driving. They were heading back to Seattle PD, having been called in by the chief of detectives herself. Jerry already knew what was going to happen—they were going to strip him of his temporary consultant's ID. They were going to pull him away from all this.

Jerry didn't know how to feel about it. On the one hand, it was his wife, his Annie, who was somewhere out there, and nobody wanted her found more than he did. But on the other hand, he knew he was too close to the situation. His hysteria would not make for good police work.

"You know I'll keep you posted about everything. You'll hear it from me, I promise," Torrance said, as if reading Jerry's thoughts.

A helicopter buzzed overhead, its huge searchlights scanning the fields around them. It was one of theirs, looking for Abby. They didn't think she'd be on foot, and there was clear indication at Cavanaugh's family house that another vehicle had been there recently. The tire tracks were fresh.

"We'll find them," Torrance said as the lights of the helicopter faded into the dark.

"I'm sure we will." Jerry's voice was tight. "But the important question is, will we find them before she kills them? She won't hesitate to do it, Mike. I know this bitch, remember. She'll just do it, she won't pause to think it over, she'll just fucking do it. That's what I'm scared of." *Ha. Scared* was such a small word to describe what he was feeling right now.

"We'll find them," Torrance said again. "Also, maybe you should warn Danny."

"Why?"

"Maddox liked her, didn't she? You'd better make sure she doesn't pay your girl a visit."

Jerry hadn't even thought about the potential danger to Danny with Maddox out of prison, and he mentally slapped himself. Reaching for his phone, he pressed five on his speed dial to call Danny's iPhone. It rang three times before his assistant picked up.

"Hey," he said, trying not to sound tense. He didn't want her freaking out. "Just checking in."

"Everything okay at work?" She sounded breathless, as if she'd run for the phone. "I was surprised to see your number. Are the computers okay? I left a sticky with all the passwords on your—"

"Listen, Abby Maddox has escaped from prison."

A long silence on the other end. Finally Danny said, "That's funny. I could have sworn you just said that Abby Maddox escaped from prison."

"I did. Because she did."

"Holy shit!"

Jerry couldn't tell whether it was fear or amazement in Danny's voice, but he suspected it was a lot of both. "Where are you right now?"

"I'm at home—"

"Alone?"

"No, I've got a study group here."

"Stay home, okay?" Jerry said. "And make sure your friends stay with you. At least until we find out where the hell she is."

"Jerry. You don't think . . ."

"I don't think you're in any danger." Jerry's attempt to sound reassuring was pathetic and he knew it, but he had to try. "Maddox has no reason to come looking for you. You were friends, yes?"

Danny hedged. "Well, I wouldn't go that far. She seemed to think I was okay."

"Just watch your back, is all I'm saying." He kept his voice neutral. "I just wanted to let you know the situation. If, by some small chance, you do hear from her, call the police immediately. Go grab a baseball bat. And then call me. You got that?" He didn't say anything to her about Annie or Sheila being snatched. What was the point? It would only scare her, and there was nothing she could do about it, anyway.

"Yes," Danny said.

"Repeat it back to me."

"Nine-one-one, baseball bat, call you."

"Good girl."

"Hey, Jerry," Danny said. Her voice was shaky now. She sounded spooked. "Be careful, okay? Abby Maddox . . . she's not one to fuck with, dude."

"Preaching to the choir, dude," Jerry said, and disconnected.

CHAPTER 39

The van finally stopped.

A moment later, Abby's face loomed over her in the back of the Jeep. White, ethereal, angelic. Angel Face, the media sometimes called her. Ha, right. More like the Angel of Death. There was a syringe in her hand.

"I'm moving you, so I'm going to knock you out." Abby said. She plunged the needle into the side of Sheila's neck before she could protest.

By the time Sheila registered the sting, she was out.

::::

She woke up strapped to a gurney. Wait, no, it wasn't a gurney, it was a portable massage therapy table. There was a doughnut-like cushion underneath the back of her head. And she was freezing because she was completely naked. Abby had stripped her down.

The smell hit her next. Blood, urine, and body odor, all melding together like a disgusting stew. It took her a moment to realize that the smell was emanating from herself, because she'd wet herself. She looked down and saw bloodstains on her chest and legs that had obviously seeped through her clothing. Marianne's blood. She screamed.

"Enough enough enough," said Abby's voice from somewhere behind her. "It's so annoying, you must realize that. You're going to give us both a headache."

Sheila craned her neck to see where Abby was, and finally spotted her. She was approaching the table with a small smile.

"Don't say it," Abby said.

"Say what?" Sheila's voice was raspy.

"You know, the typical cliché question all victims ask when they wake up somewhere strange, otherwise known as, 'Where am I?'" Abby sighed. "God, I hate that question."

"It's a cliché because most people want to know." Sheila squirmed but the straps wouldn't give.

Abby leaned toward her. "Does it really matter?" Her breath was soft and sweet on Sheila's face.

If I can figure out a way to get out of here, it will definitely matter, Sheila thought. "Yes, it matters to me."

"Well, guess what?" Abby's voice turned flat as she stepped back. "What matters to you doesn't matter to me. Because I'm not Ethan, you useless cunt. I'm not keeping you alive. I'm not torn by my feelings for you. I'm not *confused.* So let's be very clear, shall we? I hate you. I've always hated you, and you're in the place where you're going to die a very painful death."

Abby's face loomed over her once again. Sheila twisted violently as the younger woman moved closer. Then she let out another curdling scream.

Abby winced. "Wow. Quite the lungs you've got on you. Really, Sheila, the screaming is so irritating. Do I need to stick something in your mouth, or are you going to stay quiet?"

"I'm sorry," Sheila gasped, her back aching from the strain of pushing against the straps. They were made of canvas and very strong. "I can't help it."

"There is no terror in the bang, only in the anticipation of it." Abby smiled. "That's Hitchcock, in case you didn't know. One of my favorite quotes of all time. The waiting's the worst part, isn't it?"

Sheila disagreed. She was certain that the pain, when it came, would be worse than anything.

The lights in the room were so bright that when she looked up, Sheila's vision became blurry. It was difficult to tell what kind of room she was in. She couldn't detect any strange smells over her own awful odor. And it was cold, colder than the cellar had been earlier. There was no breeze, no dampness, no noises other than her own rapid breathing.

"I can tell you're still trying to figure it out." Abby had something in her hand, and it glinted whenever she moved it. It was the knife, the one she'd used to stab Marianne. No, wait, it was a different knife. This one was much worse. A surgeon's blade. "But really, don't worry about it. It's a place that has no significance for you what-soever. Other than the fact that you'll die here, that is."

Sheila believed her.

"Hey, look at your nipples. You must be freezing. They're like pebbles." Abby flicked one of them with her finger, and Sheila bit down to keep from screaming again. "Wow, so sensitive. Good to know."

"Abby, please." Sheila was breathing hard.

The younger woman disappeared for a moment, and then Sheila heard a click and a hum.

"There," Abby said. "I plugged in the space heater. Give it a few minutes; this place really is drafty. That ought to give you a hint that we're not in Ethan's house. Like I would actually try and re-create that. Although," she said, cocking her head, "that might have been interesting if I'd had more time. But unfortunately some kids set fire to his place a few months ago, and it burned to the ground. The lot's just sitting there now, sad and empty."

"I hadn't heard."

"That's because you're so fucking narcissistic." Abby examined the knife in her hand. Sheila couldn't take her eyes off it, either. "Anybody ever tell you that, Sheila? It's all me-me-me with you sex addicts. Anyway, I'm sure the neighbors would all move away if they thought they could, since for a time it was pretty much a graveyard. Now nobody's going to want to buy in that neighborhood. Especially not in this market." She sighed pleasantly. "Now I'm kind of wishing the house was still there. It might have provided an interesting sense of closure."

Abby held up the blade, took a good look at it, frowned, and wiped the side of it on her shirt. Then she pressed it to the side of Sheila's right breast, and slid it in. Sheila gasped. It couldn't have penetrated more than a few millimeters, and the knife was so sharp that it didn't really hurt that much, but the thought that the steel was inside her—*inside her!*—was horrifying. Her whole body turned rigid. She dared not move, for fear the knife would slide deeper.

And then it did. Abby pushed the knife in a little farther, and a white-hot pain seared through Sheila's breast. She cried out and the lights above went hazy. Sweat poured off her forehead, and yet she was shivering. She couldn't remember ever having been this cold.

"Please, Abby. Please, stop."

Abby leaned forward again, her face inches away from Sheila's own. "As much as I'd like to play games with you right now, Sheila, I'm not going to. So I'm going to tell you right now that you *are* going to die tonight. It's not going to be quick. You are going to suffer. It is going to hurt like nothing you've ever experienced before, and yes, I am going to thoroughly enjoy it. All the begging in the world won't change my mind." She smiled and withdrew the blade, examining the tip, which was now red with Sheila's blood. "Actually, begging turns me on, I should tell you that. The more you beg, the more excited I get, and the more inclined I am to draw it out. Your choice."

"You are a psychopath."

"Yes I am!" Abby said cheerfully. "Unlike Ethan, I've never had a problem with labels."

Quickly and without warning, she inserted the blade into Sheila's other breast, and the pain, once again, was searing. Sheila bit her lip, trying desperately not to cry out, and a low, agonized moan escaped her lips. Abby pulled the knife out again. The exit of the knife was almost as painful as the entry. Sheila cried silently, tears streaming down her temples, but she dared not do more than whimper.

"I'm always so interested in the sounds people make." Once again, Abby examined the blade that had been inside Sheila's body just seconds before. She seemed fascinated with blood. "I could write a book on just the sounds alone."

"Why don't you just kill me." Sheila's voice was dull. She felt like she was floating in a sea of pain. The pain wasn't constant; it ebbed and flowed, giving her no chance to try to adjust to it. There was no way she could take another hour of this, let alone another minute. "Please, Abby. Just kill me."

"Now what fun would that be?"

"You don't want to get caught, do you?" Sheila said, her eyes closing. The throbbing in her left breast now matched the pain in her right. "You want to escape, don't you? Start over somewhere else?"

"Stupid question." Abby shook her head in mock disapproval. She disappeared for a moment, and came back with a bigger knife. Christ, did she have a whole surgeon's arsenal? "Of course I don't want to get caught. My mistake was fucking around with you in the first place. By sending you those postcards. Remember when you were in rehab? I thought I could torment you from afar."

"You did. I didn't sleep for weeks after you sent them. I didn't sleep until they arrested you."

"Really?" Abby looked delighted. "That's outstanding. How sweet of you to let me know," she said with an exaggerated smile, her eyebrows arched.

Sheila kept her eyes closed, willing herself to go away. To be anywhere else but here, wherever this place was. She was probably going to die without ever finding out. A thought hit her then. Abby could not have found this place by herself while she was behind bars. And with Mark Cavanaugh dead . . .

"Who's helping you?" she asked suddenly.

"Hmmm?" Abby's voice floated over her from a few feet away. She'd obviously changed her mind about the larger knife and was back at the spot where she kept her tools. Sheila could hear her picking through a stack of what sounded like very sharp knives, not that Sheila could see them. How helpful that her imagination seemed perfectly willing to fill in whatever blanks she couldn't visually confirm.

"Where are we?" Sheila tried again.

"Someplace no one will find you," Abby said. "Someplace you can scream all you want, though I really hope you don't; my ears can't take it." She continued to tinker with her knives. "This really is the perfect place, and if the person I'm expecting ever shows up, I'll be able to express my gratitude. Have I ever mentioned how much I hate tardiness? It's disrespectful and I know you hate it, too, Sheila. Ethan mentioned once how important punctuality is to you, and on that, we can agree."

There was a banging sound, a door slamming shut.

"You're late," Abby said to whoever had just entered the room. Her voice was icy, and Sheila prayed that Abby wouldn't take out her annoyance on her. "I told you on the phone to be here before she woke up."

"After everything I've done for you, *that's* what's bugging you?" a voice said, and Sheila froze. She knew that voice. That voice was eerily familiar. Whose was it? "Well, then, I'm sorry, I guess."

"You guess." Abby's tone was condescending. "You sound like a petulant child."

"Maybe because you're treating me like one," the

other voice said. Definitely female. "And for the record, you sound like a nagging bitch."

Are you crazy? Sheila thought. *Don't say that! You'll just piss her off!*

A small silence followed, and then a giggle. And then a sigh. And then another giggle. Was Abby actually laughing? The unmistakable sounds of kissing followed, then a slight grunt, and then a groan. Whoever this new person was, Abby wasn't mad at her. Not even close. They were kissing like long-lost lovers.

Jesus Christ, who are you?

Abby stepped forward into Sheila's very limited line of sight. "I don't believe an introduction is necessary. You two have met before."

Sheila tried to focus on the figure next to Abby's, but the lights were too bright. Squinting, she said, "Who's there?"

"Hey there, Dr. Tao. It's me," the female voice said brightly. The woman leaned over and Sheila got a good look at her face. Caramel ponytail, hazel eyes, sweet smile. "It's Danny Mercy. I had a class with you a couple years back? And I'm also Jerry's assistant."

Abby laughed, and the sound was delight, ice, and evil, all rolled into one. "Not anymore."

CHAPTER: 40

Sheila didn't know what they had injected her with this time but it wasn't the same stuff as before. Abby seemed to have a whole box truck's worth of knives and drugs at her disposal. The first two injections—some kind of animal tranquilizer, Sheila thought—had knocked her out completely.

This injection was not nearly as merciful.

She could breathe easily and could feel her chest moving up and down. She could feel the sweat dripping down her neck and shoulders, and she could hear the hum of the space heater from somewhere in the room. She could feel the table beneath her.

And yet, she couldn't move any part of her body other than her head. She was paralyzed from the shoulders down. Who would invent a drug like this?

She could hear them cooing to each other, off in a corner away from her line of vision.

"How long have you two been together?" Sheila managed to ask. The cooing stopped. Footsteps approached.

"Not long," Danny answered, standing directly above Sheila. "But when you know, you know."

Abby laughed from somewhere in the room.

"You planned this?" Sheila asked. *Oh God, Jerry. Oh God. Your assistant may have helped kill your wife . . .*

"Been planning this for a while." Danny smiled. "I've been in love with Abby ever since I was your student, Dr. Tao, not that Abby knew I existed back then. We met briefly when Ethan was my TA. Ever since, I've followed every bit of news—"

"She started a fan site about me," Abby interrupted, coming closer and sounding giddy. "FreeAbbyMaddox .com. She told me about it when we met at Rosedale a few months ago. I knew she was the one from that point on."

"A few months?" Sheila said in disbelief. "I thought you just met. When you accompanied Jerry to the prison."

"Oh no, we met long before that. I used to volunteer at Rosedale." The affection in Danny's voice was unmistakable. "Best time of my life."

The women exchanged a loving glance over Sheila's naked and paralyzed body.

"You're bisexual?" Sheila said to Abby, not that it mattered. She was trying to keep both of them talking and couldn't think of anything else to say. "Since when?"

"Oh, who gives a shit." Abby's brows furrowed together. "You love who you love. I love this girl. I wouldn't be here if it wasn't for her, and that's all that matters."

"I don't know about her, but *I'm* gay," Danny said matter-of-factly. Her hands were empty. Unlike Abby, she wasn't holding any knives or weapons. "I knew when I was about twelve or so that boys didn't do it for me."

"Boys still do it for me." Abby winked.

"Yeah, we'll discuss that later." Danny raised an eyebrow in mock consternation. "One night with me, bet you change your mind about that."

"I've been with girls. Always with Ethan present, of course," Abby said, addressing Sheila. "He was big into threesomes. And foursomes. And I never minded it, really. But she and I"—she glanced at Danny with a loving smile—"we haven't been together yet. In fact, we've only just kissed for the first time today."

"And I want to do a lot more than kiss," Danny said.

"There's plenty of time for that." Abby licked her lips. "We have things to finish here first."

They smiled at each other again.

"What now?" Sheila asked, her throat dry.

Abby looked down at her. She wasn't wearing her blond wig anymore and her ebony hair trailed in waves over her shoulders. Her eyes fixed on Sheila's breasts, then moved slowly down the rest of her body.

"You're still in pretty good shape for your age," Abby said, the hunger in her voice unmistakable. "You're what, forty-two?"

"Forty," Sheila whispered.

"Yeah, you look good." Abby looked across the table at Danny. "Don't you think?"

Danny shrugged. "Yeah. She's hot. But we knew that."

"Should we fuck her first?"

"There's no time." Annoyance was spreading over Danny's pretty features.

Abby smiled at Sheila. "There's always time for what's important," she said. To Danny she held out two knives. One was long and thin, the other short and fat. "Choose your weapon, darling. I'll let you go first."

CHAPTER: 41

Jerry's phone was buzzing incessantly in his pocket, but he didn't bother to check it. He already knew who it was. He had nothing new to tell Morris, and he didn't want to be yelled at right before going into this meeting. He exited the elevator on the fourth floor of Seattle PD's East Precinct, his temporary police ID clipped to his belt.

"How long has she been here?" he asked the officer who'd been escorting him.

"They picked her up an hour ago."

Jerry followed him to Interview Room 2, the smallest of the interrogation rooms, which housed only a table and two small chairs. There were no windows, just a camera mounted in the corner of the ceiling. He'd thought he was being called in because they were going to yank his police privileges, but it turned out they wanted him in to do interviews. It was better than nothing. At least he wasn't being pulled off the case. Torrance had promised him regular updates.

Corrections Officer E. Briscoe—the *E* stood for Elaine, Jerry had discovered—was waiting for him. The blond woman sat ramrod straight at the table with an unopened can of Diet Coke in front of her. She was still wearing her uniform.

"You heard that Maddox is out," Jerry said, not bothering with formalities. He took a seat across from Briscoe and the door closed behind him. "What can you tell me?"

She shook her head. "Why would I know anything about it? She transferred out of Rosedale a month ago. She's someone else's fuckup."

Jerry inched his chair a little closer. "Do I look stupid to you?"

"Do you really want me to answer that?" Briscoe said. Steely blue eyes challenged Jerry from across the table. Of course, she was a prison guard. She spent all day around inmates who no doubt gave her plenty of shit, and Jerry was probably small-time to her. She didn't seem the least bit intimidated. "I don't have to talk to you. You guys asked me to come in, so I did, but I can leave anytime. I know my rights."

"I know you were involved with Abby Maddox."

Briscoe blinked. "I beg your pardon?"

Jerry sighed. "I really, really don't have time for this, Sergeant. We found Mark Cavanaugh's cell phone."

"Mark?" Briscoe's confusion was genuine. "What are you talking about? Why would I care about that?"

"Because he's dead. Maddox killed him."

The color drained from the CO's face and she leaned back in her chair, her pin-straight posture suddenly going slack.

"And so of course we checked his phone," Jerry said. "He's received a lot of calls and texts from Abby Maddox. Luckily for us, the guy didn't delete anything."

Briscoe, despite her pallor, did not seem surprised. "And this has what to do with me?"

"Well, it made us realize that Maddox has had a phone the entire time she was at Rosedale."

"I didn't—"

Jerry lifted a hand. "I didn't say it was you who gave it to her. Nobody's saying that." According to Superintendent Alicia Elkes, any corrections officer found providing inmates with contraband was subject to immediate dismissal. No, Jerry didn't plan to get Briscoe fired for the phone—Mark Cavanaugh had likely given it to Abby. He planned to get Briscoe fired for something else. "But it led us to call Rosedale. And have Maddox's old cell searched. And guess what we found?"

Briscoe said nothing, but her eyes were wide.

"We found her smartphone. Her cellmate—Celia, is it?—denied that it was hers, of course. Insisted it belonged to Maddox." Jerry leaned forward. "Of course the phone was wiped clean. But that doesn't matter, does it? Because we have the phone number for it. And if I were to get paid a dollar for every time her number showed up in *your* cell phone records, how rich do you think I would be, Sergeant?"

Again, Briscoe said nothing, but her face turned even paler, and her hands started to shake.

"I'm guessing pretty rich." Jerry pulled out his phone. "Should I work on getting a subpoena for those records?"

Briscoe's eyes spilled over with tears. "I'm going to lose my job."

Jerry slammed his hand down on the table, and Briscoe jumped. "My dear, that is the very *least* of your concerns." He allowed this to soak in for a moment. Pulling a crumpled tissue out of his pocket, he handed it to the corrections officer, whose eyes and nose were running. "So tell me. What do you know about Maddox's escape from Creekside?"

"Nothing, I swear." Briscoe blew her nose with trembling hands. Jerry handed her another tissue. "I didn't know about any of that."

"But you knew she escaped earlier today."

"Of course. Anybody working in the Department of Corrections would have heard about it."

"So you're telling me," Jerry said, cracking his knuckles, "that you were involved with Maddox the entire time she was at Rosedale, and yet she never said a word about her plans to escape from the next prison? I find that hard to believe, Sergeant."

"We weren't involved the entire time, not even close. It was only a few months. She started pulling away when I wouldn't give her what she wanted. Abby, she . . ." Briscoe shook her head as if she were trying to make sense of it herself. "You don't know her. She's very manipulative."

"Actually, I do know," Jerry said. "But enlighten me anyway."

"We were involved for about four months." Briscoe's tears started flowing again. "Four very intense months. About three months into it, she asked me to get her a phone. I refused. I made a lot of other things happen for her, made sure she had lots of privileges, but the phone . . . I just couldn't bring myself to do that. Way too risky. Eventually she found another way to get one, but once she had it . . . yeah, we did communicate a lot that way. It was just too easy."

This time it was Jerry's turn to wait.

"I didn't realize she was involved with Officer Cavanaugh the entire time we were together." Briscoe rubbed her face, looking dejected. "When I found out, I was furious. But she swore she loved *me*. She said with me it was real. She said she was just using Mark for the phone."

"You're the one who got Officer Cavanaugh fired."

"Yes, but not because of the phone. He is—was—a drunk. I couldn't trust him to do his job."

"Did Cavanaugh know about your own involvement with Maddox?"

"I don't know. She said she didn't tell him, but it wouldn't have mattered anyway if he'd known, he wouldn't have ratted me out for that. Because it would have gotten her in trouble, too."

It was dizzying, the amount of people Maddox had been able to manipulate from a prison cell. Mark Cavanaugh, Jeremiah Blake, Elaine Briscoe, Sheila Tao . . .

"Have you been in contact with Maddox since she was transferred out?" Jerry asked.

"No." The hurt look on Briscoe's face told Jerry she was telling the truth. "Once she got to Creekside, she was supposed to find a way to get in touch with me. She hasn't."

"Be glad she hasn't," Jerry said. "Cavanaugh's throat was slit. That could have been you."

Briscoe lost it. Putting her face in her hands, she sobbed.

Women crying always made Jerry feel like shit. He stood up and headed for the door.

"Hey," Briscoe said weakly, her voice cracking through her tears. "When you find her . . ."

"Yeah?"

The corrections officer lifted her head. "Tell her Elaine says hi."

::::

Bob Borden was a much tougher interview. The defense attorney's office was only five minutes from the precinct and it took no time at all to bring him in. Jerry hadn't even finished his coffee.

"If you're not going to charge me—" Borden began, but Jerry cut him off.

"I don't have to charge you with anything to hold you for twenty-four hours."

"Fine. But I don't have to say anything, either."

"Mr. Borden." Jerry paced the room. He couldn't sit still for this one. "Your client, Abby Maddox, has escaped from prison. I know you were in contact with her regularly. It would be the easiest thing in the world to charge you as an accessory in her escape."

"Because I'm her lawyer?" Borden gave a short laugh that sounded like a bark. "You can't prove what I knew. Which, for the record, was nothing."

"Because she had an illegal cell phone."

Borden blinked, but regained his composure quickly. "I don't know anything about that."

"So if we subpoena your phone records—home, office, and cell—Maddox's number won't show up?"

"I knew nothing about her having a cell phone. And even if those records show she called me from a cell phone, you can't prove *I* knew it was a cell phone."

Fucking lawyers. Jerry gritted his teeth. They never seemed to care about true guilt or innocence—it was all about what they could *prove*. "I can prove it if you exchanged text messages with her," Jerry said. "You can't send texts from a prison pay phone."

Borden's face reddened.

"Look," Jerry said. "I don't give a shit about the cell phone, okay? What I need to know is who else she was in contact with on the outside."

"I can't tell you anything. Confidentiality."

"Okay then. I'll get that subpoena going. Exchanging texts with your client while she's behind bars won't put you in jail, but I'm sure it won't make for good publicity. And what will your wife say? Divorces are so expensive. Nice chatting with you."

He was at the door with his hand on the knob when Borden said, "Wait."

Jerry turned. "I don't have time for games and legalese, Mr. Borden."

"Turn off the camera," the man said, looking up at the small camera mounted to the ceiling.

Jerry hesitated, then looked up at the camera and nodded. A second later, the flashing red light turned off.

"This is off the record, or I get disbarred." Borden gripped the table with both hands. His knuckles were white. "And if I do, then I sue you for harassment. You, personally, along with the police department. You understand? I should absolutely not be telling you this, and if you say I did, I will deny it and I will sue your ass. It completely violates the rules of confidentiality."

"I understand."

"Abby didn't have many friends that I knew of." Borden spoke slowly, as if he were weighing his options. Which he probably was. "A lot of fans, maybe, but not many friends."

"She didn't mention anybody who might help her? Because she couldn't have done this by herself."

"There was only one person she ever talked about with me, and it was only once," Borden said. "Someone named Danny. Danny Mercy."

Jerry's throat went dry and he stopped pacing. "What about Danny Mercy?"

"Abby wanted the funds she was paid from *The Pulse* moved from her bank account to Danny's account, and she asked me to handle the paperwork. Naturally, I was concerned, and I asked her what the nature of their relationship was. She made it clear that they were . . . involved. Romantically." The attorney's face was pained, and Jerry realized then that the man was jealous. "She said she trusted Danny with all her heart. So I did as she asked. I can only assume that this Danny is her boyfriend."

Jerry let out a puff of air, feeling the onset of another headache.

Not boyfriend. Goddammit.

Girlfriend.

CHAPTER: 42

He didn't have Danny's home number, because as far as he knew, she didn't have a landline. All he had was Danny's cell phone number, and she wasn't picking up.

Jerry had called Torrance from the precinct and the plan was to meet the detective at Danny's loft. As he drove, his mind raced. He knew what Borden had told him, but could Danny really be involved in all this? She was a nice kid, a smart kid . . . but then again, what did Jerry really know about his assistant? He had done a quick criminal background check when he'd hired her last year, and nothing had flagged—she'd never been arrested. Her parents had died when she was young and she'd grown up with her grandfather. The man had passed away two years before, leaving her a sizable inheritance, which paid for school. She was in a rock band. She was good with computers.

Beyond that, he knew nothing about her. Because he never thought it would matter.

His phone rang, and he jumped. It was Torrance. "What's up?"

"The techies finally found out where the FreeAbby-

Maddox site was registered," Torrance said. "It was set up here, in Seattle. The exact address is on Collard Road."

"Which is where we're headed, because Danny lives on Collard Road." Jerry's voice was so dry he could barely speak. "You're telling me she's been the creator of that sick fan site all along? Why?"

"I don't know, pal." Torrance's voice was heavy. "I can only think she did it to call out the crazies, so she could recruit someone like Jeremiah Blake to do her dirty work."

Jerry tried to process his former partner's words, but it was really too horrible to contemplate.

"I just ran a detailed background check," Torrance continued, "and a large sum of money was deposited into her account about a week ago from Bob Borden. Fifty thousand. Her bank account has since been cleaned out, sent to an offshore account. Did you know your girl had over three hundred thousand dollars?"

Jerry said nothing, narrowly missing a student on a bicycle who'd pulled out into the street without looking. He honked. The kid gave him the finger. "I don't know why anything should surprise me anymore."

"Guess this has all been planned for a while," Torrance said. "Sorry, pal. I liked her. I always thought she was a great kid."

Jerry had thought so, too. He stepped on the gas.

"I'm ten minutes away from her place," Torrance said, as if reading his mind. "I'm sure we'll find something there that tells us where Marianne and Sheila might be. It'll be okay. We'll find them in time."

"Don't make promises you can't keep, Mike." Jerry's voice was strangled but his throat was so tight, he couldn't speak any louder. "As a cop, you know better."

"I was speaking as a friend," the detective said gently, and his sympathy was almost unbearable.

CHAPTER: 43

Sheila opened her eyes and focused on the shape that seemed to be floating right above her.

"You keep passing out," the voice said with just a hint of accusation. "How can you enjoy it if you keep passing out?" A giggle followed.

The pain, which came and went in waves, suddenly came back with a vengeance, and Sheila moaned. Her entire torso was on fire. No, that wasn't even quite right—it was like somebody had cut her open and poured gasoline into the wounds and *then* lit her on fire. She moaned again, then started crying.

Abby's gaze was fixed on her, watching her with a curiosity that was frightening. There was none of the detachment in her eyes that Sheila had read about in textbooks. Most serial killers had to distance themselves from their victims and objectify the person in order to do what they did, but Abby knew exactly who Sheila was. She didn't seem crazy at all.

And *that* was what was so damned scary.

Sheila gathered up her courage and attempted to lift her head to look down at herself. The sight of her bloody, carved abdomen filled her with horror, and she screamed.

"Oh relax," Abby said dismissively when Sheila ran out of breath, her scream ending in a whimper. It was the most absurd thing she could have said under the circumstances. "It's just blood. I haven't even gone that deep yet."

"You cut me open?"

"Do you see your entrails hanging out?"

Sheila couldn't bear to look again, so she simply shook her head.

"Then that would be a negative." Abby cocked her head. "You know, I seriously considered carving a spider-web into you, considering you're a giant spider yourself, attracting younger men to you with your beauty and your brains and your goddamn *authority*. You make me sick." Abby smiled, but it didn't touch her eyes. "But I didn't. I just carved a word on you, is all. One that I thought was fitting."

"Abby, please . . ."

"And now I'm seriously considering eating your heart for dinner."

Sheila screamed again.

"O.M.G.," Abby said, mimicking a Valley Girl accent and rolling her eyes. "I was kidding, Sheila. Relax. Seriously, it was a joke. That's Hannibal Lecter's bullshit, not mine. Yuck."

"I'm laughing on the inside," Sheila said in a small voice.

That got a chuckle out of the younger woman. "Now, see? Isn't it good to retain one's sense of humor, even in a situation like this? Nice one, Sheila."

"Just kill me, Abby. Please. Get it over with." Sheila

knew there was no point in negotiating. This had all been planned from the beginning, from the moment she and Ethan had engaged in their affair well over a year ago.

"Yeah, that's what Danny keeps saying. I realize we're a bit pressed for time. But why would I rush? I've been waiting a long time for this. You fucked up my life." Abby leaned over, putting her face close to Sheila's. "Why shouldn't you suffer like I did? My beautiful man died because you couldn't stay away from him. You got him killed. You brought this on yourself."

"*He* couldn't stay away from *me*," Sheila said, unable to resist a jab of her own.

Abby made a hissing sound of displeasure, and a second later Sheila felt Abby's blade slide across her thigh. Sheila shrieked, and the room spun out. The pain, sharp and dull and throbbing and steady all at the same time, was unrelenting.

"Ethan didn't love you, Sheila." Abby's voice was hard. "You know that, right? He might have thought he did, but he wasn't capable of those kinds of feelings. Which is why he did the things he did. He desperately wanted to feel *something*. Anything."

Sheila barely heard her. The pain in her leg was overshadowing everything else.

"Don't worry," Abby said. "You won't bleed out, I didn't go too deep. Hurts like a sonofabitch, though, doesn't it?"

Sheila passed out.

When she came to—moments later? hours?—she could hear voices arguing. But she was dizzy from the pain, and she couldn't seem to focus long enough on what was being said. All that registered were bits and pieces.

". . . enough already . . ." Danny was talking. ". . . no time . . ."

". . . not a game to me." Abby's voice, aggressive and irritated. ". . . knew the plan when you started this . . ."

". . . massive manhunt for you . . ."

". . . coward . . ."

Sheila forced herself to concentrate, and finally, her mind cleared a little.

Danny's voice was low and agitated. "If you don't kill her in the next five minutes, I'm going to have to. Because we need to get out of here. I'm serious, Abby. They're coming for you."

"It's not up to you."

"You're not in charge of the entire goddamned universe," Danny snapped. Sheila managed a smile through the haze of pain. Never in a million years would Ethan have said that.

Abby laughed. "Says who?"

"You're not hearing me. I told you, I heard on Jerry's police band radio that they're looking for us."

Abby snorted. "So what? They won't find her in time." Raising her voice, she said to Sheila, "Did you hear that, Sheila? They won't find you in time. Think about that for a moment."

Sheila was definitely thinking about it.

"Fine," Danny said, sounding irritated. "I got some last-minute stuff to finish up. I'm not going to stick around here while you do this shit. Mark may have been your bitch—"

"Hey now. Don't speak ill of the dead."

Sheila heard the door slam shut.

Abby's face loomed over Sheila's once again. "She's pissed off at me, but she'll get over it. Now, where were we?"

::::

"Don't cut my face," Sheila begged as the knife hovered over her right eye. "Please, don't cut my face."

"Why not?" Abby said, sounding genuinely perplexed. "Oh. Right. Open casket. Not my problem. Of course I'm going to cut your face. It's all I've been thinking about for a year. Now don't move. You'll only make it worse." She sliced the tip of the blade across Sheila's forehead.

Sheila whimpered as the blood trailed down over her orbital bones and across her temples. "Just kill me. Please."

"You said that already. Though I do like that you always say 'please.' How very Emily Post of you." Abby stepped back to admire her handiwork.

Sheila didn't know how long Danny had been gone. It felt like hours, but for all she knew it could have been five minutes.

Her body burned all over. Letters that Sheila couldn't make out were carved into her stomach. The wounds were deep enough to hurt like hell, but they weren't fatal. Yet.

It wasn't that she wanted to die, but she finally understood that by begging Abby to kill her, it was prolonging Abby's satisfaction in torturing her. The begging made Abby want to draw out Sheila's pain.

It was a fucked-up, twisted way to try to stay alive, but it was working.

"What time is it?" she said, her eyes closed and her teeth clenched.

"And why would that matter to you?"

"Danny's been gone a long time."

Abby scowled. "Yes, I know. It's something we're going to have to discuss once we get out of here."

"Where are you going?"

"Mexico. *Soy fluido en español*." Abby smiled. "I learned Spanish in prison, picked it up pretty quick. Gonna work on my tan. If I get dark enough, I think I can pass for a Mexican. Danny, too." She sighed and glanced at her watch. "I wish I could prolong this a little more, but we're almost out of time." She smiled fondly at Sheila. "I feel so close to you right now, you know. Death brings people really close together. It always did for me and Ethan."

"Danny's a poor substitute for Ethan, though, don't you think?" Sheila said. "I mean, she's nothing like him."

"You have no idea what you're talking about," Abby snapped.

"Ethan was an alpha male. Danny's . . . softer. How could that possibly turn you on?"

Abby snorted. "You thought Ethan was an alpha male? Wow. You really didn't know him at all, did you?"

"You and Danny have been arguing half the time we've been here. How is that supposed to work?"

"That's not arguing, darling. That's foreplay."

"What if she doesn't come back?"

Abby paused over the knife. "Why wouldn't she?"

"Why *would* she?" Sheila looked up at her captor.

"You're the one who's into this sick shit. Not her. She hasn't hurt anyone. And now all your game-playing is going to get you caught. Why would she stick around for this? Sure, she might have been fascinated by you when she didn't really know you, when she only knew the image you were trying to portray, but now that she does know you, I'll bet anything she's going to split."

"Shut up," Abby hissed, holding the blade to Sheila's throat. "You don't know what the hell you're talking about. We're in love. And she set me free."

"Just like you and Ethan were in love?" The blade, cool and smooth, pressed against Sheila's throat, making it difficult not to gasp. "Look how well that worked out."

"Oh, shut the fuck up, you stupid, arrogant, petty bitch." Abby leaned in, moving the knife away so she could get close, her spittle hitting Sheila's face. Sheila could now feel the cold steel brushing against her hip. "You're not going to psych me out. She's coming back."

"I bet she's not. So you might as well kill me and move on, because they're coming for you, Abby. They're coming for you and they're going to put you back in prison and you're never, ever coming out, and everyone will know what a sick, twisted bitch you really are."

Sheila would have liked to say something more, because she could see that her words were stinging Abby, but the knife was now slicing into her thigh, and she could feel that this time, it was cutting very, very deep.

And then she heard a popping sound.

Before she could decipher what it meant, the world went white again.

You win, Sheila thought. *You win.*

CHAPTER: 44

Torrance's unmarked was already parked in the lot in front of Danny's loft when Jerry pulled up behind him. Jerry got out of the Jeep, his heart on fast-forward but his legs in slow motion. Everything seemed surreal. It felt like this was happening to somebody else. What did Danny know? Had she helped Abby snatch Annie and Sheila? Would she actually hurt them? She was a sweet girl. Why would she do this?

He had a bad feeling. A bad, bad feeling, and no matter how hard he tried to reprogram his brain, the bad feeling wouldn't go away.

Torrance was watching him closely. "You all right, pal?"

"I think I should go in alone," Jerry said.

"Absolutely not."

"Danny has worked for me for the last year, Mike." Jerry looked up at the warehouse. He had never understood why anyone would want to live here. He supposed a twenty-three-year-old would find it cool in a grungy way, but he was a long way from being in his twenties. There were lights on in some of the converted residences, but other than that, the whole street was dark. And quiet. "We have a good relationship. I can make her talk to me."

"Talk to her all you want. But you're still not going in alone." Torrance's eyes lingered on his backup Glock, which was holstered to Jerry's side. "You know how potentially dangerous this could be."

"Danny's probably not even in there."

"Probably not. But the warrant says we can search, and we will. It's gonna be okay, pal. We'll find Danny, we'll find Annie, we'll find Sheila, it's all going to be fine."

His former partner's reassurances were not helping. If anything, they were grating, like nails on a chalkboard or the sound balloons made when they rubbed together. He didn't want to hear it.

"After you," Jerry said, gritting his teeth.

They entered through the main doors and buzzed Danny's apartment. Of course there was no response, so Torrance pushed all the buttons until the inside door finally buzzed open.

Danny lived on the second floor, and they took the stairs two steps at a time until they were outside her door. A quick knock, again no answer, and then Torrance used his shoulder to push his way in.

Empty. A few bits of mismatched furniture, a bed that was neatly made, but the whole loft was one large space and it was clear there was nobody here. Torrance checked the apartment's one bathroom, then pulled open the doors to the freestanding wardrobe in the corner.

"She's gone," the detective said. "Looks like most of her clothes are gone, too."

Shit. They really weren't here. Where the hell could they be?

"Let's start canvassing the neighbors." Torrance was

already heading toward the door. "There were only a dozen names on the buzzer downstairs. Shouldn't take long."

"We're not going to find them, Mike," Jerry said, his voice faint. He could feel his hope slipping away with every passing second. "We're not going to find Annie in time."

"You can panic later." Torrance punched his arm. "Right now, we've got a job to do. Start moving. I need you, pal."

CHAPTER: 45

When Sheila opened her eyes again, it was Danny's face that loomed over her. "Hi, Dr. Tao," she said. Sheila tried to speak.

"Don't try and talk. Just listen." Danny looked down at the floor and grimaced. "I shot her. God, I hated to do that. I love her, I really do, but this was just getting ridiculous. Vendettas get people killed. Abby's always been too emotional. It's the reason she got caught in the first place. I've been telling her to chill out when it comes to you, but she's just so obsessed with you, you know?"

Sheila blinked and tried to focus on the young woman through her haze. She opened her mouth to say something but all that came out was a moan. Every part of her body was screaming, especially her face. The paralysis was wearing off, but she didn't dare try to look down again. She didn't want to see how bad it was.

"Try not to move too much, okay?" Danny said. "There's a lot of blood, and I've wrapped your leg really tight so you won't bleed out. I hate to leave you like this, but I gotta go." Her voice seemed filled with regret, or maybe that's what Sheila wanted to hear. "You'll tell them I saved you, won't you? You'll tell them that, okay? I never wanted this. I just wanted Abby. This wasn't part of my plan. I hope you believe me. And tell Jerry . . ." A pause, and then in a softer voice, "Tell Jerry I'm sorry about Marianne."

Somewhere in her delirium, Sheila thought she could feel her head nodding, but whether she was actually moving, she didn't know.

"Hang in there, Dr. Tao."

Those were the last words Sheila heard as she drifted out of consciousness and into a warm place where there was no more pain.

CHAPTER: 46

Torrance was leaning against the unmarked, smoking a cigarette. His efforts to quit hadn't lasted long. The detective was annoyingly calm, lost in thought.

Jerry, on the other hand, couldn't stay still. They had opted not to leave Danny's parking lot just yet, on the off chance she might show up. It was a long shot, but hey, stranger things had happened.

And frankly, they had nothing else to do. They were fresh out of leads. A whole goddamned police department was searching the city for Abby, Danny, Sheila, and Annie, and yet nothing had turned up.

He paced the side of the road, feeling hot and bothered despite the chilly night air. He was trying to think of something, any possibility for where they might be. There were four of them, for Christ's sake, and one of them was a high-profile escaped convict. How the hell could they all just disappear?

Continuing to pace, he stared up at the warehouse that had been Danny's home. He had always thought of her as so young, and while in some ways she might have been, it would have taken months of planning, strategizing, and patience to pull this off. He could hear her voice in his head now, sounding exasperated. *You never give me enough credit, dude.*

His phone vibrated in his pocket. His heart sank when he saw who was calling. *Shit.* He'd forgotten he owed someone a phone call.

"Hi, Morris."

"Anything?"

"Nothing yet."

The phone went dead.

Jerry stuck the phone back in his pocket. He would be truly amazed if their friendship survived this night. He turned to Torrance. "Hey, man. Do me a favor and take off your friend hat for a minute."

"Okay." Torrance exhaled. A thin stream of smoke wafted out from his nostrils into the cool night air. "What's up?"

"Tell me the truth. Cop to cop. You think they're gone?"

Torrance sighed, dropping his cigarette and stomping on it. "I don't know, pal. But the longer it takes . . ."

He didn't have to finish his sentence, because Jerry already knew how it would end. The odds of finding kidnapped people dropped dramatically with each passing hour, especially in a situation like this, where no ransom note was expected.

"They could be anywhere by now," Jerry said quietly, the constant throb in his temples growing stronger.

"Yes, they could be," Torrance said. "So now I'm putting my friend hat back on. You stay positive, you hear me? It's not over till it's over."

Jerry's phone buzzed again. He checked it. A text had just come in. It was from a number he didn't recognize.

CHECK NEXT DOOR.

"What the hell?" Jerry muttered.

"What?" Torrance said, lighting another cigarette.

"Just got a strange text. Probably a wrong number." Jerry typed a reply.

WHO IS THIS?

And then a few seconds later:

DUDE. CHECK NEXT DOOR.

Jerry looked around, half-expecting to see someone playing a practical joke. The street was quiet. Nobody was outside but the two of them. He showed Torrance the text.

"Any idea what it means?" the detective said, frowning.

Jerry stared at Danny's loft and his head began to pound so hard he could feel it all over. What did it mean, the apartment next door? They'd checked every loft in that goddamned warehouse and had found nothing other than sleepy residents who hadn't appreciated being woken up at this time of night.

Then suddenly his mind flew back to the conversation he'd had with Danny when he'd dropped her off with her bike. *We practice in the abandoned building next door. Some kind of machinery used to be manufactured there, and the whole place is soundproofed. We can play as loud as we want.*

"They're in there," Jerry said, pointing with an arm that felt like it weighed fifty pounds. Torrance followed his gaze to the warehouse beside Danny's. It looked completely deserted. His hands started shaking and he balled them into fists. "That's what she's trying to tell me, Mike."

"Who?" Torrance said.

Jerry didn't answer. He simply started walking. He would have run if he could, but his legs felt like lead. He was terrified to see what was inside that warehouse, but he knew he had to look.

He wasn't entirely surprised to find the main door open.

::::

The warehouse was a maze, and Jerry felt like a rat making his way through it.

Old, rusting machinery filled every inch of the first floor. The windows of the warehouse were filmed over with a thick layer of dust, allowing a little light in from the outside parking lot, but not much. Torrance had his Maglite but all Jerry had was his crappy pocket flashlight. They weaved their way around strange objects that cast even stranger shadows, careful to avoid anything sharp. After a few minutes, they'd determined there was nobody on this floor.

"Second floor?" Torrance said, but Jerry was already at the back heading for the stairwell.

The second level of the warehouse looked like a series of offices. Some doors were open, some doors were locked, some had bits of old furniture, some were completely empty. As Jerry entered the last room at the end of the hallway, a lightbulb string grazed his face. He yanked on it, and the huge space flooded with light.

Right in the middle of the room was a massage table. And on it, a nude body. Slender, female, black hair that trailed off the table about eight inches. Bloody from head to toe save for a torn, blood-soaked T-shirt wrapped around her thigh.

Annie. Unmoving. Dead.

Jerry sprinted toward the woman. When he reached the table, he looked down, his whole body freezing when he realized it wasn't Annie.

It was Sheila.

The relief that it wasn't his wife was so powerful that Jerry's knees buckled, and he grabbed the edge of the massage table for support. A wave of guilt, almost equally powerful, threatened to knock him over once again. Sheila was his friend. He cared about her well-being almost as much as he cared about Annie's.

The key word being *almost*.

"Sheila," he said, when he regained his balance. "Sheila, it's Jerry." Morris's angry face flashed through his head. *Let her be alive. Sweet Jesus, let her be alive.*

Torrance was behind him, and soon the detective had his fingers on Sheila's wrist. "She's got a pulse and she's breathing. But the cuts, Jesus Christ—" Torrance's face, normally set in stone, was a mix of horror and concern. He looked quickly at the floor around the table. "She's lost a lot of blood but I can't tell how bad it is. I'll call for an ambulance."

On the table, Sheila moaned.

"It's me." Jerry took her hand and squeezed gently. "It's Jerry. I'm here, Sheila. I'm here now. You're going to be okay."

Sheila's eyes flickered open. "Jerry," she whispered.

"I'm here," Jerry said again. "You're going to be all right, honey. Do you know where Annie is?"

"I . . ." Sheila looked on the verge of passing out again.

Gritting his teeth, Jerry closed his eyes briefly and prayed for forgiveness for what he was about to do. Sheila was in terrible shape, and yet . . .

He touched her cheek, the only part of her face that wasn't covered in blood. She had a deep gash on her forehead that was open and oozing. She was bleeding from both breasts, and her stomach . . . there seemed to be a word carved on it, but Jerry would have had to wipe the blood away to read it, and of course he couldn't do that. There was blood on her legs, but Jerry couldn't tell if there were multiple open wounds there or if the blood had trailed down from her torso. God, the pain must be terrible. She moaned again.

"Sheila," he said, leaning in. *God forgive me.* "Sheila, please. I need to know where Annie is."

Sheila's mouth opened, but no sound came out. Then her eyes rolled back in her head and she was out again. Behind him Torrance's phone rang, and he could hear the detective muttering to someone over the phone. He heard Torrance say "Marianne," but at that same moment, another moan escaped Sheila's lips.

"Sheila, stay awake," Jerry said, panic beginning to set in. He touched her cheek again, but this time she didn't respond. "Stay with me, honey."

Torrance disconnected his call. "Jerry, the EMTs will be here any moment. You tell the good professor to hang in there." His voice, normally blunt and gruff, sounded strange.

Jerry turned to look at his former partner. "What do

you know?" he said clearly into the silence. "I heard you say Annie's name. Twice. What do you know about my wife?"

"Stay with your friend." Torrance wouldn't meet his gaze. "I'll wait for the EMTs downstairs."

"Tell me, you fucking asshole!" Jerry felt like he was on the verge of losing it. He'd never felt such a heated mixture of emotions before—rage, fear, violence. They were rolled up into each other, writhing in his gut, and he felt like if he didn't get some answers, he just might shoot somebody. "If you know something, you tell me right now." His teeth were pressed together so hard, his gums ached. *Where is my wife?*

"I'm sorry, Jer," Torrance said, his voice cracking. "I'm so sorry. They found her. They found Marianne."

Stay calm. Keep breathing. Let him finish what he's going to say.

"She was on the side of the road. Out on Route Twenty, about thirty-three miles west of Cavanaugh's house." His voice broke down. "They've got her on a bus, but it doesn't look good, Jer. I'm so sorry."

No. No, no, no.

"You're wrong," Jerry said, sounding much calmer than he felt. "You're totally wrong."

"I'm so sorry, pal."

It hit him then. All the air went out of the room, and Jerry crumpled to his knees.

CHAPTER: 47

The smell of disinfectant, the hushed tones, the mint-green wall paint. Hospitals never changed.

Morris was saying something comforting, but Jerry wasn't listening. He was staring at Sheila, reminded of a year ago when it had been him in the hospital with bandages around his throat. But he knew Sheila had it much worse.

In a shaking, raging voice, Morris had explained to him earlier that morning that Sheila's body had been carved up pretty bad. Thankfully none of the wounds had been life-threatening, as most were superficial, other than the one on her thigh which had already been wrapped tight at the warehouse. She would heal. A top plastic surgeon had already been consulted, and while the surgeon was confident he could minimize the scar on her forehead, it would always be visible.

On Sheila's stomach, Abby had carved the word WHORE. Christ Almighty. The surgeon was certain this one could be eliminated entirely, and thank God for that.

Jerry took one last glance at Sheila as if to reassure himself she'd be okay. He shook Morris's hand, allowed himself to be embraced by the big man, and left the room.

A moment later he was on a different floor of the hospital, back in the same chair he'd been sitting in for the past few hours until Morris had come up to check on him.

Around him, the machines beeped steadily. Annie was covered with the hospital's sheets, her face pale but peaceful, the only movement coming from her chest as the machines helped her breathe. There were bruises on her forehead and multiple cuts and scrapes on her cheeks, neck, and arms. The abdominal wound had been operated on, but she had lost the largest amount of blood a person could lose and still be hanging on. She was stable for the time being, but the doctors who'd worked on her couldn't guarantee she'd make it through the night.

He stared at her, touching her hand, caressing her face. His beautiful, brilliant, vibrant wife. It was his fault.

This was all his fault.

Jerry buried his face in his hands, and sobbed.

CHAPTER: 48

Van Morrison's "Into the Mystic" was playing on Danny's iPod, and the song was fitting. It was a warm day, and the windows were down, rustling both Danny's hair and Abby's.

"I might never forgive you," Abby said beside her, her voice low and husky and intimate. Her shoulder, bandaged tightly, was in a sling. "I can't believe you actually shot me, you bitch."

A small smile crossed Danny's lips, but she kept driving, her attention focused on the road, which seemed to stretch on forever in front of them. "You didn't give me a choice. You'll be fine. Chill."

"The hell I will." She felt Abby's eyes burn into the side of her face. "Once my shoulder heals, I'm going back for her. And then I might just put a knife in *your* throat for not letting me finish it, you stupid cunt."

Danny placed a hand on Abby's thigh and rubbed it lightly. Immediately, Abby relaxed. She always did when Danny touched her. "You know killing Sheila was never the goal," Danny said again. "The only goal was getting you out. And now you're out. Be happy, baby. It's a new day. Everything worked out perfectly."

"It's not over."

Danny looked at Abby, looked at her beautiful face, all fine bones and fair skin and Elizabeth Taylor eyes, and said, "It is over. It has to be."

"They're looking for you, too, don't forget."

"So what? I didn't kill anybody."

"No, but you helped me. You recruited Jeremiah, you got him to do your dirty work, and then you made sure he was attacked in prison . . . you might as well have killed them all yourself."

Danny's jaw tightened. "But I didn't kill them myself. And anyway, I did all of that for you. As a means to an end. I had a plan, I accomplished everything I set out to do to get you out of prison, and now it's over. We're moving on." She looked back at the road. "I know you think you have a choice in this, but you don't. Let's be crystal clear about that. We're never going back. And if you do go back, you go without me, and we're done."

Abby was silent. Danny knew she wasn't accustomed to having people talk to her this way, but she'd damn well better get used to it.

A moment later, Abby said, "Why did you save her?"

Danny knew she was referring to Sheila Tao. There could be several answers to this, and Danny mulled them all over as she drove. Perhaps she'd saved Dr. Tao because she'd had the woman as a teacher, and Danny had learned a lot from her. Perhaps she'd done it to prove to herself she wasn't a psychopath. Or perhaps she'd done it to make up for what Abby had done to Jerry's wife, Marianne, who'd been an unfortunate casualty in Abby's war.

A pang shot through Danny. *Poor Jerry*. Wherever he

was, he was hurting. And that hadn't been part of the plan. Jerry had always been good to her. She forced the thought out of her head.

Ultimately, the real answer was simple. Ridiculously so.

Danny had saved Sheila Tao to let Abby know who was in control here. Who had *always* been in control here. There could only be one alpha female in this relationship, and Danny had never been the submissive type.

"I saved her because I wanted to," Danny finally said. "And because I could. Now do you have the passports? We're almost there."

They were approaching the U.S.–Mexico border, having driven all night. Danny pulled into the far left lane, where her old friend Pedro was working. It had all been arranged.

Abby pulled out their passports, which Danny had bought for the low, low price of five grand apiece.

"By the way." Abby sounded cross as she handed the passports, which were Canadian, not American, to Danny. "Clarissa Butterfield? What the hell kind of name is that? I sound like a fucking bimbo. I totally hate you. I hate you so much." But she was smiling.

Danny chuckled. Her passport said Sarah Butterfield. They were going to pass themselves off as sisters. They were going to settle somewhere along the Pacific, and maybe run a restaurant or a small resort or something. Or maybe they'd keep driving, all the way down to South America. It really didn't matter. They'd figure it all out when they got there. Hopefully the Spanish lessons would pay off.

As they pulled into the queue for the border crossing, Danny kept one hand on the steering wheel and leaned over for a kiss. Abby's lips met hers hungrily, her sweet tongue flicking hers, sending a white-hot tingle through Danny's body.

Almost a year of planning to get to this point. Everything she had done, from the internship with Jerry, to volunteering at the prison, to creating the FreeAbbyMaddox .com site to attract just the right obsessed freak to help her, which turned out to be Jeremiah Blake . . . it had all come to fruition.

They were home free.

"También te amo, mi amor," Danny said, when they broke apart. *"Todo lo que hice, lo hice por ti."*

I love you, too, my darling. Everything I did, I did for you.

AUTHOR'S NOTE

The prisons in this book are fictional, but if it wasn't for a visit to the Washington Corrections Center for Women in Gig Harbor, Washington, I would have had to invent many of the descriptive details. Thanks so much to Superintendent Jane Parnell and Sergeant Bassetti for the interview and the tour. As an author, I took artistic liberties with what happens inside prison to make it work for my story, but readers should know that the WCCW is an impressive facility with a dedicated, hardworking staff.

I'm also grateful to S.P., an inmate currently serving out a life sentence at Folsom State Prison in California, for generously sharing so many details of his day-to-day life with me.

Gallery Books proudly presents . . .

CREEP

JENNIFER HILLIER

Available now in hardcover and mass market

Turn the page for a preview of *CREEP* . . .

Three months. That's how long Dr. Sheila Tao had been sleeping with Ethan Wolfe. Three months, four days, and approximately six hours.

The problem wasn't the sixteen-year age difference. It wasn't even that she was his professor and he was her teaching assistant. The problem was that Sheila was engaged to Morris, and now the affair with Ethan had to stop. No more weekly "meetings" at the Ivy, the motel just off campus that rented rooms by the hour. No more sneaking around. No more lying. No more falling into that chasm of depression that consumed her for days after each of their trysts.

It had to end. All of it. Sheila and her therapist had been working hard on this. Yes, even psychologists had psychologists.

It wouldn't be easy. Ethan was good-looking and prone to getting his way. Hell, he had seduced her, though Sheila suspected not even her therapist believed that.

They were in her bright corner office on the fourth floor of the psychology building at Puget Sound State University. He was relaxed, casual, his jean-clad legs spread open in that cocky way he liked to sit. The desk between them was strewn with papers, an organized clutter that served as a makeshift barrier.

Observing him, she watched his full lips form words she only half-heard. There was nothing vague about Ethan's attractiveness, but he downplayed it by wearing ratty vintage T-shirts, worn jeans, tennis shoes. His hard, flat stomach wasn't evident through the loose-fitting shirt, but Sheila could damn well picture it.

She had no idea how he was going to react to her news. She'd known him long enough to understand his propensity for structure, and she was about to upset the routine they'd established over the past three months.

Of her five teaching assistants, Ethan was the brightest and most ambitious. His intelligence and drive had been a big part of his appeal. They were discussing grades for her popular summer-session undergraduate social psychology class, and so far neither of them had commented as to why they were meeting here this morning, in her office, instead of room sixteen at the Ivy Motel. She knew he had to be thinking about it, because she was thinking about it, too.

She forced herself to focus on what he was saying.

"Danny Ambrose doesn't deserve a B," he said, fingers resting lightly on the arms of his chair. He never talked with his hands, even when he was passionate about something. "The similarities he drew between Milgram's experiment and the Nazis? Too obvious."

His brows were furrowed. Sheila was about to overrule the grade Ethan had assigned to one of her undergraduate students, and he didn't like it. He wasn't used to it. They didn't disagree often.

"He loses points for originality, but don't you think his argument is solid?" Sheila smiled to soften her words. "This is only a sophomore class. He did what was asked of him and it was better than average. I spoke to Danny personally the other day. He risks losing his scholarship if we give him that C. He's a good kid. I'd really hate to see that happen."

She could almost hear the wheels in Ethan's mind turning as he thought of a counterargument. Most of the time she encouraged healthy debate, but she wasn't in the mood this morning. There was a conversation they needed to have, and she was having a hard time steering them in that direction.

She waited, saying nothing. If she didn't push it, he'd come around. The key was to let him work through it on his own.

"Okay," Ethan said finally. "You win, Sheila. Danny gets a B. Lucky bastard. God, I hate it when you assert your authority over me." Lowering his voice, he glanced over his shoulder at the open door behind him. "You'll have to make it up to me later." He leaned forward and ran a finger down the back of her left hand, lips curled into the half-smile she liked so much.

His finger brushed over the band of her new diamond ring, turned inside out so the stone was tucked into her palm. His gaze dropped down to her hand.

She was surprised it had taken him this long to notice. *Here we go.*

Her first instinct was to yank her hand away, but that would only make things worse. Willing herself to appear relaxed, she twisted the platinum band around. Ethan's eyes widened at the sight of the four-carat diamond.

"What's this?" The lightness of his tone did not match his face. A flush emerged just above the neckline of his T-shirt. He touched a finger to the top of the stone, leaving a smudge.

She resisted the urge to wipe it off. The face of a diamond this size was like glass. Morris was a senior partner at Bindle Brothers, the largest investment bank in the Northwest, and he hadn't held back.

She withdrew her hand. "Could you close the door?" she asked. "Just for a few minutes. There's something we need to discuss."

Ethan stiffened, as Sheila knew he would. He was fine in a lecture hall, but they both knew he didn't like closed doors in small spaces. Something to do with his childhood and getting locked in a closet for hours—she didn't really know, he'd always been vague. In their tiny motel room, the windows always had to be open, even if it was raining.

"Please?" she said. "Just for a bit so we can talk in private. I'll open the window."

He closed her office door reluctantly while she cranked open the casement behind her. A blast of August warmth entered the air-conditioned room. Ethan waited in silence, his expression betraying nothing.

There was no way around it except to be direct. "Morris and I are getting married."

Ethan leaned back in his chair and stared at her with unreadable light gray eyes. Again, she waited. The thrum of the air conditioner reverberated in the room.

"When did this happen?"

"Saturday." Five nights ago.

He looked around the office. He wasn't one to avoid eye contact, so she guessed he was digesting this information. His gaze focused briefly on a small, framed picture of Sheila and Morris on the window ledge before returning to her face. "Well, this is big news. But it doesn't change anything between you and me."

"It changes everything." The words were out before she could consider their impact. Biting her lip, she forged ahead anyway. "I can't be involved with you anymore outside of class."

He didn't blink. "Just like that?"

"I'm sorry."

He exhaled and she caught a whiff of the cinnamon gum he'd been chewing earlier. He always chewed cinnamon gum, and if she closed her eyes, she could almost taste it, could almost feel his sweet, spicy tongue in her mouth—

"Congratulations." The smile didn't quite touch his eyes.

"Thank you," she said.

"When's the wedding?"

"October tenth."

His smile turned into a grin she couldn't read. It wasn't amusement, or annoyance, or even a desire to please; it was something else entirely.

"So soon. Why the rush?"

She had prepared for this question, rehearsing the answer in her head during the drive to work that morning, and it rolled off her tongue. "I'm thirty-nine and I'm not getting any younger. I'm tired of living alone, Ethan. I love Morris. We want to start our life together. We—there might still be time for kids."

"What should I wear to the wedding?"

Shocked, she opened her mouth, but no words came out.

"I'm kidding," he said, his eyes finally showing a hint of amusement. "Joke, Sheila. I wouldn't come even if I was invited. Isn't there a rule about going to the weddings of people you used to fuck?"

She winced. She had no problem with cursing, but here, in this moment, it sounded unreasonably harsh.

"Ah, well. It's better that it's over anyway." He ran a hand through his short, mussed hair. "It really should have ended ages ago, now that I think about it. Remember when your father died? How messed up you were?"

Her stomach lurched. "Of course I remember." It had only been three months since her estranged father had passed away from liver cancer. Three days before the affair had started. She knew it had been the trigger.

His voice became low, accusing. "I never wanted this to be a long-term thing. But you were so goddamned needy. You kept telling me not to go."

It was a subtle but unmistakable slap in the face. *Please don't go.* Oh, yes, those had been her words exactly, words she'd whispered to Ethan the morning after her father's funeral while lying next to him naked under the scratchy motel bedsheets. It hurt to think he could bring it up now as if they were talking about the weather.

"The timing was bad," he said with a shrug. "I couldn't do it to you. But really, it should have ended right after it started."

"You said that already."

"Are you mad?" His face was open, interested. "Don't be mad, Sheila. I don't regret that it lasted as long as it did. But all good things must come to an end. This won't change anything professional between us. We still work really well together."

He sat back with a Cheshire-cat smile.

She was suddenly infuriated. Exactly who was dumping whom here? She had agonized over this conversation for days, wondering what to say to him and how to say it, alternating between supreme bliss at her new engagement and pangs of regret over the affair, worried about hurting Morris, hurting Ethan, hurting herself. Nothing about this had been simple. Nothing.

But here he was, easy like Sunday morning, his handsome face a mixture of pity and regret.

She arranged the papers on the desk into neat stacks to keep her hands from trembling, thinking hard about what she wanted to say next.

"All right, about that." Sheila's words were tight as she forced herself to stay calm. "I don't think we should continue to work together. I'm going to recommend you work with Dr. Easton from now on."

This caught him off guard. "You're not fucking serious?"

"I am." She smiled, pleased at his reaction, then made a grand show of wiping her brow. "You know what, I need to close the window. It's really hot in here and the air-conditioning's escaping. You know how I get when it's stuffy."

"Sheila, don't close—"

She stood up quickly and cranked and latched the window. By the time she turned back to Ethan, his body had gone rigid. She sat down again and crossed her legs, not bothering to hide her own little smile.

"I promise you it'll be an easy transition. Dr. Easton was impressed with the work you did in his advanced personality theory class last term. His expertise on deviant behavior can only help your thesis." Sheila's smile widened. "Don't worry, the department won't have a problem with the switch. You can stay until the end of next term as my TA, but after Christmas—"

"I don't want to switch," he said. Beads of sweat appeared at his hairline even though the room was cooling. "I have less than a year to go. I don't want to work through the kinks of a new adviser."

"I'll do everything I can to help."

They sat staring at each other. It was awkward waiting out the silence, but she knew whoever spoke first would lose.

"You're trying to get rid of me," Ethan hissed. Circular sweat stains had formed at his armpits, soaking through the cloth of his gray T-shirt. "Well, guess what, I'm not switching. I've been working with you for going on three terms now. You're not passing me off to someone else because you're getting married and don't want a reminder you fucked the help. My thesis is nearly done." He was breathing hard. Perspiration trailed down his left temple.

She had about thirty seconds before he'd totally lose it; claustrophobia could be debilitating. "And I promise you nothing will change," she said again. "Dr. Easton's always admired you and—"

"Dr. Easton's a fucking fag!" Ethan slammed his hands down on the desk and the stack of term papers fell over. At that moment the air conditioner paused and the room was suddenly quiet. Pointing a finger at her, he stood up. "I am not working with him. You *are* going to finish what you started with me."

Sheila did her best to appear impassive. "You don't have a choice. I can reassign you anytime I like, for any reason."

"Really? And what would the dean say about that?" Ethan was towering over her desk. Little drops of sweat hit the term papers, blurring the ink into shapeless forms.

"Dean Simmons will back me up, of course," she said, looking up at him.

"Even after he sees you on the Internet taking it up the ass?"

"What? What are you—" She stopped. Her throat went dry and she swallowed. Her heart started thumping in her chest so hard she thought she could feel her silk blouse moving. "You deleted that off your phone. I watched you do it."

"Are you sure about that?" His eyes were flat, devoid of emotion. He was still sweating but his voice was once again controlled. "I didn't e-mail it to myself first? You're absolutely sure?"

Her temple began to throb. The fluorescent lights overhead were suddenly too bright, the walls too yellow, the air conditioner too loud. Her armpits tingled and she could smell onions. Ethan's body odor. Or was it her own?

"You wouldn't dare," she whispered.

"Wouldn't I?" He grinned triumphantly as he wiped his sweaty brow with his hand. Turning away from her, he finally yanked open the office door and stepped out, taking deep breaths of the semi-stale hallway air.

Sheila sat, dazed. There was a 99 percent chance he was bluffing—her gut told her there was no video anymore, he wouldn't have had time to send it somewhere else from his phone before she'd made him delete it—but goddamn it, it wasn't good enough. If anything like it ever showed up on CampusAnonymous.com, a website notorious for outrageous gossip and nasty comments about all things involving the university, she'd be ruined. The video would go viral before she could blink twice, and two decades of hard work would be snuffed out like a campfire in a thunderstorm.

Having an affair with a student was one thing. It happened all the time—she could think of three professors who'd been involved with students in the past, who'd gotten nothing more than slaps on the wrist. And Ethan was twenty-three and neither of them were married, which counted for something.

But a video? It wouldn't matter whom she was screwing—a video of her writhing naked on the Internet would get her fired. No hearing, no chance to defend herself, just an hour to collect her personal belongings and she'd be out the door on her ass. Do not pass Go, do not collect two hundred.

How could I have been so fucking stupid?

A voice broke into her thoughts, and she looked up. Valerie Kim, one of Sheila's other TAs, stood in the doorway just behind Ethan.

"One sec, Val," Ethan said to the petite young woman. His tone betrayed no hint of the tension that filled the office. "The professor and I are almost done here."

"That's cool." Valerie looked past Ethan into the office at Sheila. "I can come back in five."

"No need." Sheila's smile felt clownish. "Come in, Valerie."

Ethan stepped back into the office and made a show of bundling up the scattered term papers on the desk. Slinging his worn leather bag crosswise over his torso, he grinned at Sheila. "Dr. Tao, I'll see you next week. Thanks for your time."

"Sure," Sheila said. Her shoulders slumped and her back ached.

Ethan winked at Valerie as he left the office. "She's all yours."

She heard him whistling as he ambled down the hallway, not a care in the world, and her mind reeled. What the fuck had just happened?

"So, Professor Tao, did you hear?" Valerie's voice was breathy. The ponytailed teaching assistant plopped into the chair across from Sheila and rummaged in her bag for her own stack of papers to be reviewed. "Diana St. Clair's body was found this morning."

"Hmmm?" Sheila could not process what the graduate student was saying. Somehow, she had completely underestimated Ethan Wolfe. He had outsmarted her, and how was that possible? Damn him. *Damn her.* This was a disaster. Could he really still have that video? He'd made it several weeks ago, and maybe her memory was foggy, but she was certain she'd seen him delete it right afterward, could remember her relief when she saw it was gone . . .

"The swimmer? Diana St. Clair?" Valerie was saying.

"Yes, of course I know she disappeared," Sheila said, irritated. A drop of Ethan's sweat remained on the desk and she swiped at it. She forced herself to focus on Valerie's pretty face. "What's the update?"

"I don't know all the details yet." The grad student sounded appropriately somber, though her eyes were alight with morbid excitement. "She was found floating in Puget Sound early this morning. A ferry rider spotted her."

"She *drowned*?" Sheila's hand flew to her mouth. Valerie had her full attention now. "How is that even possible?"

Everyone was familiar with the story. It had been all over the news. Diana St. Clair was the pride and joy of PSSU, a champion Division I swimmer and Olympic hopeful. She'd gone missing after swim practice over a week before, and it was all anyone on campus could talk about. There'd been multiple theories about her disappearance: she'd eloped to Brazil with a guy she'd met online; she'd quit swimming but didn't have the heart to tell her parents; she was pregnant and hiding it from her sponsors . . .

"She didn't drown, that isn't how she died. I heard she was stabbed first." Valerie paused for dramatic effect. "Multiple times."

Sheila sat up straight. "Holy shit!"

Valerie looked pleased to hear her professor swear. "I heard they're going to be putting new security measures in place because of this." Clearly Valerie had heard a lot. "My boyfriend works part-time in the communications department. They're sending out a bulletin later today."

"Holy shit." Sheila felt disoriented as she tried to process the news.

Diana St. Clair had been her student. Sheila had never known someone who was murdered.

Until now.